LOCA

a novel

ALEJANDRO HEREDIA

SIMON & SCHUSTER

*New York   Amsterdam/Antwerp   London
Toronto   Sydney   New Delhi*

Simon & Schuster
1230 Avenue of the Americas
New York, NY 10020

This book is a work of fiction. Any references to historical events, real people, or real places are used fictitiously. Other names, characters, places, and events are products of the author's imagination, and any resemblance to actual events or places or persons, living or dead, is entirely coincidental.

First Simon & Schuster hardcover edition February 2025

SIMON & SCHUSTER and colophon are registered trademarks of Simon & Schuster, LLC

For information about special discounts for bulk purchases, please contact Simon & Schuster Special Sales at 1-866-506-1949 or business@simonandschuster.com.

The Simon & Schuster Speakers Bureau can bring authors to your live event. For more information or to book an event, contact the Simon & Schuster Speakers Bureau at 1-866-248-3049 or visit our website at www.simonspeakers.com.

Interior design by Carly Loman

Manufactured in the United States of America

10 9 8 7 6 5 4 3 2 1

Library of Congress Cataloging-in-Publication Data has been applied for.

ISBN 978-1-6680-5046-0
ISBN 978-1-6680-5048-4 (ebook)

For Junior

friendship is so friendship   *& ain't it*

—DANEZ SMITH

Santo Domingo me deja sin palabras,
y sin palabras yo no puedo vivir.

—JOHAN MIJAIL

I.

SAL STANDS BY THE KITCHEN WINDOW BATHED IN MORNING light. If I catch the next train . . . he thinks as he hurries to scrub a plate clean. His résumé is in his bag. His shoes are by the door. His speech is coiled tight in his mind. "I'm ready," he whispers to himself. But then he looks out the window to the sky blemished by a flutter of birds. Pigeons are pigeons everywhere, he thinks. In that city and in this one.

Suddenly he can't move.

The suds on his knuckles turn translucent. The faucet drips and drips.

An hour later, all he can move is his hands. He palms his burning forehead. Runs his fingers atop his small fro to make sure his head is all there. Then he pulls the handset sitting on the counter and braves the call.

"Oh, you're back already?" Charo says.

"I didn't go."

"What?"

"I was standing in the kitchen, and . . ." he says. But how to explain it?

In the background, Charo's daughter yells above the noise of plastic toys clattering together. "She barely slept last night. Now she's at a hundred. Come over. We can talk here."

"I don't know if I can."

"Salvador." She says his name the way his mother would, and for a second he detests her for it, his best friend's cutting tone.

"Okay," he says. "All right."

Charo's place is far enough to justify taking the D train two stops up to Tremont. But now that his legs are working again, he prefers to walk on The Concourse. Maybe the breeze will soothe his mind and calm the fever. He walks past kids playing hopscotch on the sidewalk, men lounging by bodegas, and women crowding the front of salons in their rolos waiting their turn at the secadora. On the corner, he stops under a tree and loses himself in the sunlight burning through the acid green leaves.

"Fuck out the way, nigga!" a boy yells, speeding by on his bike. The hooded teen is down the block by the time Sal comes up with a good response.

On 170th he passes a man using a metal hanger to search the inside of a blue mailbox. Whether he's picking up a suspicious package left for him or stealing people's mail, Sal doesn't know, though he wonders what the man might say if he were asked. If, once confronted, he'd run away in shame or flip Sal the middle finger.

The letter inviting him to interview arrived a week ago, his little American dream folded into an envelope. The months of English classes he took when he arrived in New York. The extra semesters it took to get an associate's degree in education. Countless evenings working at the Cuban restaurant to make ends meet. He even visited the museum a couple of times a year, hoping to absorb something useful every time he walked by a tour guide. Almost five years. So much time and effort, he thinks, and I couldn't even make it out the door.

In front of Charo's building, through the glass-and-metal door,

Sal makes eye contact with a man carrying grocery bags. Something like pity forms in the old man's eyes, but he turns and slips into the elevator. Sal curses the dead intercom in Charo's apartment. He rings half a dozen other tenants, hoping he'll get lucky.

Upstairs, the apartment is raptured by the whirlwind of a cleaning day. Folded pants on the couch, Robert's polo shirts hanging by the open window, the sharp scent of Clorox wafting from the bathroom. In the living room, Carolina hammers a pink plastic spoon against a glass table. Sal plants a kiss on her head, then follows his friend to the kitchen.

Charo plants herself in front of the stove and goes on scrubbing black grime. Her hair is tied up in a ponytail, her eyes are bloodshot. As long as he's known her, she's been beautiful. Her deep brown skin, high cheekbones, big dark eyes, all reduced now by a tormenting night of childcare.

"You've been talking about this interview all week. What happened?"

Just like Charo to get straight to the thing at hand.

"I don't know," he says. Admitting this doubles his regret.

"So you don't want it, then."

"I did. I do. I keep seeing myself at the museum."

"Getting paid to talk to people about planets and moons and shit."

"Jódete," Sal says, but that manages to make him smile.

"Just call them tomorrow and try to reschedule," she says over the rattling stove. "Tell them you got a stomach bug or something."

"Maybe," he says with hesitation, though the thought gives him some relief.

A loud bang reaches them from the living room. Charo slips off her rubber gloves and runs over to check on her daughter.

A younger Charo would scoff at what Sal sees now. I'm never gonna be like those viejas locked up at home tending to a man, she said to him once. But who is she doing this for, if not for Robert?

The immaculate kitchen. The ironed work clothes. The urgency with which she moves about the apartment, like she's running out of time. He can't help but feel that things should be different. Wasn't that the point of leaving everything behind to come to this country? To live entirely unlike who they might have been on the island?

When she returns, Charo wears a mischievous smile. Sal should see it coming, the idea brightening her eyes, but his heart still flutters when she says it.

"Let's go dancing."

"No way," he says in the middle of a halfhearted laugh.

"C'mon! You'll be braver after a good night out," she says.

But that's only half the reason. Charo has been hinting at going out to celebrate for weeks. Ever since she finished paying off some money she owed her uncle, all she can talk about is dancing.

"You know I don't like the scene."

"Well, you can't keep avoiding gay bars forever."

She winces like she's the one her words have hurt.

"It's fine," he says, to get ahead of her apology.

"You feel so far away sometimes."

"I don't know what that means."

"Do you want to talk about it?"

"Charo, please."

She bites her lip, but he sees a hundred questions in her eyes. If he doesn't get ahead of it, they'll be here all day, having the same tired conversation, digging up what should be squarely in the past.

"If I say I'll go dancing, will you drop it?"

"Wait, really?"

"Really," he says, trying to sound convincing.

She turns and scrubs the stove with more vigor now. A strand of hair falls over her face. She uses her forearm to tuck it back behind her ear.

"If you want to talk, Sal. I'm here to carry it with you," she says to her hands.

But Carolina has walked in with her ruckus, demanding their attention.

The eyeliner on her left eye is darker than the eyeliner on the right. She adds a few soft strokes to bolden the wing, then swivels her head to look at her work. Close enough.

"I just think you should've told me before making plans with your friend," Robert says. He wraps an arm around the baby, while the baby hugs her favorite cow plush toy.

Charo stands in front of the bureau mirror and looks at him in its reflection. He's lying on their bed shirtless, his body a muscled homage to the hour he spends at the gym every morning. He must have stopped at the barbershop on the way home from work, because his hair is lined up. His retouched Caesar cut reminds her of their youth, so distant to her now though it's only been a few years. The first couple of months, all they did was fuck. In the bathroom, in the car. Once, at Randall's Island during a friend's birthday party. She was bubbly off a few beers. He was high off of male company. She sat on his lap as he talked to his boys, just to feel close. Eventually they snuck away into the forest, yards away from the echoes of bachata, hidden in the wild and verdant trees. The sex was clammy in the summer heat, uncomfortable, angled as best as they could manage perched beside a brittle trunk. They went to great lengths to feel that quickening burn between their bodies that first summer.

A year later, Charo was pregnant.

"I took a test," was all she said, after biting her tongue for a week. She sat on his couch. He played with the radio, as he always did those days, intent on nurturing his side dream of being a DJ.

"That's okay," he said, like she'd just apologized.

"You don't understand," she said. "Like, a baby."

7

"I know what a baby is. You don't want it?"

"What?"

"I mean, I'm ready," he said, and moved from behind the radio to sit at her feet. "I can do it. Be a dad. A really good one. But we can wait, if that's what you want. I have a tía that knows a lot about herbs."

She thought she should be upset by his suggestion, but Charo slept well that night, knowing he'd be okay with whatever she chose. She didn't have hang-ups about abortions. She'd seen enough girls in high school forced to get secret procedures by their parents. Her Catholic upbringing couldn't shame her away from the truth that was all around her. And besides, now she was in America. Whatever she decided, it wouldn't have to be in secret. The next day she posed the news to her mother as a question, hoping to find some wisdom only seasoned mothers could offer.

"My daughter, finally with a good and stable man? God grants his miracles after all," she said. It hadn't occurred to Charo that she'd never told her mother about Robert in the year they'd been dating. It was all business and bills with her parents. Even when they asked, she couldn't bring herself to share much about her real life in New York.

"Ta bien, Mami. He's good and all. But what about me? I've only been here a few years."

"Did he say that he'll take care of you?"

"Well, yes, but—"

"Then what else is there to think about?" her mother asked.

Charo thought about it so long she began to worry her options were dwindling. It tired her, the idea of taking care of a baby when she was still sleeping in cramped rooms with question-able roommates and working long hours to make very little. Her doubt deepened, but as the weeks passed, Robert grew more en-amored with the idea of keeping the baby. He assured her again and again that it wouldn't be like her cousins and the girls at the supermarket who ended up raising their kids alone. He promised he'd be good.

One morning, straight from a tender dream about tiny fingernails and soft baby scalps, she finally made her decision.

"Okay."

"What?" he said, still half asleep.

"Let's have a baby," she said. She was tired of looking for a reason where there was none. Every time she asked someone around her, they made trite promises like "Being a mom will be the best thing you'll ever do" and "You won't know until you get there, there's just no words." At first all she wanted was words, anything to help her through this paralyzing fear. But she realized after a dozen sleepless nights that trying to push away her fear was not going to work. It's okay to be afraid, she told herself again and again, until she found enough clarity to make a decision.

They moved in together a few weeks after that. Robert sold his radio and his giant speakers to make space for his growing family. "A baby's no joke, I have to get serious," he said when she tried to dissuade him from selling the set. They danced for hours the night before his buddy came to pick up the radio. He showed her how to transition smoothly from one song to the next, what all the lights and buttons meant, even played her the best playlist he'd ever made, which he'd never played for anyone, out of fear they wouldn't vibe with his taste. Charo had known Robert to be calm and measured. He never strayed too far into emotional extremes. But that night he was ecstatic to share his love of music with her. And the next morning, he was equally morose as he lifted the speakers into his buddy's truck. It surprised her to see this side of his temperament. There was still so much about him she didn't know.

Toward the end of her pregnancy, Robert took care of the bills when Charo couldn't bear to stand those long hours at the supermarket. When the time came, he let Charo pick Carolina's name.

He let her pick Sal as the godfather, though she could tell how badly Robert wanted to gift the title to one of his best friends. He gave in to her needs a lot. He was there when things were smooth and easy. He was there when they were not. Like the night Carolina got a fever at three months and had to be rushed to the hospital. Or the first week Charo went back to the supermarket, at ten months. She called him every day while they were both at work to ask if it really was okay to leave their daughter with a babysitter so soon. Parenting an infant was tough, but they always got through, together.

The change has come in the last few months, since their daughter's first birthday. Things have started to feel tenuous between them. Robert spends less time at home, more time at the barbershop or out with his friends. It's made her anxious to be in the apartment alone with the baby. Like she's being left behind. Now she thinks maybe going out will help smooth out this rough patch. Give her some relief from her life. Make him miss her a little bit.

"It'll be good to have hija-and-papi time," Charo says as she adds a touch of powdered blush to her cheek.

"Ven, mi amor. Mami is leaving us today, it's just you and me."

"Are you mad that I'm going out?" She puts the brush down, rummages through her jewelry box to find her hoop earrings.

"You have a daughter."

"And she has a father." She can't help it now, the edge in her voice. "Who's perfectly capable of babysitting his daughter for one night."

"Also, those people," he continues like he hasn't heard her. "You don't even know what goes down in those places."

She can see where the argument is going. Robert has never been explicit, but his discomfort around Sal is clear. Better to leave before they spoil the night with an argument. Charo grabs her bag, kisses her daughter goodbye. She hears him follow behind her but doesn't turn until she's at the door.

"I watch her when you're out at the gym or playing pool with your boys. Why do you have to give me shit about this?"

He opens his mouth to defend himself, but he softens at the hurt in her eyes. He massages his temple with his middle finger. "Okay, you're right. I'm being an ass," he says through his teeth.

"A burro, a brute," she says, though she's surprised by how quickly his apology came.

"Here. I don't want you on the train on the way back." He hands her a couple of twenties for a cab.

This wave of gratitude and bitterness. It's always like this, these days. Polarized emotions, sentiments to the extreme. Sometimes she wants to run out the door and forget her life. Other times she wants to fold in his arms, make herself as small and pliable as he wants her. It feels impossible, with Robert. But if it were all bad, she wouldn't feel this overwhelming pull to forget the club, to stay in the comfort of his arms tonight.

"Don't wait up for me," she says, and turns to go.

It's 1999—everyone is existential, Sal knows he's not the only one. Everyone thinks about the senselessness of time, the black of space, microwaves, the man acquitted for the hot fluid on the dress. Orgies, intoxicating pop music, the blue or the red pill sitting in the quiet of an open palm. The whole world waits in anticipation for the new millennium. But the future is already here, in this two-block strip filled with queer people from every walk of life. Sal and Charo pass a drag queen carrying a bag of dildos for her next show. They slow down by a group of daddies crowding outside of a bar, cackling and eyeing the occasional twink. They skip ahead of a solemn group masked in leather discussing the fall of democracy and the plight of the proletariat. One of them shoots Sal a compliment as they walk through the glaze of time. Despite how hesitant he was a few hours ago, he's taken over by the excitement of this street, where everything is subversion, an undoing of the norm, a leap.

The Shade Room, at the end of the strip, stands out for its Latin parties. For just one evening a month, it's transformed into a portal to San Juan, Santo Domingo, Havana. Myth goes that the Latin parties began in the early nineties with a group of Puerto Ricans who got tired of listening to the latest white-girl pop star. They were Puerto Ricans straight from the island, not the Nuyoricans who helped build hip-hop culture in New York. They wanted to move to the rhythms of the island they yearned for, so they made a deal with the Shade Room's manager. If they could bring in three hundred people once a month and hire their own DJ, they could have the space to use as they pleased. As much as New York changes, in Chelsea and everywhere, the parties have been going strong for years. Sal has never been, but he's heard about the myth. Now, as he and Charo near the bar, they find that the line goes down to the end of the block.

"I can't wait to dance," Charo says, holding on to Sal's arm. In all his denim, Sal guesses that he looks younger, more like a blooming adolescent than his twenty-five years. Charo wears her favorite black wedges, high enough to accentuate her ass, comfortable enough to dance for hours. We look good, Sal thinks as they take their place on the line.

Once inside, they squeeze their way through the haze of bodies to order something sweet at the bar. Bachata blasts from the speakers. All around them people dance and sweat and yell above the music. When they both have drinks in hand, Sal grabs Charo and pulls her to dance. They ease into it, slow and careful movements at first. But before they know it, they're dripping in sweat. He is with her, he is watching all around them. In this country, Sal has seldom seen two men dance bachata together so intimately and publicly at once. Maybe a few times when he arrived in New York and tried going out to bars, before he realized he couldn't be in these spaces for too long. A man's arm around another man, the two of them glued together, dicks hard, hips moving to the rhythm of Antony Santos's heartbreak oeuvre. Scattered on the dance floor are new and old lovers alike, holding each other as if only this night exists. Sal knows. He can feel it too. This is the closest they can be to their respective islands without hopping on a plane. The safest they can feel in public holding another man. He sees the sweetness in their smiles, the bitter wanting in their drunken eyes. The night will end. In an hour or two, they'll scatter back to their lonely lives. But for now, this. What's the use of longing when you have the dance floor?

"The music is so good," Charo yells, once, twice, before Sal can decipher her words amid the blaring horns.

An hour later, as they dance to a fast merengue, a circle gathers around her. The crowd cheers her on. Here, she's not the woman Sal is used to seeing at home, scrubbing grime or changing her daughter's diaper. In the center of all this energy, she looks so free. Closer to who she was when they first met.

"Oh my god, that was crazy!" she yells when the circle breaks.

In the midst of unfiltered joy, specks of sorrow. When was the last time Sal had this much fun with a friend, surrounded by the exuberance of gay people? It must have been a lifetime ago. The memories unfold their paper wings in his mind. His breath shortens, a knot dense as a stone forms in his stomach. Sal signals to Charo that he's getting another drink, but she's talking to strangers, already making new friends.

"Give me a second, amor," the bartender says as he wipes off the counter.

Sal's feet are starting to ache from all the dancing they've done. The rum will numb that too, he hopes. But his lungs. There's not enough air. He looks for the orange exit sign. He scratches at his throat. Just as he decides to go, someone sits on the stool next to him.

"Yo, this party's the shit," says the stranger to no one in particular. He sounds more jovial than drunk. Still, Sal doesn't respond.

He's older, at least thirty. Bald, dark skinned, brilliant smile. Dominican or African American, Sal can't tell at first glance. Sal nods and turns back to face the bar. He occupies himself with the bottles behind the counter, the pulsing lights reflecting off the glass. Slow and steady, he thinks as he catches his breath.

"Rum and Coke," Sal says when the bartender returns.

"Make it two," says the stranger next to him.

"I'm here with my friend." Sal decided before arriving: no boys tonight, just Charo and the dance floor.

The stranger doesn't hear him. Sal doesn't know if it's his accent or how loud the music is. Before he tries again, the stranger leans in and puts a hand to Sal's hip, as if that will help him hear Sal better. He smells of cool cologne mixed with sweat. Sal leans in and repeats himself.

"Oh, that's cool, that's cool," the stranger yells over the music. "Make it three."

"Thank you," Sal says after a pause.

"I love these parties. Spanish people know how to get down."

"It's not Spanish." It's a reflex, to correct him. Sal feels dread rising as soon as he opens his mouth but he can't stop himself from talking. "It's Latino if you're speaking generally; Dominican, Puerto Rican, whatever, if you want to be specific."

The man's smile disappears, but he doesn't seem insulted. "You're right. I live in The Bronx, I should know better," he says.

Half the people I know in New York call themselves "Spanish." What does it matter if this guy says it, Sal thinks, scolding himself in his mind.

"Technically, y'all are all Black anyway," the man adds playfully. Sal is relieved. He breathes a little easier.

A drop of sweat rolls down the man's forehead, reflecting the violet LED lights. It triggers a flashing image in Sal's mind. He imagines himself kissing the stranger's full, sweet lips, tracing his hands down the length of his back, inhaling his quickening breath, made more hollow and hungry by Sal's palm around this stranger's bulge. A night turned animal, compressed to a second in Sal's mind.

Before he can collect himself, their drinks are served.

The stranger signs the check, hands Sal a piece of paper, then disappears into the whirling body of the crowd. In Sal's palm, a number and a name. *Call me.* A gesture toward the future, calling it here.

Onscreen, a ship traverses the black of space from one planet to another. Flicker. The narrator's voice prophesizes an intergalactic battle. Flicker. Cut to next episode's preview.

Kiko jumps up from the floor where he's been sitting. He's tall for eleven, but his missing bottom teeth, his big ears, his animated eyes, all of it reminds Sal of his little brother's lingering innocence. Kiko goes on about what he thinks the heroes will find on the green planet. This is his favorite part about watching anime, making predictions about what will happen next.

"You gotta catch up on these reruns," Sal says. He sits on the couch behind his brother, chugging a gallon of water to ease his hangover. Another reason to not go dancing again, he thinks.

In the kitchen he hears his mother cleaning up after their breakfast. She hasn't brought up the job yet, but any second now. His headache intensifies. He brings the water bottle to his lips.

"I liked how they were training on the spaceship," Kiko says. "Que bacano."

This is Kiko's new word, bacano. His punctuation to everything he deems cool. He wasn't born on the island, so he must have learned the word from a cousin or a friend in school. Lately, he's been mimicking Spanish from back home. Not the halfway incarnation American-born kids like Kiko learn in New York, a version of both languages puzzled into one. Parqueo. Janguear. Frizado. What Kiko has been practicing lately is Santo Domingo's street slang, those words and colloquialisms that are sometimes forgotten when people leave the barrio to come to New York. Vaina de tiguere, his mother calls it.

"You know, people can't really fly to another planet like that. It'd take forever."

"Dude, who cares?" Kiko says, and goes on to explain another theory.

Just then their mother calls Sal into the kitchen.

Teresa puts down their coffee cups on coasters to avoid staining her precious tablecloth. The stitching of red fruit and green leaves stands out in the otherwise plain apartment. The rest of the place is white walls, pale curtains, functional furniture, but the tablecloth's bright decorative fabric is an homage to the tropics. It was there when Sal first joined his mother in New York, through the three years that he lived with her, and has remained in the same place since he moved out two years ago. Once or twice a month Teresa removes the cloth, wipes down the table with a steaming towel, then takes a toothbrush and a drop of stain remover to the spots on the tablecloth that might be marked by food, coffee, or time. Even Kiko, hyper as he can be, has learned to be attentive around the kitchen table. In the past, Sal tried to avoid sitting in the kitchen altogether, but that only enraged his mother more.

"The kitchen is to eat and drink coffee. Just be careful, coño. Is that so hard?"

Now he traces a red apple with his finger, careful not to pull or pick at the stitching.

"They called to say they went with another candidate," Sal says. He presses his finger against his brow, looks out the kitchen window to avoid her eyes. He's been dreading telling his mother about the museum job all morning, if only to avoid the burden of her disappointment weighed upon his own. He feels bad for lying. But he'd feel worse telling his mom the truth. What could he say to her, anyway? I froze, Mami. It sounds ridiculous just thinking it.

"Did you ask them when they'll have another opening? That can't be the only role they're looking to fill." Her hair hangs at her shoulders, freshly straightened yesterday. She wears her nurse's uniform, ironed and crisp. Sal imagines the other nurses at the hospital, how they might carry themselves with fatigue or boredom into their late-night shifts. But not his mother. She never lets them forget about how much she's had to sacrifice to get here: her old friends, the warmth of her country, and Sal, only just a year old, whom she left to be raised by her own mother. She used the pain from this loss to create her new life. Learning English when she first migrated to New York at nineteen. Getting her GED, then college, then a nurse's certification, and even after she became a professional, when she attained the job of her dreams, how she insisted on leaving the broken-down Lebanon Hospital for the more middle-class services of Presbyterian Hospital in Washington Heights.

"Salvador, you have to ask those questions. You have experience dealing with people, at the restaurant. Did you tell them that?"

"I don't think restaurant hosts qualify as tour guides."

"So you don't think you deserve the job." Teresa sits back in her chair and purses her lips to show her disappointment.

A sudden rain saves Sal from further scrutiny. Teresa rushes to close the window, mumbling complaints about how she just got her hair done. When Kiko is done stuffing two days' worth of clothes into his book bag to stay at Sal's place, she follows her sons to the door.

"I'll make sure he does his homework," Sal says, and pats his brother on the head. Kiko slaps his hand away and rushes downstairs to face the storm.

"Call the museum, Salvador," she says, holding his gaze.
"I'll call, Ma. I will."

Outside, the world is water.

"You know, gravity's doing all the work to make rain happen," Sal yells over the drum of droplets falling on their umbrella. "Otherwise it'd just be water vapor, floating in the atmosphere."

"This storm's not gonna beat me!" Kiko yells from inside his hoodie. He pushes against the wind with fervor, as far as he can go while remaining under the protection of Sal's umbrella.

By the time they arrive at Sal's apartment, his brother's clothes are heavy with rainwater. He sends Kiko off to a hot shower, hangs his small jeans and white T-shirt on top of his bedroom door.

"Hey, you home?" Sal calls for Don Julio, his roommate. For two years they've shared the apartment equally. The older man sleeps in the living room–turned–bedroom, and Sal sleeps in the actual bedroom, where he keeps a bed, a small television on top of his nightstand, and a bureau with a square mirror. They share a kitchen, the bathroom, and occasionally, on a warm day, the fire escape. There they sit to talk about that other country, what they miss, what they want to forget most of all. At first Sal was hesitant about living with someone more than twice his age. Would he be subject to the man's moods? Or his aged homophobia, strengthened through the decades, two countries, a war?

But Don Julio's moods only vacillate between deep interest in Sal's life and total indifference. Some days they sit out on the fire escape for hours over coffee and good conversation, once so long that they met the golden sunrise with energy to spare. Sal talked to Don Julio about the sky, all he'd learned from the documentary series that changed his life. He was thirteen when he happened upon *Cosmos: A Personal Voyage* on a Saturday morning flipping through channels on the television, trying to quell his boredom. What piqued his interest first were the images: drawings of the sun, Venus, Mars. Then the image of that plain gringo in his beige blazer, legs crossed, hands gesturing as he explained the nuances of astronomy as if he were explaining how to light a candle or start an oven.

In response to Sal's musings about space, Don Julio mostly talks about La Guerra de Abril. The fighting gave him purpose, a sense that he was a part of something alongside the common man. He was proud of his people, and for the first time felt he was helping to make his country a better place. But it ended quickly when the gringos came with their guns and soldiers and interventionist policies. He mourns the pueblo-centered future his people might have had. He also mourns his family. The days it took to find them, among the chaos. The yellow dress his daughter wore, sticky with red.

"Ironic," he always says. "I spent a month shooting at Americans only to come here, to live on gringo territory."

One late afternoon, just as they settled on the fire escape, the topic of love burrowed its way into their conversation. Sal pointed at a bright dot flickering by the horn of the moon.

"It's funny, Venus is supposed to be the planet of love," he said, taking another sip of his coffee. "But it's actually the hottest planet in our solar system. No amount of love could live there. It'd just shrivel up, dead as a raisin."

"And you, and Venus?"

"I don't have a girlfriend," Sal said.

"Oh, I know you don't have no *novia*. I'm asking you about love." The rest Don Julio said with his eyes, hazy with drowsiness, soft with compassion.

Sal looked up at Venus, brighter than any star in the sky, and laughed with relief.

Other days, like today, Don Julio just wants to be left alone.

"Did you hear back from the job?" Don Julio calls from his room.

"Not yet," Sal says. This is the first time he's lied to his roommate.

"Hopefully soon, then. Tell Kiko I made cookies," Don Julio says.

Sal hears his roommate shuffling to shut the heavy curtains that serve as a door.

Once he's out of the bathroom, Kiko follows the smell to the kitchen. Sal serves him a plate of warm microwaved cookies with a glass of milk. So American. As Dominican as Kiko is, with all the slang he picks up from school, all the stories he absorbs when he talks to his grandparents back on the island, he is still of this country. No Spanish accent plagues his tongue. No arbitrary document marks him resident or alien. Would everything be easier if Sal had been born here and not there? It's so stupid, he thinks. So much of a person's life is dictated by when and where they're born.

"Done!" Kiko gives Sal his empty plate and glass. Sal leans in to clean a chocolate smudge from his brother's face.

"Mi hermano, I'm eleven. Chill with that," Kiko says, and goes to watch TV in the bedroom.

Sal stays to wash the dishes, if only to get a few seconds of clarity away from his brother.

The museum closes in an hour. Sal knows he should call. Lie and say he got a stomach bug, like Charo suggested. It might not work. But he'll only find out if he focuses, like his mother is always asking him to do. If he tries. Sal flips through his address book for the museum's number. On the page where he's written it is a folded receipt. He doesn't remember putting it there when he got home drunk last night. The stranger hasn't crossed his mind all day. He was charming, sure, but Sal isn't moved by outgoing men who talk a lot. And yet. Now that the piece of paper is in front of him, he's curious. But what if it's a fake number? Or what if it's the right number, but Sal can't find what to say?

He closes the address book and throws it back on the kitchen table. He decides he will put the dishes away and call the museum. It's the responsible thing to do. The way forward, if he's to find one. He puts a glass on the drying rack, then glances back at the address book. Puts a plate away, then glances back at the phone.

"Hello?" It's a familiar voice on the other end.

"Hi, this is Sal. You gave me your number, at Shade's."

Silence. For a second Sal thinks the man must not be interested and is pretending he forgot all about last night. That's it, Sal's certain. He gets ready to hang up and run. Then, "Ah yes! The I'm-not-Spanish-I'm-Dominican guy."

"One of the many Dominican guys you gave your number to last night, I imagine," Sal says.

"Oh, he's got jokes!"

Sal feels his heart drumming in his chest. "Yeah, just, thanks for the drinks. I appreciate it."

"No problem," he says. "So, you called to thank me?"

The taunting in his voice pulls Sal closer, even through the phone.

"Do you want to go out sometime? I owe you a drink."

"Yeah, yeah. For sure. I'm actually having a get-together at my spot next week, if you wanna swing by."

When they're done, Sal slams the phone on the receiver. He paces the kitchen a few times. When the excitement finally overwhelms him, he calls Charo.

"Wait, wait! So you, Mr. I-don't-chase-anyone-ever, you actually called him?"

"Shut up," he says, but he knows she's right.

"And you like him?"

"Yo no sé, Charo. I don't even know him. You have to go to this party with me."

"I don't know. Robert was being difficult about me going out, and I'm not even sure if I work that day," she says. "Anyway, I gotta go, Carolina woke up. But wait, his name?"

"Vance," Sal says. Just one syllable. If he could elongate a name, stretch the sound out to contemplate all of its components, what would he find there? This name with its smooth, velvety start. Then the sizzle at its end, like the quiet hiss of fire.

THE CARIBBEAN SUN BURNS OVER LA ZONA COLONIAL. ON ONE corner, a band of lawless musicians sync tamboras and guitars to the tune of an old merengue. A pack of schoolkids chase after a one-eyed stray dog who's run off with their ball. And police officers stand in every corner, batons ready to protect tourists from the locals. Sal and Yadiel walk past a tourist burnt like a cereza and laugh off their nerves. Sal told his grandmother he'd be at Yadiel's tonight. Yadiel told his father he'd be at Sal's. They have just enough money for a cup of coffee and for the bus back to school in the morning. Who knows where the night will take them.

From the bus stop, they walk to Parque Colón. People crowd the benches under the shade of tall trees, chatting in groups or perusing the day's paper alone. At the center, a statue of the colonizer looms over the square. One arm down, the other raised to the sky. He points his index finger north, as if to say, *Look what I've discovered.* As if to say, *All of it is mine.* But he's not alone. Under him, at the base of the pedestal, looking up in reverence or fear, is a statue of the queen Anacaona. Yadiel stops to admire her as they walk by.

"I read about her," Yadiel says. He launches a rock at the dirty pigeons resting on her shoulders. Even the sound of their flapping wings makes Sal queasy.

Next to them a group of girls stand in a circle talking over one another. The boys still wear their school uniforms, light-blue polo shirts with khaki pants. They hate the uniform policy, though they know the privilege of attending a private school over a public one. In the ladder of education, their school sits just above the public sector, a privilege gifted to them by Sal's mother, who works in New York, and Yadiel's ease with words, which earned him a scholarship. Still, they don't come from the same world as the girls next to them. They know this just by hearing them talk. The girls are part of the true elite, schooled in some private corner of the city, taught by gringo foreigners to speak proper Spanish, English, French. If Sal and Yadiel were remotely interested in girls, they would offer them unwarranted compliments, as they've been taught to do.

"Mira," Sal says, and pulls two fat yellow mangoes from his book bag. Yadiel curses at him for hiding them for so long. He claws for his mango, bites a small hole in its flesh, massages the pulp, and sucks from the fruit every last drop of juice. Sal does the same. When they're done, the skin of each mango is wrinkled and saggy. Only the pits remain.

Next to them, one of the girls says something to her circle that makes them all laugh. Yadiel flips them a middle finger. Sal tries to stop his friend from walking over to escalate things further, but he squeezes the mango in his hand too hard. The seed breaks through the rubbery skin, falls wet and sticky on his shirt. The girls laugh again.

"Let's just go." Sal throws the seed into a nearby bush and pulls his friend away from the park square.

"I fucking hate girls. I really do," Yadiel says.

They sit at La Cafetería Colonial and order one coffee to share, negro con azúcar. Yadiel drinks most of it and explains that this cafeteria is famous for hosting some of the nation's most illustrious minds. Painters, writers, even revolutionaries have met here, as far back as the 1930s. Men who would later become leaders of the pueblo and enemies of the nation's authoritarian elite. All these heroes strung together by the coffee he drinks from now. It's rumored that even Pedro Mir once sang his most famous poem here, that the walls of the cafeteria were filled with laments about the tierra, this sad, old country.

"I bet he's a maricón, too," Yadiel whispers in Sal's ear. The only thing Yadiel loves more than the great Dominican poets is twisting their poetry to create gay alternatives of their lives. Pedro Mir isn't sad about the country. He's sad 'cause he's not getting fucked. Aída Cartagena Portalatín writes about una mujer sola not because of the great social burden placed on Dominican women, but because she's a raging lesbian. The dream she writes is about finding another woman, eloping under the Caribbean sky. Even Salomé Ureña, founding mother of Dominican letters, is a subject of Yadiel's queer reconstruction of history.

"Why do you think she started that school for girls?"

"You're sick," Sal says, but he laughs. Their minds are what draw them together. They're not particularly excellent at school. Yadiel gets better grades to keep up with his scholarship, but for the most part, they go unnoticed by the teachers and authority figures in school. Rather, it's their particular obsessions that bind them. Sal with his facts about the planets and the nature of light. Yadiel with his queering of Dominican poets.

And, of course, there's the secret that everyone knows. They've never had serious girlfriends, not anything of significance. And anyway, no relationship status could hide their mannerisms: their walk, the way they hold their hands, how their eyes roll to the back of their heads when they're annoyed. They're far too flamboyant to go unnoticed, especially Yadiel. While Sal is shy, Yadiel is unapologetic, so much so that Sal thinks sometimes Yadiel exaggerates his mannerisms, just to piss their teachers off. Any attempt to justify these mannerisms was thrown out the window in eighth grade when Yadiel got into a fistfight with one of the popular girls in school. Maricón, she called him, back when that word was still a fresh wound. After Yadiel's fight, there was no question. Yadiel was a girl-fighting maricón, and Sal, by association, was maricón adjacent.

"Where did you meet this guy, anyway?"

"I told you, loca, friend of a friend. You know how that goes, everybody has a gay cousin," Yadiel says. Sal likes the sound of that, *loca*. They've been doing this new thing where they refer to each other in feminine pronouns, and it feels good. Simple. Like seeing each other better.

An hour later he finally comes through the door.

"¿Yadiel, verdad? Ren," he says as he sits next to them.

He has the eyes of a fox—playful, seeking. Ren takes the boys in, their uniforms, their smooth faces round with youth. He wears a red shirt, which accentuates the constellation of freckles on his cheeks and nose. Sal also notices that both of Ren's ears are pierced. Most of the men he knows only have one pierced, and certainly never the right ear. Everybody knows a piercing on the right ear makes you a pájaro, Sal thinks.

They talk until the café closes at nine. Ren tells them where he went to school, the part-time jobs he does now to get by, mostly in hotels. They circle around the topic but never enter into it, past that hidden door. Sal looks around to see if anyone will notice. Maybe the old couple sitting by the door. Or the owner, who doesn't come out from behind the counter to ask them what they'd like. They must see it in Yadiel, how he fills the place up with his voice. They must see it in Ren, too. He exudes feminine energy out of some hidden core at his center. The way he wipes sweat from his forehead with an open palm. The way he puckers his lips, just so, to accentuate a joke. Or how he squints his eyes when he's listening to Yadiel, those vulpine eyes glaring with a hint of wisdom, a hint of wickedness. He even crosses one leg over the other, the way men shouldn't, the way these boys have been instructed not to do their whole lives.

Sal wonders if this is their future, if they will look and speak and move like Ren one day. The thought of it is as exciting as it is frightening. Sal can't tell which feeling dominates the other. The one that comes rolling down his temple in the form of a sweat droplet, or the anticipation that moves him to shake his leg under the table.

Outside, a moonless sky blankets the city.

"Okay, chicos," Ren says, and they follow him down Calle El Conde. They turn into a dark alleyway, away from the streetlight. Ren says he will go first, tells them to keep watch for the stray drunk or militant officer doing his rounds. He goes into the shadows with his bag slung over his back.

When he returns twenty minutes later, he is a new person. Sal looks at him with his mouth open.

"Wow," Yadiel says for the both of them. Ren wears a long, wavy black wig that falls to the middle of his back. A loose red dress hangs off his shoulders, revealing a tattoo of a rose right below his left collarbone. He continues the rest of his transformation before them, in the dim glow of the streetlight. Two small hoops replaced by large silver earrings. Worn-down sneakers replaced by black strappy heels. His makeup takes the most time. He looks at himself in a small compact mirror to powder his forehead. Finally, when his eyeliner is done, he pulls out a tube of red lipstick. The boys stare as Ren paints a line across each mound of flesh. He presses them together, then puckers his mouth.

"This is what I spend all my fucking money on," he says. "How do I look?"

Yadiel looks at Ren as if he's found a pearl after searching long and hopelessly in the dark. He's too stunned to speak. Next to him, Sal is unnerved. He feels as if he might laugh at the sight. A man turning into a woman right before his eyes. How absurd! Then there is the other. Or the others. The multitudes within him that fight to push their way to the front of conscious thought, like a field of fireflies suddenly flickering in synchrony, as if to say, *You have arrived.*

"Can't be seen out here looking like a maricón, can't be seen at the parties looking like an ugly man. Qué maldito lío," Ren says, rolls his eyes, but smiles at his reflection in the compact mirror. Yadiel goes into the shadows next, and when he's done he comes out wearing his aunt's blue blouse and tight black jeans. His skinny arms stick out awkwardly, and the blouse drapes around him. He parts his small fro and, in it, places a white flower. "Oh, she's virginal," Ren says, and fixes the flower on Yadiel's head. Then he takes a few pins from his bag, uses them to tighten Yadiel's blouse in the back. Now it looks as if the blouse were made not to be filled with breasts and an older woman's heft, but for Yadiel's body exactly. Ren puts orange color on Yadiel's lips and uses a hint of highlighter to accentuate his cheekbones.

In the alleyway Sal dresses up like the partygoers he's seen in music videos. Tight jean shorts, a white tank top, a shirt tied around his waist.

"What are you doing? I thought you were taking something from your grandma," Yadiel says when Sal returns.

"Do I look bad? I don't know, I wanted to look more cool than girly, you know?"

"You look like a boy. That's not the point," Yadiel says, gesturing to his own outfit.

Ren jumps between them. "You look cute as a boy, it's okay. But we gotta get some paint on your face. You'll like it, te lo prometo." Ren draws bold eyeliner onto each eye. Sal likes the way Ren holds his chin up to the light, this sudden intimacy between them. In the small circle of the compact mirror, he looks like an owl or some other bird of the night. He looks away from his reflection. A rush of shame warms his face.

Ren tells them they'll go through the back alleys to avoid crowds. Sal refuses to turn the feeling into thought for fear that it will paralyze him. But he feels it there underneath his skin. His body responding to danger, to the possibility of meeting the baton of some cop or the ire of a stranger, dressed as they are. He looks next to him to find in Yadiel's face some semblance of what he feels, but his friend is shaking with excitement.

Not so long ago, they were boys playing baseball in the street. Raging against some inner beast. Or not resisting at all, taken over by its might. The wrath of boyhood—a scream, a belch, unabashed laughter. The soles of their naked feet slapping the concrete. A bloody knuckle crushed against another's cheekbone. A bruised lip, a cutting joke, a chorus of argument. And when coupled or in a small group, sudden gentleness. Loyalty, when needed, like showing up to a friend's fight just in case, or lying to another's parents to get away with disobedience. The ever-present shyness in front of girls, in front of teachers, in front of the mirror, facing their own naked bodies. Skinny or fat or too small or too big or smooth or growing hair, each day something new. The fear of jumping but jumping anyway, even if only to impress one another. They were everything, everything. Boys.

Now look at them. Girls, or adjacent to them. Girly boys, maybe, gliding through the streets of Santo Domingo, protected by the night. Soft as feathers. Quick as shadows. Hiding, but filled with a gust of pride for everything they've made of themselves, what they've managed to take from the corner of the mind or a dream. A fantasy materialized.

They arrive at a white-and-yellow house. Sal doesn't come to this part of the city often. Whoever owns these pastel houses must have money, more than he and any of his family have ever had as far back as he can trace. Maybe his uncle who married a wealthy doctor from La Romana. But his uncle entered the world of the Dominican elite and never looked back, not even to thank his mother, Sal's grandmother, for everything she'd done to finish raising her kids alone after her husband died from a liver disease.

Ren leaves them on the sidewalk. He walks through an alley toward the back of the house. His heels click-clack on the pavement. Sal listens for the echo of Ren's walk until it disappears.

"Are you mad at me?"

"I wish you weren't such a coward," Yadiel says.

What does Yadiel know about courage, hidden in the shadows same as him? He's about to protest when they hear someone running up behind them. Sal shrieks. Yadiel jumps to defend them, but instead of a hostile attacker, they turn, and it's the one-eyed dog they saw at the park earlier, jumping at their thighs, begging to play. The socket where its eye was caves into its face. Yadiel throws a rock for the dog to follow.

"It's so ugly," Sal says, and sighs in relief.

"Not like us."

"Not like us," Sal agrees.

When Ren returns, he confirms that he has the green light to enter.

"Listen to me," Ren says. He's taller than them by a few inches. More so now in his heels. "This is fun and all, pero tienen que tener cuidado. No drinks, no going home with no viejo, no calling the girls men. If she says she's a woman, you believe her. I'm serious. Make friends, but don't lose sight of each other. You're the only one the other needs tonight. Got it?" Ren grabs them by the shoulders and pushes them together. He leads them through the back, up the stairs to the second floor. A boy like them opens the door. He wears a brunette wig that stops at his shoulders, a blue dress that stops at his knees. He screams, "Renata," and Yadiel looks behind him to see who he's talking to. But Sal has caught on. Ren is someone else here. Renata turns and puts a finger to her eye, as if to say, *Eyes open*. Then she disappears inside. An intoxicating smell of rum and tobacco wafts from the party. It beckons them in and repulses them at once.

Ready? they say to each other with their eyes.

Yadiel finds Sal's hand, and they step forward together.

For the first time since her daughter was born, Charo conquers her guilt and slips into a clothing store.

No me compro ni un panti, she often jokes, and says it with pride, all she sacrifices for her family. Even her beauty, which at one point was of great importance to her, she's set aside to privilege her domestic life. When she first arrived in New York, she couldn't afford to go to the salon every week like some of the girls in the supermarket. But every now and then she bought herself cheap earrings or a blouse on sale. It wasn't a lot, but it was enough to show she cared about her looks. This was the woman Robert met, the woman he lusted over for weeks until she finally let him take her out. After dinner, he brought her home to his apartment, a humble place with a leak in the bathroom and not enough sunlight, but still a place of his own. Charo, who'd been bouncing around rented rooms for two, was enthralled. Here he was, a young Dominican immigrant like herself, who had his own apartment and a good job at a warehouse for a fruit juice company, with a union and vacation days and a growing pension waiting for him at the end of his life. He was everything she'd been taught to look for in a man. They had sex that first night. He was rough but controlled. She came twice as he held her to him, and she liked that most of all, that he wanted her enough to put her pleasure first.

What has she been making of her life? When she was a teenager she swore she'd never be like the lineage of women before her, shaped by the hands of their husbands, the demands of their children. It'd be fine if work was inspiring, if her social life was exciting. But she's been working supermarket jobs since she arrived in New York over five years ago. And she only has one friend to speak of. Is this it, then? Is this as good as life gets in this country? The thought makes her cold inside.

Now, at this off-brand boutique on 170th Street, she rummages through stack after stack of clothes, looking for something to wear to Vance's party. She finds the perfect pink silk blouse on a mannequin, the last one in her size.

"It'll look better on me than on this plastic dummy, I promise," she says to the floor manager as he strips the mannequin naked.

Outside, the block is hot with the anticipation of a Friday afternoon. Charo passes schoolkids crowding outside a video game shop. Men old and tired gather around a rowdy game of dice, gambling away the few dollars in their pockets. One of the men moves a bottle from his lips and whistles at Charo as she walks by with her stroller. She ignores him and stops by a woman selling dulces and arepas. Food carts sit on every corner of 170th, exchanging American dollars for dishes from all over the world. At the top of the hill, on The Concourse, Salvadoreñas heat up pupusas until cheese oozes out of the warm tortillas. Down the strip, a quiet West African man sells yam by the pound. At the bottom of the hill, under the 4 train station, a Puerto Rican man with a round belly shaves ice into fruit juice piraguas and boasts about the ten summers he's kept the block cool and hydrated, even though it's only April. Charo knows slices of their personal lives, like the pupusa lady's abusive husband, whom she refuses to leave, or the piragua man's cat, who has run away from home more times than he can count.

She's not done gossiping with the arepa lady when a familiar voice calls behind her. It's her father's friends, though how and when they met her father, she can't recall. They look like a pair of ostriches: no chin, big bulging eyes, neck skin sagging. And they're unusually tall, the wife made taller than her husband by her church-lady heels.

"When are you coming to visit?" the man says. His wife next to him stretches her long neck toward the carriage and coos at Charo's daughter. You'd think it's been months since they've seen each other, by how excited they sound. But it was only last week that Charo ran into them on her way out of the supermarket. And a few weeks before that, the same conversation with a different couple, that time her mom's acquaintances. Charo wonders how many friends her parents have on the block. If they'll ever tire of inviting her to gatherings she'll never attend. She's sure they still keep in touch with her parents. She knows she's not being paranoid because her mother has let it slip once or twice that a neighbor saw her running to work late, that another saw her wearing too short a skirt. Much as she likes gossiping with the arepa lady, or standing under the piragua man's umbrella listening to cat stories, the block feels claustrophobic. Like she's still back in the barrio under her parents' intrusive eye.

Because she can't tell them to go fuck themselves, she smiles and promises to call soon. Yes, the baby would love to meet their Chihuahua. Yes, she's sure it would make her father happy. She tells them she has an appointment to run to, but yes, yes, of course she'll call.

As soon as she walks into the salon, stroller in front of her, the women reprimand her for being gone so long. They complain about her dry hair, how it must miss their expert hands, their special prod-ucts. They go on and on, talking of her hair as if it were a thing with its own vitality. Then they circle around Carolina to offer a barrage of compliments and blessings. The baby stares back at them from her stroller, her hand clutching a clump of arepa.

"Una morena tan fina como tu, con ese pajón," the saloneras complain. Charo's small nose, high cheekbones, unassuming lips. People have called her "morena fina" all her life to make her exemplary, to suggest that she's beautiful not because of but despite her deep brown skin. She's used to these backhanded compliments, but it still stings. She offers a smile of apology to excuse this untamed hair that so betrays her.

They rush to lather her scalp with their strongest conditioner. The hot water loosens her temples, smooths the edge of the women's insults. She's missed this process, all of it long, tedious, burning, itchy, but so full of latent satisfaction.

Charo feels a quickening pulse in her chest, something deep inside her flickering to life.

The next day Charo takes extra measures to avoid a fight. She hires the babysitter, since Robert is working a rare overnight shift. She cleans the apartment. She even makes Robert's favorite meal, rice and oxtail.

"So you weren't going to tell me? You're going to leave our daughter with a stranger and just sneak out?" He's taller than her by at least six inches. His full lips. The strength of his jaw. White tank top tight against his muscled chest. His collarbone, that sleek, curved bone she's kissed a thousand times. He looks good today. That makes it harder to detest him.

"Eunice has been taking care of the baby for months."

In her towel, Charo tries to move with ease, as if they're discussing the weather. She goes to the bathroom to wrap her hair up in front of the mirror, yells back to him, "I put red wine in the oxtail this time. The gravy came out great."

"Where are you going?" He stands by the door and crosses his arms.

"Your clothes, they're folded and put away. I didn't put the button-downs away 'cause you like to do that yourself." She turns from him, leans into the tub. The faucet spits out water a few times before it turns into a steady stream.

"I don't mind you going out, but the least you can do is give me a heads-up."

"Just make sure to put the shirts away, que no se te olvide. They'll get wrinkled if you leave them on the couch."

"I'm talking to you," Robert says.

Charo tinkers with the shower knob, trying to find the right temperature.

"Are you going out with him again, el maricón ese?"

He opens his eyes wide, like he, too, is startled by his words.

"I didn't mean—"

"Get the fuck out," she says, and slams the bathroom door in his face.

They meet up on The Concourse, then take the 4 train down to 138th. Sal wears a dark blue corduroy shirt. It's a long-sleeve, cozy enough to keep him warm on this cool April night, but he looks elegant, more so than Charo is used to seeing him. The top buttons are undone, revealing a small patch of chest hair. His curls are wet and defined.

"You look so handsome," she says. She's still bitter about her fight with Robert. But she's also happy to see Sal this excited to go out. She can't tell where her own feelings begin and end. Everything floods together. Is she wrong for leaving her daughter with a babysitter? This is the first time Carolina has stayed the night somewhere else. Just outside the train station, under the highway where pigeons and the homeless gather, an unexpected sob comes rushing out of her.

Charo holds her hair back with one hand, wipes her tears with the tip of her finger, careful not to smudge her makeup. "It's okay, it's okay," Sal says until her breathing settles and she's ready to walk again.

The resident drunk at the liquor store opens the door for them and guides them through the small, cramped space. He tells them about how much New York has changed since the eighties, how much the streets have cleaned up, how the moon landing was staged, probably, and how maybe Clinton isn't really that bad 'cause the intern was pretty. Beautiful women will turn you lunatic, man, he says through missing teeth. Charo pulls a dollar from her purse. He looks down at the gift with joy. Then he lifts his chin and swallows his gratitude. What will a dollar get him, his new face says, though he pockets the crumpled paper anyway.

"I know it's not easy. You're doing good," Sal says once they're back outside. She doesn't ask what he means; he doesn't elaborate. Silence settles between them like a balm.

A pale Puerto Rican kid opens the door and rushes them inside. Charo's first thought is that his brain is strung out to a higher frequency by some psychedelic drug. He talks a mile a minute as he leads them to the kitchen, hands them red cups full of a bubbly blue drink. Two others join them in the kitchen, chatting them up as if they're old friends. It becomes clear, as they direct their attention toward Sal, that they've been sent by the party's host to take care of them. Once he's described the contents of their drinks, how he's styled his cargo pants and plain white T-shirt, the pregame he went to before arriving here, the Puerto Rican kid grabs Sal by the wrist and pulls him through a crowd into the rest of the apartment.

Charo wants to follow her friend down the long hallway, but she's caught in conversation with a stranger. The man before her reminds her of Robert—muscled build, fresh Caesar cut, light skin.

He has a noticeable scar where an eyebrow piercing used to be, and a dark, flirty gaze.

"I know she's just another blanquita, but I really dig it," he says.

The teen pop idol fills the apartment with a song about blooming sexuality. Charo doesn't have to keep up with American pop culture. She lives in her own little bubble in The Bronx, where Dominican culture dominates most of the spaces she inhabits. The bodega, the salon, the taxicab. Her people have created a village in their own corner of the city. The closest she gets to American music is at birthdays and holiday parties, when Charo's cousins put her on to their favorite rappers. She's seen how hip-hop makes her cousins feel tough, protected, cool. Charo often wonders where her daughter will fall in that cultural divide. She and Robert do their best. They only speak to her in Spanish. Robert plays merengue from the small battery-run radio he keeps at home. But what if it's not enough? What if Carolina likes American music more? Is that all bad?

Just as the urge to run back home emerges again, the man in front of her breaks out in dance. For a second, Charo worries that he'll bump against the kitchen counter or a cabinet, but his moves are controlled. He executes the choreography from the music video with precision, twirling and kicking and moving his muscled arms in swift, elegant strokes. The pout, the sensual swing of his hips. It's an unusual sight, a man with arms that big performing as teenage gringa longing for love, but Charo can appreciate talent, and he's captivating in the kitchen's low light.

She gathers that his name is Mauricio from the chorus of compliments around him. Charo holds his drink, waits for him to be released from the hands of his admirers.

"So how do you and Sal know each other?" Mauricio asks, catching his breath. Another agent sent by the party's host.

Two cups of the blue drink make her brave enough to tell Mauricio about all the trouble she got into as a teenager. Escapades with dangerous boys. Arguments with her parents. That one time her mother sent her to an aunt's house for a week for sneaking around with a boy.

"Wait, you fucked him in your house?" he screams above the music.

"It was on the veranda! And it was like three a.m., my parents were out of town. How was I supposed to know the vieja next door got up that early to pray?"

"Girl, you were wild. And you're married now? And a kid?"

"Well, not legally married yet. But I'm twenty-five, I have to settle down eventually," she says. At this, he lets out an exaggerated laugh. It stings, and with the rush of shame Charo realizes that an inane part of her desperately wants Mauricio to like her. She brings the cup to her lips to hide her face.

Just then, a woman walks into the kitchen. She wears a violet spaghetti-strap dress, tight against her thin figure, her dark brown skin. She looks like she's on her way to someone's high-end event somewhere on the Upper East Side, where gringos reign.

"I'm thirty-two. It's a new day. Fuck that marriage shit," Mauricio says. Charo gulps down the rest of her drink. Before she can respond, the woman wraps her arm around Mauricio's waist.

Her name is Ella. Her perfume is floral, and she is taller than Charo by a few inches, made even more so by her heels. Charo's mind immediately snakes itself around mistrust. She becomes a younger version of herself. In high school, Charo was never invested in being popular. She didn't want attention and all the work one had to do to keep such a rank. She preferred the currency that came with being desired by boys. And not just the boys who talked hot shit, who bragged about fucking, grabbed their dicks in public, even smacked an ass here or there during recess. Those boys told every story around the thing but had never felt the intensity of being desired in return. Charo liked the cool tigueres with experience, or the quiet, focused types who, so tired from the pressure to be excellent student athletes, channeled their self-hatred and rage into their libidos. Even if there were more popular girls, girls who got better grades or had pretty straight hair, Charo felt confident in that covert circuit of desire.

"Baby, it's almost a new millennium. Let the girl be married if she wants. Long as she loves him," Ella says, and winks.

This close up, she can see that Ella's bottom teeth are misaligned. A single flaw in all that beauty. It gives Charo some relief.

"C'mon. That idiot will talk your ear off all night if you let him," Ella says, and pulls Charo into the rest of the party.

The living room is divided into clusters of conversation above the music. Sal notices the vibe is different here than it is downtown. Most of the people here are men of color. A little bit like Latin or hip-hop night, though those spaces, white people tend to infiltrate. Many of the men here are masculine, some so steeped in their hood-dude veneer that Sal wouldn't guess they're gay if he passed them in the street. He can't imagine some of these tatted men, in their baggy pants and tank tops, sucking dick or taking it up the ass. Whatever his own limiting views about gay men might be, it's clear he's been missing out on the gay scene in The Bronx.

Sal and the Puerto Rican kid pass the bathroom, where through the door that's just ajar, Sal sees someone bent over the sink, snorting a line.

The Puerto Rican kid leads Sal to a door, knocks, then pushes him inside. It takes a second for Sal's senses to adjust to the bedroom. The lights are dim. A thin screen of smoke wafts and fills the room. A young man lies on the bed, head in a hoodie, mumbling in a drunken language only he understands. Vance sits on the bed with him and rubs circles on his back.

"I know, Luis, I know," Vance says.

Sal senses he's intruding. He reaches for the door, but Vance gestures for him to come closer and hands him a joint. Sal wraps his lips around the joint where Vance's mouth must have been seconds ago. He's as handsome as Sal remembered. Same keen eyes, same playful mouth. The drunk guy tries to stand, but Vance cradles him in his arms.

When he falls asleep, Vance covers his friend with a blanket. He places a hand on Sal's hip, gestures toward the window. Vance climbs out onto the fire escape first. Sal notices the outline of a crab tattooed on his right arm, right above the elbow. The ink is faded into his skin. Must be old, Sal thinks. He wants to ask, but he climbs out quietly and sits at the very edge of the metal railing. They dangle their legs and look out at the street below.

"Sorry about Luis," Vance says. "It's Mauricio, my roommate. Can't keep his dick in his pants." He takes the joint from Sal and lights it. His beard is fuller than when Sal last saw him, though it's clean and shaped. Sal tries not to look too hard, focuses his attention on the street below. In front of a bodega, two men yell at each other over the speakers playing bachata. People gather. The scene balloons with the promise of violence. But then a police car drives by and flashes its lights to break up the crowd.

"I didn't think you'd come," Vance says, and blows out a stream of smoke.

"Why did you think that?"

"You seem, uh, uninterested," he says, stretching the last word carefully.

Sal thinks back to the few interactions he's had with Vance. At the bar, then on the phone. His intention was to seem self-possessed, to mask the dizzying doubt blurring his thoughts. Was he cold? Too guarded?

"I'm here," Sal says, half to Vance, half to himself. "Your friends are nice."

"They're crazy."

Vance tells him about Mauricio, whom he's lived with for years. They went to high school together here in The Bronx, though Mauricio dropped out right before they finished to chase after some wealthy white guy he met at a bar. The man was married, two kids, corporate job, very cookie-cutter closeted faggot trying to have his cake doubly. But the sex was good, the money better. Mauricio followed him down to a small town in Florida to live a life among the citrus trees. He promised Mauricio that he would leave his family once the kids got old enough, that he would relocate to another city where they could be new and anonymous. He promised a lot, but the man got bored with time, found himself a Cuban from Miami to fulfill his Latin-lover fantasies, and put Mauricio out. Mauricio wandered around Miami for a few months, tried to find himself another daddy to put him up, but after a close scare with the virus, he gave up and returned to The Bronx, ashamed of whom he'd become for what he thought was love. Then there's Luis, college educated and brilliant, except he fell in love with Mauricio, Vance says, so he can't possibly be that smart. And Ella, who's wiser than all of them together, though he doesn't know if she went to school, where she lived before New York. He doesn't know much about her past at all. Sal listens quietly as Vance draws the links between his friends and acquaintances, all these people strung together by sex, parties, feuds, happenstance. Sal wonders if he, too, will become a dot in that constellation.

"You get really upset, talking about Mauricio," Sal says.

"Must mean I love him, that idiot."

Below them, a fire truck rushes by. They wait until its horns are at a distance.

"We're getting older," Vance says. "We can't keep partying forever."

They're both high now, light as a breeze. Vance takes one last pull and offers it to Sal, who shakes his head too quickly. His vision blurs. To avoid getting nauseated, Sal trains his attention on his hands squeezing the metal bars.

"I just talked a lot. What's up with you?"

"I'm good with listening," Sal says.

Silence falls between them again. For a second Sal thinks he can get away with forfeiting little about himself, but Vance meets his eyes and waits.

"I think my mom is disappointed," he says between his teeth. Out of all the things to say, Sal thinks to himself. But Vance gestures for him to go on, and he does. Sal tells him about his job at the restaurant, his mother's crushing expectations, Kiko's love of anime, his concern about Charo's relationship. He worries that he's gone on too long. But Vance puts his arm around Sal's waist to reassure him. Sal goes on mapping out the uncertainty of his present life, as if he's pouring himself into a well with no end.

"I mean, she was barely there the first eighteen years of my life. She visited every couple of years. But she was here, preoccupied with her own stuff. Sometimes I wanna tell her she has no right to care now. Is that too harsh?"

"Nah. We have a right to resent our parents."

"Though she's not all wrong," Sal says, and sighs. It's been a week and he still hasn't called the museum to reschedule his interview. "Sometimes it feels like I'm just floating through life."

"You strike me as someone who's smart in all the right ways. You'll figure it out." He opens his palm in front of Sal. "How about we go float together, back at the party? I'll stay with you."

"You're so corny." Sal elbows Vance in the ribs. They cackle like they're teenagers. An hour ago, this familiarity would have been impossible. He might have even argued against Vance's optimism.

Sal hates when people talk about the future with certainty. It only makes him think about the fractured past. He has to repeat the thought in his mind: Be here. As he feels pulled to this man he barely knows, as he offers glimpses into his life, as he laughs and laughs till his head is numb. Be here, be here.

"To be clear, I'm interested," Sal says, and plants a kiss on Vance's lips. "Let's go float."

ALL NEXT WEEK, ON TOP OF ROBERT'S POINTED SILENCE, CHARO has to deal with bathroom floods from the upstairs apartment that ruin her rugs, curtains, towels. When she gets home from work on Monday, Carolina in tow, the bathroom floor is a pool of brown water. She's up late into the night disinfecting everywhere the brown water touches, but when she's back from work the next day, the ceiling is leaking again. She calls the super, who promises he'll go and talk to the upstairs neighbor. But she's greeted with a third flood on Wednesday. This time she doesn't wait. Charo marches upstairs to confront her neighbor.

"Non-flushable, coño," she says, and points to the packaging that the Mexican woman has handed her. The woman apologizes, tells her that this is her first baby, she had no idea. Charo knows she should be kind, extend her empathy to this young woman just like her, disoriented and made stupid by the demands of being a mom. But she's jaded by fatigue. Charo sucks her teeth, threatens the woman, and slams the door to show she means it.

On Thursday, after she's cleaned everything again, she buys new bathroom linens and threatens to sue if the super doesn't repaint the bathroom ceiling. Charo is relieved when Sal calls to invite her out again. She says yes on the spot, thrilled by the prospect of leaving behind the baby and Robert and her flooding apartment for a few hours.

Sal usually works at the Cuban restaurant Friday nights. It's the busiest night on account of the corporate crowds who come in for happy hour. He's been a host there for over three years, longer than all the waitstaff have worked there, and even longer than some of the cooks, so he's trusted to manage the staff while the manager takes care of their most valuable customers. Seniority also gifts Sal the privilege of changing his schedule with freedom. When he tells the manager he won't make it Friday night, the old Cuban man grumbles but doesn't resist.

"You'd think you guys are in your sixties, with the shit you gotta do to go out one night," Mauricio says to them when they're the last ones to arrive.

"Leave them alone," Ella says, welcoming them into the apartment with a kiss on the cheek.

Ella and Charo sit next to each other on the couch, making idle conversation about work and Ella's secret thrift shop where she gets all her dresses. Luis likes this conversation and finds his way between Ella and Charo. His black hair, drooped shoulders, still mouth, all of it gives him a gloomy disposition. But talking about style brightens his eyes. Mauricio serves them all his new sage-and-orange cocktail. Luis takes a glass, but he doesn't say thank you, doesn't even look up at his boyfriend. Every now and then the circle comes together to form a single conversation, usually with Mauricio at the center telling some story about a night at the club. Sal sits next to Vance, close enough that their thighs touch.

"All right, my man," Vance says. "Can you shut up and tend to the music? I made another mix."

But just as Mauricio pops in another CD, Ella jumps up and stands in the middle of their circle. She puts her hand on her neck, and from her throat escapes her voice. It's deeper than Sal expected but still soft. She sings a song by another Ella, about a paper moon lighting a love affair. She points her finger in the air, twirls in one direction, then back again. Her movements are flirtatious. Sal almost believes it. It's not that Ella isn't a good singer. She sounds nice enough. But it feels strained, like she's trying to fit someone else's voice in her mouth. And yet, the look on Charo's face. She doesn't seem to hear where Ella's voice leaps and flounders. His friend is enthralled.

"Coño loca!" Charo yells. "Do you sing? Like, are you a professional, in front of audiences and stuff?"

Ella waits tables at a restaurant downtown and features during jazz night once a week. Nothing too serious, she explains, except it's the only time she's the woman of her own dreams, on that little stage singing away the night.

"We all have fantasies about our lives. I'm trying to live my own," Ella says.

After Ella's performance, they go around telling stories about their first times. First time driving a car, first time getting disrespected by a gringo, first time having sex.

"Do you want to know about my first time when I wanted it? Or like when I was a kid, and my uncle touched me?" Mauricio's smile is wicked.

"Dude, c'mon," Vance says.

"I'm just saying! We all have a story like that, no?"

Sal doesn't say so out loud, but he agrees with Mauricio. He's always believed that every gay kid has a story of being molested. So many of the sexually confused boys he knew as a teenager, boys who suggested themselves to him by grabbing their dicks in front of him or who groped him before calling him a maricón, all those boys had a story to tell. About a cousin or neighbor or uncle or aunt who had taken advantage of their innocence and thrust them into the world of desire too young. These boys were tough, detached, but the few who told him their stories, during recess or in the back of an empty classroom, they talked about it like what happened to them was a day of inevitable rain. Only one boy cried on Sal's shoulder like he was really living with the haunting of his uncle's touch every day. Sal thought this intimacy would make them friends. But the next day the boy started avoiding him. Told their mutual friends Sal tried to kiss him. Even got a girlfriend soon after, as if to prove to Sal that there was nothing wrong with him, after all. Sal often wondered how many there were. A hundred? A thousand? Dominican boys everywhere carrying secret stories of sexual violence, a country of drowning boys.

For Sal it was a neighbor when he was nine. The neighbor was five years older. Never penetration, never a kiss or any sign of affection. He only fondled Sal while he masturbated. The neighbor's probing was methodical, a search for whatever part of Sal pleased him most that day. They were left alone when Sal's grandmother was out running errands. Sometimes Sal tried to go out on the veranda, where the wandering eye of a passing pedestrian might deter his neighbor from touching him. Other times, he would lie in bed unmoving, let his mind wander until the neighbor finished. This went on for a few months. Eventually, his neighbor got bored of sneaking around and found himself a girlfriend he could touch and kiss in public. Sal sometimes saw them in the barrio holding hands, and he'd feel a mixture of relief and jealousy at once. What had his neighbor found in the girl that Sal couldn't give him? What was it about girls? he wondered. Did she feel herself changed, as Sal had felt, beating to the time of his neighbor's touch, transmuted by desire from innocence to whatever lies beyond?

Sal never grew to hate the older boy who molested him. He imagined confronting him, demanding that his neighbor apologize, that he explain what Sal himself couldn't put into words. But that resentment never grew. Instead, he bent all of his will into variations of the same question: Would I be straight if my neighbor hadn't molested me? Is sexuality that malleable, that a few months of sexual experience could reshape my personality so deeply, so without return? It's a senseless question. It has no end. But he's never been able to get it out of his head.

"That's just some shit straight people say to make us sound fucked up, and you know it, Mauricio," says Ella from the couch.

"Oh, c'mon, Ella, I didn't mean it like that."

"Nah, motherfucker," she says. "I grew up a quiet little Christian boy in middle-of-nowhere Pennsylvania. There wasn't a creepy priest or fucked-up uncle that could get past my grandmother's eye. I was always a gay boy, and then I knew I wasn't. I was a girl; I didn't have to be touched as a kid to know it. Your bullshit is your bullshit, don't drag the rest of us into it."

"You're a dickhead," Luis says to Mauricio, and storms out to the hallway to hide from the secondhand shame. Mauricio runs out after him.

"I'm sorry. I didn't know," Charo says.

"Girl, that's the point," Ella says, and laughs.

Charo has a million questions on her face. Sal tries to mask his own surprise, but he's afraid that Charo might blurt out whatever comes to her mind first. Their eyes meet, and in that exchange she assures him they're not seventeen anymore. She knows better now.

"Okay. It's not my business," Charo says. She grabs a fashion magazine and delves into a drunken critique about the cover model's outfit, which sends Ella into a laughing fit. Ella's laugh is infectious. Sal and Vance join them, though Sal cares very little about fashion.

When their voices strain from talking and whiskey, Ella offers to take Charo downstairs to hail a taxi.

"I'm fine," Sal says to Charo at the door, to get ahead of her concern. She knows the kinds of conversations that thrust him back into the past.

"I believe you," Charo says. She hugs him again and turns to go.

Vance's room is pristine. Next to his made-up bed is a modest collection of books on a shelf, organized by color. The wall above his bed is decorated with half a dozen photos of famous Black actors. The largest photo is of Eartha Kitt, framed in gold. She lies on the floor with a book in one hand. The other hand is placed lightly on the soft brown of her cheek. Her feline eyes are piercing, even as she looks away from the camera. In a corner is a luminous tank filled with orange-and-black fish. Some glide through the water after one another, others float idly by a plant or in the crevice of a rock. The tank's blue light and the hum of the filter make the room feel serene, like it's a running river. How did I miss the fish tank last time I was here? Sal wonders. He sits next to Vance on the bed.

"I've never seen any of her movies," Sal says, looking up at Eartha. "Wait, seriously?"

Vance grew up going to the movies with his aunt. One Saturday a month, they'd take the train downtown, buy a big bag of popcorn, and sit through whatever film she was most excited about that season. While other parents dressed up for Sunday service, Aunt Meena wore her Sunday best to the theater. Floral dresses, a touch of makeup, and her favorite gold brooch pinned to her hat. Movies were her religion, the scripture she quoted and from which she learned her most valuable lessons about the world. It was habitual for her to use a line from her favorite films to teach Vance a lesson. The week after they saw *The Color Purple*, Vance broke a girl's heart by not showing up to a date. He was young, unwilling to turn her down for fear that it would reveal his disinterest in girls, so he bailed on her, only to receive a barrage of calls from the girl the next day. Aunt Meena scolded him about the importance of taking care of Black girls. She began talking about the girl in the film but quickly transitioned to a monologue about herself. She spoke in Sofia's voice about her own absent father, her abusive work supervisors, and the man who broke her heart when she was young, leaving her sour to the possibility of finding love again.

"Aunt Meena's something else," Vance says. They lie on their backs and face the ceiling like they're looking up at stars. Vance explains that Aunt Meena is sick. A cancer that's gone from bad to worse in just a few months.

"She's my mom," he says. "Still calling me out for shit. But it's good, it means she's got plenty of fight in her. She's gonna beat this thing. I know it."

Sal wishes he could say something to soothe him. But sometimes silence is the best relief. They lie there quietly for an hour, it seems, before Vance kisses the soft of Sal's skin above his collarbone. Gently at first, then with increasing intensity, his tongue burrowing along the length of Sal's neck where his heartbeat pulses. He feels in Vance's quickening breath a desperate longing. Like Vance is coming up from underwater, and Sal's the air he needs. Sal grunts as Vance presses up against him, as those stern hands wrap tight around his throat, making him stupid with wanting.

"Do you want to fuck me?" Sal asks.

"Absolutely," Vance says. He reaches over and pulls a condom from his nightstand. "I work at a gay center. Gotta set a good example."

Sal wishes they didn't need protection. That sex didn't have to be half pleasure, half risk.

"I got it," Sal says. He slides the condom on Vance's dick with such tenderness he feels ridiculous. They laugh to ease the edge.

Their bodies fall into a practiced position, Vance on his back, Sal sitting on top. Their naked bodies are illuminated by the fish tank's undulating light. Vance enters him slowly. He stops every time Sal winces or catches his breath. When the sharp pain softens into warmth, Sal looks up in relief and sees through the window a horned moon. Inside, Sal pushes down and rides his lover. Outside, the slice of moon pulses in the dark sky. Everything blurs in the middle. Vance, Sal. Grief, Vance. Sal, sky. Sal, cutting the night in two with his moan.

From the crowd, Renata emerges dressed as a boy. The sun lingers; the streets are busy even for a Friday. Sal waves to her from where he's sitting on a bench. Beer in hand. Under a tree moving in the wind. Someone approaches Renata as she walks to Sal. He doesn't know who the woman is, but Renata seems to know. She touches the woman's shoulder. Laughs at something she says. Hugs her before ending their quick exchange.

"I can't stand that bitch," Renata says, and offers Sal a drag of her cigarette.

They meet here at Parque Duarte a couple times a week. Sal doesn't know where Renata lives. They've been meeting out in public the whole year he's known her. If he tried, he might imagine what her life looks like when she's not at a party or at the park surrounded by maricones. But he doesn't. Better to take her as she is. Splendid yet mysterious, now dressed in a red shirt, red corduroy pants. Her way of standing out, even in boy's clothes.

"I'm good," Sal says, and gestures to his beer.

"Are you? You haven't been coming to the park lately." Renata doesn't sound accusing. She'd never be so up-front about her probing. Her style is sly, shrouded in questions. Half the time he doesn't know there's a secret meaning behind her words. Even when he notices, he doesn't mind. To be questioned by Renata is to be enveloped in her care. Sal feels comfortable there.

"School," he says, and finishes his beer. That feels like a justifiable reason.

"Good," Renata says. She blows out smoke, eyes the men gathering on the other side of the park around a game of dominó.

La Kali comes next. She's short and round but her raspy voice makes up for her size. She comes with a story about some tiguere who flirted her up last time they were here. Now she's looking for him and their future together. Then Morena comes around with Lolo, both of them drunk and giggling. They smell like cheap cologne. Morena in a hot-pink tank top she probably stole from a women's department store. Lolo with his usual masculine swag smoothed out by whatever cheap rum they drank. Sal kissed Lolo on a night like this a few months ago. They were drunk. The girls were distracted. It happened during a piss break in a dark alley. Sal liked it. How Lolo's mustache rubbed against his lips. Lolo is older, more experienced. But that was also the problem. Renata only had two rules for Sal and Yadiel. No dating boys until they turned sixteen. No taking money and gifts from wealthy men until they were old enough to disobey her. Maybe in a couple of months, Sal told Lolo in the alley, and that was that. He's never wanted to disappoint Renata. Even now, as they stand around the park telling stories. Sal likes the feeling of a group of them together. A group means power. He'd do anything to keep them together like this. Even suppress his want for Lolo, dizzy as it makes him.

Renata goes off to the colmado to get them another round of beer. She always pays for their drinks. She's the only one among them who can keep a job for more than a few months at a time.

"That fancy hotel pays well, huh," La Kali says as Renata walks off.

A minute later, Yadiel joins them.

"Y este grupo de feas?" he says. Yadiel's shorts are short, that's the first thing Sal notices. Did he always show off so much skin? And his face. Were his cheekbones always so round? Was his skin, brown like a coffee bean, always that smooth? They're almost sixteen, but Yadiel looks more mature than Sal. He goes around hugging the group and lands on Sal last. "Except for you, Salvador. El niño mas lindo de la bolita 'el mundo."

Yadiel is late. Sal doesn't hug him back. Who knows where he was, where he's been. Morena calls him out on it.

"Estaba con mi marido, since you're curious," Yadiel says.

Morena wants to know more. What he looks like. If he's a tipo maduro or just a boy their age.

"Of course he's a man," Yadiel says, and crosses his legs on a bench.

"Is that where you got that little bracelet you're wearing? Looks like gold," La Kali says.

Sal looks up from the empty bottle he's fidgeting with. Morena coughs midlaugh. Lolo's thick eyebrows rise to his forehead. They're not used to hearing La Kali sound so serious.

"I have two more at home, pero hay que ser humilde," Yadiel says.

"You know Renata's not gonna like hearing that," La Kali says.

"It's a little gift, what's so wrong about that?" Morena asks.

"Men don't give nothing for free."

"Oh, please, how old were you when you started fucking for money?"

"Yadi," Sal says.

"It's fine." La Kali tightens her ponytail. Her hair has a new gloss to it. Word is she finally found a good salonera that treats maricones. "She's the one that'll have to hear Renata's mouth."

Yadiel waves his hand to dismiss La Kali. Something about the gesture. Like they're all flies and he's the honey. Sal rolls his eyes.

"It's Friday, let's keep the energy up. Look what I brought." Like a magician procuring a bunny from a hat, Yadiel draws a blond wig from his backpack and pulls it over his head. Morena and Lolo scream. Even La Kali laughs, though she looks about her to see if anyone has noticed. Sal, too, looks around. The park is more crowded than when he arrived. The dominó game surrounded by men. Couples sitting under the shadow of trees. Another big group gathered around a radio, beers in hand, itching to dance. The sun has set. But its orange glow remains. It's not dark enough for them to go unnoticed.

"You should put that away," Sal says. He jumps from his seat and tries to reach his friend. But Yadiel turns away and begins to strut. Like he's a superstar in the kind of high-fashion show they've only seen in magazines and telenovelas. His walk is slow and sensual.

"Si, coño, como la Marilyn Monroe," Morena says.

"Dale, manita, que tú puedes," Lolo adds, and laughs a hearty laugh.

Yadiel is radiant. For a second, this joy washes away Sal's worry. Maybe it'll be okay. No one will notice. They'll go on laughing like this as they've done many nights. They'll go on like this forever. But then they hear someone calling from across the park.

"Ey! Aquí no, eso aquí no." It's the same woman Renata greeted when she arrived at the park, now burning the distance between them. Sal's stomach tightens. "Y esa pajarería?" the woman says. Her hair is up in a doobie. A vein runs along her forehead.

"Maybe you should mind your business," Yadiel says without skipping a beat.

"It's one thing we let you maricones crowd the park. But this," she says, her arms waving at Yadiel in his wig. She's struggling to find the words. So big is her anger. Her shame.

"What's going on here?" It's Renata, back with a handful of beers. She puts them down on a bench.

"It's too much, Ren. Get these carajitos out of here."

"Ay, Mari, please. They're not hurting anybody," Renata says, with fearsome calm. They know that maricones out in public, loud and taking up space, is anything but mundane. But the ease with which Renata stands now in front of this woman.

"I'm going to get the men; they'll take care of it if you don't."

"Mari, do you know what they're saying about why your brother's wife left him?"

At this, the woman freezes. Her upper lip quivers. "What are you talking about?"

"I heard he likes it in the butt," Renata whispers, just loud enough for them to hear.

How Renata knows a little bit about everyone's lives, Sal doesn't know. This isn't like the benign facts about planets he's learned. Or the monologues he's memorized from watching countless hours of Carl Sagan on his television. Secrets. Promises. Betrayals. That's what Renata stores within her, ready to weaponize at any second: all this knowledge about the barrio passed to her in whispers.

"Maldito maricón," the woman spits, but by then Sal and his friends are laughing over her insult, ushering her out of their corner of the park. Renata's won. She always wins. But Renata herself looks unappeased.

"Put the wig away," she says coolly.

"Oh, please, who gives a fuck what that rat has to say?"

"That rat could have gotten your friends hurt, Yadi. I've taught you to be smarter than that."

For a second it looks as if he'll defy Renata. But he slides the wig off, tucks it back in his bag like he's handling something delicate and vital.

"Speaking of what we have and haven't learned," Yadiel says. "Do you know the story of Anacaona? The Taino chief. She was murdered right here on this plaza. Hung dique for plotting against los españoles."

"Okay," Renata says. She's waiting for the point.

"They killed her right where Pablito stands." Yadiel gestures toward the center of the park, where a statue of Juan Pablo Duarte looms over them. "They say she was beautiful. A real queen of the people. And that's why they murdered her. Not because she did anything wrong. But because she made the Tainos brave. With her beauty and her poems and how wise she was. A real matatana. And I just wonder sometimes. If we could do to them what they did to Anacaona. If we could hang the conquistadores and the corrupt government and the people who make us feel like shit for being maricones. Out here in this same park where they ridicule us. Line 'em up and . . ."

No one knows what to say. But they all feel it, this lingering tension between Renata and Yadiel.

"You scare me sometimes," Renata says, and chuckles. Sal's not sure if she's joking. But Yadiel takes it like a slap to the face. He recoils. Then finds his footing again.

"That's the point, ese maldito miedo que utede tienen. Look at Salvador. Why do you think he hasn't been coming to the park lately? It's scary to be a maricón. But I'm not a coward like you all. I don't need to hide."

"Just because we want to protect ourselves doesn't mean we're cowards," Sal says.

"Keep telling yourself that, manito," Yadiel says, and winks.

"All right, all right. This is supposed to be a fun night, dejen su vaina," La Kali says.

But Sal can't let it go. Because he hates to be embarrassed in front of Lolo. Because Yadiel brings out the worst in him sometimes. But most of all because somewhere deep inside himself Sal knows his best friend might actually be right.

"If you're so brave, why don't you tell Renata where you got that pretty bracelet?" Sal says. He puts the beer bottle to his lips. It's so cold it numbs his throat, dulls his forehead.

In the haze of the argument, Renata hadn't noticed. But now her gaze lingers there. Even though Yadiel puts his hand over his wrist to cover it. Like she can see through flesh and bone to where the gold glitters. She just stares.

"You're young. You should be focused on love. I spent all these years focused on using men for money. Now look at me, old and alone," La Kali says.

"Mejor con un tiguere con dinero, que con bugarrón," Lolo adds.

"And aren't you twenty-nine, Kali? What are you talking about, old?" asks Morena. Lolo spits out his beer. La Kali gestures for them to go fuck themselves.

"We need to have a talk," Renata says finally. Sal's never seen her so angry. If people could erupt. Like a volcano on Venus. But also, something else he's never seen on Renata's face, twitching there between her brows. Is that uncertainty? Sal thinks maybe he should interfere, try to squash this new trouble he's started. But what could he say to make it go away, to salvage the night?

Renata doesn't wait for Yadiel to respond. For his snark. His smarts. His good way of using words to get out of trouble. She pulls him by the wrist, away from the group, away from the park, out to the darkening streets where the light can't touch them.

SAL AND VANCE MEET ON THEIR DAYS OFF. THEY VENTURE OUT TO corners of the city Sal has never been to but has heard about in the way people speak of New York like it's more myth than place. The Staten Island Ferry, where they catch the sunset; Green-Wood Cemetery, where they share ghost stories to see who gets scared first; Rockefeller Center, where they sneak into a tour of the sixty-fifth floor. There's no trite sentiment that they've known each other forever. Instead, the feeling is fresh, and Sal likes getting to know New York better through the lens of his lover. Vance is well connected from all his years out partying with Mauricio. He knows what DJs will play where, which drag queen's set is sweeping the scene.

"But I've been doing that stuff forever," Vance says after the first week. "I like hanging with you outside."

On a warm Saturday at the end of May, they stumble upon a large community garden on the Upper East Side. Half of the garden is filled with common flowers, daffodils, and bright daisies dancing in the late-spring wind. The other half is a vegetable garden. Rows of zucchini and squash grow on one side; on the other, red-orange grape tomatoes hang from rows of wooden trellis. Sal says he doesn't know a lot about plants but goes on a full tangent about how energy is turned into food, how miraculous it is that life begins with light.

"What it's called? Photo who?"

"Photosynthesis," Sal says, and laughs. He has the urge to kiss Vance, but the nerves stop him. What if someone sees them? What would they say? Just then, a middle-aged woman approaches them.

"That's right, that's right," she says casually, like they're old friends. She wears a mud-stained apron over ankle-length cargo pants and a green T-shirt. Her graying hair is tied in a ponytail, and half of her face is shrouded behind thick corrective lenses. The woman seems loopy, a little more attached to the circles in her mind than what's in front of her.

"Uh, what?"

"I've been following you." A brief, dense silence falls between them. Then the woman pulls out a wrinkled piece of paper from her apron pocket. "You really know your plant stuff. I'm looking for gardening and plant experts to work with kids. Support the after-school and weekend programs, teach classes, garden a little, here and there," she says in a flat tone, and goes on to explain timeline, pay, all the paperwork particulars. If her cheeks weren't smudged with dirt, if she weren't holding a pair of shears, it'd be hard to believe she cares about gardening at all.

Sal wants to explain that he's not really interested in plant science, that he's never worked with kids before. Besides, it sounds like a lot of work for less pay than he's making at his current job. And no way he'd be able to work at the garden five days a week and have the energy to stay at the Cuban restaurant. He starts to decline the offer, but Vance snatches the paper from his hand and thanks the woman for all the information. She meets Vance's excitement with the same indifference with which she admitted she'd been following them.

"Come back soon," she says, then walks down the path she came from, kneels in front of a cluster of vines, and starts admonishing the tomato vines for growing so quickly.

"What are you doing?" Sal says quietly.

"This is perfect, Sal. You have to apply," Vance says. He looks the job application over, then folds the piece of paper neatly into the back pocket of his jeans.

"I don't know," Sal says, scratching his temple. "It doesn't seem like the most lucrative gig. And anyway, what about the winter? She said the job is temporary."

"No, no, listen," Vance starts, and offers a series of solutions, none of which ease Sal's worry. Sal knows Vance is trying to help, but he's repulsed by all the enthusiasm.

"Can we just drop it?" Sal walks ahead to show he's done with the conversation. On their way out of the garden, they see the woman with the large glasses carrying a crate of grape tomatoes. She stops and stares into the fruit as if they're splendid little suns. She pops one in her mouth, groans at its sweetness, pops in another.

They walk ten blocks, down to Eighty-Sixth Street, before either of them says a word.

"I didn't mean to pressure you. I'm sorry," Vance says.

"I've been good where I am, at the restaurant," Sal says loudly above the screeching of a passing bus. Those aren't the words, he knows it. He wants to think of a true thing to say, but his mind is a scattered mess. "I'm scared, I guess."

"Well, it's okay to be scared when you're putting yourself out there," Vance says. Two white women speed by pushing strollers that look more expensive than anything Sal owns. One of them confirms she'll confront her husband about all his traveling for work, the other hums and nods in approval.

"If the rich white lady is brave enough to call out her absent husband . . ." Vance says. A taunting smile spreads across his face.

"It's a hard life she's living," Sal says, and laughs.

A few days later, he arms himself with two copies of his résumé and a speech to explain his work history. He doesn't have experience teaching, but he has an associate's degree in education. Back in his community college days, the education program demanded the least credentials and courses, and though he had no intention to teach, no desire to embarrass himself in front of kids and their sharp criticism, his mother assured him that any degree would do, he just had to keep pushing on, finish his two years, then get his bachelor's, and on and on until the gates of opportunity opened before him, as they had done for her. His degree has been useless until this point, but now, as he walks to the interview, he rehearses how he'll stretch the truth to make a case for himself.

When he arrives at the garden, a group of kids are gathered around an instructor as she explains how bees pollinate. That could be me soon, Sal thinks. The thought makes him want to run out of the garden back home where he'll be safe again. It's okay to be scared, he says to himself in Vance's voice, and drags his feet toward the office in the center of the garden. Inside, a small staff of three in an open space, working quietly from their respective desks. The woman from the other day welcomes him into her office, a quaint room filled with photos and diagrams of mushrooms. He hopes she won't notice the sweat on his forehead, the wet stains under his arms.

"Martha," she introduces herself, like it's their first time meeting. She skims over his résumé, asks him a few slack questions about work ethic and physical labor before she offers him the job.

"I like the way you talk about things, like you care. Reminds me of Martha when she was younger," Martha says, and claps her hands together.

Sal leaves her with the second copy of his résumé, just in case she changes her mind. He hurries back uptown to Charo's place to share the good news.

"Okay, and it's two dollars an hour less than the restaurant? That adds up, Sal." She sits in her living room across from him, her eyes heavy with fatigue. Carolina sits on her lap, mumbling.

"I can still make rent, just gotta be smarter about buying groceries and not buy any books for a bit."

"And not go on so many dates with Vance." Carolina jumps from Charo's lap and zooms out of the room making helicopter noises. "I mean, c'mon, Sal, I know he's trying to help, but why would he push you to do something like that?"

"Okay. Weren't you the one encouraging me to apply to the museum two months ago?" He tries to keep his voice from rising. Carolina comes back to the living room gripping a doll by the mess of her blonde hair.

"Yeah, 'cause that job has security, better pay, benefits. Tell me something. Did you even call the museum to reschedule? Or have you just been running around with this guy, pretending you don't have responsibilities?"

Something about the doll in her hand has upset Carolina. She wails. Charo doesn't rush to calm her. She just looks, waits, her piercing eyes unmoving. She's right, he hasn't called. He kept pushing it off, and as the weeks passed, it became harder and harder to come up with a reasonable excuse. Instead of calling, he focused on planning the next date with Vance. That, he could control. Sure, it's stupid, he thinks now. But I can't be the only one making stupid choices if she's still with Robert.

"I'm just gonna go, okay?" he says, before harsher words escape him.

The first few days at the garden are smooth enough. Martha gives Sal the basic rundown of the job in a single afternoon: the workbooks they use to teach the kids, the most arable plots this season. She even spends a few hours teaching him to harvest, where to cut zucchini from the plant, how to tell if a tomato is ready for plucking or if it needs a few more days to ripen. "You'll get it with time," she promises him. "It took Martha time, but it all becomes instinctual." She speaks with reverence for the soil and the sun, and for the first time he understands why she's the garden's boss.

By the fifth day, Sal is helping to lead lectures for the kids. He finds talking to them natural, in large part because of his practice with Kiko. Except unlike his brother, these kids seem interested in what he has to say. For once, he has an invested audience, whether they're in the program by choice or because their wealthy parents want them out of the house for a few hours after school or on weekends. It fills him with purpose, a reason to look forward to getting up in the mornings. It's not the museum job. But it's close enough.

"Sometimes the kids are difficult, but it's going great," Sal says to his mom after the first few days.

"As long as you like it," Teresa says with some trepidation.

"And you were right, all I needed to do was focus and take the leap," he says, trying to sound convincing.

Now Jenna, one of two lead educators, interrupts him as they're giving a lecture about sunflower seeds. This is the third time today, probably the hundredth time since he started the job a week ago. Sal catches on quickly that no one else seems to like her. Every time she interrupts, he looks up to meet the eyes of one of his co-workers. The session ends and the students, mostly white kids from wealthy families in the area, are sent to examine the sunflower beds scattered across the garden. As soon as they're off, Sal rushes to Amy's side.

"Why is she like that?" Sal says. Above them, the sun beams on the earth with little care for what it burns.

"She just has to make sure we get it right," Amy says, mimicking Jenna's high pitch exactly.

Amy left her close-knit family behind in the Bay Area a few years ago to attend one of the prestigious universities in New York. She's almost finished her undergraduate degree in biology and uses her time at the garden to get away from the lab, where she spends most summers closed off from the world. And though her stature might suggest she's unassuming, and her pimple-mapped face might make her a target for cruel kids, she's one of the best at the garden. The kids are either scared of her or drawn to the way she breaks down plant science to its most basic components, making learning science engaging and exciting, even for fifth graders.

"She wants Martha's fucking job, that's what it is," Amy says.

Sal thought the garden would be less competitive than his old job hosting at the Cuban restaurant, with its high-strung atmosphere, quick-tempered manager, tired cooks. Even the waitstaff, some of whom were Sal's closest friends at the job, tried to outdo each other to get the coveted evening shifts with the best tips.

Still, as he looks up now, walking next to his new friend, for the first time in a while he feels that he makes sense under the blue sky.

"Chin up, here comes the terrorizer," Amy says.

That night, Sal picks Kiko up from his mother's apartment and they head to his place. When Vance asked if he could hang out with them on Friday, Sal had to think about it for a full twenty-four hours. He's never introduced his family to a boyfriend, though of course they know. He's frightened about what his brother might say. Kiko picks up so much language from his older cousins, his friends at school, neighbors around the block. Sal's certain by now he's learned a slur or two about gay people. What if he repeats what he's heard in front of Vance? Not out of hate or derision, but just to test the bounds of what's appropriate, as Kiko likes to do with words.

Vance arrives with a box of brownie fudge cookies from a local bakery.

"He's gonna love you for this," Sal says in the hallway.

"That's the goal," Vance says.

The velvety smell of chocolate melting in the microwave draws Kiko into the kitchen.

"Did Sal tell you cookies are my favorite?" He looks suspiciously at Vance and strokes his chin. Some gesture he probably picked up on TV. Kiko grabs two cookies and runs to Sal's bedroom, yells at them to hurry, that the show is starting soon.

"You guys are such brothers," Vance says. "It's nice. I didn't grow up with siblings."

"You'll get tired of him soon. He doesn't stop until he knocks out," Sal explains.

In the room, Kiko has created a tent made of pillows and blankets. He's even taken down Sal's sheer white curtains, the ones he keeps all year round to welcome the unencumbered light. Sal wants to reprimand him, but the shock of the whole thing holds him back. He was in the room five minutes ago. The fact that his brother managed to make a tent so quickly is a miracle.

"Dude, this is fucking awesome," Vance says.

"Yeah, it's fucking awesome," Kiko says. He eyes Sal to see if he'll be scolded for cursing. When his brother says nothing, Kiko nods proudly. "Bet you can't make one like this," he continues. He says this with a new severity in his voice. Sal can't tell if he's trying to compete with Vance or if he's trying to impress him. He wonders if there's a difference for a boy Kiko's age.

"I'm pretty sure I can smoke you in a tent-making competition," Vance says, and they dive deep into a spirited debate about cushions and the gravity of blankets. Sal is surprised to see this side of Vance, a glimpse into the competitive kid he might have been. Would they have been friends, if they found each other in their youth? Gay kids are so lonely. Was Sal lonely? He met his first real friend when he was seven, despite his grandmother's warnings not to talk to the boy at the end of the street. Word was that the boy's father beat his mother, that's why she ran away with another man. Once, a few of his neighbors stopped the boy's father in front of his house, suggesting that he let the bottle go, or at least send his son to a grandparent or aunt who could take care of him properly. He's not going nowhere, he's my son, the father yelled at his neighbors, and pulled out a handy machete he kept out front, to show he was done with the intervention. The neighborhood gave up and left them alone, no matter how loud the boy cried when his father punished him for wandering too far from home, or for not cooking while the man was out fixing motorbikes for a few cheles, or just because. You don't want that kind of trouble, his grandmother told Sal. Sometimes on their way to church he saw the boy reading alone in front of his house and felt bad for him. Cheeks dirty, skin tight around his ribs from malnourishment, eyes mean and sharp. Still, he didn't feel bad enough to bridge the distance between them. On a hot day, Sal got into it with a boy and a girl from the barrio over a game of marbles. When it was clear he'd lose the fight, he tried to run back home, but they threw him flat on the sidewalk and kicked him. The air left his lungs. The sight of the sky above him blurred blue and yellow. He would have passed out if the mean boy from down the street hadn't come, broomstick in hand, to swat the kids away. By the time Sal sat up, one of his bullies was running down the street; the other stood motionless, assessing her next move. She tried to dive at the mean boy, but he swung the broomstick at her head. She yelped, spat in Sal's direction, and then ran off, clutching the growing knot on her forehead. Sal got up to thank his savior, but the mean boy turned on him and slapped him with the stick. Why me? Sal groaned as he held his throbbing knee. You gotta be tough, that's what Papi always tells me, the boy said. There on his face was a tinge of pride. He was pleased with himself for saving Sal. But he must have noticed how much Sal was hurting, because the mean look vanished from his face. I can't always be around to protect you, he said by way of apology. Stay for a little bit, Sal responded, not because he was scared of his assailants coming back, but because he was curious about this boy he'd been avoiding for so long. They were similar, Sal felt. His mom, too, had gone away somewhere and hadn't come back. The mean boy stayed for hours, talking Sal's ear off like he hadn't talked to anyone in months. What are you always reading? Sal asked. It's called poesía, the boy said. They're Mami's books, she left them. I don't really know what the words mean, but I like how they sound, you know? Sal didn't know, but he nodded like he did. In return, Sal showed him a trick he'd learned by putting a glass bottle under the sun and manipulating the refracted light. They placed the refractions on their arms, on their foreheads, laughed and laughed like the light was funny. Eventually the boy's father came stumbling down the street. Yadiel, he called. The man's voice gave Sal chills. How did the mean boy live with that voice all day, just the two of them in that dilapidated house? It made Sal grateful that he'd never met his dad. Before he ran off, Yadiel turned and eyed Sal like he was contemplating staying, like he was sorry to go. I'll come back tomorrow, he promised. Just in case.

"All right, the show is starting. Pay attention," Sal says now to his brother, to his lover, mainly to himself.

THE TELEVISION ALONE ILLUMINATES THE LIVING ROOM. TO AVOID waking her daughter, Charo keeps the volume at just above a whisper. Her world is quiet for the first time today. She finds comfort in a science fiction movie, something about an alien invasion and the subpar human response. She likes the way these fictional worlds can make her own life feel small in comparison. It's Sal's fault that she's so into these films, all the hours they've spent hate-watching these intergalactic battles. Sal points out all the scientific inaccuracies, Charo tells him to hush, why does it matter, what's key is the hero's chiseled body as he saves the world. She misses him. They haven't talked in weeks, not since the argument about his new job. She can't quite place where her frustration came from that day, hasn't had much time to give that or anything else much thought. Carolina got sick, a cold that kept her up for three long nights. And one of the girls at her job went back to the island to care for an aging parent, so Charo has been putting in extra hours at the supermarket, double shifts that weigh on her knees. She's grateful for their babysitter, Eunice, who lives upstairs and is accommodating enough. Still, every night when she lies in bed she's surprised to have made it through another day.

The phone rings. She's surprised to hear Ella, calling to invite Charo to one of her performances at the bar later in the week.

"One hundred percent, I'll be there," Charo says. The thought of going out with friends is thrilling. But the energy deflates almost immediately when she thinks about facing Robert's scrutiny. I'll just call Ella back later to cancel, she thinks. Better to avoid another fight.

From the couch, she hears the front door unlock, open, then close again. He walks through the dark, drawn to the living room by the television light, and greets her with silence. He unbuttons his shirt and fumbles to roll off his pants. Then he slides onto the couch next to her and plants a wet kiss on her cheek. He's been drinking, she can tell. He wraps an arm around her waist, presses his hard dick against her. A part of Charo wants to push him off, to yell at him for coming home drunk. Any excuse to let loose the rage that's been bubbling within her all these weeks he's shunned her.

"What do they give you that I can't?"

"You're drunk, Robert."

"I do my best, no? I do okay."

She's only heard this quiver in his voice once. When she was pregnant, he told her about his father, whom he never met. Knifed down in a robbery so senseless it was almost comical. That's how he talked about it, like it was a joke, his father murdered at dusk on his way home from the colmado. They left the yuca but took the beers and the few pesos he hid in his shoe. Took the shoes, too, to honor the ritual of robberies so common in the barrio. His mother was six months pregnant and showing. She almost lost the baby from a weeklong shock, then spent the next two decades telling Robert what a good father her late husband was. But Robert was their only child. How could she know what kind of father he was or might have been? It made Robert curious about the whole enterprise; why it takes so little to be deemed a good father, why so many men around him struggle to show up for their kids. Charo knows Robert uses Carolina to fill a pit in his own life. But is that so wrong? she wonders. We all have myths about what makes us good. He's a great father to their daughter, that's all that matters.

"You're amazing. It's just . . . it's hard to explain."

"You feel alone when it's just us. That's it, isn't it? You feel alone."

All these hours complaining about Robert, wanting to escape him and this life they're building together, yet here he is in her arms, seeing her better than she sees herself. What the fuck is wrong with me? she thinks.

"I'm sorry, baby," he says with his rum-sweet breath on her neck.

Charo pulls him closer.

They sit at the bar next to a Johnson or Smith, a tall man who has taken off his suit, rolled up his sleeves, and is deep in a conversation about baseball with his white-collar co-workers. The sports enthusiast turns around, asks Robert what he thinks, Yankees or Red Sox? Robert, in his thick Dominican accent, offers his analysis of the teams' storied history, flexing his knowledge of the sport. They go back and forth like this, in the way men debate to feel close to one another.

Charo looks around the restaurant for Ella. At first, she thought they'd come to the wrong place, but then they met Jimmy the bartender. Jimmy is a lanky dark-skinned man with long locs falling over his shoulders. He looks regal and relaxed at once. When people yell at him from across the bar asking for another drink, Jimmy smiles, but he doesn't hurry. He moves at the speed of his own clock.

"She probably in the bathroom getting ready. You know Ella, she do a lot," he says, affection like honey in his voice.

Charo finishes her whiskey ginger. Next to her, Robert is fully engaged in a conversation about the league. She likes to see him like this, outside of their routine. They haven't gone out together since their daughter was born. Robert was traditional from the start. He paid for every meal at a restaurant, every outing to a bar. She liked getting courted. Those early gestures made her feel desired. But they also made her anxious about money. She wasn't dumb enough to tell him about the debt she owed her uncle, or the money she sent back home to her parents. But it made her wonder, Is he any good at saving? Is he just showing off? If he's willing to spend money on drinks and party entrance fees, how responsible can he be? With time, she learned that he was frugal, same as her. But those early days, all the fun she had with him was mixed with money worries.

Now she's just happy that he came out tonight, even if it took some convincing. He argued that he didn't even know this woman who was singing. Why should he come? But he gave in, if only to prove that his apology from the other night was earnest.

Ella emerges from the back in a tight-fitting olive dress. Apple-red lips, gold hoop earrings. The crowd parts for her; some even turn to look at her as she passes by, squinting with curiosity. Charo jumps out of her seat to embrace her.

"Got something good for me?" Ella says to Jimmy. He mixes together a concoction of lime, ginger beer, and whiskey. "I'm so glad you made it. Is that your man?"

Charo pats Robert on the arm to get his attention. He's cordial enough, even laughs at one of Ella's jokes. Good, Charo thinks. They've met, the hard part's over.

"Magic always starts with whiskey," Ella says, and downs her drink in one go. Then she climbs the stage to help the pianist set up.

The piano man's friends sit by a table. They kiss the mouths of beer bottles and whisper under their black fedoras. Opposite them, a group of European tourists sit and talk loudly as they pick at fries and nachos. They have no idea that they're about to witness an incredible performance. Charo is so excited she can barely stay in her seat.

Ella starts with a slow jazz number about a duplicitous lover. She's a bit off-key, even Charo can't deny it. But the piano strings help. Charo looks at her in wonder, how she holds the mic to her lips, how she glistens in the light.

But the rest of the room ignores the performance. In the back, a kid throws a ketchup-dipped fry at another, and the table erupts in laughter. This sets off the other tables. Robert, next to Charo, picks up his conversation about baseball.

"Robert, callate," she whispers to him, but he ignores her.

When Ella finishes her set, Charo is one of a few people clapping.

"I'm so sorry," she says, and holds out her hand for Ella to join them at the bar.

"Girl, what are you sorry for? I got five motherfuckers to clap. That's as good as it gets around here most days."

"But you were good. I just wish . . ." Charo says, feeling her excitement sink.

Just then, the white-collar who's been talking to Robert comes around and stands before Ella. Mop of brown hair tousled on his head, unfocused drunken eyes, white shirt wrinkled and unbuttoned. Ella plays it cool, nods to welcome his compliment, the hunger in his pink, wet lips. Maybe he has no wife to go home to, unlike the rest of his white-collar buddies, most of whom have left the bar by now. Or maybe he does, and that's precisely why he stays.

"I've seen you a few times. Incredible," he says, and kisses his fingers like he's complimenting a dish.

He reaches for her shoulder and places a bill under her bra strap. The movement is practiced, smooth. He's done this at least a hundred times before. He continues flirting as if nothing has happened, but the mask of idle interest falls from Ella's face. She pulls the bill from under her bra strap.

"Fifty bucks? That's it?" Her smile broadens, revealing her teeth. Jimmy, from behind the bar, moves to intervene, but Ella puts her hand up. Charo, too, freezes in place. Ella tosses the bill on the floor and kicks it as far as it will go. "I think my pussy costs a little more than that."

The man looks behind him to see where his gift has gone, then back at Ella in front of him, as if he's trying to locate himself between this woman he desires and where his offer has gone wrong. Shame rises to his face, bright and red.

"What the fuck," he says. He bends over to pick up his crumpled ego, but he trips and falls under his own weight. The people around him chuckle, no one helps him up. Before he can stand up to face Ella again, Robert stands between them as a warning. The man considers Robert. A few minutes ago they were baseball buddies sharing beers. It didn't matter that they speak different languages, that they come from different worlds. What mattered was the game. But now? Robert stands before him like a wall. The man frowns. More than Ella's rejection, more than the crowd laughing around him. This brotherly betrayal is what hurts most of all. He looks back one last time, then stumbles quietly out of the restaurant.

"I used to make ten times that when I was fucking yuppies. That's not my life anymore," Ella says.

For a second, as Ella drinks what's left of her whiskey, Charo thinks she sees a shadow of sadness come over her friend's face. A part of Charo wishes she could ask about this unspoken history. The other feels shame for wanting to pry. Ella notices and shakes her head.

"No pity, no pity. It's regular shit you gotta deal with as a transsexual girl in the big city," Ella says, like she's introducing an episode of a tragicomic television series.

Robert raises an eyebrow. He's probably never heard the word before, at least not in English. *Maricón* is all-encompassing in the lexicon of men like Robert. Everyone who deviates from being a regular macho is assigned the term. If he's lazy and doesn't work. If he's a bad father and mistreats his children. If he does, indeed, fuck other men. She's heard him use the word passively at times, at other times with acuity and intention. They've had arguments about it, but he's never cared much about the nuances of identity, not enough to care about how trans women are different from gay men. She can see in his raised brow the machine of his mind trying to catch up.

"Can I meet the piano man? He was so good," Charo says, and jumps from her seat.

They leave Robert alone at the bar, mouth full of questions.

THE TEACHER ANNOUNCES THAT THEY'LL WORK TOGETHER FOR their first big project of the year. Charo sucks her teeth so loud kids two rows back chuckle. Sal ignores her and keeps his gaze ahead of him. The two don't know each other much. She mostly hangs around baseball jocks he wouldn't even think of talking to. Not out of fear. But because he thinks those boys are stupid, careless, violent. Why should he waste his time befriending them?

Though he's never spoken to Charo, years in the same classrooms have revealed to him all he needs to know. She's always surrounded by snippets of rumors, usually to do with stolen boyfriends or who she's fucking at any given time. There are signs everywhere that he should stay away. But if he were to dig deep, he might find that he's more curious about her than he cares to admit. What if they lived in an alternate world where boys get to go on dates with boys, and girls get to go on dates with girls? Like it's no big deal. Like it's all just normal. And what if Sal were at the center of the boys' attention? Would that feel like belonging, to be desired like the boys want Charo?

Charo only knows Sal as a shadow. There are two maricones in their year, though it's the loud one who gets all the attention. Yadiel gets into arguments with girls, talks back to teachers, flirts with boys to disarm them. She likes interesting people. That's why she notices Yadiel and not his shadow. Salvador doesn't speak. Doesn't cause a scene. He always has his head in a book but never the good grades to show for it.

She truly sees Sal's face for the first time when he opens the front door of his house. He's cute, but what a waste, she thinks, which is the immediate thought that comes to mind every time she sees a handsome maricón. She doesn't even know where she learned the phrase. There are probably a dozen other phrases like that stored in her mind. She'd never say she hates maricones. Not like the people at her mom's church hate gay people. But she's never befriended a maricón before. They're all opaque in her mind, painted in broad strokes by ironic phrases she's learned from church, family, cruel kids in class.

Inside, his grandmother serves them coffee and bread. The old woman throws a few niceties her way before she disappears to her bedroom. She has to watch her novelas, she says, but tells Charo to feel right at home, any friend of Salvador's is welcome here.

"Friend," Charo says, and snickers. Sal ignores the remark and gets to the point. It's health class, not pertinent to anything either of them care about, but they have to pass this class to graduate high school in eight months. Sal walks Charo through the research he's found on the family planning centers across the country, mostly in and around Santo Domingo, a few in Santiago. Offices made to promote women's health and support families through tough economic choices.

"Que chévere," Charo says. "I mean these offices are helping women. God knows the rest of the country doesn't. Este país odia a las mujeres."

"Right," Sal says. He looks up from his book and meets Charo's eyes for the first time. "Did you know it was Americans who opened those offices here? To tell all the campesinos to stop having kids. It's population control."

"Okay, then. Way to ruin it."

Sal ignores this too and continues reading. She looks around his living room. There are no family portraits on the walls, no ornaments decorating their furniture. Only a large image of a long-haired, fair-skinned Jesus pressing a hand to his chest. But everyone has one of those at home. She was hoping to find something specific, like photos of extended family, an altar to a dead relative, or collections of tapes from musicians they worship. Anything that might reveal him or who he comes from.

"So what's your deal? You don't talk at school, and you don't have any friends."

Sal stops reading midsentence. "You don't really have friends either, right? I mean, all the girls hate you, and the boys you hang out with, I doubt they're just your friends."

She should be insulted, she knows. But his quip pokes at her curiosity. She expects this kind of response from his friend Yadiel, but not from Sal. She tries to pull more out of him, but Sal insists on getting their work done. He wants to get this over with. She lets him lead the way. If she's quiet, maybe he'll do all of the work, like the other neurotic try-hards she gets stuck with sometimes. He should be easy, like the rest. But Sal asks her questions about the content, forces her attention back to the subject every time she wanders.

She's just about to call it a night when Yadiel walks in through the front door. Sal introduces Charo to Yadiel, and they nod to each other like it's their first time meeting. Charo hasn't seen him in some time. Yadiel rarely comes to class anymore. Another dropout, Charo's assumed, though now that she's in front of him she's curious about where he's been all these months away from school.

"Are you done? I have to get ready," Yadiel says impatiently, even though he's just arrived.

"We're done," Sal says. He packs up his books to gesture to Charo that she should leave, but she ignores him.

"Where are you going?" she asks. Sal makes up a story about some family event, but it's an obvious lie. It only makes Charo more curious.

"I'm not in a rush. I don't mind hanging out," she says, and looks at Yadiel, who rolls his eyes to say he doesn't care.

Sal leads them down the hallway to his room. The rest of the house is plain and opaque, but Sal's room is of another world. One of his walls is covered with a giant poster of an old space film she's never seen. Above his bed is another poster of an animated movie, a man in a red jumpsuit walking toward a red motorcycle, huge Japanese letters written at the bottom. Next to that there's a third poster of a cluster of stars, with the text "Cosmos by Carl Sagan" big and bold.

"Wow, you really are a nerd," she says.

"You have no idea," Yadiel says. Charo hears a tenderness there, behind his words. She stayed for the snark and entertainment. But this softness he exhibits for Sal makes her wonder if she's figured him out all wrong.

Yadiel drops his duffel bag on Sal's bed and pulls out an assortment of smaller bags. A bag for his makeup, a bag for his dress, a bag for his heels.

"Wait, are you dressing up as a girl?"

"Do you want me to kick her out? I don't mind," Sal says.

Yadiel looks her up and down as if he's contemplating her again.

"You can stay. Just, no jodas," Yadiel says.

She sits on Sal's bed, thrilled that she's been given permission to be a proper spectator. This close, cramped in Sal's room, Charo notices that Yadiel has no facial hair. His brown skin is spotless, and his eyebrows are thinly trimmed. She's always seen Yadiel as the more feminine of the two, the way he speaks, his mannerisms, but she's never noticed how pretty he is up close. Now he strips to reveal a lean silhouette. Charo covers her eyes as he adjusts his underwear, slips on a black dress, then adjusts again. She figures it's going too far to ask where he puts his penis. Though a base, inane part of her wants to know, she keeps her mouth shut. Sal points a flashlight to the wall, and Yadiel uses the reflected light to see himself better in front of a small square mirror. Sal stands off to the side and hands him a brush, a pencil, whatever Yadiel needs next. Where his jaw might grow wide, he thins. Where his forehead might crease, he smooths. Yadiel knows his reflection well, the dips and curves he has to accentuate to pull from his face his most feminine features. Charo can tell he's done this a hundred nights before.

"Maybe you could put a little more contour on your nose, like down the bridge," Charo says.

"Niña, didn't I tell you que no jodas?" Yadiel scorches her with a side eye.

"I'm just trying to help."

"Yes, I know. You all are always trying to help. Like femininity belongs to you only."

"What do you know about being a woman?" Charo says. She feels suddenly defensive.

"Nothing, and thank god for that. But I'm not trying to be a woman like you. I'm trying to be a woman like me. Catch my meaning, linda?"

A part of her wants to understand. It must be hard for Yadiel, having to hide this big part of who he is. But she can't contain the bitterness rising up inside her. Sal sees that she's about to open her mouth again and cuts her off.

"Ay, loca. I don't know if you should be going out with that man again," Sal says. He helps pull a wig cap over his friend's scalp. Then, together, they place over Yadiel's head a long black wig that goes down the length of his back. Sal ties the wig back in a ponytail as Yadiel makes final touches on his red lip.

"Mi marido ta buenisimo, I'm telling you," Yadiel says.

"Even if he had the best dick on earth, you don't know this man."

Charo feels a wall between them now. She doesn't know about the underground queer life in Santo Domingo. The parties in La Zona Colonial, the private dinners at resorts just outside the city, the parks crowded after midnight. It's been a few years since Renata led Sal and Yadiel to their first party. Sal loves the music and the adrenaline of stepping out into the night ablaze with rum, but he finds the lifestyle draining. He prefers to meet his friends at the park, where it's more intimate, where it's just them. Meanwhile, Yadiel can handle drunken night after drunken night with ease. He's not afraid of the occasional horror that La Kali and Morena tell Sal about, stories that always involve men, be they cops, gringos, or tigueres, gone berserk after a drunken night with a maricón. All those dead gay people at the hands of men who couldn't live with their shame. No way Sal can risk that. But Yadiel says he's excellent at the art of manipulating men. Despite Renata's talks, her scolding, her warnings. None of it deters Yadiel from finding his novios. They're weak. They're desperate. They all want it differently, Yadiel says, but I'm the bone they want, those dogs. I just have to push the right buttons, and bam, Yadiel explains, as if loving men were simple.

The gringo Yadiel prepares to see now he met at a party a year ago. Yadiel didn't fuck him the night they met. Instead he played the long game. Like a serious woman should, Yadiel joked. Now they're steady lovers, the first person the gringo sees when he visits the island. Their meetings are always private dinners in hotel rooms or walks on the beach at night, where no one can see them together.

"Do you even know what he does for money?" Sal asks.

"He's a diplomat," Yadiel says.

"So he works for the consulate?"

"You know the right kind of gringo doesn't have an actual job. He just knows people."

This is the kind of ambiguous power Renata has always warned us about, Sal thinks. The kind of men who come to the island, make us dependent on them, and then leave us when they get bored. But Yadiel doesn't care. For him what matters is that the diplomat can offer hotel rooms by the sea, extravagant gifts, a chauffeur, and a car that smells clean with power.

"Yadiel is planning to use the diplomat to get his visa," Sal says to Charo.

"That's right. Not everyone has a mom in New York like you, Salvador."

Charo tries her best to keep up with their coded language. She imagines a dozen problems for this covert relationship with the diplomat but doesn't ask. She's heard rumors that Yadiel's father finally kicked him out for being a maricón. Men don't have patience for the obscene and the social stigma that comes with it. I hate shows, I hate people knowing my business, she's heard her own father say often. But how many women fight against such stigma every day? Like her cousin, who chose to raise her kids alone rather than stay with an abusive husband, despite how much people in the barrio criticized her. Or unmarried middle-aged women like her aunt, judged for worrying too much about her teaching career and never settling down with a man. Is that how Yadiel feels? Like his options are limited by other people's shame?

"Una mujer está sola," Sal says, completing the thought in Charo's mind.

"No one gets me like Aída gets me," Yadiel says of his favorite poet. He turns so that Sal and Charo will get a better look.

The final touch, a pair of sapphire earrings. Charo gets real close, says again and again that they can't be real, though she knows they must be by the way they glisten.

"These earrings, that's how I know it's a good investment."

"He must really like you. If he only wanted sex, he would pay a bugarrón and call it a day," Charo adds.

"I like her," Yadiel says to Sal, and gives Charo a high five.

Charo welcomes Yadiel's touch. She likes that she said the right thing. She likes to feel like she belongs. She's been lonely. Reading magazines during recess. Going from school to work, then straight home. The occasional hookups never help, though she always thinks they will. She always hopes the touch of a boy will give her whatever she's missing. She tried to ask her mother about it once. When will men be enough? But just as she was arriving at the question, her mother gave her a warning look. There are bridges you don't cross, the look said. She feels especially alone when her mother is in the room.

"I gotta get ahead in life, corazón. This is the ticket," Yadiel says, not to Sal or Charo in particular, but to the air, like she's flirting with fate.

They wait out on the veranda. For fifteen minutes they stand there in idle silence. They get so bored Sal starts talking about the stars flickering above them. Then a black car glides to a slow stop in front of Sal's house.

"Tranquilo, Salvador," Yadiel says. She presses Sal's hand, and then she's down the road, wherever the car is taking her.

"Does Yadiel always come around to get ready?"

"Almost always. She doesn't really need much help, but . . ."

The neighbor next door walks out onto her veranda, cradling her cat. She sits in the shadow where they can't see her. Her rocking chair creaks. The cat purrs.

"She," Charo says, turning the pronoun in her mouth like a cherry pit.

"Sometimes she, sometimes he. Anyway, Yadi says it's better to get ready in good company."

From where he's standing, Sal eclipses the light from inside the house, so that his face is in shadow. This is what he's looked like in her mind all these years, faceless and always on the periphery. But watching him and Yadiel tonight . . . This little ritual they've built for themselves. The way Yadiel looks to Sal for confirmation every time she speaks. Confident as she sounds. So unafraid of life. And yet, from all that Charo's seen tonight, Yadiel needs Sal more than she lets on. Maybe, Charo thinks, there's more to Salvador than I expected.

"Don't tell anyone about tonight, okay?"

"Who am I gonna tell?" Charo says as she opens the front gate. "We have a lot of work to do, nerd. I'll be back around tomorrow."

A PANEL OF SUNLIGHT ENGULFS THE GARDEN'S DAFFODILS IN A deep orange glow. The flowers stand up straight as if they, too, sense the day's end, the encroaching darkness.

Students run around the garden, excited to get on stage. Some of them stand behind bushes and rehearse their lines, others practice their short dance routines, and the rest, the ones who are confident about their performances, those kids run around the garden wild and worriless. Sal stands with Danny, one of the quiet kids, who shakes with fear.

"You know your lines, just have fun," Sal says, but the boy doesn't look convinced. Sal pats him on his head of red curls, then moves on to the next problem. One kid tries to switch roles with his friend last minute. Another gets her shirt stuck on the tomato trellis but doesn't cry out for help, just hides deeper in the vines until Sal finds her holding her knees, snickering like she's been found in a game of hide-and-seek.

"These kids are fucking insane," Amy says, though she, too, is excited. They've been working on the show for a few weeks. It's a simple play about a farming family who struggles with a season of bad crops. The kids are smart enough to get the simple plant science depicted in the story but young enough that they don't mind dressing up as talking carrots and potatoes. The center lawn is lined with foldable chairs in front of the stage. Teachers, parents, and neighbors all come out to support. The staffers, too, are encouraged to invite their friends and family, if only to help raise funds from ticket sales.

"Do you think Jenna's gonna steal half the money and use it to bury Martha? After she murders her, I mean," Amy says.

"You think that gringa is gonna get her hands dirty? She'll definitely hire someone to do it for her."

On the other side of the lawn, Jenna jumps from parent to parent, raving about how amazing it's been to have their kids in the program. Her tight blond ponytail bobs up and down as she nods and laughs along. A tall man who must be her boyfriend follows her around and holds her bag while she sweet-talks the parents. It's been a month since he started, long enough for Sal to learn that the only way to survive Jenna is by laughing at her from a distance.

Right before showtime, Sal and Amy stand off to the side as the kids prepare to go on stage. Through the crowd, Sal spots Vance, standing in the very back, and waves.

"Oh my god, is that your man?" Amy whispers.

"Shhh!" He feels warmth rise up to his face.

When the play stumbles on to its last scene, after two boys get into an argument on stage and the tallest girl in class throws up all over her broccoli costume, the kids get a standing ovation from their overzealous parents.

After the show, Sal and Amy rush to fold chairs, pick up trash, dump the vegetable costumes back into the main office. When they're done doing their part, they run out before Jenna gives them more to do.

Vance waits for them just outside the garden gates.

"Whoa, buddy," Sal says when Vance tries to kiss him. He wants to be careful, there are kids still roaming the garden with their parents.

"Stop being paranoid, kiss your man!" Amy says, nudging Sal's shoulder.

Maybe it's the evening's excitement, or the fact that Amy is finally meeting Vance. But he feels braver. He kisses Vance on the lips. Too quickly, maybe, but it's more physical affection than he's used to out in public.

They walk down the street to the train station. Vance and Amy do most of the talking, ask each other about work, school, their summer plans. He tells her about working at the Gay and Lesbian Center, how it's always been his dream to support the community after years of organizing in the streets.

"I'm getting older, though. Pushing thirty-three. I don't know if I can do it forever." Vance shrugs like it's no big deal. But Sal has seen what a toll his work life takes on him. The days he walks around worried about a sick elder in the community. Or how he stays up past midnight scribbling notes for a new grant proposal, trying to come up with ways to get food and medicine and a stable roof for young gay people.

"We gotta treat the old dude who's down-low and in danger of contracting HIV with as much dignity as we treat the young kid who just got kicked out of her home for being gay. And don't get me started on trans issues. The center is still called 'Gay and Lesbian' like it's fucking 1989."

"Shit, dude. That's a lot," Amy says.

"It's a lot," Vance agrees, and wipes a droplet of sweat from his forehead.

"Well, it's nice to finally meet you. You better take care of our friend here," Amy says. "Or you'll have some gardeners to answer to."

Sal can tell she's been waiting for this moment, and though it feels rehearsed, he appreciates the allegiance.

"It's been so hot lately," he says to move the conversation along.

Even with the sun gone, a thin layer of sweat glazes their foreheads.

"Days like these make me miss the Bay Area. The Pacific. You guys don't know anything about that," Amy says, and sighs like she's sorry on their behalf.

It occurs to Sal that he's never asked her how it feels to live so far from home. There are more miles between New York and the Bay Area than between New York and Santo Domingo. It's the same country but still so far from everything Amy has known most of her life. She seems okay, always tough, always a second away from cutting someone down with a clever joke. It's never occurred to Sal until now that she might be lonely.

"We should go to the beach. Tomorrow," Vance says, and stops in the middle of the sidewalk.

"We don't really have nice beaches in New York, do we?" Sal has never been to one, as long as he's been in the country. Amy mentions the horror stories she's heard about Coney Island.

"There are plenty of nice beaches on Long Island. Fuck it, we're going. I'll borrow a car. We'll get a whole group of us to go."

Sal knows it's hard to dissuade Vance once he's made up his mind. He shrugs, and Amy hollers a loud "Fuck yeah." Before she crosses the street to catch the downtown train, Amy gives them her address, her pimpled face spread into a toothy smile.

"We'll pick you up," Vance says. "Bright and early."

Ella calls Charo with the invitation.

"I have this cute little two-piece, you're gonna die," she tells Charo.

But Charo and Sal haven't talked in weeks. What if he ignores her? Or worse, what if their tension creates ruptures within the group? Charo hates making a spectacle of her problems.

"Girl, they're my friends too. I'm inviting you," Ella says. She refuses to take no for an answer.

The next morning, Charo rises before the sun. She slips into the kitchen to prepare food for the beach day, a ritual that reminds her of her childhood on the island. Sometimes, her mother would wake her up at dawn with a sudden itch to spend the day by the sea, away from home, away from Charo's father. They always made the same recipe together, spaghetti cooked in a thick red tomato sauce. Green olives, cubed salami, crushed garlic. They'd drive out to the beach, just the two of them, with containers of food in the backseat. Her mother was usually serious and reserved, but on those getaways, she surprised Charo with stories about growing up in the campo, all the trouble she and her siblings got into swimming in rivers, hunting for crabs, riding their father's mule.

Now the sweet smell of tomatoes and olives fills the apartment. She hears Robert peeing in the bathroom, then the bedroom door shut as he slips back in bed. She invited him to the beach last night, hoping it'd become a regular thing, going out with her friends together.

"You go out and have fun. Llevate a la niña, she'll love it," he said, which was just as welcome a relief. And maybe he's right. Maybe Charo can create a new tradition here in New York with her own daughter.

Once the sauce has settled, she moves the spaghetti from her biggest pot to disposable trays and seals them with aluminum foil. She hopes her friends will like her food. They're all good at something, she thinks. Ella the singer, Mauricio the dancer. Even Sal's nerdiness got him a job. All of them except Vance. She can't see what makes him special, why Sal is infatuated with him so quickly. He better like my spaghetti, Charo thinks as she places the aluminum trays in a big bag.

Downstairs, Ella honks her horn three times to announce she's arrived. Charo makes her first trip downstairs with the trays of food. Luis offers to come back up to help her with the rest, but she declines, afraid to wake Robert up with a visitor at six in the morning.

She doesn't want to push him too much. But when she's struggling trying to get the car seat and her wide-eyed daughter out the door, Robert swoops in, face still swollen from interrupted sleep. He walks them downstairs, waves a groggy hello to her friends as he straps the baby's seat to the car.

"Charo's a backseat driver, don't let her boss you around," he says to Ella. They laugh. Charo kisses him goodbye. When they hit the highway, Charo feels relieved. She looks out at the pink sheen of sunrise, thinking it's the start of the day, making her soft. But no. It's not out there. The source of the feeling is inside of her. For the first time in months, she's excited by the thought of returning home to Robert.

In the other car, Mauricio's playlist shakes the seats. From the backseat, he directs Sal to skip songs or to switch over to a new CD. Amy sits with him in the back, and Kiko is plopped in the middle, sleeping through the music.

Mauricio is on his third beer this morning. He tries to get Vance to drink, tells him he'll hold the can to his mouth so he can drive.

"You're not drinking and driving," Sal says.

"Take the stick out of your ass, man." Mauricio flicks the back of Sal's neck.

"I prefer the stick there," Sal says. "Keep your alcohol in the back."

"I'll take it!" Amy says. She downs the beer in a matter of seconds. They all stare at her in bewilderment. "What? I can't drink 'cause I'm an Asian nerd? Fuck off."

Amy wipes the beer foam from her lips, asks for another.

"I'm not stopping when y'all have to pee," Vance warns.

An hour into the Long Island Expressway, both of them ask to use the bathroom. Vance teases them until Mauricio swears he'll pee all over the borrowed car. They stop at a large gas station lined with trucks. The air smells of gasoline and hot tires. Mauricio and Amy trip over each other running to the bathroom.

Sal thinks maybe he should go say hi to everyone in the car behind them, where the rest of their friends wait. But the thought of Charo's face keeps him in his seat. He hasn't been angry with her for some time, but he doesn't know if he'll be his normal self with her, or if he'll be cold, distant. Vance must sense that this drift between them has something to do with him. He asked about it once, but Sal shrugged it off and explained that they fight like this sometimes, though in truth no argument between them has stretched this long.

"You can't avoid her forever." Vance looks at the car behind them through the rearview mirror.

"I'm thirsty," Sal says.

It's close to ten but the sun already stings. Sal walks to the store next to the gas station, picks up a plastic container of cold cubed watermelon.

"Beef jerky's half off," the cashier says through his thick brown beard.

"I'm good." Sal hands him a five-dollar bill.

"Where you from, man?"

"The Bronx."

"No, I mean, before." He's holding the container of watermelon hostage. Sal considers walking away without his fruit.

"The DR. It's an island. Or half of one."

"Ah, yes, yes! I know that place," the cashier says, and rubs his beard. "It's like paradise, right?"

"Something like that."

Back on the road, Mauricio and Amy's liquor high crashes, and they fall asleep next to Kiko. Sal turns the music down, grabs Vance's hand, and faces the window. The white moon is a vague thought in the sky. It was an early morning in Santo Domingo when he discovered that the moon is visible during the day. He and a gang of kids were out on the sidewalk, chasing each other up and down the street. One of his neighbors invited his visiting cousins to hang out with them outside. The cousins were loud kids from the campo, accustomed to life outside the traffic and density of the city. One of the girls suggested a baseball match, the city kids against those from the campo. Soon a competitive fervor rose between them. The kids from the campo declared they would win because they had the most practice playing in open fields, unperturbed by cars and traffic. Sal, Yadiel, and the other city kids argued they would win precisely because they were used to playing with so many obstacles in the way.

They had passion but no equipment to carry out their game. The only kid who had a sleek wooden bat and a rugged ball was out of town for the weekend. He came from the richest family on the street, the only house where the lights stayed on when power went out in the barrio, on account of his family's fancy generator. Suddenly, Yadiel ran off without a word to the end of the street, where his house was. He returned a few minutes later with a plastic bottle in one hand and a wooden broomstick in the other. The city kids laughed at the faux bat, but the campo kids clapped in approval of Yadiel's ingenuity.

Sal saw the moon at the height of their game. The teams were tied. The campo kids were up to bat, last chance for either team to score. A tall girl swung the bat and hit the bottle far out to where Sal stood. He felt his stomach tighten as he saw the bottle ascending. When the bottle arrived at its zenith, Sal stretched skyward, as far as his fingers could reach. Just left of the descending bottle, Sal spotted the moon, a white coin in the sky. The bottle fell right in front of him. The campo kids cheered as the girl with the long legs landed at home base, giving them the win. They banded together and chanted, while the city kids surrounded Sal to reprimand him.

Where is your head at? they yelled. It was right in front of you, how could you miss it?

It was a plain fact about the world that had eluded him the first nine years of his life. How long had the moon been there on his way to school, or as he ate buttered bread dipped in coffee on the veranda with his grandmother?

What, you've never seen the moon? Yadiel asked, rolling his eyes. But he didn't wait for a response. Yadiel pulled Sal away from the game and started running. They entered a ruined two-story building through the back. The building had been abandoned many times in their short life, businesses that kept failing for one reason or another. Once it was a regular colmado, another time a hair salon, for a few weeks even a clothing store till they were shut down for selling drugs; at least that's the story the barrio kids spread. Sal hesitated in front of a red ladder with missing rungs. They'd snuck into the building before to play hide-and-seek, but never up to the roof. Sal gestured that they should go back and join the others. Yadiel waved away Sal's worry and climbed up ahead.

When they emerged on the roof, there it was in the sky. Sal was convinced it was another moon, different from the silver disk he saw at night. This moon was pale, almost translucent, and the depressions on its surface looked blue as day, instead of the usual lead gray. He grew up hearing stories about the moon from his grandmother, about where it went and what it did when they couldn't see it. This was before Sal learned scientific facts about the moon's tumultuous origins, its storied affair with gravity, before the moon solidified as a giant, solid fact in his mind. Back then, the whole sky was a series of tales his grandmother strung together to keep him occupied, especially on the days he fixated on the same tired question: When would he glide through the clouds to meet his mother in New York? When he turned nine, he stopped asking about his mother. He felt how sorry it made his grandmother, who tried to explain things about borders and papers he couldn't wrap his head around. He stopped asking about New York. But he still asked for stories about the moon. It was the best way to spend time when the power went out.

Once, on one of those dark nights, his grandmother told him about the oceans. Long ago, she explained with her coffee breath, it was believed that the moon was filled with water. Those depressions, the dark caves of the moon, were evidence of the moon's oceanic depths. Sal didn't want to imagine all those fish up there, stuck in perpetual night. But the moon above him as he stood on the roof, he really could believe that it was filled with blue-silver days, tempestuous seas, fish in every color. The morning moon was something more fantastic.

"Water!" Kiko yells now.

Sal looks down from the sky.

To the right of the road, they have met the rolling sea.

It's not noon yet when they arrive, but the whole world burns with the intensity of the July sun. Only the occasional breeze from the sea breaks the heat. Sal and his friends drive through a small town lined with ice cream parlors, restaurants, souvenir shops. Vance drives slowly and rolls the windows down.

"Uh, are we in the right place?" Amy says.

"This is a lot of fucking white people," Mauricio says. "And, like, rich motherfuckers. Look at that gringo's shades."

They gawk at the wealthy townspeople like they're at the zoo. Even Sal wonders out loud if maybe they should have gone to a beach closer to home, a place that's more familiar.

"Guys, this is the most beautiful beach I've ever seen. Pink and white rocks everywhere. You'll love it, I promise," Vance says.

"It's about to get real uncomfortable." Mauricio rubs his temple where his fresh Caesar has left a scratch.

"Mauricio, you have this idea that we can't be in a place because white people are there. Frankly, I don't give a fuck. If a whitey has a problem with my Black ass sitting on a beach, he can come and chat."

For once, Mauricio is out of words.

"It's the beach, it belongs to everybody," Kiko declares in that serious tone he picks up when he's trying to emulate adults. It doesn't settle their anxiety altogether, but Kiko's simple understanding of the world is helpful. At a stoplight, Vance turns around and gives Kiko a fist bump.

"You know, Kiko, this is supposed to be the easternmost point of the whole island," Sal says. He unfolds a map on his lap, points to where they are.

"So we're at the end?"

"The very end," Sal confirms. "Montauk."

The sand is hot and grainy on their feet. The shock of it sends a scream out of Amy. Mauricio hops around until he gives up and slips on his sandals. Ella brings a large blanket from her car. Luis carries an umbrella and opens it over the ice coolers.

"This is Amy. Best teacher in the garden," Sal says. Amy hugs everyone she hasn't met.

Charo senses Sal avoiding her. It's too hot to focus, so she narrows her attention on slathering Carolina with sunscreen. Her daughter laughs at the cool touch of the cream, takes some of it from her own skin and rubs circles on Charo's face.

"I don't believe in that 'Black don't crack' bullshit," Ella declares, and opens her arms for Mauricio to slather her in sunscreen. Sal rubs it on Vance's shoulders, down his back. For a second the crab tattoo above his elbow looks as if it's made of sand instead of ink, as if it might wisp away into the wind. Sal covers it in a thick layer of sunscreen.

Vance and Mauricio race into the water first. They look like children, small against the vast blue before them. They run until they can't, then they dive headfirst into a wave. Charo and Luis take Kiko and Carolina to dip their feet.

"You two are gonna have to talk eventually." It's Ella. She lies behind him on a towel with her eyes closed. The wind carries Kiko's laughter and the baby's shrieks. Sal looks toward the water, where Vance is chasing after his little brother. Mauricio sneaks behind them, tackles them both back under.

"Eventually," Sal says, and crushes a watermelon cube between his teeth.

As they lie there in silence, an old couple red as tomatoes walks by and gawks at them. Ella pulls her shades up and clocks the old man eyeing her yellow bikini.

"It's nice, right?"

The man tightens his lips into a strained smile and hurries along with his wife.

When Charo returns, she sits Carolina in Ella's arms and hands her a slice of mango to keep her busy.

Charo eclipses the sun in front of Sal.

"Let's talk."

They walk along the water where the sand is wet and heavy. Their feet make spongy prints. Sal looks out toward the ocean as they walk. Always daydreaming, Charo thinks, but doesn't say anything until their group is far behind them, swaying dots in the summer haze.

"I need you to tell me when you're upset."

"What do you mean?"

"You keeping quiet doesn't help. Why don't you just tell me if you're mad at me?"

"You can be intense."

"C'mon, Sal. Be fucking for real."

"I'm serious," he says.

"Almost ten years of friendship," she says, because she's not in the mood for half truths. "That's a long time."

"Okay, fine," Sal huffs. "I'm scared to fight. I don't want to lose you."

She can tell he's uncomfortable, but she pushes anyway. "You think us fighting means you're going to lose me?"

They stop in front of a fish head washed ashore. A cluster of flies hovers above the half carcass. Where its eye was is now a black circle. It smells sharp, like it's freshly dead.

"This is about Yadiel."

"You think everything is about that," Sal says, and walks ahead.

Charo catches up to him, pulls his hand, and sits him next to her, facing the ocean. A current of wind passes between them. Strands fly loose from Charo's bun, into her face. She tucks the loose hair behind her ear.

"We've been trying to help you out of this rut for years," she says eventually. "Your mom and I, we've been here the whole time. When you got here and couldn't get out of bed. When you finished school and didn't know what to do with yourself. And then comes this guy, de la nada, and suddenly he moves you. Everything we've done to help, you've resisted. It seems so easy with him."

"Charo."

"I know. This is my shit. It's not that I'm not happy for you. It's just that, well, a part of me wishes it was me, that I had helped you find a job." As soon as she says this she feels ugly, trapped in her skin. She crosses her arms. In front of them, a wave crashes onto rocks, seaweed, desecrated shells.

"What is it about him? It can't just be that the dick is good," Charo says.

"You can't make fun of me."

"You know I'm going to make fun of you." She nods for him to go on.

"He doesn't know my life before he met me. It's easier to let someone help you like that when they don't know your past."

"It's that simple?"

"I'm trying to be simple, tranquilo."

"I think I know what you mean," she says, and turns to face him. Sal is lighter than her, but after just an hour in the sun he's already taking on a deeper color. His cheekbones look round and bronze, a richer hue that makes him radiant. As much as she knows him, there are still parts of Sal she doesn't know, parts of him she might never know. He's changing. She's changing, too. "Things have been better with Robert. He's trying. It feels good when it's like this. When it's simple."

"See? Tranquilo, smooth," Sal says, and pats the wet, flat sand to make his point. They sit in silence for some time, listening to the waves, tending to the circling thoughts in their own heads. Sal pokes at the sand with one finger, then another, until the smooth sand next to him is dotted with holes.

A flock of seagulls cry about them, ravenous.

"That first night we went out with Renata, Yadi called me a cobarde. That keeps playing in my head. Like the VHS player is broken and I'm in a loop. Maybe she was right."

Sal pushes sand over the holes he's made, all those little imperfections.

"And you were right. About the museum. I fucked up for not going to the interview, and I fucked up for not calling. But I'm focused now. I'm getting things together."

"I believe you," she says. And then, because she can't help it, to love him the way she knows best, she continues. "And I'm not trying to tell you what to do . . ."

"Here we go."

"But! I don't know, I don't think you have to pretend. You don't have to forget the past to survive it, is what I mean."

He wrinkles his nose like he's smelled the fish head again. "This is what I'm talking about. Pushy."

"Just trying to be wise and boring like you."

Charo stands and brushes off the wet sand sticking to her ass and thighs. Most of the walk back is quiet except for the rippling waves and the white birds crying above them. Their friends in the distance clarify from mirage to dots to recognizable bodies running between sand and water.

"You'll have to tell him eventually."

"Eventually," Sal says. He rubs his hands together to get rid of the sand caked between his fingers. "Just don't leave me, okay?"

She wants to make fun of him to mask this sudden tenderness between them. They're good when they're going back and forth with biting jokes. Or when she's lecturing Sal about some mistake he's made. Their common ground is built on irony, humor, the occasional scolding to cut through the bullshit. Isn't that what makes relationships work? Keeping to a shared script, sticking to one tone. But now Sal's honesty disorients her. She wants to return it, to follow him to this new place between them where they point directly to their wounds. She thinks, Isn't this what I've been asking for?

"Okay," she says. It's all the softness she can manage for now.

When they return, Kiko has made half a sand fortress. He's surrounded by a bucket for sand glue, a second bucket for rocks to build a base, a third for water. Sal doesn't know how his brother moved so quickly in the time he was walking with Charo or where the extra buckets came from. Vance must have something to do with Kiko's determination, Sal is certain.

"I'm gonna build this thing in record time. That'll show him," Kiko says as he hauls a bucket of rocks to his working masterpiece.

"You got it, buddy," Sal says.

Mauricio and Luis have gone on their own walk. Sal sees them in the distance.

"Everybody is trying to have a moment," Ella says to Carolina, like she understands.

Charo uses the opportunity to start preparing her pasta. She hands Ella a plate and watches as her friend takes the first forkful.

"Oh, this is bangin'," Ella says.

"Really, you like it? Here, I'll serve you some more," Charo says, ecstatic. "Sal, go find Vance. It's time to eat!"

Down by the water, Sal feels the crackle of white foam on the soles of his feet. Out where the water meets the sky, that hazy blue line in the distance, everything looks still. The waves, the sky, the horizon. All of it should be a comfort. But it's too much like the lavish beaches of his home, so beautiful they obscure the harsh reality of the people living in those perfect places. *Paradise.*

In the distance, he notices Vance in the water among a crowd of pale faces. Vance rides a wave, then emerges a few seconds later, his bald head shining in the sun. He yells something the wind swallows. Then waves and waves until Sal gives in and joins him in the water.

"I didn't know you like to swim so much," Sal says.

Vance leads them deeper in, the crab tattoo flexing on his arm as he wades through the teal sheen. It's colder than Sal expected. His legs tense up in reflex. His stomach tightens. They swim out until they have to stand on their toes. Vance hauls him up on his back. A mixture of fear and excitement catches in Sal's throat.

Vance points to a wave accelerating in their direction.

"You're crazy! What if we drown?" Sal is a good swimmer, but the wave looks mighty.

"You gotta trust me," Vance yells. Then he pulls them under.

Sal opens his eyes as the wave rolls over them. He can't see much except the sun above. Light slows down when it moves from air to water. The thought unravels slowly in his mind as he stares at the sun rays made pale by the undulating current. The only time he went to the beach with Yadiel, they filled coconuts with rum and got drunk off their minds. Why now, why light? He wishes he could stay here. Go on back to the city without me, he wants to tell his friends. I'll be here a long time, refracted by the sea. But a second later, Vance pulls him out of his dream, out to the world to gasp for air.

It's a hot July day and the kids are being particularly difficult. They don't want to play in the sun or sit in the shade to listen to the day's lesson about natural insecticides. They don't want the lunches their parents prepared for them, but they grow sluggish and irritable from hunger. Water, only water. Nothing else will do. On days like these, Sal feels like a babysitter without the perks of air-conditioning. He's relieved when he sends the last kid off with her parents at the end of the shift.

Amy, who has a date she can't stop talking about, asks Sal if he can take care of the cleanup alone, just this once.

"If it doesn't work out with this guy, I'm going back to only dating women," she says as she rushes out.

When he's done picking up candy wrappers in the daffodil beds, Sal stops by the cherry tomatoes. The vines grow wild and rebellious around the wooden trellis. Other than annual mulching and regular weeding, they require little work, compared to how much fruit they produce. The staff isn't supposed to eat food from the garden, but they all do it. Sal reserves his picking for the end of long days like this one. He plucks a single cherry tomato and crushes it between his teeth. Juice explodes in his mouth, warm and sweet.

Jenna catches him as he's leaving the office. Sal holds back a groan. "We have to talk," she calls out to him.

"Can we wait until tomorrow? It's been a long day," Sal says, and points to the darkening sky to make his point.

"It can't wait, it can't." She marches toward him in long, hurried strides. Her blonde ponytail bobs above her head as if it's taunting him. "I got a call from a very concerned parent. She says her son was asking questions about boys kissing."

"Wait, what?"

"Apparently the kids have been talking about it for weeks. I don't know how we didn't notice," Jenna says, her face growing red. She looks down at her notepad like it'll save her from whatever she's embarrassed about. "He saw you kissing a man in one of the gardens."

"What student?"

"Danny," she says. The boy with the red curls. "Fuck, I shouldn't have said. It doesn't matter. That is completely inappropriate."

"Jenna, they're kids. Kids make things up. I mean, I have a boyfriend, and he came to watch the show, but I'd never kiss someone in front of the kids," he says. This isn't a complete lie. They were technically outside the garden gates when Sal kissed Vance at Amy's request.

Jenna raises her eyebrows, as if he's given her what she was looking for. Before she can jump on this new opportunity, Sal continues. "You brought your boyfriend to the play."

"That's not what we're talking about."

"You were holding his hand, your boyfriend, in front of the parents."

"Sal, Sal, please," she says, chirping like a bird. "It's just not appropriate here. It's not. I'm sorry."

Sal knows she's not sorry. The decision was probably made before this conversation even started. Jenna is just delivering the verdict. Does she feel bad about it? Is that why she's biting her lower lip? He wonders if this will be the task that gets her a leg up in the race to become Martha's replacement when she retires next year. He wonders, too, if when Jenna says "it" what she really means is Sal. If he has changed from person to thing before their eyes, now that they know he loves men the way he does.

He's done looking in her eyes for understanding. He feels stupid for thinking he could find it there in the first place.

"Fuck you, Jenna," he says, turns on his heel, and leaves the garden one last time.

A couple argues outside of their apartment. She yells her accusations of infidelity. He makes his claims of innocence. They're a floor below, but the hallways carry the echo of their hurt. Sal isn't sure why they've left the apartment to argue, but he's certain the whole building must hear them. They come in and out a few times, each time slamming the door harder than the last. Finally, the man leaves, and she locks the door from the inside.

Sal snuck in as someone was leaving the building. Now he sits on the stairs outside of Vance's apartment. He came here right after his argument with Jenna, expecting Vance to be home on a Tuesday after work hours, or to find Mauricio, who starts his bartending shifts much later in the night. When he realized no one was home, he decided to sit. His head is lighter now, less dense with thought. He focuses on the hollow sounds traveling the building. Bachata playing a floor above. A pushy tenant interrogating the mailman in the lobby.

Vance comes an hour later, carrying a bag of groceries in one hand, handling his keys in the other. He wears a blue button-down with a checkered pattern, khaki pants, Chelsea boots. Sal is not used to seeing Vance in his work clothes. He looks so different, this man who works at a community center, who talks to funders and takes business calls and runs community programs that affect a lot of people's lives.

"What are you doing here? Why didn't you call?" He sounds apologetic, as if it's him that's late, not Sal who has shown up unannounced. "What's wrong?"

"Nothing, my head, I have to lie down."

"Sal."

Vance drops his groceries. A few tangerines roll out onto the dirty floor. Sal falls apart in Vance's arms.

Speeding through the crumbling streets of Santo Domingo, the bus breaks down again, third time this month. It always happens when Sal's on his way home from the electronics store. At this hour, the streets are packed with people on their way home from work. But given the state of the highways and how old the buses are, it's a miracle the commute is reliable at all. Last two times it was a popped tire. This time, an exhausted battery. They have to wait a whole hour to cram the complaining passengers into a new bus. I'll get a car once I start university, Sal promises himself as he walks home from the bus stop. That's the whole point of this job. A yearlong break between high school and college to get some money together. He's done a decent job at saving since he started working at the electronics store eight months ago. At this rate he'll be able to afford the freedom of a car very soon. He imagines it now as his knees ache. Driving to university with ease. Leaving the city whenever he wants. He's seen all the ads dedicated to American tourists, how his country advertises its beaches, its colonial history, the serviceable locals, all for the consumption of foreigners. But of the locals, eight million Dominicans in the country, most will never know anything beyond what's in their backyard. Sal doesn't want to be like everyone around him. He wants to experience his country for himself.

He'll go out to Barahona first, where his family is from, before they all moved out to the capital. Then he'll travel north, loop around the national park, stay in Puerto Plata to meet the sea. He'll stretch the trip to last two weeks, staying with cousins and friends of cousins. Then he'll return, and in another few weeks start his new life as a college student.

At home, his grandmother is waiting for him with the phone in hand. He mouths to her to say he's not home, but she shakes her head and passes him the phone. It's clear where her allegiance lies.

"How am I going to get through to you? You tell me. I'm done trying to figure it out."

"Mami, I already told you. Estoy cansado de hablar de lo mismo. It's not happening."

"Sal, this is an amazing opportunity. Do you know how many people wish they could live in New York?" Her reasoning always starts like this. The state of the island, compared to America. The lack of jobs, the violence. She doubles down by telling him of a friend's uncle, who was shot and buried in his own backyard. They looked for him for days. Didn't notice the dog sniffing around in the backyard until, a week later, the sad old thing unearthed a cold hand that had just begun to rot.

"Do you know how many of my friends at work are waiting to get their kids a visa?" his mother continues.

She never mentions that she longs to be with him, after all their years apart. That she wants to work on their relationship. Or that she wants him to spend time with the little brother he's never met. His mother isn't sentimental in that way. Most of his life he's been here, she's been there. But if he knows one thing for sure about her, it's that she has strict ideas about what her life should be like. If Sal doesn't go through with the final stage of the visa process, ace that interview, join his mother in New York, she won't be able to brag that she finally got her firstborn to America. It makes him feel like a project. Less a person and more a shiny symbol of all her hard work. Some of that weight was lifted when his little brother was born.

But her husband left her a few months ago, and now she's back to obsessing over Sal to keep herself busy.

"I want to go to university, get my car, and keep working my job when I can. I'm good here," he explains.

"What about your friend? What's her name? Look how quickly she jumped on the opportunity. She's smart, Sal. You have to be smart about your future." He listens to her go on about Charo. It's not the first time she's brought her up. Charo and Sal spent almost every day together their last year of high school, making up for the years they'd known so little about each other. Then, six months after graduation, Charo left. She got the call for the interview suddenly, though she didn't expect to get a call for another year. Even Charo, always so cool and controlled, let herself be raptured by the promise of New York those last few days on the island.

When he's off the phone, his grandmother eyes him with worry. If he leaves, she'll be alone. There will be no one to get groceries with, no one to rub her callused feet, no one to climb the avocado tree in the backyard when it's time for harvest. But she doesn't want him to stay. She echoes his mother's sentiments, tells him there's nothing here for him but struggle. And anyway, she has her church friends, she explains, and the Duartes next door have four sons. More than enough able hands to help her if anything comes up.

"You know your mother's right," she says, though her sorry eyes betray her.

"I'm not going," he tells her, then walks off to shower.

That evening, the power goes out just after eleven. It happens a few times a week, but tonight they're especially disappointed. On nights like these they rely on their rickety fans to soothe them, even if it's more a trick of the mind than anything else. But as soon as the power goes, the fans slow to a hot stop. The house swelters with heat. They are faced with the same old choices. To pray that the day has tired them enough to sleep through the discomfort. Or to wait it out outside until the power comes back on. Sal rolls around in his bed for some time before he sighs in defeat. His grandmother is lying quietly in her bedroom down the hallway.

"You up?"

"Yeah," she says, rising to her feet. She unplugs all the electronics on her way out.

They sit on the veranda, a rocking chair for each. Sal passes his grandmother a piece of cardboard to fan herself with. Others in the barrio have come out to do the same. Across the street, Benito and his family sit out on the sidewalk with a dim kerosene lamp. He hisses at his kids to go back inside, tells them to pretend they're in an icebox or at the North Pole, but they're excited to be let out past their bedtime.

In the sky, a slice of moon is pale and distant. He can't make out his neighbors' houses. The darkness swallows everything but the kerosene lamps dotting the street. The barrio's sounds are more pronounced: children screeching, viejas whispering, crickets chirping from their hiding places.

"If you talk, you put more heat into the air," his grandmother says, and laughs, because what else can they do but laugh at their luck.

Sal's mind wanders in the dark. He misses his friends. Charo, whom he didn't like at first, had no reason to befriend him except they were paired together for a school project. She snuck into his life; that's how it felt those first few weeks. After school, she'd come over with an excuse. She needed help with an assignment, or she forgot something at his place. Eventually she stopped making excuses and settled for just saying she was bored at home. Sal suspected she was lonelier than she cared to admit. He asked about it once, but she laughed it off and started telling him a rumor about one of her ex-boyfriends.

Sal grew to welcome her company, in place of Yadiel's absence.

He was spending more and more time with the diplomat. Investing in his future, Yadiel called it. When Charo got her papers and left six months after graduation, Yadiel cursed her.

"Una tipa como esa, what is she gonna do there? I'd take that city by storm, do something real," Yadiel said. He sounded bitter, more so than usual. But Sal knew it was out of desperation. The diplomat was taking too long. Sal guessed that the gringo really had fallen in love and wanted to keep his friend in a golden cage. But Yadiel wasn't worried.

"I'm going to New York," Yadiel said with such certainty there was nothing to do but believe him.

Yadiel has no family in the United States, Sal thinks now. An uncle got Charo through by claiming her as his daughter. Yadiel's only relative is his father, who barely makes enough money from the occasional gig fixing motorcycles to keep a roof over his head. And anyway, his father kicked him out months ago. The diplomat, who pays for the apartment where he lives now, is Yadiel's best option.

Next to him now, Sal's grandmother snores. He waits another half hour before shaking her.

"Go to bed while you're still sleepy," he says, and helps her out of the chair.

Sal decides he'll call his friends tomorrow on his day off. It's been too long since he's heard from them. Charo in New York. Yadiel who knows where. And if Yadiel doesn't pick up the phone, Sal will stop by his apartment early in the morning, wake him with a café negro con azúcar, the way he likes it. He'll tell Charo about university coming up. He'll tell Yadiel about the trip he'll take cross-country. The last few times they spoke, Sal felt bad for rejecting Yadiel's invitation to go out drinking. That's just not my life right now, he said. But maybe he can convince his best friend to come along on this trip, maybe they can see the island together.

It's about two in the morning when the power comes back on.

He must have dozed off; he didn't realize how late it'd gotten. The kids from across the street groan. Sal turns on the porch light and waves to Benito as he ushers his kids inside. The man doesn't wave back. Instead, he points in Sal's direction. Sal looks back to see if it's his grandmother, but there's no one behind him. Maybe a rat by his feet? Nothing. He can't see what the man is pointing at.

"Afuera, en el piso. Te dejaron algo," Benito calls out. His Cibao accent is strong. He just moved to Santo Domingo a year ago. From the little Sal knows about him, he left the campo and moved to the city to put his kids in a better school. Everybody's dying to leave their home for somewhere better, Sal thinks.

Benito goes inside and shuts his door. Sal steps out from the veranda. There on the ground sits a large yellow envelope. The paper is clean and crisp. On the front, written with a black marker, the words *our little secret* in English. The envelope wasn't there when Sal got home from work that afternoon. And someone, anyone from the block, would have taken it and checked for money if the envelope sat there for more than a few hours. It must have been done in the dark, when the lights were out. I would have seen a car stop in front of the house, he thinks. Did someone walk by and drop it?

Sal opens the envelope and pulls from it something round and rubbery. It fits neatly in the cave of his palm. Even as he sees it, he can't process the object in his hand. It feels too much like flesh to be flesh. And the mound is wrong. Not because it looks any different from a regular ear, but because he's never seen an ear not attached to someone's head. It could be any ear. But attached to the lobe is a sapphire earring. His breath stops in his throat when he sees the red staining his palm. He looks around to see if anyone's noticed. The last of his neighbors throw their cigarettes to the sidewalk, take their madrugada conversations back inside. He throws the mound of flesh, earring still attached, back in the envelope.

Inside, he places the yellow envelope on top of the cabinet next to his bed and waits, like it'll reveal itself if he just stares. Whoever left the earring on the lobe knew Sal would recognize it. For a second, it occurs to him that it might be a request for ransom, like in the movies. But there was no note requesting money. Only silence. And anyone who wanted money wouldn't have left an earring worth hundreds of American dollars on a mound of flesh. There's only one person who knows where Sal lives that isn't in any need of money, power, or influence.

The hours pass him like this, thinking. How did I get here? But the envelope won't answer. And the night won't answer. He starts to feel his body flare. When was the last time I had a fever? I must have been ten, maybe. He washes his face in the bathroom, drinks three cups of water, but his body is still hot. His limbs grow heavy. He lies in bed and stares at the ceiling. Time hammers away at the psychic wall between him and the realization all the signs point to. But he can't go there yet. The mound is just a mound. Not an ear, he thinks. Not something that was once attached to a person I love.

Sometime later there's a knock on the front door. He looks out the window and there's the sky, brightening again. Why didn't it wait, the sun? Why won't the clock stop? He's not sure if he hears the door or if his mind wills it into being. He's half asleep, certain this side of consciousness is just a dream between dreams. But the door, his mind warns, and another knock follows. His feet slap heavily on the floor. One second the door is closed. The next, there's Renata, in her wig and makeup from the previous night, standing like a tired messenger after a long journey.

"She came to the park right before the sun set, bereft, out of her fucking mind," Renata says. She doesn't sit, she just paces in the middle of the living room.

"My grandma, she shouldn't see you dressed like that."

"Are you listening to me? She had bruises on her shoulder,

down her back. Bruises everywhere. He kicked her out. She tried to fight him, the diplomat."

"Renata, I—"

"I told the girls to grab her, but she busted La Kali's lip. Almost knocked Morena out. Kept saying she was gonna go back and give him an ultimatum. The visa or the truth. Even if she had to march to the embassy to out him. I spent the night looking. But even if I find her, she won't listen. I need you to come with me."

"Wait," Sal says. He must sound too calm, because now she's looking at him like he, too, has lost his mind.

The envelope is stained now. But it was clean a few hours ago, Sal thinks. Does blood do that? Spill from an ear overnight the way it's draining out of Renata's face now, the way its absence now makes her look aghast, like a ghost, like something that was living and is now dead? He pulls the mound from the envelope. The cartilage bends between his fingers. It smells sharp now, like an infected piercing. The sapphire winks at them in the growing light that enters through the window. It looks beautiful in the dawn's glow, Sal thinks. He holds it out in front of him as if to offer it to Renata. This last bit to complete her story, the evidence they need to close the door to wishful thinking.

"A warning, for me. For us, to keep us quiet," Sal says.

Renata lets out a cry, an animal emotion. It triggers something similar within Sal, scratching at his throat. He rushes through the long hallway to the backyard. His body is scorching now. Outside, he kneels on the ground and bends over. The early breeze caresses the hair on the back of his neck. His vision blurs but he can still see his hands stained red in front of him. He vomits bile thick and yellow. The world goes black.

THE BODY WASHES ASHORE AT EL MALECÓN, SALTY AND SWOLLEN, A brine of sorrow. It takes a few months for authorities to identify the corpse. By then Sal is in New York. His grandmother calls to tell him. Says he should come back for the funeral. Says Ren is looking for him. Says she understands his pain. But how could she? This wound. He left the island. Doesn't want to know about the state of the body or the funeral or his grandmother's vicarious pain. He's in New York now. He says it to himself and to Charo again and again. I'm okay. I've moved on.

This feigned peace is only interrupted once, when Renata finally reaches him.

"Do you blame me? Is that why you won't call? I know it's my fault. I shouldn't have taken you two to those parties. You were too young. But I'd seen gay kids like you. Like us. Who kill themselves because they're lonely. Or who get destroyed by drugs, the bottle, fucked-up families. I thought if I gave you a little vision of belonging . . . If I kept you close . . . I know we weren't perfect. But I didn't have a lot of options."

Renata never let anyone touch her. But every now and then, when it was de madrugada and it was just them left at the park, tired and drunk, she would place her head on Sal or Yadiel's shoulder.

I gotta lay my head down somewhere, she'd say, and stay there un-moving for a long time. That's how she sounds on the phone with him now, like she's desperate to find someplace to put it all down.

"Only one newspaper covered her death. Can you believe that shit?" Renata says. Her voice is muffled, her sorry mouth too close to the phone.

"Yeah," he says. Becase he can believe it, that no one would care to cover the death of a maricón spit out by the sea.

"I can send it to you, manita. The paper. Proof that someone cared."

"Keep it, Renata. And just . . . Don't call me anymore," Sal says. Then he hangs up.

II.

THE NEXT TIME SHE GOES TO WATCH ELLA PERFORM, CHARO plants a few audience members to stir up the crowd. A young European tourist and her American friends, a married couple bored with each other's company, a tipsy loner sitting at the bar. The loner says he's seen Ella perform. "It's old-people music," he complains. But Charo promises a free drink for their cooperation, courtesy of Jimmy the bartender, who's in on the plan.

When the show starts, her planted audience members clap at the end of each song. The applause is timid, weak as a broken faucet, but it draws the attention of the other patrons. They start nodding along to Ella's songs; some even mouth the words to the old jazz hits. In the middle of her set, the loner at the bar wobbles toward the stage as if Ella were a mermaid, he a seasick sailor. "Kiss!" someone yells from the audience. The man stumbles onto the stage, but before he reaches her, he bends over and empties his stomach over her shoes. Half-digested burger chunks splatter on Ella's ankles. The crowd groans. Ella runs off.

Later that night, after Ella washes her feet three times and switches shoes twice, they sit on a bench outside the restaurant. Sweat sticks to the back of their necks. Charo ties up her hair into a messy bun that droops from her head. Tonight Charo saw what a difference a good audience makes. Ella looked like one of those stars on television, lifted by the admiration of a crowd that was curious, that wanted more.

"You felt it, right? I mean it was short, but they loved you."

"You shouldn't come anymore," Ella says. She sits deflated, her shoulders hunched over. "I get paid for these gigs. I just want to make a few bucks and go."

Charo feels stupid all over again for having tried. But after seeing Ella shine tonight, even for a few minutes, how can she give up? Ella might not see herself the way Charo sees her. But isn't that what friends are for? To reflect the best of what they see back to each other? If only she could find a way. She's about to fill the air with a new idea, but Jimmy walks out of the restaurant, car keys in hand.

"Y'all ready? I'll drive you home too, Charo," he says.

Charo follows behind them up the empty street. He puts an arm around Ella to keep her from wobbling on her heels. His hand is firm around her waist; his walk is steady.

Charo wonders how long it's been, if Ella will ever notice that Jimmy is in love with her.

The last customer this shift places her items on the conveyor belt. Pureed banana, so there must be a baby at home. Black beans and yuca, so she must be Dominican. Charo's been working here long enough to know people well by what they buy. The woman puts in the wrong PIN for her EBT card once, twice. Charo wonders if there's nothing wrong with the card and the woman's faking it. Jose, the store owner, has gotten in her head. He's always training them for theft. Customers who use stolen cards and pretend to forget their PIN. Elders who stumble in with walking aids and stuff the most expensive items into their carts. Even kids, he says, can be used creatively to steal, or to draw attention from the person stealing. It's always the meat, he explains every time he calls them into a meeting. They have to be careful with the meats, especially beef. He is obsessive about beef. Jose has a beef-theft story for every year he's owned this supermarket, as far back as the eighties.

The customer in front of her now has no cart or baggy clothes to hide stolen meat. That makes Charo feel better. The woman presses the four-digit PIN a third time like her life depends on it. The reader approves the transaction. They both sigh in relief.

Robert arrives just as she finishes closing the register. He comes inside to greet Jose. They've been friends for years, a friendship, like hers and Sal's, that survived the move from Santo Domingo to The Bronx.

When Charo met Robert, she worked at a different supermarket owned by a man who was taking money from the registers straight into his pockets. Everyone knew, and they all went along with his anecdotes about what he'd do when he found the thief.

But stealing wasn't the worst of his crimes. It was a few weeks into her relationship with Robert when she learned what only the women at the supermarket knew. The owner called Charo upstairs. He started by scolding her for being late. Then, halfway through his halfhearted speech, he put his hand at the small of her back. I know what you're doing, he said. Coming in late. Arguing with customers. These pretty jeans. You're just acting up to seduce me. That word, *seducir*, it sounded wrong in his mouth full of spit. Charo held back her disgust. As she walked out, free of his grasp, she turned, tried to say something, anything that might return to her an ounce of power. But fear paralyzed her. How would she pay for her room without this job? Her uncle? Her parents? Where would she get the money? It'd take her at least two weeks to find another job. She bit her tongue and walked out quietly.

That night at Robert's apartment, she complained until her throat ached. It felt good to have a lover to vent to. But what Charo really wanted was revenge. For Robert to explode in masculine rage, find her boss, and beat him till he bruised purple. Instead, Robert did what Charo would later learn was truer to his sensibilities. He made a few calls, found the building superintendent's number, and tipped him off to where he could find the rent that hadn't been paid to him in months, all that cash carelessly stashed in the store owner's office.

The next day Robert took her to Jose's supermarket. He trapped his friend in the upstairs office for thirty minutes, and when they came back out, Charo had a new job, starting the next day, with the power to choose her own schedule. The other women working the cash registers had been there for years and were demoted to give Charo preference. They detested her for it, but she felt protected by Robert's influence; that's all that mattered to her then.

Now Charo goes to the bathroom to change her clothes. When she returns, Jose is telling Robert about the new camera system he installed. She looks for Robert's eyes as she walks toward him, hoping he will notice her white summer dress.

"Oh, wow," Robert says, and wraps his arm around her waist.

At the restaurant, they sit among a crowd of other couples. Slow salsa plays in the background. The room is dimly lit. The waitstaff is kind enough.

"Jose's serious about those cameras," Robert says.

"He's crazy."

"I think it'll work. You gotta be smart, keep up with the times," he says, and lathers their complimentary bread with butter. "All these Dominicans act like they're still home. They don't think. In this country, you gotta think to get ahead."

"Well, not everyone has a rich uncle on the island who can help them open up a supermarket," she says. That makes him laugh. She smiles too. She likes that he's trying. Asking her out to dinner, like the old times. Picking her up at work. It's these gestures that paved the path of love for them at first.

"Let's not talk about work. La niña," she says, opening up a conversation about the best thing they share. Robert's been talking about putting their daughter in school before kindergarten, an early program he heard about at work. He wants his daughter to get every head start possible. He tells Charo about his grandparents, how they grew up in the campo and never learned to read and write beyond what's needed to survive. Street signs, labels on food, but that was it. His grandparents were people of the earth. All their lives, they worked with their hands. Plucking passion fruit from trees, uprooting yuca from deep within the soil. To get by, they sold some of the produce they grew. His grandfather fixed wooden furniture for neighbors. His grandmother sewed up holes in old dresses and shirts for a few cheles. They didn't need language to work with their hands, to survive in the monte. Except for the occasional trip to the nearest town to buy clothes, they had little reason to leave and engage with the rest of the world.

Robert was the youngest grandkid, the only one who still spent vacations in the campo, away from the capital, where his mother worked. He saw firsthand how peacefully his grandparents lived. The only time he saw them struggle was on Sundays. Instead of going into town for church, his grandparents hosted small ceremonies in their house, for the family and their closest neighbors. Hard as they tried, Robert's folks struggled to read from the Bible. Most times they improvised verses before swallowing their shame and handing the Bible off to the next person in the circle of prayer. In the afternoon, when everyone went home, they'd force Robert to read scripture out loud for them. His grandparents sat in front of him like a girasol faces the sun and let the scripture wash over them. Then, as thanks, they made him fried fish, his favorite, and took him to the local river to spend the lord's day in the water.

"I came from nothing. No money, no dad. That's why I get it, what it's like to work hard. Everything we've done to get here. And it's not just me. It's everyone. My grandparents working the farm, my mom moving to the city, me coming to this country," he says now. "Sometimes I wish I could have stayed with them, worked my abuelo's land."

This is the first time Charo has heard the full story of his grandparents. She didn't know he had all that inside him. *I think I know him, then I don't,* she thinks, and reaches across the table to hold his hand.

"Who knows, maybe I'll go back one day," he says, and laughs like it's a bitter joke. "But while we're here, we have to focus. La niña, she needs us. I know you want to have your fun, but we're parents. La calle, friends, it's all distractions."

The waiter drops off their plates in front of them. Steaming moro, steak and onions, red beans, and salad on the side.

"It's okay to have friends. I don't think it's one or the other, home life or personal life," she says.

"I'm not saying it's one or the other. But one needs to come first, no?"

"All I ask is a few hours off. Once a week, just a few hours for me," she says. Even though he's not disagreeing. Even though he's been so lax about her going out lately. She pulls her hand away from his.

A middle-aged man walks up on stage with a microphone and interrupts their conversation. He sings a Juan Gabriel ballad, sounds and even looks like the famous singer. Hair brushed back, thick eyebrows, a red suit making him a velvety dream before them. The audience cheers like it's Juan Gabriel himself who's graced them with his presence. When he sings his fifth and final song, a table of older women hop on their feet and raise their napkins in the air.

"I want you to leave your job," Robert says when the crowd has quieted. "Stay at home with Carolina, just until she starts pre-K. I can do overtime at the factory to make up the difference, but if you're there with her, it'll be good. It'll be good for us."

"It didn't occur to you that I might not want to be stuck at home all day?"

"I'm confused. Isn't this what you want, more freedom?"

"Freedom," she says, the word sour in her mouth. She parts the rice on her plate into two small hills. "Maybe you're right. If I don't work, I can manage my time better. Take care of the baby, have more flexibility to see my friends."

"That's all you seem to care about, your friends."

"What are you giving me, then?"

"What am I not giving you, Charo?"

She's being difficult, she knows. She should be grateful that he's offered to take on extra work to make her comfortable. He's making sacrifices. Isn't that what being a parent is about? Centering their daughter, even if it's to the detriment of their own happiness? Besides, Charo has no allegiance to her job. Shouldn't this be easy? But the thought of not making her measly checks, of having to ask Robert for money . . . She's been working since she was thirteen. She has no idea who she is without a job. And the prospect of being a stay-at-home mom, like her mother, and her grandmother before her. She jumps to her feet without excusing herself, dodges the table of drunk women on her way to the bathroom. The air around her thins. A dull pain forms in her chest like there's a hand there pressing to get out. Her knees are weak, but she manages to make her way to the bathroom mirror and practices her breathing there, where she can see her chest rise and fall.

She hears the door behind her, looks up, and there stands the Juan Gabriel impersonator. Startled, she points to the "Women" sign on the door.

"Ay, niña, calmate. It's a fucking bathroom," he says, without looking away from his reflection. Her stomach turns, her balance droops to the side. She'll either fall or throw up. Her mind races to choose the least embarrassing of the two. Right here on the sink is fine, she thinks. Just let it out here. But her racing thoughts stop short when she feels a hand making circles on her back.

"Keep breathing," he says. "Don't move, I'm gonna get you something."

"My partner, he's waiting for me," she says, but he's already gone.

A minute later, he returns with a small glass bottle. He puts it up to her nose and asks her to inhale. The scent of peppermint enters her like a winter breeze. Harsh at first, then with cool relief.

"You have a nice voice," Charo says as she massages two drops of oil on her temples. "Not that it means much, coming from a girl about to throw up in a public bathroom."

"I know, linda, it's what I do," he says. "Pregnant?"

"Hell no."

"Good. He can't be that good if you're in here and he's out there."

She feels instinctively like she should say something to defend Robert. But the diva just saved her from passing out in the bathroom. Choose your battles, she tells herself, and breathes in more peppermint. "You sing here often?"

"Tuesdays, Fridays, Saturdays. I play a different diva each night. And before you say no, Juanga is a diva," he says. He smiles and looks ten years younger, though he must be fifty under the layers of foundation.

Charo puts her palm on her chest. The pressure is almost gone. Then the idea clarifies in her mind, though it doesn't feel seren-dipitous, sudden, and flashy, as good ideas often come. If she tried hard enough, she might have noticed the thought forming a few minutes ago when she was leaning over the sink, or when she was talking to Robert, a thought as old as the instant the Juan Gabriel impersonator took the stage.

"So, I have a friend," Charo begins.

THERE'S ALWAYS A FIGHT IN FRONT OF THE SCHOOL, BUT THIS ONE'S different. For starters, it's not happening around one in the afternoon, when class is over and kids are antsy to let out the energy they've been bottling up all day. It's late enough that the sun has stopped burning. The schoolkids are gone. The street vendors selling caña de azúcar and chickens as pets are all gone too. Charo never stays around school this late. But she told her mother she had a shift at the clothing store after school. That's the only way she can stay out late. She lied so that she could hang out with a boy she likes. He doesn't make her feel like the fairy tales. He doesn't make her feel much at all. But he knows a good spot behind a staircase where they can act grown-up, like the world is theirs. He always chews gum before they kiss. He always asks before touching her somewhere new. That's nice enough.

Now the street is desolate except for the grunts and groans of the boys before her.

The fight is odd. It's three against one, but the one seems to be doing the ass-kicking. He dodges and swings one of his assailants by the backpack. He ducks and kicks another to the floor. They're all the same size, similar build to all the boys her age, just starting puberty, lanky and bony, but almost too strong to have these regular fights in school without causing each other serious damage. How is he winning? Charo wonders as she watches from a few yards away. She has the urge to go, but she's curious about how it'll all play out. Is this a reversal of fortune? Can the underdog really win?

The other thing that's different is so striking she doesn't fully register it until the fight is almost won. Maybe because he's moving too fast for her to recognize him at first. Maybe because it's usually the other way around, maricones getting their ass beat. Maybe it's the way he moves about them, not aggressive and thoughtless like most boys fight, but with a lithe precision—twirling on his toes to dodge a hit, slapping another boy across the face with an open palm, scratching wherever his nails can dig and let loose blood. By the time it's all formed in her mind, Yadiel has brought his three enemies up against a rusty fence. He picks up his bag, asks them if they want more. But the boys are stupefied with shame. Not only because they've lost a fight they should have won on account of their number, but because they're fighting a pájaro. The only thing worse than losing an unfair fight in your favor is losing a fight against a maricón. What will everyone say tomorrow? they must be thinking. It all looks just about done, so Charo fixes her own bag to hurry on home before her mother gets suspicious. But then the air of the fight changes. Yadiel freezes. The one with the tattered shirt smiles with delight. It seems as if he's staring at his friend's crotch. Charo stretches her neck to see what's changed the mood. And there in the middle boy's hand is a blade, about eight inches long. Suddenly they're no longer a couple of boys ganging up on a maricón. Now they're something else. The third boy must not like it, because he grabs his bag and runs. But the boy with the tattered shirt is excited. And his friend's face next to him is so serene it scares Charo. If he's so calm, he might really do it, she thinks. A second ago this was fun. Just a fight between boys. A sight so regular she might not have stopped if it weren't Yadiel at the center of it, beating the odds. But now . . . This is the kind of scenario that fuels her mother's worry, why Charo can never go anywhere that's not school or work. "Nope, no way," she whispers to herself, and turns to go. There's no one else on the street. The sun is starting to glow orange as it nears the horizon. As she walks away, she can hear the boy with the tattered shirt egging his friend on. "Hit him with it one time," he squeals. And that's what he sounds like to her, like the pigs she sees when she visits her family in the campo. Then there's the image of her mother cutting a pig's belly open. The organs falling sticky to the ground. The sharp smell of unclean intestines. The mess of blood everywhere. It's crystal clear in her mind, how easily flesh can be sliced with a knife. "No way," she whispers again. She'd never be so stupid as to get involved.

"What's going on here?" It's not her voice she says it in, but the voice of her schoolteacher. Why say that, of all the things to say? But that's what her mind has picked, in the moment's hurry, from the second ago she was walking away to this instant, as she stands before the boys, closer now than she was before, so close she can see details in the jagged knife. Yadiel stands with his book bag covering his chest. It looks like he had no intention to run before Charo intervened. Is he fucking stupid? she thinks. The two boys are just a few feet away from him, ready to leap.

"Mind your business," the boy with the tattered shirt says. He throws his shirt on the floor, like he's embarrassed by it, now that there's a girl in the mix.

Charo doesn't move.

"You want some of this? Huh?" says the boy with the knife. Now that she's closer, she realizes that he looks a bit older than the rest of them, at least sixteen, by his height and posture. Though she thinks she remembers him from gym class. The big ears, that's what triggers her memory.

"Richard, if you don't put that knife down, I'm telling everyone your little secret." This, too, isn't her voice. She hopes to sound taunting, like the sharp fourteen-year-old she ought to be, but she sounds like a little girl. She opens and closes her sweaty hands.

"What are you talking about?" Richard waves the knife to shoo her away.

"I'm good friends with Mariana. She told me about your small dick," Charo says. Yadiel scoffs next to her. But it's a lie. Mariana and Charo haven't been friends in months. Not since Charo missed Mariana's birthday party for the second year in a row. You don't know what they say about that girl's family in church. I don't want you in that house, her mother warned. Charo's guess was that there was no rumor in church. Just her mother's general paranoia that everywhere is dangerous except for home. Charo didn't go to the birthday party. And Mariana stopped waiting for her at the school gates as she once did every morning. But Charo knows Mariana and Richard are on-and-off-again lovers. Inseparable when they're together, insufferable when they're apart. Last Charo heard, they'd broken up again.

Richard points the knife away from Yadiel and toward Charo.

"I have a big mouth. Pack up your shit or half the school knows about your little pistol, first thing tomorrow."

Finally, she sounds like someone brave.

Richard throws the knife in his bag and tells his friend they're leaving. On his way past them, he coughs up phlegm from the back of his throat and spits it like a seed at Yadiel's face. Charo can hear them laughing up the street. She waits till they're gone to turn to Yadiel as he cleans his face with a balled-up uniform shirt.

"Mind your business next time," Yadiel says. He fixes his tank top and turns to go.

"Whatever," she says, and follows behind him.

The sun is going. She'll have to hear her mother's mouth all night. But right now she doesn't care. Her heart is still beating a mile a minute. She doesn't want a thank-you. But she wants to talk about the moment, the way people commiserate after leaving a movie theater. Except this is real life, and she can feel the moment's shock burning through her body.

"You fight like a girl," she says.

"Are you going to follow me all the way home?" The way his head snaps to the side when he speaks. The inflection in his voice. The way his hand moves with the rhythm of this one question. When a boy does this, people say, "Se partió." The phrase is said when a boy suddenly moves and sounds like a girl. But Charo has never really understood why people say that. What does it mean that a boy breaks? Is it kind of like when an actor breaks character? She doesn't get it, but her choices are to laugh or to be disgusted, so she laughs.

"Well, I live this way too, so I guess we're going together."

He looks focused, like he's trying to solve a math problem in his head. But then something changes. His eyebrows come apart; his face relaxes. And then he looks behind them, as if to make sure they're not being followed.

"Fine," he says. He sounds tired. Like it's all finally catching up to him.

At home that night, her mother isn't waiting at the front door with a broom and empty threats, as Charo expects. You wanna end up in the street, como una loca? Her threats always bend into that question. Charo thinks about the woman who roams their street at dusk. She's seen her from the window. Sometimes the woman coos and places her breast to a balled-up red blanket, like there's a baby there sucking for milk. Other times she runs around crying and moaning that the river took her baby, though there isn't a river here for miles. Does her mother mean loca like that? Or crazy like she talks about the sisters two streets down who run a brothel above a colmado? Or her friend from church whom she unfriended after she saw her coming out of a santera's house? There are a hundred ways to fail to be a good woman. Her mother reminds her every time.

Now the front door is open and the fan is going. This is what they do when they have visitors. Maybe it's the neighbor. Her mother shit-talks the vieja from next door, but they have coffee together every now and then, and they pretend. But instead, the face that greets her is so familiar she feels as if she's known him all her life, though she's only ever seen him in photos. She is giddy meeting her tío from New York. Like meeting someone from the TV. This is how it must feel to meet a famous person she's sure of it. She sits by the table facing her mother. To her right is her father, leaning on the blue cushion that helps his back. To her left, the New York tío.

"I'm so excited to see you," Charo says. This isn't untrue. Except by the look on her mother's face, it looks like Charo interrupted an important conversation.

"Last time I saw you, you were this tall," the New York tío says. "You don't remember me, do you?"

Charo shakes her head. The New York tío cackles. Her mother's mouth spreads into a tight smile.

"Your tío Leo is in town for some business," her mother says.

"Business, that's what we're calling it?" Her father taps on the table with impatience. She notices for the first time the yellow envelope on the table. The thick vein pulsing on his bald scalp.

"That's all it is, manito," Tío Leo says, like he's talking to a little boy. Though her father is older. Way older, she thinks as she notices those deep, dark brown lines on his face. She should hate the way her uncle's tone agitates her father. But she seldom sees him like this. He's always so calm. In church. At dinner. When he plops himself in front of the TV after a long day at a construction gig. The only time she ever saw something like anger on his face was when a man stopped by the house a couple of years ago with a bouquet of flowers for her mother. From her room, she heard how he beat the front door and yelled. Twenty years I've been waiting for you, Mercedes. Leave that Mario and come with me, mi amor, mi alma. He sounded like he was half singing, half crying. Charo had never known her mother to have loved any man other than her father. In fact, Mercedes often told Charo that her father was the only one. If you do it right the first time, you don't have to be out in the street sullying yourself in the eyes of god, she'd say. But who was this man banging at their door? And Charo's father's name is Francisco, so who the hell was Mario? Another lover her mother had lied about? Her father refused to go to the door to tell the drunk to leave. He was trying to play it cool. But Charo saw the vein on his head pulsing. Go take care of it or I will, he warned her mother, in that way men tend to hide their shame with anger.

Now it's the same vein pulsing on his head, the same wide-eyed expression.

"You're taking me for more pesos than I'm worth."

"Dollars, hermano. I only speak in dollars," Leo says. She can tell he's only half joking.

"Eight thousand fucking dollars? Not even 'cause I cleaned your ass when you were a baby?"

"You should see what other people are paying to sell off their kids."

Charo looks to her mother for some clarity, but her mother averts her eyes.

"Not in front of la niña, please," her mother says. Charo hates that phrase, *la niña*. It makes her feel infantile. She wants to tell her mother that a few hours ago, she was hiding under stairs, getting fingered by a boy she barely likes. Maybe that crude image would show her mother that Charo's not a little girl anymore.

"What does that mean, sell off your kid?"

"No one is selling anything," her father says. "Your uncle just has a funny sense of humor."

"So what are you giving him money for?" Charo asks, ignoring her mother's warning glare. It's the same stupid face she makes when she wants Charo to shut up. But she's tired of waiting for someone to explain. She looks to her father, who looks at her mother, who bites her lip and looks down at the table. Next to her, Tío Leo fixes the straw hat on his head. Now that his forehead isn't covered, she can see the resemblance. If her father were a decade younger, had more hair, were less tired. This is what he'd look like.

"Your parents propositioned that I adopt you. If I'm your legal guardian, I can petition for you to come live abroad with me. It's one of the ways people are getting to New York."

"You mean, like, leave right now?"

"No, no, nothing like that," her uncle says. He puts his hands up to deflect the urgency in Charo's voice. "Nothing would change right now. You keep living here, normal. It takes a few years for it all to happen. For now we gather the few photos we have together when you were a baby. We snap a few more. Come up with a nice sob story. Fill out some forms. For now it's all just paperwork."

Her father scoffs at this.

"Me preocupa, of course," Leo says. "You're not really working, right, manito?"

"I have plenty of people who owe me. Don't you worry about the money," her father says. It sounds more like a threat than a promise.

"I'd like to go to New York," Charo blurts out. She looks to her father for a reaction.

"You don't know what you're talking about," her father says.

"It has to beat living here, with you two," she says too quickly. Her father frowns. Her uncle laughs. Immediately she feels sorry.

"You shouldn't speak if you have nothing good to say. Go to your room. Now," her mother says, doing her best to hide her anger in front of Tío Leo.

That night her mind is filled with New York. She's never been curious about that place. It's only ever come up when they talk about her uncle, who's lived there over a decade and has a thriving restaurant in Queens. She's seen commercials on the TV about new Dominican businesses in every borough, moving images of skyscrapers, photos of that green lady holding up a torch. But going there has never been an option. Now that it is, it's all she wants. Not because she knows anything about living there, except all the money and *opportunity* people go on about. But because it has to be better than here. Though she'd never say she hates her mother, she feels something expiring between them. Lately it's been nothing but fights. About how Charo has been altering her uniform to show more skin. About that one time Charo insinuated she might have a boyfriend. Her mother thinks she's helping, that the fights will mold Charo into her mother's image of what good girls do. But all of it only makes Charo want to push back more. This is a real chance, she thinks. Alongside a wave of excitement grows something like dread. What if her parents can't pay the amount?

For a long time they didn't struggle with money. Her school payments were always on time. She knows because she delivers the envelope of cash to the school administrators herself every month. They used to go out to eat pica pollo sometimes, just for fun. And she always got a nice dress for Día de Los Reyes. It was never as good as some of the girls in her school, whose parents take them to Puerto Rico for vacation. Or the boy she's talking to right now, whose family has a backup generator. Somehow it came up in conversation in the middle of their make-out session last week. Sometimes when the power goes out, he said to her, I wait an hour, maybe two. Then I serve myself a cup of orange juice with two fat pieces of ice in there. And as I'm drinking, I'm thinking, Yeah, nobody else on the block has ice. Everybody's sweating their asses off. She laughed. But it hurt. What she'd give to have ice when the power goes out for a whole day. No, she's never had it that good. But once, it was better. Then, around the time she turned twelve, her father hurt his knee at a construction job and had to stay home for a few weeks. Charo thought it would be temporary. And anyway, having her dad around redirected some of her mother's attention away from her. But a few weeks turned into six months. The knee problem revealed a severe back problem, which turned into a shaky leg problem, which turned into an insomnia problem, and on and on.

A year into her father's unemployment, they had to get serious. Charo was tired of getting disappointed looks from the school administrators every time she delivered an incomplete tuition payment. And though her mother always played the dutiful wife, people at church started talking. That's where her mother drew the line. Her father said again and again that he'd be back on his feet in no time. But eventually her mother got a part-time job at a flower shop. Charo got a part-time job at a clothing store. It all barely adds up to what they need. But they make it work. She tries not to resent her parents every time she puts her earnings on the table for them. She calculates the conversion now, in the only currency that matters: ten American dollars. That's what she gives her parents every week. If her mother weren't doing all the math, Charo might be tempted to pocket a peso for herself. But the only time she treated herself with her own money, her mother almost kicked her out. That was another big argument, another splintering between them.

It'll work itself out, she thinks to herself about New York. It's only paperwork.

Outside her room, she hears her parents send her uncle off. Their muffled whispers as they speak through the headache he's left behind. The creak of their old bed as her father lies on his bad back.

Then the house is quiet, lonely to her as it's ever been.

It's part-time, minimum wage. Inconsistent hours, two dollars less an hour than what he was making at the garden. But it's a job, Sal thinks as he scrapes another ball of ice cream onto a sugar cone.

He got the job through Vance. A friend of a friend worked here, years ago, and said they were looking for extra hands in the summer season. After he was fired from the garden, Sal fell into a deep slump. He stopped calling his friends. Stopped going to the kitchen, where his roommate sat around with a hundred questions. When Charo called and asked if he needed anything, he said, Tired, just tired, like he was fulfilling a promise by keeping to these daily rituals. Bed. Bathroom. Kitchen. Bed. Bathroom. Kitchen. It began to scare him, how good he was at tending to his melancholy. And there was Kiko. Who still needed to be picked up from school when their mom was working, who still needed an engaged response when they watched anime together. It took him two weeks to gather the energy to care enough to call the number Vance had given him.

In another life, Sal would love working at an ice cream shop. He doesn't have a strong sweet tooth. He prefers his chocolate dark, his coffee bitter. But the ambiance always seemed exciting. Clean white walls, radio on a loop playing American pop hits, the cold air a refuge from the summer heat. Maybe the television brainwashed him. Onscreen, there's always an ice cream parlor in a small town where people gather to have epiphanies.

It should be a joy to work here. But the customers are picky. The intoxicating smell of milk and sugar gets tired after the fifth hour of scrubbing stains off the counter. And his co-workers are miserable. Like Goth Derek, who complained on Sal's first day about having to take his piercings off at the job. We're not trading stocks, he said, what kind of white-collar shit is this? He complained about the cold, the paper hats, the petulant customers. Sal realized quickly there is no end to his grievances. Derek is a vacuum of negativity.

Now, as another customer walks in, Sal fixes his paper hat, tries best as he can to smile.

At the end of his first week, the owner, Lena, stops by the shop to talk to him. She tells Hamburger Derek to go home early, says that she'll help Sal close down. Hamburger Derek's face goes salmon pink, like he's done something wrong. He's the opposite of Goth Derek. Hamburger Derek rarely talks, and when he does it's always polite muttering between his teeth. He hesitates, but Lena ushers him along. He throws his apron in the back and leaves the store, though his bovine smell lingers.

Sal's heard rumors that Lena is almost sixty, but he'd never guess she's any older than forty-five. With her drag queen makeup. Extravagant boob job. Blonde extensions that make her hair look full and healthy. Lena is the shop's second owner, after George Bryant, who brought his shop to the East Coast after his success in San Francisco. Rumor goes he wanted to bring his family's ice cream recipes to as many gay people as possible. New York seemed like the obvious next step, but shortly after opening the shop he found out he had contracted the virus. He barely fucked anyone, according to some versions of the story. Instead, he lived a celibate life and poured his vitality into his business. No one knew how or when it happened, if it was a one-night stand or a steady lover, only that it got bad quickly. At the end of his life, he isolated himself in his studio. Only Lena saw much of him those last few weeks in the fall of '95.

Missed the cocktail by just a few months, Goth Derek said when he was telling Sal the story.

George's dream withered with his illness, but it didn't die with him. Lena bought the business—his last wish, she told everyone who would listen. No one knew much about her except that she was a European immigrant with ambiguous wealth, and that she loved gay people, a real fag hag who spent most of her weekends on Christopher Street. She changed the ice cream parlor's name to "George's" and promised to only hire young gay people looking for honest work. Kids running from home, the brokenhearted, the disenfranchised. Some in the gay community say George damned every faggot in the city those last few months, spoiled in self-hatred by all the virus took from him. But Lena clung to who he was before life ruined him.

In the photo by the shop entrance, George is handsome. Square jaw, thick glasses, full brown hair. *He lived for his community*, the plaque under his photo reads. *Every fulfilled sweet tooth is his legacy.*

When they're done cleaning, Lena serves them each a scoop of black cherry vanilla. The fat under her arms flaps like wings, and her hands tremble. Sal's never seen anyone so bad at scooping up ice cream. His stomach turns at the thought of eating black cherry vanilla after smelling it all day, but Lena is his boss, what option does he have? They lock the door and sit on the bench out front.

"I like your look," Sal says.

"Little Edie stole her look from me, don't let anyone tell you otherwise," she says, adjusting her blue silk headscarf. "But tell me about you. How are you liking it?"

He gives her the rundown of his first week. The nice customers, the nice space, the nice work environment. Everything, nice.

"Oh c'mon, don't give me that bullshit. Tell me, really. I know it's no heaven."

Lena waits for him to run through a list of complaints, like Goth Derek might. But he can't come up with anything that feels safe enough to share.

"The people who work here. Everyone just seems sad," Sal says. "Seems hard to make friends here, is all."

"Everyone thinks the gays all love each other," she says, like she knows all the gays. "But that's not always true. The people who come here come to work. They come to work and make their money, and when the season slows down and it gets cold, they leave. That's what it's all about, getting people on their feet. That's what my George would have wanted, for sure, for sure."

Sal wants to believe the ice cream shop is a gay haven. But his cramped wrist. Goth Derek's attitude. The overzealous customers. It's all bullshit, Sal thinks. Just Lena's way of grieving for her friend. Because that's what people do with the dead, turn them into symbols to serve the living. The world is cruel. Sal wishes more people would accept that.

He dumps the unfinished cone in a nearby garbage can.

"Anyway, you don't have to love them to see they're just like you," Lena says as she licks at her spoon. "You're all trying to figure it out, right? All my gay children in this crazy city, just trying to figure it out."

The next day, Sal meets Vance in front of Aunt Meena's building. He walks around the block exactly seven times before Vance pulls over in a cab, but he doesn't mind the wait. It's a cool summer morning, a nice relief from the August heat.

In the elevator, Sal looks in Vance's face for any sign that will reveal how he feels after another of his aunt's stays at the hospital, but he's so focused he doesn't even remember to introduce Sal to Aunt Meena. Vance pushes Aunt Meena's wheelchair out of the elevator, Sal follows quietly behind.

The inside of Aunt Meena's apartment is filled with dying plants. Under a hanging vine by the window, a bed of dried-up leaves. Vance explains that he's been coming over once a week to water them, but he doesn't have the touch, not like she does. They sit on the beige couch in front of the television. A few minutes later, Aunt Meena turns and looks at Sal as if he's just walked into the room.

"You must be my baby's special friend." She cups his face in her palms and presses his cheeks. Her hands smell like clean linen. Her eyes are hazy, but her voice is strong.

The screen lulls them into silence. A pigeon lands on the windowsill. Vance drinks two coffees to stay awake. That's how the morning goes, time passing through them nice and slow. Eventually, Vance walks Aunt Meena to her bed. When he returns, he lies down on the couch and rests his head on Sal's thigh.

"Hey," Sal says. He massages the back of Vance's head and notices a long, thin scab stretching down to his neck. He must have shaved his head in a hurry this week.

"I fucked up," Vance says. "I should have come twice a week to water the plants."

"You're doing your best."

"She's getting worse." Vance closes his eyes. "The home attendant is going to stay with her half the week. But I'm gonna have to stay the other half. It's that or hospice, and I know she wants to be home."

Sal tries to find something useful to say, but nothing comes. He holds Vance close and turns his attention to the screen, but he can't focus on the flashing images either. Another pigeon lands on the windowsill.

"You said she loves the movies, right? Let's take her to one."

"All she does is sleep these days, with all the drugs they're stuffing her with."

"I know, but we can take it easy, move at her speed. Dress her up and make her feel special, like the old days," Sal says, as if he lived the old days with them.

Vance sits a phone book on his lap and calls a few local theaters. The first theater manager hangs up before he's done explaining Sal's idea. The second waits until he's done before explaining that it'll cost them to rent out a whole theater for three people.

"I'll pay in advance, you don't have to worry about money."

Some of Vance's vitality returns to him after that call. He jumps on his feet and smacks the window, sending the pigeons flapping.

"I would have never thought of that," Vance says by way of thanks.

Sal nods to play it cool, but inside he's gushing with excitement. He likes to be useful.

Vance gives Sal a tour of the many photos decorating Aunt Meena's living room. Birthdays, graduations, portraits of Aunt Meena wearing a series of stylish hats. He gets so nostalgic he climbs a chair to find hidden on top of the living room bureau a thick, dusty album. Each photo has a note written on the back, ribbons of black ink transcribing each moment. Who took the photo, what year, what happened right before, and what resumed after they were frozen in time by the camera's flash. The oldest photo they find is of a small girl standing in front of a towering white house, holding a bucket with one hand, scratching her head with the other. The note on the back only says *Florida, 1947*.

"She used to clean houses when she was a kid," Vance explains. After school Aunt Meena and her siblings would ride the bus out to the white neighborhoods and clean their homes. They'd earn two dollars every week. Half of that would go to the bus fare and making their lunches for the long days, the other half they would give to their father. Nothing about the photo's wide frame and flat lighting suggests care for what it captures. It was probably taken by a white homeowner playing with a camera, using Aunt Meena more as a prop than subject.

"She looks beautiful in this one," Sal says. He pulls from the stack a photo of two young women. They look almost identical. The same shade of brown skin, same long legs. Even their outfits match. A younger version of Aunt Meena dons a blue bowl hat, a loose blue blouse to match. Over the blouse, a leather jacket paired with a black leather skirt and flat black shoes. The young woman next to her wears the same outfit, except her hat and blouse are maroon. The note on the back reads:

> Look how pretty we were. Nobody could tell us a thing, not on our block. Remember Chewy chasing you up and down, talkin bout he gonna marry you? That dog. You was always more popular than me. I mean, we was equally pretty, but you had that fire, you know? Boys don't like quiet girls like me. I mean, they say they do, but they always chase the ones that put up a fight. I do hope one day you'll come back to New York, visit an old friend. Remember that one time we ditched the boys at the old theater? We told them we were going to the bathroom, ended up drinking their flask of whiskey in the back alley. You always knew how to make them want more. I fell for them like a fool. Especially Raymond. He was my one and only. I wish you had stayed long enough to meet him. I was shocked when that doctor swept you off your feet, took you all the way out there. A Harlem girl in California. Imagine that. My Cleo.
>
> Harlem, summer 1966

Vance tells Sal she didn't meet Raymond until the 1970s, so she must have written the note later. What sudden longing brought her to write a letter that she would never send? Sal imagines Aunt Meena hunched over the photo at the end of a long workday. Jazz in the background, glass of wine by her side, or something stronger, like whiskey. She's a whiskey lady, I can hear it in her voice, Sal thinks to himself.

Next, they find a photo of two lovers. They're leaning over a window ablaze in sunlight, backs turned to the camera. The man they guess is Raymond has one arm around Aunt Meena as they bend toward the window. She pokes her head out, but whatever he's pointing at is burned out by the sunlight.

"We don't have to talk about it. But I'm curious."

"You can ask, whatever it is."

"Was Cleo your mom?"

"Oh, no. My birth mom's name was Elba. Or is. I barely remember her. Even when she was around, I stayed with Aunt Meena most of the time. It wasn't a man, or drugs, I don't think. Maybe she was restless? I don't know. When I was seven she left for Florida. Who knows where she ended up."

"You say it like it doesn't hurt," Sal says.

"It hurts less than it used to. That's what matters."

When she wakes up, they bring the two photos to Aunt Meena. Sal and Vance sit by her side on the bed.

"Oh," she says as she stretches over to the nightstand for her glasses. He's only just met her, but it scares Sal to see her so frail, so loopy from the drugs. He thinks maybe they shouldn't agitate her with the past. But she clings to the photos.

"I don't even know where to start with these two."

"How did you and Cleo meet?" Vance asks.

"Ray broke my heart, you know. Left the city and never wrote. Never called. I didn't hear a single word. They say the heart heals with time. But with no words, how?" she says. She puts down the photo of her lover and holds up the photo of her friend. And then it's like they've left the room, like it's just Aunt Meena alone with her memories. "Look at those hats. That jazzy outfit. We were young birds. Good girls, most of the time. Oh, my Cleo. Why Elba would leave her baby like that, I'll never understand. Twenty-five years and I still don't get it. I must have pushed him out through her, I think. He's my baby now. I'm gonna raise him, make him a good man, I will. When Ray comes back, we gonna raise him together. Only thing I told my Vance about loving men is that they hurt you. If you gonna love men, you got to be ready to fight for them. I never did, never fought for him to stay. Is that why Cleo leaving? She don't wanna end up alone, like me? That's why she choosing the doctor. A fancy house on the West Coast. I told her she should go, but she like my sister, better than my sister. God forgive me, but I did. I loved her better than I ever loved Elba. My best friend, my best girl. I'm gonna miss her all the time."

TURNS OUT HIS NAME IS JUAN, LIKE THE DIVA HE IMPERSONATES, though today he wears an electric-blue cape that makes him look more like an astrologer than a singer. No es ironia, es destino, he says in his best Walter Mercado voice.

Charo, Ella, and Carolina make themselves small in a corner as Juan directs the restaurant's transition to the evening shift. The workers cover the tables in black cloth, light candles, change the music from fast merengue to smooth bolero. They run around like ants before a storm. Even as they mumble under their breath. Even as the bravest among them show their disdain on their tired faces. There's no one to complain to about Juan's tyranny. For this two-hour gap, the restaurant owners forfeit their authority to Juan's keen eye for style and beauty.

"We can't have these tables so close to the reserved party," he says to a manager. "Coño, use your brain a little. And those curtains? Where are the velour curtains I ordered last month?"

A jittery waiter who must be new drops a tray of plates. Juan floats across the room, takes a gulp of air like a dragon readying to set everything ablaze. But Carolina laughs at the shattered plates, deflating the moment's tension.

"I like her," Juan says, and motions for the waiter to pick up his mess.

When the fray finally slows, Ella hops on stage. Juan closes his eyes during the first song, opens them for the second. When she starts the third, he claps his hands together. The restaurant's pianist stops before her voice does.

"I need to hear you sing," Juan says as he puts out his cigarette on a tray.

"I'm singing." Ella moves her braids out of her face. She looks nervous, for once.

"No, you're performing. And you're good at it. But you're not singing. This, this is boring," he says, mimicking the way Ella moves her arms on stage.

"What do you suggest, then?" she asks.

"You have a nice voice, and the cabaret bit is cute, but if you can't command the stage from in here, then it don't mean nothing," he says, and palms his chest.

Ella tries again, but Juan claps again to stop her. Charo can't see what he sees. She's usually mesmerized by her friend's voice. Did I fuck up by bringing Ella? she wonders, not questioning her friend's talent but her own judgment about Juan. He's sharp, she knew that much before coming here, but he seemed generous when they met in the bathroom.

"What now?" Ella says. She looks as if she's ready to throw the microphone across the room.

"If you think you're doing the Queen of Jazz any favors up there . . . I mean, really."

Ella walks offstage to face Juan. For a second, Charo thinks she'll have to jump between them, but Ella gestures for a cigarette, pockets her lighter from her bag, and walks out.

"I didn't know he was gonna be such an asshole," Charo says when she catches up to her outside. Ella stands under the shade of a lamppost. The sun burns everywhere else.

"I'm not used to someone telling me I'm not good. Not to my face, at least."

"Ella, I'm sorry."

"Maybe he's right," she says. "I told you, girl, I do this singing thing to have fun, make a few extra bucks when I can, but this . . ." she says, and points toward the restaurant.

"Well, you can't give up just 'cause it's hard," Charo says, too harshly by the wounded look on Ella's face.

"Girl, fuck you. I'm not Sal; stop trying to make me your little project."

Carolina climbs down from Charo's arms. She walks over to the front of the restaurant, pulls from a decorative plant two green leaves. Charo's attention is divided. But Ella looks at her, waiting for a response.

"What is it about your life that you're trying to fulfill through mine?"

"What are you talking about?"

"You wanted to be a singer? Too bored at home? What is it?"

"Wow, okay," Charo says. Ella knows about her troubles with Robert, her fears about the baby, even about the dizzying stress that's been making it hard to breathe sometimes. Ella's words sting. She wants to return the poison, but Carolina palms a crushed leaf to her mouth. Charo rushes over with a napkin.

"I'm just gonna go," she says when her daughter starts to whimper.

"Stop being dramatic."

"You don't get to hurt people 'cause you're scared, Ella. That's your shit, not mine."

"Okay, all right, you win. I'm scared. You got your confession. Happy?" She spits out the cigarette and crushes it under her heel. "People want to fuck me or kill me, there's little in between for women like me." ·

"Well, I'm not people. And I'm not society or whatever, out to get you. I'm your friend," Charo says. But by the look on her face, Ella's not satisfied. What else can she say? Charo wants to scream. People keep asking her to have words for things she can't explain. Robert, Sal, Ella, even her daughter. Last week, when Charo scolded her for jumping around the couch, Carolina responded with a straight-faced "Why?" She sounded so clear. The defiance in her big eyes was clearer. How could she explain to her daughter that she'd had a long shift at work that day? That afterward, she'd rushed to Fordham to contest an electric bill with a haughty service worker, and then ran home to make dinner for Robert before he got home? Or that she'd gotten into another argument with her father a few days before? When she called, he asked for a hundred bucks on top of what Charo already sends every month. I want to go to the río with my buddies to play a round of dominó, he explained, like a boy asking for an allowance. When she reminded him his knee was fine now, that he could find himself a part-time job, at least, he called her ungrateful, then passed the phone to her mother to make his case for him. Why did Charo feel the unreasonable urge to explain all of this to her daughter, who barely had any words? I'm the mother. I should have the answers. Get down, was all she said to Carolina, because she didn't know how else to express that she had limits, too.

"Maybe you're right," she says to Ella now. "Maybe it is that your life as a woman is different from mine. When I'm with you, it's like I get to leave my bubble for a little bit, like I get to be out in the world. If that means I'm using you, then . . ."

"Then," Ella says, and leaves it to the wind. She looks down the street in silence so long Charo fears that this is it, this messy ending to their friendship. Her honesty has won her nothing.

"We have a word for straight women who are obsessed with gay people," Ella says, and laughs. She picks up the baby and walks to the door. "You coming?"

Inside, the whole place has been transformed in just a few minutes. The windows have been covered, the lights are dimmed, the scent of chicken, herbs, and vegetables wafts in from the kitchen.

"Oh, she's back," Juan says. "You ready to follow instructions, or . . . ?"

"I think it'd be helpful if you explain what you mean, Juan," Charo says from her table.

He looks at Ella and puckers his lips, trying to decide if he'll go on giving her his time. There are a hundred other things at the restaurant demanding his attention. Like the host and cook arguing in the back. Or preparations for his own performance later that night. He groans and rises to his feet.

"Look, the first problem is that you're dated. I love the Queen of Jazz, but there's a dozen divas from this decade you can imitate. Why go old school?"

"That's my grandmother's doing. We didn't have anything fancy in the house but the piano and her dresses. She used to sit on her stool, and . . . look. I'm not here for therapy."

"No, no. Go on," he says, and for the first time he looks at her with something other than disdain. He takes the piano man's place at the keyboard and hums loudly to himself as he tries to recollect a song in his mind, then on the keys.

"Okay, well . . ." Ella says with some trepidation. She finds Charo's gaze and focuses her attention there, so that it feels like it's just the two of them alone together, like there's not a dozen other people scrambling about the restaurant. "With Grandma Nettie, it was easy. She was always talking about how our family was well-to-do way back when, but I never knew how serious to take her. Except she'd pull out these beautiful dresses, real fancy stuff. The first time I asked to dress up with her, she didn't berate me with questions. Or treat me like an abomination. She looked at me all quiet, like she'd been waiting for the question. I mean, it's not like she had words for it. No one had words, except maybe the cruelest words. But when she got on that piano to sing her tunes, when I sat by her side and sang along with her, I never felt like a boy with her. It was just me and my grandma in our own world."

"There it is. 'Little Girl Blue,'" Juan says, his nose to the keys. "You were a little girl trapped in a boy's body. Or you felt a boy until you found the girl within. Or you always knew you were a girl but the world did not. Whatever story you tell yourself about your life, use that to get there, to the feeling. Can you sing it?"

Ella closes her eyes. Charo can feel it from her seat, her friend searching for something behind her eyelids, a place within her where light doesn't touch. This time there's no twirl, no flirtatious swing of the hips. She opens her mouth, and from her throat escapes a song so sweet her lips tremble, her lashes flutter. She sings from an untouched place within her, if Charo had to guess. The little girl Ella was but could not name, all the years it took to find her, the struggle, even today, to keep her safe from the cruel world. She stretches the last word, fills the note with a sorrow so lonesome she drowns the room with all of her blue.

GOTH DEREK WALKS IN A HALF HOUR LATE TO HIS SHIFT, complaining about the long commute from East New York. He takes off his choker, his rings, his septum piercing, but keeps the metal bar on his left ear as a symbol of his rebellion.

"If Lena sees you taking off your piercings by the counter," Sal warns. But Derek shrugs and goes on complaining to their co-worker Katie, who doesn't talk much unless someone's asking her about how she got her hair so flaming pink. She gives Derek a blank nod to urge him on. The shit MTA. Violent police officers. Oblivious tourists. All reasonable complaints about their city. If it were anyone else, Sal might entertain the conversation by complaining about the D train, which is always late in the Bronx. *They don't give a fuck about us uptown,* he might say. But he knows Derek would find a way to make it about himself.

In the middle of Derek's rant, a customer returns to the counter with a sour look on his face.

"This isn't what I ordered. I wanted the peanut butter," he says through a mouthful of braces.

"C'mon, man, you know that's not what you ordered," Derek says.

"It's okay, I got you, buddy," Sal says, even though he clearly remembers the boy saying butter pecan, even though the boy has licked all the way through his first scoop, well into the second.

"He's just trying to get free shit."

"Fuck you. I said peanut butter. Peanut butter!"

Sal would rather have the boy blow up with ice cream than fight about it. He tries to hand the boy what he's requested, but Derek reaches for the cone in Sal's hand, and it slaps sticky on the floor. Katie squeals, a second too late. They all stare at it for a second, as if some truth were hidden in the pointy end of the waffle cone.

"Now you have to make me a new one!" the boy yells. Sal puts together a large cone, follows the boy's instructions as far as his whims will take him. Peanut butter and strawberry ice cream. Cookie crumbs and extra fudge, a mound of gummy bears to top it off. The boy chews loudly, the metal in his mouth slushing through the gummy texture.

"Thanks, assholes," he says as he walks out of the shop.

"Derek, what the fuck?" Sal says. Katie stares quietly. Derek shrugs and escapes to the back to change for his shift. Sal is both infuriated and relieved by Derek's presence. For once, he doesn't have to close the shop. It's his least-favorite part of the job. Sometimes Lena shows up during closing unannounced and watches over them to make sure they wipe every milk stain on the counter, sink, refrigerators.

He's out the door before Derek replaces him at the counter. The air outside is hot and stuffy. But he's grateful to be outside again. A block away, he almost steps on a large ice cream cone, half finished. He recognizes the exorbitant amount of gummy bears, though they've fattened in the summer heat.

"Asshole," Sal says out loud, thinking of the boy and Derek all at once. He walks the familiar route to get to the 4 train, passing the same shops, the same food trucks sitting idly on the street, selling coffee, bagels, bottles of ice-cold water. By the time he arrives at

Union Square, the last bits of orange sky are fading. People young and old line the edge of the park. They're separated into subgroups of cultural and aesthetic differences. The skaters to one side, the faggots to another. The drug addicts quiet and mumbling, the alcoholics loud and bickering. The groups rarely intermingle, except to exercise power over another when one feels that their territory has been encroached upon. The rest of the time, they're peaceful, isolated to their own corners of the park.

Sal walks along the perimeter. He's not afraid of the groups; it's the lone wanderers he keeps an eye out for, those looking to pick a pocket to make ends meet or fund their addiction. He walks along the lampposts, where everything is visible, and notices the stark difference between the people in the trees and those outside. Inside the park live the lost or forgotten or those hoping to forget the pain they come from. Outside, out on the sidewalks lined with stores and restaurants, people rush by with bags of clothes, surplus groceries, and souvenirs. Sal wonders what separates them, if it's money, opportunity, or if all of it is random, if it's an amalgamation of accidents and choices that make up a life. He wonders, too, where he stands. He has a job, and though he hates it, he makes just enough to pay for his room and the subway. Maybe this is where most New Yorkers live, somewhere in the gray, on the brink of ruin but not quite there, grasping on to civility best as they can.

He's lucky enough, he recognizes, yet he can't help but see himself in the man a few feet away, carrying his life in a shopping cart. Lost, wandering, hoping to find some semblance of belonging. What if he were to leave his life, become one of the park people? Anchor himself to an addiction, a bad habit, or his own destructive pack. Would he be stupid for making that choice? Would it be a choice, when so much of his life propels him to want to escape it by any means necessary? A thought enters his mind suddenly and forms fully before he can suppress it. Is that how Yadiel felt, trapped by the whims of whatever life meant to do with him? All those nights out fucking whatever man paid his sum, was that his friend's way of escaping? Or was it his way of carving out his own slice of meaning?

He goes down University Place to 13th Street, 12th, 11th, until he loses track of the blocks and avenues. He notices the neon eye at the end of a desolate street, almost hidden behind a large white truck. He wouldn't have seen it in the day, but now that the sun is set, the neon eye pulses in the dark. Pink oval, blue lashes, a green circle inside the pink to mark the iris. If he were a photographer with a film camera and a taste for the esoteric, this is the kind of image he would capture. But that's another life that is not his.

Two young women walk out, chuckling like they're hiding a secret. They notice him staring.

"You should go in, if it's calling you. She in the back," one says. She has a vague Caribbean accent. Her friend next to her doesn't speak, but she grabs Sal's hand and walks him to the door. He wishes the stranger would hold his hand longer. But she lets go, they smile at him like they're in on the same joke, then they head down the street.

He lingers by the neon eye. Doubt scratches at the back of his mind. What am I doing? he wonders. But the warmth of the woman's hand. He wants to find whatever made those women so bubbly.

Inside, a jukebox illuminated in neon light plays trip-hop. A woman's entrancing voice sings above a steady beat. The rest of the space is filled with voices talking just above a whisper. It's as if everyone here has a secret they don't want the next person to hear. In the back, two red velvet curtains separate the establishment from whatever lies beyond it. Sal sits at the bar, looks toward the back in case anyone comes in or out, but the curtains are still, heavy as doors.

"Here, this will help." The bartender drops a shot of whiskey in front of Sal. He has olive-green eyes, brown locs tied up away from his face, a soft pink mouth. Sal has the sudden urge to kiss him, but he puts his lips to the glass instead.

Beyond the red curtains is a long hallway. At the end, a door ajar. A blade of yellow light escapes the room and cuts the hallway in half. He's more curious than afraid. Wants more to be cradled by the warmth at the end of the hallway than to run away. Two voices whisper from the room. He can't make out what they're saying. He follows them anyway.

The first thing he notices when he opens the door is that the room is lit only by candles. A woman sits by a computer, typing on a keyboard. She appears to be middle-aged, but she wears black leather head to toe. A white scarf holds her fro up from her face. She looks too old for her clothes, or her clothes too edgy for someone who's graying. Next to her stands a lanky bald man. He wears a long purple silk robe tied around the waist.

"Ooh, we got a cute one!" The man waves his hand to usher Sal inside. His robe dances like it's caught on a breeze. The room pulses with the candles' flames. Like a heart, Sal thinks. A drop of sweat rolls down his forehead. The room is burning, but he's the only one who seems to mind.

"Where you from?" she says. It takes a second for his mind to wrap around her meaning. He doesn't respond in time. She stops typing. The man sitting next to her laughs into his sleeve.

"Name is West. Haiti, by way of Montreal. Lionel, my assistant, he's from Mississippi, by way of Ohio. You?"

"Santo Domingo. That's where I was born," he says.

"Now that everyone's place has been established . . ." Lionel says. He rises from his seat, regal as the wind, and leaves from where Sal came. From her seat, West hands Sal a box of matches. He bends over the candles that Lionel snuffed on his way out the door. The first match he breaks in half. The second he swipes so many times he dulls the head. The third match he swipes once with force. Fire crackles in his fingertips. The rusty smell of phosphorus rises to his nose. He bends over each candle slowly, as if he's bringing a dead thing back to life.

Sal turns to meet her approval, but West is focused on her computer screen again. She asks for his birthday, his time of birth, first name, last. He feels like he's at a hospital visit about to undergo invasive surgery. A tiny voice in the back of his mind calls for him to take caution. Why should he give her so much personal information? He answers anyway, though he doesn't know his time of birth or why he might even need to know such a thing. Sal tries to see what's on the computer behind the woman's halo of hair.

"So you're a psychic?"

"That's not what I would call myself," she says, but doesn't turn to face him.

"That's cryptic."

Her fingers tap quickly on the keyboard. Scroll. Click. Scroll. Then, finally, "Ah," she says, like she's sorry. "Scorpio north node."

"So you do astrology? Is that it?" He's disappointed. He loves learning about the moon, planets, and stars precisely because they have nothing to do with people. Plasma radiating from the sun. Dust on Earth's moon. Acid rain on Venus. Storms as big as planets on Jupiter. But from what he's gathered, astrology is all about delivering fortune-cookie musings about people's futures, about personal identity. Why should he make the stars about himself? The whole thing is ridiculous.

He feels grounded in his truth, but when West rolls her chair back a few inches, he can't help but look. On the black screen, a green circle is crossed by a web of lines. Next to each line is a symbol, some of which he recognizes.

"Mars," he says.

"So you know something about the placements."

"I know about astronomy. Science."

"And this isn't science, of course," West says, and smiles.

He can't tell if she's making fun of him. He crosses his arms.

"It's not complete because I don't have the time of birth, but the north node is revealing."

"I don't know what that means."

"That's the problem, isn't it? That particular relationship with uncertainty. You want everything practical and crystal clear."

She turns to look at him. For the first time, he notices the wrinkles around her lips, the lines on her forehead. But her button nose, her long lashes. She looks old and young at once.

West bends over to rummage through a drawer under her desk.

"A people so attuned to nature, to the ways of the village. Now separated over every city in the Western Hemisphere."

She sucks her teeth, closes the first drawer, and opens a second.

"Look at what they've made of us, what we've accepted."

He can't tell if she's angry at her own words or because she can't find what she's looking for. Finally, out from the second drawer she pulls a resealable plastic bag filled with cherry lollipops.

"You hate cities?" Sal tries.

"Especially this one."

"What are you doing in New York, then?"

"What *am* I doing here?" She pops a lollipop in her mouth. Her eyes are dark, probing, like she's waiting for Sal to tell his half of a joke.

"I guess I just feel lost," he says.

"What are you running from?"

"I'm trying to move forward."

"Without looking back?"

"I'm just trying to find a job I don't hate."

She waits.

"It hasn't been this bad in a while, the memories. They jump out at me. Maybe in your astrology there's something—" As soon as he says it, he regrets it. How many just like him must come to West, wanting the future laid out before them, seeking easy solutions to complex problems? He's always judged people who go to psychics and astrologers. But this need rising up inside him overwhelms every defense created to protect himself against magical thinking. Here he is, same as others, pleading for certainty. She must sense his desperation, because she rises from her seat and comes around the table. She's taller than Sal expected, as regal as her assistant, but still homely, like she could be somebody's edgy aunt sitting in the living room complaining about the weather. She crosses her arms, holds her lollipop like a cigarette.

"For some people it's astrology, church, drugs. It's fine if god is dead and all of that. But we all need something between us and the world. For our people, it's always been each other."

"Our people," Sal says, like he's savoring new words.

"Who are your people? That's the thing to ask yourself." She brings the lollipop to her mouth and ushers him over to her desk. This close, he smells an aura of shea butter and earthy sage around her.

"I don't know what that means."

"Then it's time you started looking at your wounds, Salvador."

"Aren't you supposed to read me my future?" he asks, growing frustrated at her riddles. He feels like a kid who's been shown a glimpse of a magic show. He wants to know the rest of it, if she'll finally give him something that will offer some relief.

"Oh, I don't know. I'm no oracle," she says, and winks. "Candy for the road?"

Last night it snowed, today is quiet. From her window, Charo watches the empty streets. It's her third winter in New York, but it still surprises her how quickly the world fills with snow overnight. What was once a row of cars is now just mounds of white. What was just yesterday a bustling sidewalk is now just wind and ice. She's lucky to be off work today, as she is every Sunday. She's luckier she doesn't have to go all the way out to Queens. Sometimes her uncle gets sentimental and wants her to deliver the monthly check in person. Especially since his son got locked up upstate for running one of the most successful cocaine spots in Queens. Tío Leo must be lonely. This morning he called and said, No way I'm making you come out in all this snow, but he paused, like he was waiting for Charo to volunteer anyway. She complained about the useless trains and hung up quickly.

Her toes touch the cold wall. Her room is small, but it's nice enough. She likes it more than she's liked any other place since she moved to the city. The first few months, in the winter of '94, she bounced from apartment to apartment, all through The Bronx. The first spot was on Fordham with some friends of her father's. The family was zealously religious but generous enough, until it got in the woman's head that Charo was trying to seduce her husband.

Charo was always working, rarely accepted their invitation to join them for dinner. And she never left the bathroom in her towel, to avoid these kinds of accusations. But none of her attempts to make herself small as a mouse worked. They were kind when they kicked her out, though Charo could see the glint in the woman's eye, how good she felt about winning the war she'd created in her mind.

The second place was further down The Concourse on Tremont. The room came with a minifridge, and her new roommates were never home, on account of their work. But after a two-month battle with a roach infestation, she gave up and started looking elsewhere. Her uncle offered to bring her to Queens, to stay with him until she could figure it out. But the thought of owing her uncle another dollar made her sick. She got off on the excuse that her supermarket job in The Bronx was too far from Queens. And to assuage his need to be useful, she took him up on a connection with a buddy of his and rented a room on Brook Avenue and 138th Street. This third place should've been the worst. Even her mother warned her about the neighborhood, all the way from Santo Domingo. The dark sidewalks. The abandoned building across the street inhabited by a band of lawless boys. The apartment on the second floor that Charo heard was a heroin spot. But her new roommate worked at night and slept during the day. The boys who crowded the sidewalk were always polite, even when they hit on her. And whatever business was happening in apartment 2F didn't impact her, as long as she minded her business.

One day, as she walked upstairs after another elevator failure, Charo passed the boss outside 2F. His name was Malibu, or so he said. He had a four-leaf clover tattoo on his left temple, big brown eyes, a stupid laugh. Charo had seen tougher tigueres back home. He didn't scare her. I haven't bought my Cali ticket, but maybe I'll bring you with me, he said the second time they ran into each other. The third time, she found him smoking a joint in the hallway, contemplating whatever trouble the drug trade was causing for him. Charo heard a roomful of chatter inside 2F. She wanted to ask him what was happening in there, just to see if he'd tell the truth. But he must have seen the question in her eyes, because he sucked his teeth and frowned at her like she'd ruined the innocent game of flirty neighbors they'd been playing for weeks. A part of her felt stupid. What did she want Malibu to say that she didn't already know? And what if he did invite her inside, and she got wrapped up in the kind of mess her parents had been warning her about all her life? But another part of her liked the thrill. She wanted to know who she really was. What better way to see the stuff you're made of than to put yourself in the face of danger? Her heart fluttered the next time she saw him there in the hallway. Curiosity was driving her mad. She opened her mouth to ask about his business, but he stopped her and spoke first. What are you doing tomorrow night? he asked. The clover on his temple pulsed as he chewed gum. Finally, she thought, the guy has the cojones to ask me out. But before she could play coy, pretend she was busy with work or made-up errands, Malibu went on. I got a big deal coming through tomorrow. I'm feeling lucky, he said. But just in case, I don't want you around tomorrow night. His face was serious and brooding. Charo wanted to send him to hell. She wasn't his woman, what right did he have to tell her where to be? But the next day, she stayed with Sal. At that point Charo had been in New York almost a year, but Sal had arrived just a few weeks before. That night she talked his ear off about Malibu. How a drug business was a business all the same. And what if he did go out west? What if she went with him?

When she arrived home from work the next day, the building lobby was littered with a dozen cops. They questioned her on the way in. She said she'd never met a man with a four-leaf clover tattoo. And I better start acting like it, she said to her deflated heart. She knew she'd never see Malibu again.

That was two years ago. The building she lives in now is calmer. Made more so today by the snowstorm. For hours she's in and out of sleep, lulled by the world's silence. A pang of hunger finally pulls her awake. She skipped dinner last night. She only has two eggs and three potatoes in her minifridge, just enough for a meal. She can't afford to buy groceries again this weekend, so that'll have to do for the rest of the day. When was the last time I ate? she wonders again as she slips on her boots, pulls her yellow beanie over her head.

Outside, her block is quieter than she's ever heard it. It's like snow swallows all the sound. She makes a mental note to ask Sal about it later. He'll know the science of it.

A whistling wind ushers her on as she takes big steps through the snow. It's all the way up to her knees. She shudders at how quickly she feels it in her bones. It's so warm inside. She wants to run back in. But you play with snow, that's the thing to do. She sees it on TV, she sees it on the block. With a gloved hand, she writes her name real big. Then she circles her name and draws lines to denote a sun. She doesn't long for Santo Domingo, where it's always hot. She's never been one of those immigrants who prays to return home one day soon, like her co-workers at the supermarket. New York's no Eden. But it's not her mother's house, that's all that counts.

She hears a scraping sound down the street and follows that. A man in a black coat shovels snow from a bodega front. He spreads rock salt as he goes. When she moved in a couple of months ago, it was another bodeguero running the place in the mornings. They called him Gago because of his stutter, but she didn't know him, she hadn't earned the right to call him that. She opted for Mr. Rivera to be respectful, though he couldn't have been more than five years older than her.

The flirting started with free coffee. Every time she stopped for her dollar cup on her way to work, he told her it was free if she smiled for him. He seemed too boyish to her, with his lazy eye and thin goatee. But a dollar is a dollar. Of course she smiled for him. She grew to like Mr. Rivera's faltering attempts at flirting. And soon the free coffee turned into free cartons of eggs, milk, cans of red beans, even free bread, the whole wheat kind she never bought because it was an extra one fifty. She touched his arm across the counter, laughed at his jokes, talked to him real nice. And every now and then, she actually gave in to the distant thought of fucking him. She hadn't had sex the whole time she'd been in New York. Maybe being horny is making me stupid, she thought. But a few weeks ago, when she stopped by for her morning coffee, Mr. Rivera was gone. In his place was the evening bodeguero, who explained the change of schedule. Mr. Rivera got jumped. Not a targeted attack, as far as anyone knew. The guy don't have no enemies, the evening bodeguero explained. Just bad luck. He's stuck in a hospital bed. I heard he can't even shit without help.

Charo walks past the bodega, down The Concourse to 170th. This is where she sometimes drops off her checks to her uncle. Now, she packs snow on top of the blue mailbox, hoping to make it disappear. She feels like a kid, but she likes having a project, something to distract her from her hunger.

From the dust of a passing snowplow, a young man emerges riding a bike. He's smiling. Charo can't tell if it's stupid or brave to bike on the snow-covered street. Maybe it's both. What she would give to be that reckless. The young man turns down 170th. Charo follows behind him. In the distance, she sees him hop off his bike and disappear inside.

The smell of oil, vegetables, fried food; it disorients her. Half a block away, she can smell it. She never had Chinese food her whole life until she got to New York. Her uncle took her to her first buffet. His way of welcoming her to the country. His way of dropping the truth bomb. She should have known. But she was too excited by the thought of leaving her life. The endless fights with her mother. The responsibility of helping to sustain her parents. But there was her uncle, chowing down on fried rice, delivering the truth her parents had withheld from her for years. He said he was so lucky to help his family. So blessed to offer Charo the possibility of starting a better life. But her parents hadn't paid off what they owed him. Not even half of it. Five thousand dollars was her debt. There's no rush, he said in response to the horror he must have seen distorting her face. Your parents missed a lot of monthly payments. But you're young. And smart. You'll get to it with time.

It's surprised her, how good she is at restraint. She buys just the right amount of food to last her the week. Fifty dollars weekly to her parents for their expenses. The same eighty-dollar payment to her uncle every month. In just two years, she's almost done paying half the debt. She follows a strict calendar to help her keep track. At this rate, she'll be done paying her uncle in 1999. Three years is around the corner, she tells herself. It helps to stick to a budget. Though that doesn't stop life from happening. Like six months ago, when her father asked her for money for the knee surgery that might finally get him back on his feet long enough to hold a job. For five months, Charo sent her parents double the usual. To get by, she had to curb the few luxuries she afforded herself. No occasional blouse on sale. No monthly visits to the salon. She stopped taking the train and instead walked the twenty-five blocks to her supermarket job. She even sacrificed ordering Chinese food on Sundays. Those five months of extreme restraint she barely talked to her father on the phone. Even the thought of his voice made her fume with anger.

Now she knows she shouldn't go in, she can't afford it this week. But the thought of her debt. And her parents' betrayal. Though they say it's for her. She can't shake the thought that her uncle put a price on her future, that it's now her responsibility to pay for this dream that only serves her parents.

"Fuck it," she whispers.

As soon as she pushes the restaurant door open, the snow's spell is broken. Clanking pots. A ringing phone. People yelling in a language she doesn't know. To the side, the boy that was riding the bike outside, preparing for his next round of deliveries. Charo drops her hat on one of two tables in the restaurant. The woman behind the bulletproof glass looks at Charo like she's crazy for coming out.

"Four chicken wings, pork fried rice?" the woman says.

Charo nods to say, yes, please, the regular. Her mouth waters.

She's sorry when she's outside in the cold again. But her stomach is full, and it lifts her spirit about the snow. Above her, new flakes begin to fall. She pulls her yellow beanie to her forehead and walks down to Jerome Avenue. The passing 4 train sends clumps to the street below. Charo doesn't bother dodging them.

She hears laughter; that's what draws her from under the train tracks and toward the jungle gym at Mullaly Park. They're circling each other, three short hooded figures and a taller one doing the chasing. She likes the echo of their laughter. It helps her feel less alone. To pretend she's enjoying it as much as them, she pokes holes in a perfect mound of snow atop a bench.

The kid with the baby-blue coat breaks from the circle and runs toward Charo. A snowplow zooms by and swallows whatever the girl says as she approaches. She extends a clump of snow, but Charo shakes her head, smiles like she's sorry. She's no fan of kids, even less so of confident ones who approach strangers. "Leave that lady alone," the father says from a few yards away. But he's too busy chasing after his other girls. The man is handsome, from what she can see of his nose and beard. What lucky lady struck gold with that one, she thinks. The thought reminds her of Mr. Rivera with his charming stutter. And Malibu with his dreams of travel. These men who were almost hers. And what if they had been? Would she be popping babies out for them? Would they be at a park together like this?

The girl in front of her falls to the ground. Immediately Charo's heart flutters. It reminds her she has a heart, beneath all these layers of clothes. But the kid is laughing. "Look," she says, "like this." Her arms go up and down, her legs open and close. The girl's face is all mouth, since her beanie covers her eyes. Charo can't help it, she laughs too. And though she rolls her eyes every time she sees people make snow angels in movies, though they don't even look like angels to her, she lies on her back to face the silver sky. So stupid, she thinks, but she laughs and laughs.

When she rises from the snow, the girl is gone. She's back with her family, and they're leaving the park. Baby-blue coat on her father's shoulders. The two other girls circling as they go.

She's alone in the park. The snow falls harder.

Charo looks down at the angel she's made. In an hour it'll be gone. Her name circled in the sun will be gone too.

The evening of Ella's performance, Charo schedules to drop her daughter off at the sitter's apartment.

It was hard to find a good sitter when Charo first went back to work. She was suspicious of every person she and Robert came across. Young women who were confident but didn't know what they were doing. Viejas who had way too many kids to meet the needs of a ten-month-old. When she called back home to complain, her mother offered her lifelong friend as an option. Eunice was confident, old-school Dominican, had years of experience running a day care center from her big apartment, and even had assistants to divide up the work. In the end the choice came down to Eunice or staying home to care for her daughter full-time. The thought of being a stay-at-home mom had made Charo claustrophobic. One fear overcame another. She acquiesced to her mother's suggestion and entrusted her daughter to Eunice.

When she arrives with Carolina now, the apartment is littered with the last few kids of the day. Parents working a second shift or whose trains are running late. Eunice invites her in for coffee. Charo tells her she has to go, but the older woman insists, more so than usual.

"Lily, take the kids to the playroom, I'm gonna sit for a cafecito," she says to her assistant.

Eunice returns to the living room with two cups of coffee a minute later. Almost like it was planned, Charo thinks, and braces herself for a metiche's interrogation.

"Where are you going tonight?"

"Just going out to dinner," Charo says, looking down at the cheap ring she got on sale last week.

"Oh, Robert is going with you. That's good," she says. She looks up from her coffee, expecting Charo to accept or deny what she's just said. Her graying hair is tied back in a ponytail, but for her age, Eunice is strong. She has to be, to care for half a dozen rowdy toddlers every day. Nothing like her own mother, who grounds her personality in slow mannerisms, a soft voice, gratitude for god at the end of each sentence. Eunice is loud, almost too charismatic to be likable. Charo looks at her now and wonders how she and her mother have stayed friends for so long. Eunice has been in New York for three decades, an entire lifetime away from her youth on the island. They must still be using their childhood together to sustain their conversations now. Charo doubts her mother would approve of Eunice's brash personality in person, the same way she disapproved of Charo her entire adolescence for being anything other than the mold of teenage purity.

"You know, si hay otro hombre, you can tell me. I wouldn't tell Robert," Eunice says.

"Oh my god, doña. Why would you think that?" Charo says, exaggerating her surprise to show she means it.

"Men do it all the time! It's okay, it's okay." She pats Charo on the leg, then keeps her hand there, waiting for a confession. Eunice speaks to her mother on the phone more than Charo does. Even if she were cheating on Robert, Eunice is the last person Charo would tell.

"I'm happy with my man," Charo promises.

Carolina comes running into the living room babbling for Eunice's attention. Something hilarious has happened in the playroom, by the sound of the other kids laughing. Charo waits to see if her daughter will want her attention too. But Carolina doesn't even look her way. Just tugs at her babysitter's hand to get her off the couch. Charo turns her gaze to pretend she doesn't see the gesture. She's surprised by how quickly her daughter's need has shifted elsewhere. Just an hour ago, the whole world was centered around mami and daughter time. But now? Charo has the sudden urge to take Carolina home and forget the night ahead.

Instead, she lands a kiss on the baby's head and sneaks out before her nosy babysitter can say another word.

The dressing room is about the size of a closet. A bar for hanging clothes. Lightbulbs surrounding a stained mirror. The smell of perfume mixed with dust.

Charo helps Ella get ready. She doesn't say so, but Charo knows her friend is nervous. She's been practicing all week to prove herself mighty in the face of Juan's criticism. Though she says she doesn't care, Ella respects him. He has real fans who come out to see him a few times a week. Despite the exquisite Dominican food, the elaborate decorations, the fine-dining experience seldom afforded to their people in this country, Juan is the main attraction. And now he's extended his space to her, given her one of his nights, just this once, to prove she can move a crowd enough to keep the gig.

"Jimmy is here. He likes you, you know."

"Is water wet? Here, help me get these earrings on."

They're gold earrings, paired with her lilac spaghetti-strap dress.

"Don't do it," Charo says, right next to Ella's ear. She's never this close. It makes her nervous. Outside of the occasional hug, Ella hates being touched. She smells like lotion and hibiscus. Softer than Charo expected. "Not now, anyway. This gig could be amazing. You don't want a man to distract you."

"Funny that to you a man is a crutch. That's all I want sometimes. Someone to want me enough to show up for shit like this, to love me in public."

Outside the dressing room, they hear Juan arguing with the manager about the lights.

"Robert is doing better. He drives me crazy, but he's trying. We're trying."

She unties Ella's braids and they fall down her back.

"Okay, done," Charo says. "Just remember. No turns, no dancing. Just stand there and sing. Like one of the divas. Keep it light on the jazz. A ballad, maybe?"

"Damn, I didn't know I hired a manager," Ella says. She finds herself in the mirror. "Don't worry. I'm gonna show that motherfucker."

At the front, their friends crowd around a table. It's the first time they're all together since their trip to the beach.

"The Giants, man, they're special," Amy says to Mauricio across the table. She tells them about going to baseball games with her dad. Even though they couldn't really afford tickets and Candlestick Park wasn't close by. He always found a way to secure nosebleed seats. Amy never asked how he got them. She only hated that she had to be there. The only Vietnamese father-daughter duo in a crowd of pale faces. Every time she complained, he tapped on the hood of her Giants hat, told her to focus her eye on the pitcher. That's where the game really happens, he always said. She was sixteen when he died. It happened suddenly; no one saw the lung illness coming. But Amy continued the tradition in her living room. She poured a beer for herself, a beer for her father, always wore his black-and-orange hat, always tapped on the brim when her favorite pitcher was up.

"Still rooting for the Giants, the East Coast isn't gonna change me."

"All respect to your pops, but c'mon, Amy. The Yankees, that's the winning ticket. Look at the track record," Mauricio yells above the crowd.

Next to them, Luis chats quietly with Jimmy the bartender. When he first arrived, Charo introduced Jimmy to the gang as Ella's co-worker, and though she tried to hide it, her tone oozed with something hidden and unspoken. Now he grips a bouquet of flowers under the table and listens to Luis lecture about restaurant decorations.

"I would have chosen different tablecloths, but that's just me," Luis says to a nodding Jimmy. Sal, not wanting anything to do with tablecloths, listens to Vance talk about his workday.

On the other side of the room, Juan sits by a fan club of tías. They pour wine in his glass and shower him with compliments. His scarf, his eye makeup, his sleek hair. When he speaks, they listen. When he laughs, they laugh. They are satellites orbiting their star. They only quiet when Ella finally comes on stage.

She starts off with a ballad, just as Charo instructed. People want to enjoy you and still be present with their dinner, that's what Juan said. So that's how she starts, nice and easy. Then she transitions to a Spanish song to draw the mostly Dominican crowd. Her accent is meticulous. She practiced it with Charo on the phone. The audience claps lightly at the end of each song. They're not enthusiastic, but they seem to like her well enough. That's a start. If she can keep this up . . . Charo thinks. But in the middle of her set, Ella switches over to a jazz song. A classic even Spanish speakers can hum along to without knowing all of the English words. At first she thinks it'll be just one number, but as the set picks up, so does Ella's energy. She dances around the pianist, drags the microphone with her to the edge of the stage. Juan will be furious, Charo thinks as she shrinks in her seat. Even if the audience seems enthused. Even if they're clapping and laughing and singing along with Ella.

When the set is over, Mauricio hollers from his seat. Amy yells even louder.

"That was for my grandma," Ella says, breathless. "My grandma, she gave me my voice. Everything I do, I do for that lady."

The women crowding Juan rise up to cheer, this time for grand-mothers.

Charo jumps out of her seat. If she can get to Juan first. Soften him up a little bit. Maybe there's still a chance. But Juan gets to Ella first.

"They loved you," he says. He doesn't smile, doesn't forfeit an ounce of warmth. "But I don't like people disobeying me on my stage. Better luck somewhere else."

Maybe it's the hurt or the drink in her hand that's made her braver. But Ella doesn't move out of Juan's way when he tries to pass her.

"As long as you admit it," Ella says.

"What?"

"That I'm fantastic."

That finally does it, that makes Juan laugh.

"You've got cojones, kid. I'll give you that," he says, and leaves them for his circle of tías.

"You're crazy," Charo says as they walk back over to their friends.

"I do what I want."

Jimmy waits till the crowd around her thins to hand Ella a bou-quet of flowers.

Mauricio and Amy shriek.

"Y'all are doing too much. Let's go!" Charo says, and drags her friends away.

Ella clutches the violets to her chest. She leans into Jimmy like she's starting to believe those love songs she sings on stage.

*　　*　　*

At first Charo doesn't see Robert waiting in front of their building. She stumbles out of the car giggling, one shaky leg at a time. Luis comes around to help her out, but he's drunk and wobbly too. This makes her laugh more. But her voice catches in her throat when she registers it's Robert there, instead of the usual men loitering on the block.

"The baby broke a glass at Eunice's. She cut her hand open," he says through his teeth. Eunice called and called until Robert finally got home from work. She told him she thought he and Charo were out together. That's what Charo told her, that they were going out to dinner. Robert ran to the emergency room and waited an hour for the doctor to finally stitch up Carolina's knuckle. Now she's upstairs, sleeping off the medication. Charo focuses her drunken gaze on his mouth as he explains this. The more he talks, the clearer the world around her becomes.

"Is she okay?"

"No thanks to you."

"I should see her," she says. She unravels her arms from Luis, nods for him to go back to the car.

"Look what happened to your daughter while you were running around drunk with a gang of maricones."

Luis flinches next to her.

"Not now, Robert. Please," she says. She tries to sound calm, but her hands are sweaty.

"Where's Maricón Number One? He in there?" Robert says, not at her but at the shadows in the car. His voice is even, like he's running through a grocery list instead of a barrage of insults. The words are meant for Sal, but Sal went with Vance to check on Aunt Meena. It's Sal who invites Charo out at night, Robert likely thinks, whom Charo spends hours worrying about, to the detriment of their family, their home, everything they've built.

"Yo, what the fuck?" Mauricio was just as drunk as the rest of them a few minutes ago. Now he stands firmly next to Luis.

"Baby, no." Luis steps in front of Mauricio, puts his hand to his chest. Robert is taller than Mauricio, but Mauricio is bigger. He works hard for those arms. Luis says he shows his arms off to attract other men. Mauricio says his arms are his weapon. He's never wanted to be the kind of guy boy that gets pushed around by other men.

Mauricio leans forward, hot as a revolver. If it weren't for Luis in front of him, and Charo by Robert's side . . . But he's too drunk to think straight, she can see it in his face.

The muggy summer air thins around her. A familiar wave of nausea crawls from the pit of her stomach and closes around her throat. If she doesn't do something soon, the night will end in violence; she can sense it by the way Robert readies himself next to her. Robert will hurt Mauricio, Mauricio will hurt Robert. She doesn't know which thought scares her more. And Carolina. I have to get upstairs, she thinks.

Mauricio pushes Luis out of the way. He burns the distance between them so quickly Charo jumps in the middle out of instinct. Her hand goes flying at Mauricio's face. A drop of blood falls from his cheek. She's wearing a ring. She forgot.

Ella finally runs out of the driver's seat and together with Luis manages to pull Mauricio away.

"What the fuck is wrong with you?" Luis yells.

"Go home," Charo says, as harshly as she can.

Mauricio looks back at her one last time before he jumps in the car. He's looking for an apology in her eyes, something that will cushion the blow, but she can't be sorry, not yet.

Just before she slips inside, Charo looks back, hoping that her friends are waiting for her to get inside, as they usually do. But the car is gone. All she has left is to follow Robert upstairs to face this mess she's made.

ONSCREEN, ENDLESS NEWS ABOUT HURRICANE SEASON. THEY bring on meteorologists to talk about how weather patterns work. But that doesn't assuage the listeners, who call in to ask why this hurricane season is particularly bad. Is this a sign of looming catastrophe on Earth? Will the world really make it to the next millennium? The scientists offer rational responses, but the anchors keep the conversation where scientific fact and conspiracy theory meet. It's the only way to keep the news sensational, to keep the ratings high.

One scientist stands out from the crowd. She explains her story every time she shows up on television. The years she spent being the only Black girl in her advanced science courses. How she dropped out of her PhD program because she couldn't find a lab that made proper space for her. How instead, she found her passion in the field of science communication, building a career out of breaking down complex weather phenomena into op-eds, magazine articles, even a children's book.

"I want to be an example for other Black girls out there who are curious about the mysteries of the natural world," she says, looking straight at the camera.

It's Kimberly who explains that while conspiracy theories don't help us prepare properly, people's overall concern about the rain and flooding is valid. She says this is a real opportunity to educate the public about global warming.

Sal watches her on television now. She can't be more than a few years older than him, maybe in her early thirties. She stands out from the old, all-white panel. With her hot-pink blazer, her long braids. Why does she keep talking about herself every time she's on TV? It's not about you, it's about the science, Sal thinks. But really, if he were honest with himself, what he feels is closer to envy. What if it were him on television, explaining science to the masses? He's no meteorologist. He doesn't have a fancy degree. But he might do the job with ease, same as her. What separates them? Opportunity? The fact that she was born here, and he on the island? *We're just a slave-ship stop away from each other.* That's how Vance talks about it. Is that what explains why she's on television and he's here, sitting on a couch waiting for his leftovers to heat up?

The microwave beeps.

"She's so annoying. You don't think she's annoying?" Sal yells from the kitchen.

He comes back and lays out their leftovers on the coffee table. The smell of moro and pollo guisado fills Vance's living room.

"It's not every day you see a Black woman scientist talking her shit on TV, you know."

"But she's making herself as big as the storms," Sal says.

"What's wrong with that? Maybe she needs to be that big to be taken seriously."

"Whatever."

"You kind of have tunnel vision sometimes. You think immigrants have it the worst because so many of y'all have to start over when you get here. That's valid. But niggas here got it hard too. If y'all have to restart when you get here, feels like we gotta restart every day, just to stay alive. Imagine being a Black woman scientist. That's a lot of restarting."

"All right, damn, get off your soapbox," Sal says. He spoons rice into his mouth to keep himself from saying more. He wants it to be simple, like it was for a long time, this story he's told himself about his struggling immigrant life. What's worse than leaving your life, your world, to begin again in a place that wants your working hands but not your culture, language, history? Than living in this new place feeling torn in half, of two places but somehow from neither at once? Being an immigrant in this country is hard enough. But being a gay immigrant, he never gave that much thought until he got fired from the garden. Now all the stories are confused in his head. It's not enough to consider himself an immigrant. Sal also has to think about the specificity of being Dominican and how his story is different from that of Mexicans and Central Americans. Of being moreno and how that affects his relationship to Vance and other Black Americans. Of coming from an island. Of loving men the way he does. The stories get denser, more complicated. Nothing makes sense like it was promised to him by his mother, who's always repeated the same simple story over and over again: all you have to do is work hard and you'll find your place.

On television, more congratulations to Kimberly, more invitations to come back as hurricane season intensifies. Vance flicks through the channels as he eats.

"That was probably insensitive," Sal says sometime later.

"It's fine. Just try to be more open. We can't compare people's lives like that. Especially Black people. We all get fucked over. Just differently."

"You're right," Sal says. "I am. Sorry."

They lose themselves in a movie. An alien worm species invades Earth. No one knows how they got there, only that they're hungry for human flesh and that they cause tremors wherever they go.

"I think I'm just jealous."

"I know."

"I could do it too."

"I know."

Sal picks up the plates.

"Let me help you."

"I got it," he says, and takes the last plate of chicken bones from Vance's hand.

"You're going to drop them. Let me help you."

"I think I can carry a few plates on my own," Sal says sharply.

He goes off to the kitchen before he can do any more harm.

A few days later, on the morning of Aunt Meena's movie date, Sal jumps out of bed. He feels good. For having thought of the idea. For showing up for his boyfriend in this time of need. He likes showing up. Like that time his grandmother got all four wisdom teeth removed and he had to nurse her for three days. He was only ten, but he liked getting ice and handling her medicine and making soup, though it was barely seasoned water that he fed her; he knew nothing about cooking. Or that time Renata called him from her fancy hotel job. La Kali was outside the hotel drunk, asking the staff for Renata, crying about some man who broke her heart. I can't have shows at work, come handle it, Renata said. Sal felt special that she'd called him of all people to help put out that fire. But the thought of Renata balloons in his mind and spills over everywhere. What if the movie date jeopardizes Aunt Meena's health? Or worse, what if it goes really well, and Vance begins to expect these kinds of gestures all the time? Can I do it? Can I be somebody who shows up every time Vance needs me? He feels his limbs go heavy and has to sit back in bed. Get up, he thinks. Get up. Just as his forehead starts to burn, he makes a beeline for the phone in the kitchen.

"Wait, babe, hold on." On the other side of the phone, Sal hears

Mauricio and Ella, arguing over which brooch works best with Aunt Meena's blouse. Vance tells them to hurry. The movie's in an hour. He still has to pick up Sal, then make their way to the theater downtown. "Okay, what's up?"

"I can't go out today."

"What? Why?"

"I just can't."

"I'm gonna need more words than that, Sal. I mean, this was your idea."

"You go and have fun. I'll call you later to hear how it went," he says, feigning as much excitement as he can. But he doesn't have more words, and the fever's getting worse. He hangs up and passes the hours in bed, under his sheets. The whole time he imagines Aunt Meena's tired face when she walks into the theater, when she sees Eartha Kitt blown up on a giant screen. Vance by her side, holding her hand. And the empty seat next to him where Sal should be. The way he and his grandmother sat on the veranda. Rocking on their chairs and telling stories late into the night. That's the feeling he transplants into the scene of Vance and Aunt Meena in his mind. But Sal hasn't called his grandmother in months. Another thing he regrets.

On the phone, later that night:

"I'm hurt. I mean, I get it, if you were sick, but . . ."

"I'm not sick. I just started freaking out."

"About the movies?"

"About us. And not us. I mean, it's been moving really fast, the last few months. I just got scared."

"Don't do that. Don't distance yourself from me."

"I'm not."

"'Cause that hurts more. If you're gonna be here, then be here. Is this where you want to be?"

"Yes, duh." Sal laughs like he does when it's just him and Charo.

That's what they do when it gets too soft between them: they laugh. But he knows Vance needs assurance, not a biting joke. A part of Sal is repulsed by Vance's need. This sincerity. It scares him. But he tries. "I'm here. I am."

"Then talk to me."

"I will, I will."

"What if I pick you up tonight, we go to a bar."

"I didn't mean now!"

"I gotta put Aunt Meena to sleep. Wait an hour for the home attendant. Then I'm free. I'd like to pick you up tonight. May I?"

Maybe because he's tired of letting his mind get the best of him. Because he doesn't want to lose Vance like he lost the opportunity to work at the museum. Because Yadiel would say something cruel but true, like, "No seas tonto, Salvador."

"Okay," Sal says, trying his best to keep his breath steady, to stay present in his body. "Come pick me up. Let's talk."

"Hey!" It's Don Julio, knocking on his bedroom door. "Vance just rang the intercom. I think he's waiting downstairs."

Sal jumps out of bed. What night is it? He rubs his eyes to orient himself.

"You good, man? Sounded like you were suffocating," his roommate says.

"Bad dream, I think. I can't remember."

At the bar later that night, Vance tells him about the movie date. Mauricio ended up tagging along, chatting up Aunt Meena the whole ride to the theater. After the movie, they drove around the heart of Manhattan, and Aunt Meena had a story for every block: beauty stores she'd worked for, diners she'd taken Vance to as a kid, other theaters she'd snuck into. She talked all the way back uptown and as Vance put her to bed.

Now, someone drops a glass across the bar. Sal and Vance

chuckle and slump back in their seats. A cocktail of exhaustion and beer has made them loopy. Vance tells Sal about his first crush, how he bullied the boy because he didn't know how else to express his feelings. Sal tells Vance about Yadiel for the first time. Their baseball games as kids, the nights out with Renata, Yadiel's old collection of poetry, which he never added to, he just went to the same books over and over the way people go to scripture for guidance. He recounts the end of Yadiel's life as truthfully as he can tell it. The envelope, and the overwhelming fear that made him leave Santo Domingo. When he's done, it feels like he's been talking for hours. Vance holds his thigh under the bar.

"Otra porfa," Sal says hoarsely, and raises his empty bottle toward the bartender. Underneath the loose black uniform and the cap keeping her hair up, she's probably beautiful. Sal watches her as she leans over to grab the Presidentes from the fridge. In another life, the bartender is a flight attendant. She wears good jewelry and a tailored uniform to work. She feels fancy and useful and is surrounded by beauty every day: glorious sunsets, exotic meals, radiant lovers in every city. But in this life, she pops the bottles open, wipes beer foam from her stained shirt.

"Mira, mi amor," she says, and manages a tired smile.

Sal downs half his beer in one go. Everyone around them is probably straight, but Sal is made braver by the buzz. He squeezes Vance's hand.

"I really am sorry about today."

"I understand. Or am starting to. It's all starting to make sense."

"It doesn't have to make sense," Sal says as he finishes his beer.

"What do you mean?"

"It's like quantum mechanics. You get too close and none of it has any order, everything is random."

"You lost me."

"I'm just saying. We're obsessed with making sense of everything. But sometimes we just gotta let things go untouched by meaning to survive. Shit happens. Shit just happens sometimes."

"It's not that simple."

"What do you mean?" Now it's Sal who looks confused.

"We live in a fucked-up world that hates gay people. Your friend didn't die from serendipity. He died because of a fucked-up society, and he died by the hands of a fucked-up person. Somebody did that."

Sal ponders this in silence. He's the only person who knows all the lives Yadiel lived. When he was the lonely mean kid in the barrio. Their high school days filled with feverish anticipation for a better life. And when they were older and understood the possibility of what they could be, when Yadiel threw himself into Santo Domingo's party scene, living the best fantasy of his life. He did it so long that the night began to creep into the rest of his reality. He left his nails painted bright and colorful, congregated with the other girls in Parque Duarte during the day, risking the side eyes, the sharp ridicule, the inevitable confrontation with people who didn't want to see maricones out in public. And his love affair with the diplomat, weekends at a time when he lived as a woman. Like a moth trying to outlast the night, somewhere between reality and the dream in his mind, that's where Yadiel lived. Back then Sal thought it was reckless, to teeter so close to the edge of society. Shouldn't Yadiel want to be accepted and embraced, after all those years living at the fringe of their barrio? No amount of desire for self-expression would have pushed Sal to face the humiliation Yadiel faced at the end of his life. But time privileges clarity. Now Sal understands. Some people would rather be destroyed than be reduced.

"She," Sal says. "Sometimes, she. Sometimes, he. I don't think Yadiel ever arrived at one."

"Right," Vance says, nods. "She was destroyed by the world. I understand your argument about meaning. It's real intellectual, real smart. Shit makes total sense. But you can't hide behind ideas to turn from the hurt you're carrying. You been hurt bad. And you have a right to be mad at the world, at the diplomat, at the whole fucking system for hating gay people the way it does."

"I just wish I'd been braver," Sal admits. "I knew Yadiel was lonely. If I'd been at the park that night, maybe . . ."

"I get that. I understand guilt."

"What are you guilty about?"

"You sure you want to hear about my shit?"

Sal nods, because he's tired of talking about himself.

Vance wrinkles his nose. Drinks from his beer. Cracks the knuckles on his free hand.

"I was, what, eighteen, in eighty-five? That's when I started hanging out in gay bars. By then everyone knew the virus was spreading among us. Though, we didn't know how to talk about it. I didn't even know the difference between HIV and AIDS. Most of us were just running on fear. Hiding from the world, or running straight toward death. I was one of the latter. I thought, If I'm gonna die for being gay, then I'm gonna have fun doing it. I had a lot of sex with strangers. Thought I was above it all, invincible, better than all the other faggots running around crying about death and illness. That only lasted until my first scare. Pablo Negron. That was his name. He was a decade older. Took me out on dates. Bought me flowers on Fridays just because. Real Hollywood shit. We were only together six months. But the whole time we used condoms. Just in case, he said. Just in case. He told me he wanted to take me out to California, where the sun sets over the ocean, just like his hometown in Puerto Rico. He was always talking about Puerto Rico. I was naked in his bed when he told me. Playing with one of the ties he wore to his job at a local Spanish newspaper. I pretended I didn't care that he cheated on me, that he put my life at risk. I told him if I was going to die anyway, that it was better to do it with him. But when I was waiting in that hospital room for my results . . . When I thought, Shit, this could really be it. I'm only starting my life. And what about Aunt Meena? Suddenly it clicked. I took the negative test result as a blessing. Even if it wasn't certain. Even though I'd have to come back again in a couple of months. I never saw Pablo again. I stopped hanging out in gay spaces. Took me years to go back to a bar. By then I'd heard he'd died alone in a hospital room. That was common then. But still."

Sal draws a picture of Pablo Negron in his head. Not because he's jealous, though maybe he should be, hearing about his boyfriend's first love. But because he's curious. He imagines a mustache, dark eyes, the hair on his stomach, the girth of his penis. Hot-pink lilies by their bed. Spanish newspapers stacked on a small dining table. A collection of blue and tan ties in his closet. An unmade bed. An infinite six months making love under those sheets. But that's where his imagination ends. Because he can't imagine what it's like to love someone amid that kind of desperation.

"I'm sorry," Sal says, though that feels inadequate.

"I was a coward. I could have said goodbye, at least. So, yeah, there's guilt. I spent the next decade trying to make up for it, letting that shame fuel me. Any time I thought I was too tired for a protest, a sit-in, a march in defense of gay rights, I imagined Pablo alone like I left him. I blamed myself for a long time. But eventually I realized I should've been blaming the government that created those circumstances, that let all those people die."

"I hear you. But doesn't blaming the man sound too easy?"

"You have to go on somehow," Vance says.

Sal bites his lip. He's frustrated, though he should feel relieved. Here's Vance giving him an out. Telling him where to place the blame. Offering a ready remedy. And he's right. If he applies it to his own history, it's clear as day. What American tourists do to people on the island. What people on the island do to maricones. What maricones do to each other. But it feels too easy, to blame these amorphous systems, to treat his life like a social study or a set of data points. What about personal choice, where does that begin? And if he moves past his guilt, how will he remember Yadiel? How will he do better by his brother, his friends? How will he be good?

"How do you want to go on?" Sal asks.

"Oh shit, I don't know." Vance laughs. He puts the beer to his lips, looks around the room like he's lost something. He's buying time. Trying to parse his own discomfort. But then he clears his throat and looks down at his beer.

"What Pablo promised me," Vance says finally. And for the first time in the months Sal's known him, his voice breaks, his eyes water. "I've given New York everything. I just want my sunset over the ocean."

THE FIRST FEW DAYS OF SEPTEMBER, THUNDERSTORMS. METEO-rologists try to map out the cloud patterns on their green screens, only to be proven wrong again and again about the timing, the density of the rain, where it will strike. They recommend that viewers watch the news every two hours to get an idea of what's to come. But eventually they succumb to describing the sky just as it stands above them. One meteorologist, in his morning forecast, tells viewers, Stick your head out the window, your guess is as good as mine.

Charo is off work the first two days of the storms. She makes batches of sancocho from what she can find in her pantry. When lightning strikes, Carolina opens her eyes wide and leans toward the window. When thunder roars, she claps along with it. Charo lived through enough hurricanes in Santo Domingo. Thunder that loud always meant trouble—the possibility of the tin ceiling flying loose from its nails, or for trees in their backyard to be ripped clean from the wet earth. This is no hurricane, Charo knows that. It's nothing like what devastates islands. But her shoulders tighten with every rupture in the sky. There's nothing beautiful about a storm, she thinks. We only call nature beautiful because otherwise it's devastating. Still, Charo has to move her daughter from the window again and again, and every time Carolina walks back, drawn by the sky's theater.

It's been a week, but Charo can't stop looking at the stitches on the baby's knuckle. Even when Carolina stops complaining about how itchy it is, even when she's back to jumping around on the couch. Every time she has to apply ointment to the wound, Charo is reminded of her failure.

On the third day of rain, she's relieved to go back to work.

The supermarket is empty; that's the first thing she notices when she takes her place behind the cash register. As soon as she arrives, the two other cashiers start chatting her up about the weather, their day, what popular sales the customers might ask about. This is the first sign that something's off. Charo is used to other women holding her in contempt. Girls in school, at work—even her own mother held her at a distance. For a long time, Charo thought it was religion that divided them. Her mother scolded her for all the ways Charo deviated from girlhood in the Bible, at church, under the sunlike eye of god. *She's disgusted by me.* Those were the best words Charo had for a long time. The thought spoiled her mind, made her bitter. But as she's grown older and arrived at her own opinions, her own walk, as she's matured away from home, she's realized that it wasn't about religion at all. Charo's mother spent a lifetime fixing her mannerisms, dodging old boyfriends in the barrio, building a good reputation for herself at church, only to be faced with her past again in the form of a daughter.

It's not me she's ashamed of, Charo thinks now as she fixes up her workstation.

"It's slow today," Amara says. She was the first cashier to be lowered in rank when Charo started working there. They're rarely put on the same shift together. Jose's way of avoiding drama.

Why don't you pack your shit up and go, Charo wants to say.

"I'm sure it'll pick up," she says instead.

An old man walks in, dragging his wet feet down the aisle. A few minutes later he walks to her station like a snail, carrying a single can of chicken soup, as if that alone will get him through the storm.

"Be safe out there," Charo says to the old man. He opens his umbrella inside and splashes them with water, then strolls out as slowly as he came. The place is quiet again, except for the swoosh of cars outside.

"You know, Charo, I didn't see your name on the schedule this morning." It's Melissa. She's the only Mexican cashier in an establishment of Dominicans. In her short time here, she's picked up so much Dominican lingo that she sounds like she just came from the island. Charo likes Melissa. She's always been kinder than the rest.

"What do you mean?"

On Melissa's face, Charo sees a strained smile. She's trying to keep up with Amara's poison, but she's terrible at it. There's a sticky stain on Charo's conveyor belt. She wets a paper towel and focuses on making her workstation spotless.

"I did wonder," Amara says to Melissa. "I was surprised to see her here today."

The women laugh.

Charo says she has to pee, but curiosity drives out her pride. She goes to the back, where the schedule is taped to the manager's door. Jose isn't in yet. Or he stepped out and hasn't returned, she's not sure. Charo traces the schedule with her finger twice before it starts to sink in.

Just then, Jose walks up behind her. In the moment before she turns to face him, she's sure it's a mistake. She'll point to her name missing in the whole week's schedule. He'll apologize. Then tonight she'll tell Robert how silly her manager is, how he's so obsessed with catching people stealing beef that he can't keep up with who works when. But that possibility evaporates as soon as she meets his eyes.

"The schedule," Charo says, as if it hasn't already been decided.

*   *   *

She waits for him on the couch. Glass of wine in hand. TV flashing blue-gray light. Outside, the rain persists, slapping against the window.

It's just after ten when he comes home. The floor creaks under his slow, heavy walk. She hears him enter the kitchen first. The fridge door opens, closes. He probably thinks she's asleep with Carolina in their bedroom. She's usually asleep when he comes home from a double shift or from a night out playing pool with his friends. She imagines the pleasure it might bring her to sneak up on him in the kitchen. To watch his mask change from its austere concentration to surprise, then back again to stone composure. But in her mind she doesn't wait for him to turn around. She rushes behind him, pierces just to the left of his spine, his lower back, where he is softest. With what, a kitchen knife? Like cutting a pig open. Tough flesh for a second, then wet with red surprise. It's not about hurting him, and it's not about revenge. What she wants is to shake him from his center, to make a wound between where the world ends and he begins, to make him vulnerable, open, tender.

"You're up," he says when he passes the living room. He goes to the bathroom to pee. When he returns she hasn't moved, save for her eyes, which follow him as he undresses.

"I got fired today."

"Right," he says, as if she just told him that it's raining outside.

"And my boss, your friend, couldn't explain to me why. I assume it's because it wasn't his decision," she says.

His eye contact doesn't break. He is unmoved.

"Why?" she asks.

"I want you to stay home. La niña, she needs you."

"You know I can just get another job. Somewhere you don't have your hand in."

"I was scared out of my mind when I saw her like that," he goes on, like she hasn't said a word. "So powerless. Like a little kid again, that's how I felt." The fear in his eyes is true, and for a second her rage subsides, and she feels guilty all over again.

He sits next to her on the couch, and immediately she smells the long day of work at the factory on him, sweat mixed with cologne. She poked fun at him for wearing cologne to work, once. It was during their early days together. He didn't laugh at her joke. Instead, he said, It's the details that add up to make an honest man. The weekly haircuts, the cologne, the ironed shirts. You think it's just 'cause I like to look good? It makes a difference, how you present yourself. When the gringos come down from their glass towers in Manhattan to walk through the factory, that's the kind of thing they notice. They're expecting us to look and smell like rats, 'cause we're poor. But that's not me, he said. She didn't know then how sensitive he could be about work. She didn't know yet that she had the capacity to hurt him.

"I was scared too," she says now, and drinks the last of her wine. She presses her lips to his, opens his mouth, breathes him in. She loves him stupid, even now.

"This will be good for us," he says, pressing the soft of his lips against her ear. Then he lifts her shirt and puts his tongue to her nipples. His touch ripples through her. She spits into her hand and strokes him till he's grunting in her ear.

"Condom," he says, and runs quietly to the bedroom to grab one. They always have sex with protection, even though she takes birth control. Just in case.

When he returns, she spreads her legs open, pulls her head back. He kisses her neck as he enters her. Slowly at first, but the better it feels, the faster he goes. They burn where their bodies meet. It makes him tender, dumb with wanting, the way she likes him best.

"You're mine, okay?" he moans as he fucks her.

"Okay," she says, her mouth an O. Okay.

*   *   *

The rain stops two days later. Sal lies in bed reading a short account of Apollo 11, though most of the book focuses on the great astronaut. His training, the journey out of Earth's atmosphere, his first slow steps on the moon. A world of dust and rock and silver light untouched by humanity, now marked by one man's footprint. One giant leap, he says, and the whole of human history, with its wars and technological advances and endless struggle for power, all of it is suddenly made small by the possibilities of space travel.

Within these short pages, Armstrong is more myth than man. But Sal wonders about Aldrin, the nineteen minutes it took for him to meet his commander on the silver rock, what he might have thought about being the second man to walk on the moon. Or Collins, watching from the moon's orbit. The book barely mentions the third man, necessary to the mission but overshadowed by the glory of the other two. A single footnote explains that Collins never walked on the moon. The training and preparation strained his relationship with his wife and family, and he didn't think it was worth it. Apollo 11 was his last space mission. Sal wonders how often people choose their loved ones over greatness.

So much of the space race was about that flag they left behind. Millions of dollars, decades' worth of labor, speech after speech about frontiers, only to leave on the moon a sheet of cloth to represent a country where a large portion of the population was still being treated as subhuman. Sal wonders how all that money could have been used to help people in need. What if instead of subsequent missions to the moon, the government funded a vaccine for HIV? Reparations? What would our future look like if we didn't destroy so much human potential? We'd be on fucking Pluto by now, he thinks, and sets the book down on his chest.

"Sal!" It's his roommate, calling from the kitchen.

The soft, sweet scent hits him as soon as he opens his door. Some kind of cake, he guesses, by the smell of vanilla in the air.

The kitchen looks like the lab of a madman. Bottles of oil, vanilla extract, and spices line the counter. A bowl with dense whipped cream by the window, a graduated cylinder on the floor, melting bars of butter on top of the hot stove. Don Julio treats baking like a science, at first. He measures the ingredients exactly, mixes everything together with technique and precision. But somewhere in the process he gets bored and starts making up his own rules. A recipe is an outline, he often says. Carrot cheesecake, macadamia nut cookies, red velvet brownies dense in flavor. He arrives at all of his baked goods by way of experimentation, and he never remembers to write down how he got there.

"Te llaman. Un loco," he says, and hands Sal the phone.

"Okay, but are you gonna share some of that cake?"

Don Julio looks insulted by the question, as if Sal has crossed some hidden line of trust between them. He frowns and the wrinkles around his eyes deepen.

"Fuck no. This one's no good, I can tell already," he says, turns to work on his whipped cream.

"Hello?"

"Where is she?"

"Who's this?" he asks, though he knows. He's surprised it took Robert this long to call.

"Stop playing with me. Where's Charo?"

"She's not here, if that's what you're asking."

"She's gone," he says, and pauses. Sal can hear him breathe. He's trying to collect himself.

"I'm sure she'll be home soon. She probably went out for a second," Sal lies. Charo called before she left.

"No, no! All her shit is gone. Like she never lived here. I know you know where she is. Sal, my daughter. Please."

"I'm sorry," Sal says, and he means it. For the first time since he's know him, Sal feels sorry for Robert. But he has nothing else to give him. He hangs up.

"Fine, fine, here," Don Julio says. He hands Sal a slice of strawberry cake on a ceramic plate. "This thing was driving me crazy. Too much butter, I think. Or the eggs. You think it was the eggs? I don't know. It's not perfect. It's not great. But you gotta let shit go in life. If there's one thing that I've learned. Fucking eggs, right? Cool, fine, breezy. I'll just make it better next time."

III.

WE KNEW HE WAS STRUGGLING AND COULD HAVE INTERVENED—but how? Most of us were new to the neighborhood, just like him. We arrived with our husbands and our kids in waves, running away from the aftermath of the dictatorship and the civil war with the gringos that followed it. Most of us wanted what we were promised—possibility. And a few of us got that in that first decade. A bodega, a restaurant, kids sent off to college. In the early 1970s people were still calling us Puerto Rican; no one knew what a Dominican was. The Jews in The Heights and Italians in The Bronx were surprised by how quickly we took over their buildings, sent our kids to their public schools, filled every corner with dominó games and merengue. For a little bit it seemed the dream was possible. But just as many as were succeeding were getting caught in the worst of the city—gang wars, drugs, straight-up laziness. And anyway, the riches and jobs promised to us just weren't there. Factories were shutting down; gringos were running from the city faster than the rise in crime. After a few years, some of us went off to Rhode Island and Ohio, places we'd never heard of because we thought the whole country was New York. But most of us stayed in the city.

Julio Estevez was quiet when he came. We barely noticed him. Story goes, those first two years in New York he really did stop drinking. Got himself a cab license and a good routine going. Those days cabdrivers were getting killed left and right; bulletproof partitions couldn't stop that. We wouldn't have recommended the job to somebody we loved. But Julio was quiet and severe. The air around him made it clear he was a real toro bravo, not some pushover who'd let himself get robbed. Chucho the bodeguero saw him every morning as he was opening the store, walking to his cab with a cup of coffee in one hand and a cigarette in the other. He had a nice apartment, too, courtesy of a gringo client who took a liking to him. He was living good, setting himself up for better, and though he kept to himself for the most part—no ass on the side, no friends, no family anyone knew about—he was nice enough that we didn't pay much attention. We only remember those early days because of what happened after.

The tigueres who lounged in front of the bodega were curious about him. His upper lip hidden in a thick mustache, his eyes under the shadow of a flat brown cap. Sometimes they'd try to chat him up, ask him to hang out. But he always had an excuse. Too cold or too tired or "mi hermano, hay que trabajar." They almost gave up on him, but then the weather changed. Summer made the streets hot and loud. On his way out of the bodega one Friday evening, Miguelito stopped and asked Julio if he wanted to join a game of dominó.

"Julio, stop being a stick in the mud," Miguelito begged, because that's the kind of tiguere he was. Persistent. With women; with his vicio; with his mother, Doña Sulema, whose apartment he refused to move out of.

"All right, coño, vamo entonce." It was probably naïve, but most of us couldn't believe he even cursed back then. We didn't believe Julio was capable of any wrong at all.

The game started out quiet. No one knew if Julio was good or not, but Miguelito was a champion, a real tigueron on the dominó table. He could guess what fichas were in everybody's hands a few minutes into every round. And he took risks, talked his shit when he was feeling confident, blocked the game early even when the other players seemed to have the upper hand. Now he watched Julio carefully to see if he could read his moves and flow well with him as a teammate. Julio kept his hat over his eyes, scratched at his beard when he was thinking. The other players were good too, veterans of the corner, well-known borrachos on the block who could really focus when the game got serious. By the last round half the block was on the corner watching, that's what it looked like. Kids hollered from their bikes. Even the doñas with their Bibles tucked under their arms stopped to look and chat. Miguelito was quiet, which meant he was taking the game seriously. Julio was quiet too.

Eventually Miguelito broke his silence with a chuckle.

"Good try, muchachos," was all Julio said as he gently placed the dominó ficha that decided the game. Miguelito jumped from his seat and embraced him.

"Pour him up, pour him up," Miguelito screamed. From the crowd came a shot glass of dark rum. Julio looked at it real long, too long, like he was thinking hard if it was worth it. But he drank, and the crowd cheered again.

We celebrated for the game. For a hot Friday night that re-minded us of home. But most of all we celebrated because Julio Estevez, finally, was one of us.

The first incident happened that same summer of 1970. Julio be-came a regular at the dominó table, just another tiguere playing on the corner, drinking too much too late into the night.

He was high off another win when Mileidy passed the corner. Mileidy was a snappy nineteen-year-old with a big ass, big hair, a real firecracker personality. Some of us pulled her aside and gave her advice about wearing looser clothes. We knew that men's piro-pos weren't innocent. In Santo Domingo, in New York. Tigueres lounging in the street only ever want one thing with women, and once they get it, they move on to the next piece of ass. But Mileidy, she wore whatever she wanted. She seemed to like the attention and the back-and-forth. And she wasn't no delicate flower for easy picking, either. She could really hold her own.

"Mire con los ojos, no con lo boca," Mileidy would say to a viejo calling after her.

On this night, she walked by the corner with a group of girls her age. Julio shouted at Mileidy, "Coño, que belleza." Later, people recounted that he used more vulgar words. Shameful, that he'd stoop so low. And who was Julio Estevez anyway, this newcomer turned tiguere, now flirting with our girls? No one agreed on what was said, but it must have been bad, because Mileidy stopped in her tracks, pushed her curly hair out of her face, and looked back real mean.

"Mas respeto, señor. We're not cattle, for you to talk to us like that."

Miguelito slapped Julio on the chest and laughed. The rest of the men chimed in like hyenas, mocking Julio. If it was his friends laughing at him that caused it, or the winning smile that spread across Mileidy's face, we don't know. Men are much more complicated than we give them credit for. But suddenly Julio marched right up to her, pinned the girl to the side of a brick building, and closed his hand around her neck. Mileidy stood real still. If a stranger walked by, he might have thought this was the middle of an intimate moment between lovers, the way her dress climbed up her thigh, the way he breathed into her face, sweat glazing their foreheads.

"Let me go," Mileidy said.

"Al paso, niña, que tu va rápido con esa boca," Julio said, and gripped her harder to the wall.

He might have killed her if it weren't for Doña Sulema, that's what everybody said. The tigueres weren't going to betray their brotherhood. And Mileidy's girls were too scared to move.

"Miguelito!" she called as she came down the street with a bat. Miguelito ran behind a taller man, hoping to go unseen. "The garbage, motherfucker. You can't even take out the fucking garbage?"

"Mami, relax, relax, coño," Miguelito said.

But Doña Sulema wasn't looking at her son anymore. She froze and stared at Julio, still pinning Mileidy to the wall.

"Se acabó la fiesta. Let her go," was all she said.

We didn't know yet what Julio had survived. Gunfights with gringos in the middle of the street. His dead daughter in a yellow dress. The years he wasted in Santo Domingo looking for refuge at the end of a bottle. But all of that paled in comparison to Doña Sulema right then and there. With her hair wrapped up, her loose-fitting pajamas, her hand bejeweled in gold rings, nails painted red, gripping a bat with surprising force for a woman her age. Julio looked at the woman with the bat and then at the woman he held to the wall.

"Go on, then," he said.

Mileidy spit on the floor in front of him, then joined her girls.

The rest of the week, Mileidy walked around the block with a bruised neck. She didn't hide it, as some of us might have, and she didn't avoid walking by the bodega. The girl had cojones, that much was clear.

Later, we heard that she made Doña Sulema a flan as a token of her gratitude.

"It tasted like shit, but it's the thought that counts," Doña Sulema said to one of her neighbors.

"These men. I didn't survive El Jefe to be taking shit from mamaguebos in New York," she said, speaking for herself, speaking for all of us. "That curse ain't following me here."

Things went from bad to worse for Julio. He was getting drunk almost every day. Missing work. Getting into trouble with his landlord for not paying rent on time. One day he got into a fight at the dominó table, and though Miguelito vouched for him, loyal pendejo that he was, he was banished from the bodega front, where the games continued without him.

For a few summers he roamed the neighborhood drunk and friendless, until he landed a new group at the barbershop. He was older than them, loud, smelly, out of touch. But Julio was also funny, harmless, and a real good storyteller. When the barbers finished their shifts, they turned up the music, brought out their beers, and sat around this local drunk to listen to his cuentos.

"You gotta understand, in 1965 we were angry, all of us. We voted for Bosch. I know some people had their political ideas, real fancy, real educated, but a lot of us were just scared to go back to the way things were under El Jefe. I'll admit it, I was scared. That's what made me pick up a gun. I was there, you know. At Puente Duarte. Lost a few of my friends in that battle. It was bloody, but that's when we knew shit was for real, that we actually stood a chance against the military. We were just regular people, most of us. Whole families going out to fight together, can you believe that shit? Maria tried to come out with me. But I told her, I'm the man of the house, I got enough fight for the three of us. I wonder what might have happened, if I'd let her join. It was normal, women getting involved. But I didn't. And then they came, the gringos. Was like the earth was shaking. Like one of those—what do you call it when the earth breaks? You don't know nothing about that here. War, real war. We were doing good before they came. We could've had our government. Something pa' la gente. What you know about fighting for a people? You kids are American now, you love your gringo dollar. I wouldn't have come if . . . if . . . What was I gonna do there without my baby, without Maria? You got no clue, man."

He wiped beer foam off his messy mustache.

"Man, it's been ten years since that war, nobody talks about that shit anymore," one of the barbers said. But they liked hearing him talk. For months they kept him around the shop, serving him dark rum when he asked for it, contesting his stories when they seemed too hard to believe, because how could war be that horrific, how could America be as bad as Julio Estevez described it?

A sheet of snow covered the city in February 1975. No one was going to stop at the shop during a blizzard, so they started their Friday celebration early. Just as they were arguing about what music to blast, Nena's son walked in.

We watched Carlito grow up too close to his mother's skirt. We warned her. Boys shouldn't be coddled by their mothers. And the aunts? They were crazy about those long lashes, that angelic white face. They let him hang around when they talked about women's business, when they got dolled up for family parties. By the time they tried to correct the behavior, to set him straight, the boy was turning into one of those locas you saw sinning in the street. He wore makeup to family gatherings, went out with friends so late he didn't make it back in time for church services. Nena tried to beat it out of him, slapped him up a couple of times in public to show she loved her son, that she was trying. But eventually she gave up and kicked him out.

Now he stood before the barbers like an apparition. It'd been months since we'd seen him around the block. Everyone was sure he was dead or gone.

"Yo, ain't you Nena's son?" one of the barbers said, his mouth agape. He was so different. Long hair a tousled mess of curls. Red blush on his cheeks. A thin, fancy leather jacket, crop top under like there wasn't a whole blizzard swallowing the city.

"Whatever. I need a cut. I want it gone, all of it," Carlito said.

"Oh nah, we're not doing that here," another barber jumped in. He looked Carlito up and down con asco, like he was worse than garbage, a bottom-of-the-shoe kind of stain.

Carlito sat in the barber's chair anyway.

"My mother thinks it's this hair that makes me gay. But I'ma show her, hair or no hair, I'm me."

"Nah, nah, I don't want beef with Nena and I don't want whatever this is at my shop. Get up, man."

"I'm a customer," Carlito said. The barber looked around for support. When none of the other barbers moved, Julio stood up from the chair where he was sipping his drink.

"Get up, maricón," he said, looming over Carlito.

"Nigga, sit down, who the fuck are you?"

By then Julio had grown haggard from the rum. He was only thirty-five, but he looked a decade older. Big belly, crooked teeth, wild facial hair growing everywhere. No one could've seen it coming, how he dragged Carlito from his chair, out the door, onto the snow-covered sidewalk. Just as quickly, there was Julio's hand, moving at the speed of thunder, clapping against the boy's cheek. Carlito shrieked. He tried to get up but the force of Julio's hand struck him down again. Blood stained the snow crimson. Julio struck again and grunted like something beastly wanted out of him. By the time the barbers rushed outside to intervene, it was too late.

"Yo, he blacked out," one barber said. He sounded scared.

"I'm sorry," Julio whispered. He looked down at his hands, which had broken Carlito's nose. There were spots of blood from his knuckles to his palms.

"Take him to Nena's house."

"Nah, I ain't taking the fall for this shit."

"Nigga, just go. Just tell her you found him like this."

"I'll take him, I got it," Chelo the barber said, and lifted thin Carlito from the snow.

"I'm sorry, I'm sorry," Julio said. Like a muchachito caught misbehaving, that's what he looked like, muttering apologies into his bloodstained hands.

*   *   *

A few months later, Julio Estevez got his taxi license revoked after a cop found him drunk in his car at the crack of dawn. The first thing the cop noticed when he dragged him out was the sharp smell of piss. Julio's pants were still wet. He smiled and apologized real polite in his broken English, but that didn't get him out of spending a night behind bars. After that, he might have turned into another loco in the street. His landlord kicked him out, and now that he'd lost his car, he had nowhere to go. But one of his old barber friends took him in, on the condition that he join a recovery group. Julio tried to get out of going once or twice those first few weeks, but Chelo the barber insisted on walking him to the meetings hosted in the basement of an old church. Chelo came from a good Catholic family and was well respected by everyone in the neighborhood. He ran a volleyball club for the church kids when he wasn't cutting hair, and he helped our husbands fill out job applications, putting his good English to use. Real salt-of-the-earth man, real pain in the ass for Julio, who wanted to get back to his vice.

"Man, I been going for three months, you don't have to walk me every time," Julio argued once.

"I don't mind. Besides, I like these walks, we get to catch up like real roomies," Chelo said, with that saintly smile that made us trust him to cut our kids' hair and keep them out of trouble.

Close to the year mark of his sobriety, Julio was doing better. He started styling his facial hair again, the way a respectable man should. And he started doing odd jobs to make his own money, which made it possible to pay his portion of the rent. He felt things were going good for them, that maybe Chelo really was a saint sent to Julio to save him from himself. But no matter how good things got, he still longed for the bottle. He admitted his fractured state to Chelo on a hot summer night, how confusing it all was.

"Maybe now is a good time to stop our walks," was Chelo's response.

"What are you talking about? I'm trynna tell you, your help's been real, well, helpful."

"I hear you, I do. But it sounds like you've reached a real crossroads. I'm not going anywhere, I'm still here. I just want you to start going to the meetings 'cause you want to, not 'cause I'm walking you there," Chelo said, scratching his head. He was balding young, but it made his youngish looks match his wise demeanor. Aging looked good on Chelo.

"You're being a real motherfucker about this, real fucking difficult," Julio said, and slammed the front door behind him. He was walking off his anger when he saw her across the street. It'd been years since the incident. She'd moved with a cousin to Rhode Island, that's the last we'd heard. Apparently the cousin had a bakery up there and business was good. But now there she was across the street, walking with a kid in tow. She had the same great ass, same head of curly hair. Julio wanted to run up to her, but what would he say?

"Chelo, man, you won't believe who I saw across the street," Julio said when he ran back upstairs, breathless.

"I thought you were mad at me," Chelo said with his eyes on the television.

"Mileidy, man. Can you believe that shit? I thought she moved away."

"What's that got to do with you?"

"This is it, the crossroads you were talking about. They're always talking about accountability at the meetings. I fucked up bad, back then. If I apologize, maybe . . ."

"I don't know, Julio. Using other people to feel good about yourself, that can't be the way," Chelo said. But Julio was out the door again.

We don't know where he got the idea from. He'd never baked anything in his life, barely knew how to cook more than steamed víveres with eggs. But the next day he spent hours reading over a recipe book, muttering to himself. At one point he knocked on his neighbor's door to help him turn on the oven. "Como es verdad que usted no sabe prender un horno," his neighbor Marta chided him as she put on her slippers. Later, Marta complained to half the building that her neighbor had made the whole floor smell like burnt sugar.

A day before the first anniversary of his sobriety, the cupcakes were ready. He spread all twelve of them out on an aluminum tray, told Chelo he was on his way to choose his path, and only when he was outside in the hot summer sun did he realize he had no way of getting the cupcakes to Mileidy. He didn't know where she lived, where she worked. He didn't know anything about her at all. But that didn't stop him. He walked to the nearest pay phone and called upstairs.

"I think she's staying on Broadway and One Ninety-One with her aunt. But, Julio, I don't know—"

"Gracias, manito," he said to Chelo, and hung up.

Julio waited on the corner for four hours with no luck. He stood there in the shade, keeping his cupcakes away from the sun's harsh light. No one asked what he was doing there. It'd been a long time since anyone on the block had gotten involved with Julio. Most of us kept him at bay, and though Chelo told everyone at church that he was better, that things were looking up, we were on guard, we couldn't help it. He stood there all suspicious with his cupcakes; we just smiled or waved and kept it pushing. Then he finally saw her, walking out of a building with the same kid from before.

"I told you, just let me do it," he heard Mileidy say. She crouched, got the helmet tight on the boy's head, and watched as he biked down the block.

"Mileidy. Hey."

Her thick eyebrows came together as she registered who it was standing in front of her.

"What do you want?"

"I don't want to bother you. I saw you the other day, thought I'd get you these," he said, and removed the aluminum covering to reveal his gift.

"Did you make those?"

"I did," Julio said, laughing nervously. "Took me a few days to get it right, with the temperature and texture and all that. Who knew baking was so hard."

"Why?"

She didn't have to tell him to fuck off for him to get it. Her eyes were cold, her full lips puckered in disapproval. But he couldn't leave, he'd worked so hard.

"I just thought, well, I did a really bad thing. And I've been going to these meetings, trying to clean up, really trying to get my shit together. A good path is paved with accountability, that's what they say, so I thought."

"And Carlito? Are you going to apologize to him? Or do you think I didn't hear about that?"

He looked like he'd been kicked. Even Mileidy softened at the hurt in his eyes.

We heard later that she invited Julio upstairs. They ate the cupcakes over coffee. She told him about the bakery in Rhode Island. Her bitchy cousin. How embarrassed Mileidy felt coming back to live with her aunt. But where else could she go, with a kid? She didn't talk about the boy's father, but the absence was telling enough. He told her about Chelo, the meetings, the odd jobs painting houses and cleaning storefronts to get back on his feet. When she asked about how bad it'd gotten, he stuttered, smiled, said he preferred to leave the past in the past. That's the way forward, he said. He wanted to get his license again once the revocation period ended. He had big plans to get his taxi car back, save up big coin, maybe even buy a house one day. All that talk about dreams got them in a mood. Of course they kissed. The kid was asleep. Her aunt was working. The night was hot. They were both lost and searching, in need of good company. He was gentle when he kissed her. Even dared to palm her neck right there where his hand had pinned her to a wall those years ago. That night, he promised he'd come back, and he did. Once a week, always right before his recovery group meetings, when he needed the most fortification. They sat. They ate baked goods. They kissed like proper lovers.

It was a nice story we told ourselves. Not because he deserved it. Not because he was good. But because he reminded us of the worst parts of who we were. If so much tragedy could follow one man, what would become of our sons, our husbands, our fathers? Like the novelas we loved. We just wanted a happy ending.

Instead, in front of her building, Mileidy picked up a cupcake.

"I don't want your apology."

"But I'm at a crossroads."

"Fuck off, Don Julio." Mileidy crushed the cupcake, frosting first, into his face. Then she disappeared around the block.

Julio stood there a long time crying over his cupcakes.

Sal wakes up to a knock on his door. It's Don Julio, announcing a call from his mother.

"I can't leave work. Can you go?"

"Huh?"

"Are you listening to me? Kiko. In the middle of class. I think they ganged up on him. There's blood."

That last word finally wakes him up.

"I'm making oatmeal and raisin cookies. I'll leave them out for you," Don Julio calls as Sal heads out the door.

He waits half an hour outside the principal's office. Kiko is still with the nurse, and the principal is in a meeting with another student. He listens in on the administrators buzzing around the open office. Five older women processing documents, calling parents whose children didn't make it to school today, chatting across the office about what they're watching on TV. He realizes as he's sitting there that he's never given much thought to Kiko's school life. Sal drops him off or picks him up when their mother can't, and he's heard about the boys who teach Kiko Dominican slang, but that's the extent of Sal's knowledge about what his brother does eight hours a day.

One of the administrators brings him a glass of water as he

waits, but she doesn't smile, doesn't respond to his thank-you, just frowns at him like he's the one who's in trouble.

Just then, the nurse guides Kiko into the office.

"His nose isn't broken, just bleeding. You gotta take it easy, kid."

She hands him a plastic bag with gauze, then walks over to one of the administrators and starts gossiping.

"What happened?"

"I don't know," Kiko says into the gauze covering most of his face. He shrugs and looks in the other direction.

"You can tell me," Sal says. He tries to sound encouraging. Their mother would be heckling him with questions by now, her secondhand shame transmuted into anger. He could try that tactic. It might even work to get more information about the incident. But Sal doesn't want to make his little brother feel like their mother makes him feel.

Sal directs his attention to the clock. It's just past eleven a.m. He wishes he had somewhere to go after this, that Kiko's incident had interrupted some predetermined work schedule. But half of his hours were cut at the ice cream shop at the beginning of September. Now he only goes in twice a week, three times if he's lucky and someone calls out sick.

"If I'm gonna be on your team, I gotta know what's going on. You think Goku would send his friends into battle without letting them know what they're getting themselves into?"

That gets a smile out of him. Sal uses a wet paper towel to clean a smudge of blood on Kiko's nose. Kiko lets Sal clean him up.

"That punk kept making fun of my friend," Kiko admits.

"That's not a reason to hit someone."

"I just told him to back up, that's all I did. Then he called me that word and I hate it, I hate when people say that."

"What word?"

"He said I'm a faggot. 'Cause I protected my friend."

"Kiko, watch your mouth," Sal says instinctively. He looks up to see if anyone has heard. He has nothing to do with it, this world where boys use words as knives. It's been so long since he was one of them. And yet.

"I'm just telling you what he told me," Kiko says, louder now. "Anyway, he won 'cause his friend jumped in. That's all. Would have gone my way if it was one on one." He sounds older, calculated, in that voice he puts on when he's trying to explain how the world works to adults. Except this time, it doesn't sound contrived. Kiko has crossed over into another realm of boyhood. One of competition, of harsh words, of exchanging fists for blood. Sal and Yadiel had a childhood like this. Does Kiko understand the gravity of that word, *faggot*? How easily straight people weaponize it, how ugly and ashamed it makes gay people feel? Or is it much simpler? Kiko knows Sal is in a relationship with a man. He loves spending time with Vance. And he must have sensed it by now, how people respond when Sal and Vance walk into a room together. He might not have all the words, but he must have a feeling. Is he so wrong, then, for standing up for someone he loves? Should Sal offer empty words to reassert the rules of civility, since he's the older brother? Before he can formulate the thought, Kiko completes his own.

"It's not funny. What if someone said that word to you?"

That's enough to silence Sal.

When the principal's door opens again, out comes a boy around Kiko's age. Kiko moves the gauze from his nose to face his enemy, but the boy walks past them, angry about whatever happened in the office. The boy's mother walks out behind him, her hair wrapped messily atop her head, her face crumpled into an apology. "Thank you," she says again and again as she turns from the principal, a stout man with a tie too tight around his neck. She rushes after her son, trying to catch up to him wherever he's going.

Sal meets Vance at his place later that night. Vance has been staying at the office later, coming home so tired he falls asleep on the couch without eating dinner. He's trying to get city funds to support the mental health branch of the community center. He rants about the importance of mental health for gay people, what a difference this program could make, but Sal can't shake his worry. Aunt Meena has grown sicker with the shortening days. When he's not with her, and he's not with Sal, Vance is at work, leaving little room for anything else.

That night, Sal broaches the subject, lightly as he can.

"I like work. It keeps me on my feet."

"I know, I know. But when are you going to rest?"

"Sal, I'm fine, I promise."

"At least take off your work shoes," Sal says, and sighs. Sometimes, the worst thing you can do for someone is to show the depth of your concern. He keeps the rest of his worry to himself, if only for tonight.

They order Chinese food and plop themselves on the couch. There's nothing exciting on TV, so they talk over lo mein and egg rolls. Vance puts duck sauce all over his rolls and tries to feed Sal a bite.

"No! Why is it sweet? Is it even made from duck? No thanks, I'm good," Sal says, and squeezes a third packet of soy sauce onto his plate to make his point.

He tells Vance about his morning in the principal's office.

"You should sign him up for boxing."

"That's not funny. He shouldn't be doing that. Mami was freaking out."

"I know, I know. But he's fighting homophobes and he's only twelve? You got a revolutionary on your hands! How dope is that?"

Sal bites into his egg roll to stop himself from laughing. Maybe Vance is right.

They sit in the living room until the fight in the next room starts. Sal didn't know Mauricio was home, much less that Luis was in there with him. They clean up their plates, dump everything in the garbage, and lock themselves in Vance's room.

"They've been going at it the past few days," Vance says.

"Did Mauricio fuck up?"

"Haven't asked. Wouldn't be the first or last time, though."

The walls mask the words, but the tone of their argument echoes through the apartment. Luis demands more information, more clarity, more of the version of the truth that will validate his suspicions. More, more, more. Mauricio pleads for peace. He wants to forget this moment, the accusations, the senseless jealousy. Sal's heart aches for them. When he first met them, Luis and Mauricio's relationship was hanging by its last brittle strands. Mauricio had cheated. A single drunken night with a stranger, but it hurt just the same. Especially because Luis had found out through other channels. A friend of a friend, who told him not because he cared about Luis, but because he wanted to see their relationship fall apart. That was Vance's best guess, when he told Sal what happened. It doesn't help that Mauricio is desired by so many in their small community. He's tall, muscular, and carries himself with a nonchalance that makes people gravitate to him against their better judgment. Though his extraversion can be exhausting, Mauricio is a good talker, a magnificent dancer, a chameleon who can thrive in any social setting. It also helps that he's Puerto Rican, second generation. He carries with him a swagger that the white gay men in their circle want for themselves. By imitation or consumption, they want to be him or they want to fuck him, to fulfill their fantasy of the vigorous Latin lover made manifest in Mauricio. It's not his fault, Vance tells Sal often. But Mauricio loves the attention, everyone can see that.

Now Luis demands to be validated in his suspicion. Nothing will satisfy his anger but the worst possible outcome. But Mauricio doesn't give it. Either by omission or because he's telling the truth this time, Sal doesn't know.

Luis slams the door on his way out.

"I'll talk to him tomorrow," Vance promises. If anyone can get the truth out of Mauricio, regardless of what shape that truth might take, it'll be his best friend.

In bed, Vance massages lavender oil down Sal's back. He loosens the knots on Sal's shoulders with his knuckles, presses his palms down the length of his spine. The feeling is euphoric. Sal moans in delight.

"Oh, you like that?"

"Shhh, focus, focus," Sal says, and laughs.

"If you wake in the middle of the night, just tap me. Okay?"

Sal groans in agreement and focuses on the sweet smell of lavender.

When he opens his eyes again, the room is dark. The cable box tells the time in hot red numbers: 4:16 a.m.

No dreams, at least none he can remember.

He unwraps himself from Vance's arm and sits up in bed. Outside the night is quiet except for dried yellow leaves rustling in the wind.

On the nightstand is a tall glass of water, illuminated by the fish tank's blue light. Vance knew Sal would wake up thirsty, as he does most nights these days. He feels lucky. When was the last time someone cared for him like this?

I abandoned Renata. It's the first time he's allowed himself the thought. *I didn't have a lot of options*, that's what she said the last time they spoke. Did he have options? Could he have stayed? Instead of folding his feelings within him small as he can make them, Sal lets the wave of guilt crash onto him. It makes his body heavy. But he doesn't fight it. He lies there awake long after the sun outside begins to burn.

GREG'S DINER IS AN AMERICAN CLASSIC. MOST OF THE CUSTOMERS have been coming here for years, since as far back as the early seventies, when the owner set up shop. It's a quaint place with a dozen booths, a giant round table in the back for large parties, plenty of bar space. The furniture is red, the floor tiles white, and there's a giant American flag covering half a wall that's been there so long it's only noticed in its absence. Like the time in '92, when it was taken down to repaint the walls white for the first time in two decades. It didn't matter that they understood the reason, or that it'd be replaced in a couple of days. We're American! the customers complained. They were so loud the manager was forced to return the flag, leaving the wall under it dirty and unpainted. The regulars don't think of themselves as anything other than American, except sometimes fervently Christian when their faith needs reinforcement, and white only when they face the Black workers from Southwest who serve them.

In this town there are no train tracks. What separates the all-Black Southwest from the rest of town is a thin river. There are only two schools in the community, and small businesses manage, just barely, to keep their doors open, though even in Southwest there are exceptions. The Watson family, for example, owns a three-story hotel and runs so good a business even visiting white folks from out of state prefer to stay there. The Cash family, religious and strict like no other, through some secret favor, were able to get their three daughters into the mostly white high school across the river, where they received excellent marks that propelled them into private colleges across the state. Two of the Cash girls graduated and moved to Philadelphia to work office jobs. Now their mother only waits for her youngest to finish undergrad. Three educated women, that was the Cash matriarch's dream; everybody has been hearing about it at church for years. The Copperman family attained their share of wealth by way of two successful, albeit small, restaurants on opposite ends of Southwest. One of them is a dine-in restaurant with a steady clientele. The other is a small shop right off the bridge that specializes in fried okra. On Sunday mornings after church, there's a line as long as the bridge to get a serving with a side of rice. That's the only time white folks drive down to Southwest, for some Copperman fried okra. Otherwise, it's folks in Southwest who cross the river to work in white people's hotels, restaurants, hospitals.

The diner is no exception. Except for a few poor white people, most of the waitstaff at Greg's is made up of young Black folks who dream of skipping town. Big-city living, an all-Black university, anywhere beyond their isolated part of town where the future, and the whole enterprise of the passage of time, seems to tether them to the fabric of Southwest. They fear an unspoken prophecy of living like their mothers, and their mothers' mothers, stuck in the same place generation after generation, doing what their people have always done: working to survive.

The customers don't see much of the Mexican cooks in the back except for when something needs fixing and the manager wants it fixed for free. They are always undocumented, and any extra labor assigned to them is seen as payment for being allowed to work there in the first place. When they complain, the manager conceals his threats in jokes to remind them how lucky they are, how gener-ous he is. I've got la migra on speed dial, he says, in his best attempt at Spanish. The Mexican workers speak to each other in Oaxacan Spanish and do their best to stay out of trouble. The only one who makes himself known is Jaime, who's been at the diner since the eighties. He's transformed over a decade of hard work into unques-tionable respect. The managers love him for never getting an order wrong, evidence of an impeccable memory, and for adding hints of his hometown flavors to the menu, which has only increased the diner's popularity.

The owners also prize Jaime for bringing in more cheap, un-documented labor. Friends and friends of friends who travel from as far south as Puebla up to this Pennsylvania town. Usually in the back of anonymous white trucks, huddled and quiet and afraid. At Greg's, dozens of American dreams have been planted only to wither away at the speed of low-paid work.

It's taken Charo a few weeks to grasp how things work around here, but the busboys are generous with gossip. It's her own place here that still confounds her. The white people's stares. How the Mexican workers don't speak to her in Spanish. The slow pace and quiet of a small-town life, which is so alien to her. In Santo Do-mingo, people think the whole country is Nueva York. But she's starting to realize that New York is only a slice of the whole Ameri-can truth. The comfort of a flourishing Dominican community. The security of being surrounded by Spanish-speakers. The gay bars downtown where Sal and their friends dance freely. None of that exists here.

She delivers two plates of eggs and hash to table six.

"Will you need anything else?" she asks, and forces her hun-dredth smile of the day.

"Black girl with an accent," the man says to himself, and strokes his white beard. "I've never seen that one before."

It's not the first time she's heard this. She's tried to explain that she's Dominican, not for the sake of suggesting she's not Black, but for the sake of specificity. She's never been one of those Dominicans who looks down on moreno americanos, like immigrants are taught to do as soon as they arrive in this country. She has always been a negra. In her own country, in The Bronx, everywhere. But in this town her skin seems to embody and identify her completely. Most of them have never heard of her country. She nods and acquiesces to the racial category, even if she feels different from the other Black workers at the diner. To the white patrons, she's the same as all the rest, except for what makes her other every time she opens her mouth. Her accent always betrays her.

Thirty minutes is all Charo gets to break from the hustle of the diner before she goes on unthinking for another five hours. She sits on the curb of the parking lot and presses a cigarette tight to her lips. The day's remaining sunlight persists, thin as it is. She holds the lighter to the end of her cigarette, but the fire won't start. Her finger burns from scraping the metal wheel. "Coño," she curses, and the cold air catches it. One of the other girls sneaks behind her and lights it for her. The pretty one who doesn't talk to anyone. Impeccable dark skin, inspiring curves, expensive weave wrapped up in a net. They exchange a courteous nod and nothing else. Charo has been at the diner a few weeks, but she hasn't made friends. Her mind is a cloud these days. Work is the only thing that anchors it. And anyway, the other girls are distant. It's like they don't know where to place her in the fabric of the diner's social life. She is used to other women keeping her at bay, but not like this, not because her culture and accent set her apart.

Across the street, a pay phone in a glass booth. The neon light on top of the box beckons her. She waits for a pause in the rush of cars and crosses the busy avenue. The skirt of her pink diner uniform is just above her knees, too short to protect her from the crisp October breeze.

She feeds the machine a cold coin and dials Ella's number once, twice. She leaves an empty message full of echoes of her loneliness. She only dials Sal once, and is relieved when he doesn't pick up. They've only talked twice in the weeks she's been here. She wishes she had better words for him. But her leaving was without reason, is still without reason except to feed an overwhelming impulse to be far away from everything she knows.

I need the space, she thinks. I'll go back when I'm ready.

She puts in another coin. It rings and rings. She doesn't leave a voice message. Robert only picked up her call once. She didn't try to explain herself. How could she? He asked her to return, calmly at first, though she could hear the hurt in his voice.

I can't, she said.

Don't call again, then. Y la niña, you're not talking to her. You're a bad mother, a terrible fucking mother, he said with such fury it felt like he wanted to brand the words on her forehead.

Robert, I—

He hung up, and that was that, the door was closed.

Her parents, too, she hasn't spoken to in weeks. She hasn't sent them money. She can only imagine what they feel. Are they worried that she's disappeared? Or are they angry that their New York investment has backfired? She knows it's harsh to think the latter, but thinking only the former would make her a fool. Maybe it's somewhere in between. They love me, she thinks, and they also love the money.

She leans against the booth glass and looks up. It gave her solace, those first few lonely nights, to know her friends and her daughter back home were under the same sky. Then, in the middle of September, Hurricane Floyd came and covered the East Coast in clouds and turbulent rain. People at work talked about the conspiracies that were all over the news. The rapture, aliens, global collapse of computer programs. Even Jaime and the manager were chatting it up in the back, wrapped up in conspiracies. There's no science to back any of it up, she imagined Sal might say. We're hardwired to make meaning where there is none, especially when we're afraid.

Now the sky is covered in a violet sheen as the light recedes. Charo stands there until her fingers are numb from the cold.

When she crosses the street, the woman who lit her cigarette is still standing there in front of the diner, reading from a thin book. Her name is somewhere in the mist of Charo's mind, but she can't remember what it is.

"No one home?" the woman says.

"No one home," Charo confirms, and goes back inside.

That night, Charo tries to convince Clint she's better off taking the bus back to Southwest. Cooks usually finish their shift thirty minutes before the wait staff. But he lingers, bartering with Jaime about next week's schedule. It's like this every time. She wishes he would go but is relieved when she clocks out and he's there waiting for her by his car.

"My cousin asked me to help you, so let me help you," Clint says often.

It was Ella's idea to grant Charo this escape with her cousin. Clint is good people, she promised, and her hometown isn't all that bad, not any better or any worse than small towns all over Pennsylvania.

The car smells of fresh pine. It's what Clint uses to cover up the lingering smell of weed. He pretends he doesn't smoke during his lunch break sometimes. She pretends she doesn't notice.

He pops in his favorite tape, the notorious Brooklyn rapper's '94 classic. Clint was playing the same album when he picked Charo up from the bus station almost a month ago. She admitted that she didn't know the rapper's music all too well, only the really popular stuff that played on the radio. Clint was insulted by her ignorance, though Charo sensed anything but reverence for the rapper would have been too little. Surely she had heard the smooth flow, his creative rhymes, the powerful cadence that made the listener smell and feel and see the streets of Bed-Stuy from which he came, the lyrics that made death seem like peaceful relief from the endless struggle. Like his favorite rapper, Clint is tall, dark, and heavy. He talks about his hunger for money, chains, and hustling with the same severity that the Brooklyn rapper uses to defend his street cred in his music.

This is real shit, he said that first time in the car. It's music from struggle, from real life, you know? Not niggas doing Hollywood shit for money.

Charo wondered if he applied these rules to his own life, or if drugs, sex, and guns were visions of success only in the world of rap and music videos. What have I gotten myself into? she wondered then. Am I about to move into the house of some small-town drug lord? But in the weeks since she's gotten to know him, his temperament has clarified. He talks a big game, but his gentle demeanor betrays him. What he really loves about rap isn't the lifestyle, alluring as it is. Clint loves words, that's more obvious than anything else.

"I mean, the man was a genius. Listen to this next verse," he says now. He sounds hurt, as if he's still mourning the rapper's death two years after the fact.

Charo sinks into the passenger seat. She's tired from keeping up conversation with customers all day. She's relieved to sit in Clint's joy without being expected to say anything in return.

There are two ways to enter Southwest from the rest of town, and both require driving over water. The bridges are short with no tolls. They often crowd with traffic in the mornings when folks from Southwest are headed into town for work. But the afternoons and evenings don't experience the same rush. Many of Southwest's workers don't have set work hours. A mechanic might be sent home as early as noon if there are too many hands and not enough cars. A shop clerk might be asked to stay and work unpaid overtime if the store is having a good day.

It's late enough that Clint should be able to avoid traffic, but the bridges are still closed. The vein of the river that crosses them, named after the memory of an Indigenous leader, is usually tepid and quiet. It freezes over quickly in the winters, and in the summers swallows and carries away the rain. But since Hurricane Floyd passed them two weeks ago, floods have widened the river and quickened its current into a steady rage. The mayor closed the bridges to avoid a catastrophe. These old bridges weren't built to sustain rapid floods so deep into the state of Pennsylvania, he said in a press conference, but has made no further comment about how this change has made it difficult to get in and out of Southwest.

"My boy got fired for being late a few times. He tried to explain to his boss about the bridges. But you know white people," Clint complains to Charo now.

This isn't the only story of misfortune she's heard since the floods. People getting fired left and right, garbage piling up in front of homes because the garbage trucks don't come, water creeping into the homes of those closest to the river. Two days ago, the Watson family's hotel kitchen went up in flames, and the firefighters didn't arrive until half the building was burnt to a crisp. Even the wealthiest people in Southwest aren't safe. Everyone's talking about it, all these tragedies they can't afford.

When they get home, Clint invites her to stay up and watch TV. Tia, his girlfriend, comes to the living room and tries to convince her, too. Tia is short and loud and a little annoying, but she's honest; Charo likes that. She works part-time at the diner, part-time as a hairdresser, and is studying to get her GED, which she needs to get into cosmetology school. How she manages all of it, Charo doesn't know. Clint and Tia are two years younger, but it doesn't feel like they're only twenty-three. They work hard and talk about ambitious dreams of moving to a big city to open a salon that will make them lots of money. Tia's dream, which Clint is excited to support. They're focused, more focused than Charo was two years ago and certainly more so than she feels now.

"I'm really tired. I think I need to rest," Charo says, though that's only half the truth. She could use the company. But I don't want to take up space, she thinks.

"All right, girl, but this is the third time you say no," Tia says. "You gonna have to sit with me eventually."

"I will, I promise," Charo says weakly.

"I'm taking my exam in a couple of weeks. And I'm passing that shit, which means we're celebrating."

"Yeah, I'll be there."

"No more excuses," Tia says, and points a pink acrylic nail at Charo to show she's serious. Clint nods. Then she's finally free to go upstairs, where she can be alone again.

It's before seven a.m. on a Saturday morning. The only business open on the block is the bodega, where two men stand outside in their oversized coats sipping dollar coffees and arguing about the morning paper. Sal slips by them, orders a coffee and a piece of arepa. A dollar each. This cheap breakfast should get him through to the afternoon.

The liquor store is right off The Concourse on 170th. The owner shows him around. Sal is to clean the floors and all of the counters. When the place is spotless, he's to unbox a big order of wine and shelve the bottles along the wall according to brand. It's physical work and he's tired from another sleepless night, but the owner promised him a hundred and twenty dollars for a full day's work. Rent is due in a few days. He needs this.

"This is my pride and joy," the owner, Manolo, says when they're done with the tour. He is short but he speaks with his chest out and his head held high. The liquor store is filthy and small, but Sal nods like he sees it, all the work the man claims he's put into the place.

"I got you, man, don't worry," Sal says, doing his best to imitate how men speak to each other.

His mother called a few days ago to tell him about this gig. It's one day, it won't kill you, she said. Her way of offering help while still kicking him in the ass. She's never been one to treat him with softness. Besides, she was still upset with him. It was one thing to leave the restaurant job for the garden. When he told her he left the garden to go work at an ice cream shop, she almost ran out of the room screaming.

Salvador, please, I don't want to hear about that right now, she said, put up a hand to stop him, then hurried along to get ready for her shift at the hospital. It was a lie, of course. But he didn't want his mother to know he'd been fired for being gay. That would open up an argument he wasn't ready to have. *Are you sure you weren't slacking on the job?* she might ask. To his mother it's all about individual choices, all about hard work. If he got fired, he must have done *something* to make it happen.

Now Sal picks up a broom.

"Okay, hijo, I'm gonna be in and out all day. Running around, you know how it is," he says. But Sal doesn't know how it is. He wouldn't be doing odd jobs like this if he did.

It takes him hours to tame the cloud of dust and grime plaguing the liquor store. He mops the floor with lavender cleaning liquid and scrubs the cabinets with a hot towel. By the time he's cleaned the whole place, it's well into the afternoon. He's hungry, but he doesn't want to spend money on lunch. Just when he's about to unbox the first case of wine bottles, Manolo walks in with sancocho from a restaurant and invites Sal to eat with him.

Manolo has been in New York for twelve years, and it's taken him that long to open up his first business. It takes time, he says, like all good things. Manolo lives by the same philosophy as Sal's mother. The promise of hard work. But Sal worked at a restaurant for years, earned his associate's degree, had a good job at the garden, and look at him. How can hard work be so fruitful if Sal is here, eating off the plate of another man?

The second half of the afternoon is more arduous than the first.

The wine bottles are heavy and the boxes endless. Chardonnay, pinot noir, merlot. Red, white, pink. Sal didn't even know there was pink wine, though the bottle's decorative design makes him curious. Manolo comes in and out a few times to check on him and his brother, who mans the front and handles all purchases. Sal makes idle conversation with Manolo's brother, who says very little in return. It isn't till after ten at night that Sal places the last wine bottle on the shelf. Manolo comes to the back to congratulate him, unfolds a wad of cash, hands him five twenties.

"I thought you said one twenty," Sal says when Manolo hands him the cash. The amount promised is exactly what he needs to cover rent in a couple of days.

"It was the food, had to break my last big bill. But I got you lunch, that should cover the difference, right?"

Sal wants to advocate for himself, tell him what a good job he did, that he worked longer than was expected. All his life he's been taught how to haggle—at the supermarket for víveres, with his grandmother for more time outside with Yadiel, with the tigueres in the barrio for his dignity every time they tried to rob him. But now his will is weak, his fighting spirit tired.

He looks back at the liquor store one last time. The bottles neatly lined, the shelves and wooden floors spotless. Hard work, he thinks. This is what it gets me.

The month ends in a few days, and Sal is short on rent. He thought he had an extra twenty in the jar where he keeps loose change. Turns out he miscalculated. All week he's been running on small meals of plátano and boiled eggs, canceling plans to go out with friends, hopping the turnstile on his way to see Vance, but none of it has made a difference. His math is so bad that by the time Friday rolls around he's seventy-five dollars short on rent with no promise of getting his ice cream shop check for another week.

Now he looks through all of his pants pockets. It wouldn't be the first time he's come across a miraculous ten-dollar bill he forgot existed. But six pairs of pants later, he's only found a few coins, enough to buy him a bag of chips and a soda. He lies down in bed and holds the coins in his sweaty palms. His room is in disarray, jeans and shirts everywhere. The thought of asking Vance for help crosses his mind and leaves it just as quickly. He would never ask his boyfriend to help him pay rent. The only person he would feel comfortable confessing his shame to is Charo, and they've barely talked since she left for Pennsylvania.

In the kitchen, the radio is tuned to a local station. The hosts are taking listener questions and stories about extramarital love affairs. Don Julio must be home today. Either he's taken the day off or he won't start working until the evening. As a cabdriver, he works whenever he wants, as long as he wants. Some days Don Julio is up and out as early as four in the morning; other days, especially on holidays, he starts work in the evening and drives clients down every desolate avenue in the Bronx until the sun comes up.

He folds what he has of rent into an envelope, but it feels thin. I can't even lie about it, it's so obvious, he thinks. It's some time before he works up the courage to peel himself from bed.

In the kitchen, Don Julio examines a piece of cake between a fork and his fingers. When he sees Sal, he grabs a ceramic plate from the cabinet and cuts him a slice.

"Angel cake. Some gringo shit," he explains. "I read it in this book I got to help me with the baking. Supposed to be real soft pero I don't know, maybe it's too soft?"

The spongy cake melts on Sal's tongue. It's a wonder how a man like Don Julio can make something so soft.

"I, uh . . ." Sal looks down at the crumbs of cake on his plate. "Don Julio, I don't have the rent this month. I mean I have most of it. But I'm seventy-five dollars short. I can pay you in a week, when

I get my check from the ice scream spot, but right now . . . Yeah. I'm really sorry."

Don Julio bends over to look inside the oven.

"You all right, hijo?"

"I am. I just, it's been a tough few months. A lot of job transitions."

"I'm asking about you. I've heard you waking up in the middle of the night. Talking, too. Did you know you talk in your sleep? Shit was funny at first, now it's just creepy. God knows what you're saying."

"Oh. I didn't know." He's surprised to hear his dreams have made it out of his mind and into the world. Why hasn't Vance mentioned that Sal talks in his sleep?

"Gimme twenty-six minutes exactly. I'll be done with the second cake of angels in twenty-six minutes, and then we can sit outside on the fire escape. Same as always. You and me and that shit Bronx skyline."

"You gotta get your shit together, man." Very unlike Don Julio, straight to the point.

"I feel real bad about the rent," Sal says.

"That's not what I'm talking about. I mean, yeah, get me my money. Ha! Pero, I mean in general. You're walking around like a zombie."

"I've been . . . uh . . . excavating some deep psychological rifts in my mind," Sal says awkwardly. He scratches at his scalp. His curls haven't grown too long or wild since the summer, but he could use a haircut. What he'd give for a shape-up, to feel fresh and new. But that, too, costs money.

"See, that's the problem. Always thinking. Using big words. I don't wanna beat you while you're down, but all this thinking, look where it's gotten you. You stuck, man."

Sal doesn't know what to say, so he keeps looking forward.

"Just keep it simple."

Above, a cluster of small clouds eclipses the sun and makes shadows over the street.

"A friend of mine was murdered, I think. I mean, I know. It was some gringo from the States my friend was sleeping with."

"Recently?"

"A few years ago. It's why I left Santo Domingo, even though I didn't want to."

"Ah. Shit." Don Julio pulls out a cigarette. He puts it to his lips, cups it in his hands to protect it from the breeze, and lights it. When he pulls, Sal can see the lines around his eyes deepen. "What's your friend's name?"

"Yadiel." Sal's stomach turns.

"He your friend for a long time?"

"She. Sometimes he. It's complicated."

"Okay, all right. I get it, I think? I can't keep up these days, but anyway, anyway," he says. "Is that what the dreams are about?"

"I think so. I can never remember them. But I wake up feeling her presence. Like someone's been calling my name."

"A ghost calling your name. I heard of that," he says.

A flock of pigeons orbits the sky. One bird leaves the flock and lands on a gray brick building. Another joins it, and another, until half the flock is on the roof. They fight for a morsel of food, their ashen wings flapping desperately. Don Julio's eyes follow the other half of the flock until the birds are just specks in the sky. Sal thinks that maybe he's lost his roommate, that the whole thing is too morose for their sessions on the fire escape. Silence stretches to uncomfortable proportions. Then a gust of wind brings Don Julio back. He takes one last cloud of smoke into his lungs, then extinguishes the cigarette on the metal railing.

"My daughter had this dream of making bread for a living. I don't know where she got it from. I think we had a neighbor that made pan de agua. We must have taken her there at some point. Anyway, it don't matter where she got it from, point is, she wanted it real bad, her own bakery. And then, you know, the war. Yo lloraba to lo día until I found a bottle of rum. It helped to numb the pain. I didn't meet a single night sober for a long time. Years, lost. I knew something had to change. I was gonna kill myself con esa vaina. I'm not the smartest, didn't do a lot of school ni na de eso, but I had killed people and seen people killed, so I knew what it takes to make a life real small. Fast as a gun or slow as the rum. I knew what death smelled like, so I left. Wasn't easy here, either. This country's just as bad, in other ways. I was good for a little while, but eventually I picked up the habit again. Driving the cab to make some cash and every other moment, drinking. Eventually a buddy of mine took me to my first meeting. Walked me over like I was a carajito on his way to school. I felt stupid. But he was a stand-up guy, real funny, real good with the community. I know I'm talking a lot but just bear with me, I'm getting to the point. I'm getting there. I did a lot of shit I'm not proud of. Don't even want to tell you about how I got started baking. Something else I needed to repent for, someone else I hurt. I was so fixated on making amends the first time I baked I didn't even notice. But I did it again a week later, just 'cause I was curious. I made pound cake. Shit was all lumpy on the outside and gooey on the inside. Un monstruo of a cake, just wrong. But that's the moment. Baking that cake was the first time I really spent time with my baby. It'd been years since she died, and all that time I hadn't sat with her once."

At the end of his speech, his voice begins to break. He coughs. He swallows. He goes on.

"I meet my daughter every time I turn on that oven. I've never been religious, and I'm not saying you gotta believe in God if that's not your thing. Plenty of guys at the taxi base don't believe in shit. We talk about it. I'm just saying. Your friend died, and it don't seem like you ever meet him. Her, sorry. But you know what I mean."

"I've tried to talk about it," Sal says. "But whenever I do, my mom, Charo, now Vance, everyone tells me it's not my fault. That I shouldn't carry guilt around. But that doesn't help. Because I know I could have done something. Been more present. She was always asking me out. I hated those parties, but I could have tried some other way to be with her. She was lonely. I wasn't paying attention."

"Yeah, I'm sure you could have done more," Don Julio says.

He doesn't seem to notice that his words have wounded Sal. He keeps his eyes on the horizon.

"They went out 'cause they were hungry, my wife and daughter. She called me at my friend's house where we were hiding. Asked me to bring food, they were running low. But I forgot. I was too wrapped up planning the next day's battle, real macho that I was. I still remember staying up all night under a kerosene lamp. Surrounded by my boys. Drunk off the spirit of revolution, the kind of shit they write poems about. So macho I forgot my wife and kid were hungry. They went out to find food a few days later. Got wrapped up in a shooting. I don't even know if it was the gringos or our people that shot them. It don't matter now. A gun's a gun. People think it's the bodies you remember. And sure, sure, that keeps you up at night. But it's the choices you make when you can make them, that's the part of war that weighs you down and kills you, way after the fighting's done."

Sal holds his jacket close to himself. Somewhere down the hill, where they can't see, the 4 train rumbles by.

"You didn't kill your friend. You shouldn't blame yourself for that. But I'm not gonna coat it in sugar and frosting for you. We can always be better to the people we love."

Don Julio pats him on the back so hard Sal almost chokes on his own spit.

"Tienes que ponerte las pilas, hijo. I wanted to tell you before, but now seems as good a time as any, since we're getting sentimental, since we're going on about crossroads. I'm leaving. I bought a little house in Florida. It has a lemon tree in the back. I leave right before New Year's. Just feels right. I don't have no friends there and I haven't talked to most of my family in over twenty years. But I got a cousin that lives in Miami. She's helping with all the paperwork. It'll be real nice. Not Santo Domingo. I don't think I could ever go back to that country. There's nothing and no one waiting for me there. But Florida is tropical. It ain't too far from the real deal. And the lemons. I'll be able to make custard from my own lemons."

Don Julio's hands are brown, wrinkled, storied. The same hands of war that held a gun and a dead daughter and now make delicate pastries by the side of an oven. What do Sal's hands say about him? If he had gotten the job at the museum, he might have used his hands as he talked about planets and the stars to keep a tour group enthused. If he had stayed at the garden longer, he might have gained a few cuts harvesting zucchini or handling tomato vines. Even the ice cream job, if it were something he loved and could use to sustain himself, might give his hands a story to tell. Every opportunity he's tried to hold on to in the last year has slipped through his fingers. He begins to feel sadness creeping up on him, but he owes Don Julio his attention, at least.

"Lemons. A house. That's amazing, Don Julio," he says.

"That's as much of life as I want. A quiet place where it's easier to live with myself."

Don Julio sighs. He sounds tired and relieved at once. "Anyway, don't worry about October's rent, or rent for the rest of the year, until I leave. I got it," he says, before slipping back inside to tinker with his angel cake.

CLINT SAYS HE SEES THEM JUST AS HE PULLS OVER IN FRONT OF the house.

Charo looks out the window, but everything is dark.

"You sure you're not imagining it?"

"Nah, I'm telling you, they're there behind the bushes."

Clint kills the headlights, tells her to wait. After a minute, he turns the lights on again. This time, Charo catches the shadows moving. She doesn't know how she missed them. The bigger raccoon, probably the mom, is a foot tall. The smaller furballs huddle close behind her.

Charo has never seen a raccoon in person, much less a family of them. But she's not afraid. Growing up in the Caribbean prepared her for this. In Santo Domingo, it's street dogs, lizards, giant rats, flying roaches. In the campo, fat toads, fruit bats, river crabs.

Once, even an eccentric bull that jumped a five-foot fence to escape its cell. It terrorized her grandfather's small town for three nights. The first night, the bull made a brief appearance by the colmado. The crowd cut their dominó game short and scattered, spreading the news as far as the town went. The second night, they prepared. A few of the townsmen, the bravest among them, ran drills until they spotted the beast. They circled with ropes, hoping to catch the bull by its muscled neck and hold it down long enough to tire it out. But the rumors of its supernatural strength were true. It shook off four of the town's strongest men, pushed one of them so hard he hit the ground and pissed himself. By the time they dusted themselves off, the bull was gone.

Charo was visiting her grandfather and had spent most of the week playing with the neighborhood kids, until the bull came and ushered everyone inside. At first, Charo was excited by all the clamor around her. But eventually she grew bored of looking at the door, wondering what lay beyond it. Was the bull as scary as the adults said? Charo heard the rumors and warnings, but she was eleven and already starting to feel at odds with the rules people created to feel safe. On her third night indoors, when the adults settled in front of the television to watch their novelas, she snuck out through the backyard. The sidewalks were unpaved, unlit. She wandered a few streets away to where kids usually gathered to play volleyball and hopscotch. She expected at least some of them to be there. Cowards, she thought as she kicked around a deflated ball. Minutes later, a couple of men crowded in front of a neighboring house. Charo hid in the shadow of a bush and saw a boy come out to join the group. He couldn't have been more than a few years older than her, though he was tall and strong for his age. No one had seen the bull that night, but the boy spoke passionately about the possibility. Que bacano, we're about to be the talk of the town, the boy bragged. But one of the older men smacked him across the head. A wild bull was nothing to fuck around with, especially not one with supernatural abilities.

Charo followed them. If they were going to catch the bull, she wanted to witness it, to tell the story from her own point of view. But they were moving faster than she could keep up with in the dark. She turned a corner, guessing where to go next, and there was the bull standing in her path. All the fear she felt surrounding her the last few days, the rumors, the prayers, the whispers, there it all was standing a few feet ahead of her in the form of a hulking mass. Light from a neighboring house illuminated the sidewalk just barely, so she could see its muscled body, its flaring nostrils, its tail like a pendulum. The moon was a slice in the sky. The bull, too, was incomplete, its left horn chipped off in the middle. She couldn't see where its dark eyes looked, but she knew it saw her by the way it stopped and waited.

Charo should have feared the beast. And she did, as much as fear could paralyze her in place. But she also felt a sensation that was all body and no language, an electrifying realization that passed from her toes to her head when she saw the beast flare its nostrils and inhale deeply. The bull was no myth, no story, no rumor, but a body with its own vitality, its own breath, searching for its own belonging in the night, same as her.

She stood still so long she forgot minutes and she forgot hours. When it was done contemplating her, the bull turned its head, and the rest of its body followed. It galloped a few feet, then jumped over a fence into someone's backyard. She couldn't see where it went; she only heard it galloping and crossing another fence, deeper into the night.

Go far, she said, like they'd been having a conversation.

In the car now, Clint mumbles about what to do next. Charo volunteers to go out and shoo them away, but Clint locks the door and lists the numerous diseases raccoons might carry, some of which she's sure he's making up on the spot. He flashes his headlights a few times. A shadow appears from inside the house and opens a window.

"Y'all good?" It's Tia, wearing a bonnet and a white tank top.

Clint rolls down the passenger window and yells their predicament in fragments. Racoons. Teeth. Rabies. Grass.

"Oh, nah. You got it, babe," Tia says, and slams the window shut as quickly as she opened it. Charo laughs so loud Clint jumps in his seat.

"You think this is funny, man? Those shits will tear up all your garbage, make holes in your house, it's chaos, fucking chaos. Nope, I want them gone."

He tries the headlights again, but they're directed at the street and not the house, so the raccoons stay in their hiding place. Then he tries the horn of his car. The noise makes the animals alert; Charo sees them straighten up, especially the mother, who rises to her full height. But they don't leave. Next, Clint throws a water bottle across the yard.

"If I get the mom," he promises, "then the rest of them will follow."

But the water bottle misses them by a long shot. He slumps in his seat, defeated.

"Wow, you really don't like animals," Charo says.

She has a hard time feeling bad for Clint. His sweaty forehead, his childlike frown. If it were up to her, they'd run at the racoons head-on with a bat. They wouldn't even have to use it. She's sure the big rats would just run off. The whole thing is so stupid. Clint's fear, the stubborn raccoons, her being here in this town with this almost stranger, all of it.

"I have an idea," she says finally, because someone has to do something, or they'll end up sleeping in the car tonight.

Charo guides him to reverse the car to face the house.

"Okay, you're gonna flash the lights on and off and I'm gonna honk the horn. But it has to be at the same time. Focus, okay? Ready? And . . . Go!"

The raccoons are overwhelmed. They run from one side of the yard to the other, trying to find their bearings. Then the mother runs through the neighbor's lawn, past a few shrubs, and wobbles onto the sidewalk, followed by her league of children.

"Ha! I win, motherfuckers!" Clint yells out the window.

Charo laughs and laughs until her stomach hurts.

Inside, Clint takes full credit for driving the raccoons away. Tia pulls him into a hug, mouths a thank-you to Charo.

"I'm in the living room, studying with my friend. Please come chill with us, this shit is so boring," Tia says.

"Yo!" a voice yells from the living room. Maybe it's the laughter that's lifted her spirit or the long day at the diner that's beaten down some of her defenses. But she accepts Tia's invitation for the first time.

When she comes back downstairs after a shower, Tia and her friend are sitting on the ground filling out note cards. The friend stands up to shake her hand. His skin is the color of wheat. He's skinny, but his shoulders are wide and his beard suggests he must be around her age. He wears an orange durag, the length of which sits on his shoulders. Michael, his name, never Mike.

Charo sits next to Tia. The floor is littered with note cards and markers and textbooks. Michael-not-Mike has his GED exam the same day as Tia, they explain. They've sworn to pass together, so they meet three times a week to study and hold each other accountable.

Charo picks up a stack and starts quizzing them.

"Nope, it's the mitochondria," Charo says, correcting Tia, though she, too, has a hard time saying the word.

"Mitochondria, energy. Why can't I remember that?" Tia scratches at her head through her bonnet.

"It kinda looks like a bean," Michael adds. "Think beans, food, energy, powerhouse. Easy." He explains that the best way to remember things is to tell a story by connecting words to other words in a string of meaning. Little trick he learned from his grandfather the bookkeeper, he explains, who kept a convenience store running for thirty years off the strength of his memory.

"Every time you see that organelle, you're gonna think of a bean, which will trigger the rest of the story in your brain. The definition will open like a flower in your mind."

So he's poetic, Charo thinks, and looks at Michael to measure him again.

"Okay, I'm down with that," Tia says.

Charo wonders what could have gotten in the way of him finishing high school. She knows for Tia it was boys and weed. Tia told Charo the story of her adolescence one evening when Clint was driving the two women home from the diner. It was a lethal combination for her, Tia explained. Weed loosened her from her responsibilities, and boys pulled the rest of her attention. Her first year in high school she had three boyfriends, all seniors. By the end of her second year, she accumulated another three relationships. All spurts of love that lasted a few months and then burned out, leaving her a wisp in the wind. At the end of each relationship, she became depressed, smoked all day at a friend's house, in empty classrooms, a kid's jungle gym under the shroud of night, wherever she could find relief. She became lethargic, coolly disinterested, until the next boy came around and pulled her into a new adventure. School rarely mattered. She started missing days and returned every couple of weeks only when loneliness weighed on her and she felt the need to be surrounded by people. The cycle continued until she stopped going to school altogether her junior year, got a job, and moved in with one of her boyfriends.

It was that same relationship, the longest she'd ever had, that finally brought her back to herself. They were together two years, and it only happened once, but once was enough. His hard knuckles, the way her head snapped back, the cool of her own hand when she placed it quickly on her red-hot cheek. The surprise on both their faces, having crossed to some unnamed place in their relationship.

In that moment and in the days that followed, she felt she had a choice to make. She could go on loving him. Even find new meaning in his blooming aggression. It might have meant he loved her more, that he wanted to possess her so much he was willing to hurt her in the process. We make up all types of shit for love, she told Charo in the car. Why not stretch her love to hold this, too?

She didn't leave a note when she left. He would understand. They saw each other again months later at the supermarket on a Sunday morning. He wore her favorite yellow hat, the one she always said lit his face bright as the sun. Though they made eye contact and she tried her best to smile, he never tried to close the distance between them. This gave her hope. She liked to think that by letting her go quietly, he'd chosen to walk away from the violent man he had become in their relationship. The possibility that he might go on to do what he did to her, to someone else, she couldn't live with it.

In the absence of a man, and grounded in her resolution to stay away from weed and alcohol, she started doing hair with her aunt. Twists, blowouts, cornrows, weaves. Once, a short Mexican woman whose hair stretched past her ass. She wanted to cut her hair to her ears, explained in her heavy Spanish accent that she had much to let go of. Tia didn't ask, but she imagined it had something to do with a man. After she cut her hair, Tia held the woman's hand as she cried away a history of pain. Her aunt taught her everything she knew, and Tia was good at the job on account of her small, nimble hands. But the most important part was that Tia was good with people. A hairdresser needs to be as good in conversation as she is with her hands, her aunt explained. You have to hold the secrets, the laughter, the gossip, the news, all of it with equal interest.

By the time she met Clint, Tia had found a thing to do that was her own. No man could distract her from her passion of doing hair. Being with Clint was the first time she felt she could be her own person and be in love at the same time.

But Michael-not-Mike. As Charo quizzes him now, as he gives each corner of the human cell its proper name, she can't help but wonder what could have kept him back. With that kind of memory, he should have made it through school with little effort.

"You're so good at this," Charo admits.

Michael raises his eyebrows, as if to say, *I told you so*. Tia gives him the middle finger in jest, and they move on to the next set of cards.

When Clint is done getting dressed, he joins them in the living room. He asks Tia if he can invite some of his friends from the diner for a drink.

"Babe, I'm studying," she says, but her defenses are weak. She's been studying for hours, and it's Friday night, why the hell not.

They spend the next hour cleaning. Clint directs the mission. He's particular about having a clean house when people come over. Even Michael helps, though Tia tells him at every step he shouldn't.

"I'm the only one of my friends that has my own place. Everyone else is living with their parents or in somebody's attic. I'm not trying to show off," Clint says as everyone else cleans. "But if I'm gonna have my own place, it's gotta look sharp."

"Okay, great. Here's the garbage, take it out back," Tia says.

"Um, and have the raccoons attack me? Nah, man. You can cut my ass, but I ain't going out there, I don't care," he says. Michael volunteers to take the garbage out, but not before getting in a few quick jabs at Clint.

"Only a few raccoon bites, but I made it," Michael says when he returns. Charo and Tia break out in laughter.

Charo hasn't been this excited to spend time with friends since she left The Bronx two months ago. A series of memories returns to her of Vance and Mauricio's apartment, their parties, the trip to the beach. Maybe Michael is right, she thinks. Maybe memory is just a long chain of reactions, each image unlocking the next until the mind makes a convincing story. I had a solid group of friends, she thinks. A nice apartment. A good job. Then Robert went and ruined it. *Was his betrayal as bad as I remember it, or is that a story I tell myself, to justify leaving?*

Michael goes on roasting Clint. Charo sweeps a cloud of dust from under the couch.

The boys arrive with six-packs of canned beer and rolled-up joints. They are riotous and ready to have a good time. Charo knows two of them from the diner. They work in the kitchen with Clint, and though she's rarely interacted with them, when they arrive, they hug her as if she's an old friend.

With all these boys around, Tia demands they balance out the gender dynamics. She calls two of her girlfriends from the salon. One of them picks up from bed, and no amount of pushing from Tia will get her out of it. The other friend jumps at the opportunity but calls back a minute later to say she couldn't find a babysitter, she'll have to miss out.

"What about that girl that does the Tuesday shift with me? What's her name?" Charo says to no one in particular, though she says it loud enough for everyone to hear.

"Eve? Oh nah, you not inviting her," one of Clint's boys says.

"She so damn uppity," another one adds.

"She's nice! What are you talking about?" Charo says, though she's barely exchanged words with Eve. She couldn't even remember her name a few seconds ago. Their only interactions have been unspoken. Eve lighting Charo's cigarette outside. Or that one time, with the difficult customer who was raising his voice at Charo for handing him a plate of soggy fries. Eve jumped in, armored with her smile, to deescalate the situation. She was so good that by the end of the conversation the angry customer was docile as a puppy.

Charo looks across the room for support. Tia shrugs to express her indifference.

"Man, just give her the number if you got it. It's too many dudes in here anyway," Michael says. Charo smiles at him to show her gratitude.

"All right, here," one of the guys says as he pulls a tiny phone book from his back pocket. "Tried to bag her, you know I like 'em thick. It's true, she hella uppity. But you better believe I kept that number, right here with all the others on my list."

"You got swerved, nigga!" one of the guys says, and the rest of them laugh.

Charo escapes to the kitchen to call this stranger she's so curious about.

An hour later, half the party is buzzing with beer, the other half floating with burning spliffs in their hands. They gather around an intense game of *Mario Kart*. Tia has the most wins, followed by Michael, and in the very last place, after all his friends, is Clint. After every race, they argue about who the true winner is, regardless of what the points say. The guys say that Tia is winning on account of being the only sober person in the room.

"I would smoke all of you regardless, don't play with me," Tia yells above the crowd. She challenges them to prove her wrong in the next race, and they take her on, except for Clint, who's had too much to drink and is falling asleep on the couch.

At the door, a quiet knock. Charo runs to open it.

"Hey," Eve says. She is dressed in light blue jeans and a cream knitted top that hangs loosely off her shoulders. Charo realizes that she's never seen her outside of work hours. She knows that Eve has amazing curves and a nice, full ass. That she wears expensive weave, by the shine of her hair. But much of her beauty was hidden behind their dusty-pink-and-white uniform. Now the light coming from inside the house makes caves of shadow under her cheekbones. Her almond-colored skin is iridescent. She has just a touch of makeup on, thin eyeliner, a maroon lip. In a past life, in high school or grade school, where children are cruel and quick-tempered, Eve might have been bullied for being heavy. Charo sees it all the time, the way girls and women are reduced to the size of their bodies. Charo's no angel; she knows she's participated too. But nothing about Eve as she stands by the door suggests she's anything but self-possessed.

"Can I come in?" Eve raises a bottle of wine as her entrance offering.

"Uh, right, yeah, come in."

Charo introduces her to the room. Tia looks up and waves, then returns her attention to the game. The guys reorient their bodies in Eve's direction, as if they rehearsed it somehow. One by one they try to engage her in conversation. They talk about the diner, the weather; one even comments on local politics, though he tries and fails to remember the name of the Black mayoral candidate who comes from Southwest.

"I wouldn't raise a kid here," says one of the guys.

"Why, Ron? We all grew up here, we're doing okay." Eve holds the plastic cup of wine up to her lips.

"Nah, man. With all the crazy shit's been happening here? Just last year my cousin got caught up in some shit had nothing to do with him. Shot and killed—for what? Year before that, my boy's boy. Every day it's some new shit, and it's us. Fuck what that uppity nigga says, talkin' 'bout some systemic and structural isms. It's us doing this shit to each other."

Eve stands up straight, as if to ready herself for whatever else might come out of Ron's mouth. "You really believe we're hurting each other more than the state is hurting us? I mean, I don't think Williams is a serious politician. But he makes a good point. A lot of the shit keeping us down, it's bigger than the choices we're making."

"Well, I can't wait for society to change to live my life. I gotta get the fuck out," Ron says, and shakes his head. His boys behind him mumble in agreement. Michael and Tia are wrapped up in another heated race.

"You know, maybe if you paid the library a visit every now and then . . ."

She doesn't have to articulate the full thought for it to stir the room. Two of Ron's friends laugh at him. The other two shake their heads in disapproval. She's just as they expected, too uppity and good for them. Charo, sensing the tension, jumps in.

"I think it's fine. I mean I haven't been here long, but it seems like a nice place to have a family."

Ron coughs up the last bit of smoke from his spliff, turns to one of the guys, and asks loudly, as if they're the only people in the room, "Yo, didn't she leave her daughter in New York or some shit?"

Everyone pauses. Clint snores lightly from the couch.

"Ron, you ready to get your ass kicked again?" It's Michael, shifting the room's attention back to the screen.

Ron and the boys crowd around the game. Charo feels Michael's gaze, searching for her eyes. But she looks straight at the television. If she could sink into the couch and disappear . . . If she could grow wings and lunge for the open window . . . But enough time passes; the crowd forgets her and moves on to a pressing argument about gravity on Rainbow Road. She drinks the last of her wine and walks outside to meet the harsh November breeze.

The front porch is a small square with a rocking chair and dying plants littering the corners. Remains of summer, evidence that once, before this cold arrived, life could prosper in a pot of soil. Though they're not beyond return. Sal is good with plants. He knows how to make a thing close to death come back to life. It's probably just science, the way that light and water restore a thing to its former self. But Charo thinks it's magical. It's been two months since she last saw him. In between, they've only spoken on the phone a handful of times. She misses listening to his nerd talk, their hours in front of the television watching sci-fi movies.

Charo wraps her arms around her chest to shield herself from the cold. Across the street, one wild cat meets another. The wind carries their howls.

A few minutes later, the front door creaks open. Charo doesn't look up at the hand that extends the jacket, just grabs it and throws it around herself.

"I assume they've been telling you I'm a snob."

"You sure sounded like it in there," Charo says.

"Yeah, sounds like we both got our fair share of problems."

Charo wants to get up from the chair and slap her. It's the condescending tone that gets to her. But maybe Charo should be directing her anger at Clint, who she's certain spread the news about her daughter. No one knows why she's in town except her hosts, and she doubts Tia would go yapping her business to the diner cooks.

"I don't act like I'm better than anybody. I just challenge them, and they don't like that."

Eve explains that ever since she came back to town a few years ago, everybody treats her as if she's a foreigner. It's the degree, she says, as if dealing out a diagnosis. When she was preparing to go to college, everyone supported her. Even people she had never met, kids she'd shared classrooms with, neighbors she'd lived by her whole life, it was like everybody saw her for the first time. They all hoped for her success; their dreams about leaving town, getting an education, climbing the social ladder to wherever wealth leads, all of it they projected onto her. She was going to DC, where things happened and possibilities were infinite. The support lasted those few months before her mother drove her to the train with as much of her life as she could carry in a few bags. When she returned to Southwest for the holidays that winter, everything was different. The same people who had greeted her with excitement in the streets now approached her with uncertainty. When they asked, and she explained how school was going, the clubs, the challenging classes, the activism on campus, they walked away with a sour look on their faces, as if they'd smelled the first few hints of rotting milk. Eve stopped coming back to town on her breaks. She found odd jobs and internships in DC to make money and build her résumé. When her mother asked why she didn't come home, she explained that she needed to stay busy if she wanted to get into law school. But that was only half the truth. She had little to do with Southwest anymore, and the people of Southwest seemed to want little to do with her.

"Everybody likes the idea of you doing better, until you're doing better," she says.

"Why did you come back?" Charo looks up at Eve's profile.

"Nope, I've talked a lot. Your turn. Why are you here and not with your baby?"

It's a surprising relief to be asked directly. Tia and Clint never bring up her life in New York. They act as if she's materialized in Southwest with no past, no history, no story to tell or pain to lay bare. They must do this to be courteous. And a part of Charo needed this at first. Sometimes it's easier to pretend the past isn't sneaking up behind you. But pretending can be just as exhausting.

"Maybe I had a warped idea about what freedom looks like."

"Southwest not the paradise you hoped for?"

"I thought I would be figuring it out. Not right away, of course. I'm not expecting anything to fall on my lap. But all I've been doing is working and sleeping. I got here in September. It's the beginning of November, and I have nothing to show for it."

"You don't want to be a mom? Is that it?"

She doesn't not want to be a mom. She says it like this, in a double negative.

"But there has to be another way, no? A way that's not, uh, all-encompassing. That's all I was trying to do. To figure out who I am when I'm not a mom and I'm not a girlfriend."

For some time it's just the creaking of her chair, the wind rustling dry leaves about, the cats across the street purring.

"I got accepted into law school. My dream program in DC. But my mom got sick, and fast. She died two years ago. I've been stuck here since. Paying off medical bills, supporting my dad, all that."

"I'm sorry," Charo says.

"This town is driving me crazy. I'm gonna miss my mom wherever I go. Here, everything's just . . . you know. A reminder."

Two feline shadows follow each other down the sidewalk, playing a game. One hides under the wheel of a car, waits, then goes out to chase the other. Charo can't tell if they're taking turns or if it's the same one running, hiding, then jumping out to grab its friend. She follows the game with her eyes until all that remains is the cats' howling in the distance.

"You could still be nicer," Charo tries.

Eve scoffs and rolls her eyes. She pulls from her left coat pocket a bottle of wine, half full by the way the red shines in the dim porch light.

"I gotta drive, can't drink this shit alone," she says, and offers it to Charo.

Charo looks down at the bottle, then up at Eve's profile. She promised herself she wouldn't make new friends in Southwest. She's only here as long as it takes for her to figure her shit out. Getting attached to anyone will only confuse things when she leaves. Any day now, she says in her mind to convince herself.

"Don't think this makes us buddy-buddy."

"Wouldn't dream of it," Eve says.

Charo takes the wine bottle to her cold, chapped lips.

Death comes quietly on a cloudy week. The sky is a gray field interrupted by the occasional break of light. White, then gray again. The whole week is an unfulfilled promise of rain. If only it would break, the sky. Release. Instead, this quiet.

On the news, floods everywhere. Weeks after the hurricane, the water hasn't receded. In some places, it's gotten worse. Historic floods, worse than we've seen in centuries, meteorologists say. Not as bad as the catastrophes in North Carolina. But still bad in New York. From Westchester Creek, where The Bronx meets Queens. Far out as the Hamptons. Water like a hungry mouth encroaching on the earth.

Charo, on the phone: I know, Sal, I hear you. But you can't take his pain away. It's a process. Just be there, she says. Just be there.

Vance explains this to the doctor. The mortician at the funeral home. The cemetery personnel. Yes, my aunt, but really, Vance says, by every definition that matters, Aunt Meena was my mother.

*   *   *

A live debate. Kimberly the celebrity science journalist. A meteo-rologist to keep with convention. And a fanatic who argues that the storms are a warning. If not for this, then why did they come? We have to pray, he explains, that's the only way to avoid the floods. The ratings are through the roof. Callers every five seconds. Some call to debase the believer's claims on live television. But every now and then there's a frightened caller asking for guidance. Do you want your science or do you want salvation, the fanatic asks, and stares straight at the camera. It has to mean something, doesn't it? These scientists, everything's a formula, a set of numbers, a lab experiment. Do you want to live in a world like that? No meaning, just math. No, sir. Yes, yes, I know, commercial break. But let me just— If I can just— Look, we're living through some spiritually defunct times. But we've got to believe in something, no? Signs this obvious don't come to us every day. Come back after the break and I'll tell you how you can buy the videotapes, chock-full of prayers. Only $19.99 for the first bundle. Go run and grab your glossy credit cards. Salvation's just a call away.

In a quiet apartment, on a cold bed under a white pillow, a photo of two friends. Harlem, 1966.

That whole week, Vance's mourning takes the shape of a single word. Small and insignificant against this sudden truth. Why. Why. Why, he says. Not a question but a statement, a try, a small attempt against the world.

If only the weather would acquiesce to feeling. The clouds are heavy for days, and with the rising tides it seems thin, the line that sepa-rates the sea below them and the clouds above. As if the whole world will give way to water. But at night, the clouds pass. The stars wink. The moon beats whiter.

THE WALK TO FORDHAM THROUGH THE CONCOURSE IS LIVELIER than Sal expected on a Saturday morning. Maybe it's the pale sun that's inspired people to come out, this break from dark November days. On East Tremont he passes the CTown where Charo worked for a couple of months when she arrived in New York. On Burnside he passes the building of an old fling, someone he visited just enough times to remember which window was his on the second floor. In place of a Puerto Rican flag, now a Jamaican flag. He must have moved, Sal thinks as he walks by.

On Fordham, Sal buys churros from a friendly Mexican woman, three for a dollar. They're still warm when she hands him the paper bag. He wonders how early she must have started her day to make this fresh batch of churros. She asks him where he's going and is surprised to hear the answer.

"No sabía que había biblioteca por acá," she says as she hands Sal a napkin. She looks like she'll ask more questions, but then someone else approaches the cart, and her attention shifts to the prospect of another dollar.

When he arrives in front of the library, Sal has one churro left. He waits outside, bites into the warm pastry, and watches as a crowd crams into a bus across the street. All those people on their way to work, driven by purpose. Suddenly the résumé and job applications in Sal's bag feel heavy. What if I take the bus to the last stop, all the way to the end of Castle Hill? But he shakes the thought away, pats the sugar crystals off his shirt, drags his feet into the library.

Galileo would not be told how to see. The old book in Sal's hand details the man's life and his discoveries. But it's the philosophy behind his work that moves Sal to lose himself in these pages. Beyond the experiments to study the rules of velocity or his discovery of the Galilean moons, beautiful as Sal imagines them to be, what strikes him most is that the scientist insisted on clarifying that Earth, and by extension humanity, was not the center of the known universe. Most of Galileo's work challenged fundamental truths established by Aristotle, that venerable philosopher who insisted that the universe is ideal and fixed.

> Galileo's discovery of sunspots demonstrates how willing he was to welcome the world as it was. Imperfect, changing, independent of the laws and lives of man.
>
> —*A View of Galileo's Imperfect Solar System*

What a simple idea, Sal thinks, but how revolutionary, to see the world as it is and not how we want it to be. Even Galileo's supposed discovery of sunspots is imperfect. Though he's often credited for being the first observer of those dark smudges on the surface of our star, the book notes briefly that a German student discovered sunspots the same year as Galileo, in 1611. It also notes that sunspots were observed by a string of European astronomers before the supposed discovery, and by Chinese astronomers more than a thousand years before them. Chinese observers used sunspots to write predictive poetry about people's lives. Kind of like astrology, Sal thinks.

He tries to resist getting sentimental. But if the sun has its imperfections, and history its shadows, he thinks, what do I make of the sunspots in my own life?

Behind him, someone coughs and breaks his focus. Sal lifts his eyes from a diagram of the sun in his book to the floor-to-ceiling window, where the light persists.

It takes him an hour to stop distracting himself with astronomy books, another three to finish the cover letters, but by the end of it, Sal feels good about his work.

He allows himself, for the first time in months, to contemplate the future with some optimism. He could go back to work as a host at the Cuban restaurant, if he swallows his pride. They loved him there and would welcome him back with open arms. And the money was good, sustainable. Everything about the prospect of going back is comforting. But maybe it's this comfort that pulls him away from the idea. It's November; Don Julio will cover Sal's portion of the rent until the end of the year. So why not take a chance and apply to jobs that will move him forward, not back? One of his letters is for a receptionist position at the museum. It's not the tour guide job he dreamed of, but it's one step closer to fulfilling his dream. He also fills out an application to the New York Botanical Garden in the Bronx, just a few minutes from the library where he is now, and a final application for a typist position at a niche historical society uptown.

He'll edit the letters as he types them, make them even better. But his appointment at the computer lab on the first floor isn't for another hour, and he's too anxious to sit around. He finds the nearest help desk and asks the librarian if he can use the phone.

"Won't be longer than a minute," Sal promises.

The librarian stares at him blankly through her glasses. She's young, which to Sal's mind contradicts the very idea of a librarian.

Old, wise, stern, though always attentive. Those are all the stereotypes Sal expects. The woman before him now looks at him as if he were the least interesting thing in the room.

She plops the phone on the counter and digs her nose back into a stack of books.

"Just wanted to check up on you."

"I feel like shit today. Still in bed," Vance says. It's only been a few weeks since Aunt Meena passed; Sal doesn't expect anything but sorrow. Still, this kind of clarity is helpful. He wishes he could return it. He tries.

"I'm not gonna lie, I'm terrified of applying to these jobs."

"You're staying focused. I'm proud of you."

"I'm trying," Sal says.

Vance invites him over, says he can review the applications before Sal sends them out.

"It'll give me a reason to get out of bed," he says.

Sal thanks the librarian for letting him use the phone. She looks up, pushes her glasses further up her nose, and nods.

"Do you have a section for Spanish books?"

"Fifth floor," she says as she moves a book from one stack to another. Maybe it's this total disregard that moves him to say more.

"I had a friend. She's dead now. But she loved poetry. She memorized a ton of them, but she loved this one poem especially. 'Una Mujer Está Sola.' You should have seen how dramatic she was when she recited those verses," Sal says, and laughs.

The librarian doesn't reach out a hand to comfort him. She doesn't offer a lesson to be learned about his loss. She nods, unfazed, just as she did before. Her nose is long, freckled, her frizzy hair pulled back into a lazy ponytail; her lips are full, her eyes small. She's made up of an ambiguous mix of features that could situate her in various continents, as if she's from everywhere and nowhere at once.

"Who are your people?" Sal tries, just like West said it.

The question catches her off guard. She blushes. But she finally looks up from her books like he's said something worthwhile.

"I feel good around librarians," she says, and hands him a strip of paper. On it is an aisle and shelf number where he might find Yadiel's favorite poem.

THE VEHICLE VEERS VIOLENTLY INTO AN EMPTY PARKING LOT, JUST barely missing a light pole. Inside the car, two screams circle in a mixture of terror and delight.

"Bitch, are you crazy!"

"I didn't think he was gonna turn," Charo yells.

They laugh off the adrenaline until water pools and rolls down their eyes. Charo's stomach hurts, and with this feeling, longing opens up inside her.

"I really miss my baby," she says.

Eve reaches across to the driver's seat and locks Charo's hand in hers.

"Dios mío, I feel crazy," Charo says. She wonders for what seems to be the hundredth time if she's the only one. There should be a league of mothers lining the bus stops, filling the trains, hailing cabs. Women everywhere kissing their children on the cheek and promising a quick return, then leaving for unknown places. For a day or a month or a year, however long it takes each one to find herself. But the bus stop across the parking lot is empty. Even her own mother stayed, though she never liked Charo very much. The idea must have crossed her mother's mind, must have taunted her on days when Charo was being difficult or when the household responsibilities were too much, to leave for a life in a small town by the sea.

"Have you tried calling?"

"All the time. He picked up last week, said he's not letting me talk to Carolina until I stop being hysterical."

"Hysterical." Eve turns the word over in her mouth.

"I keep thinking that if I hear her voice, it'll call me back. Make me feel like I've found whatever it is I'm missing."

"Now *that* sounds crazy," Eve says. "Everybody's so sentimental about motherhood. I don't imagine it's that simple."

"If it were simple I wouldn't be here." Charo puts her arms out to mean here in this car, in this parking lot, in this town away from home.

The sky darkens. They were lucky to have caught the sun after a shift at the diner. Eve prefers to have their driving lessons in the day. Less likely that Charo will crash. She's a terrible student—makes sudden turns, accelerates to beat yellow lights, hits the brakes too soon and too hard before a stop sign. It takes some time after each close brush with death for Charo to admit she's wrong. By the end of each lesson they're sure they're done with each other, that it's the last time they'll be together in a car. But Charo comes around. This is important to me, she says every time, begging Eve for another lesson.

"We'll be two old bitches walking around on canes by the time you get your license. Hold on."

Eve goes out back and pops the trunk open. Charo steps out for a cigarette so she doesn't have to hear her friend nagging again. Eve has strict policies about what happens in her car. No food. No smoking with the windows up. No shit music, by which she means no white-girl pop trash. It's a miracle she lets Charo behind the steering wheel at all.

Eve comes back around and hands Charo a rectangle covered in Christmas wrapping paper. Charo raises an eyebrow. Eve waves away her question. Charo holds the cigarette with her lips and tears through the wrapping paper to find a yellow notebook with clean white pages and no lines. On the first page, a couple of paragraphs in Eve's handwriting. Charo holds the book up to read the note, but Eve stops her.

"Read that shit when you're alone," she says. "It was supposed to be a Christmas present, but I'm impatient. And you're a mess."

Charo throws her cigarette on the ground and opens her arms to embrace her friend, repeating again and again, "You do love me, you do!" Charo leans in for a kiss, but Eve rejects that, too, complaining about the dank smell of smoke. She runs to the other side of the car, but Charo is fast on her heels, her lips puckered to meet her friend's cheek. They run around like they're girls again.

The next day, they all meet at the house for one last study session. Tomorrow is Tia and Michael's exam day. Clint says that they should chill, what's the point of studying a day before? But Tia is wired. She takes a shot of espresso to boost her energy and brings out a thick stack of note cards. Charo quizzes them, starting with science, the subject Tia struggles with the most. Michael, too, is nervous, and though he tries his best to hide it, Charo hears it in his shaky laugh. She's finally figured out his weakness, why he might have struggled in school. He can define every diagram, remember every detail of the cell, and analyze Shakespearean excerpts on the spot. But as soon as he sits down to take a practice test, he folds under the pressure.

"It's called performance anxiety," Clint says now after Michael fumbles another practice exam. "I was reading about it on Blogger dot com."

"What the fuck is a blogger?" Michael says. "Anyway, it's not performance anything. It's the multiple-choice questions. All those options, it messes me up."

At a quarter to nine, everyone complains of hunger. They don't have to be at the exam site till ten in the morning tomorrow, so Tia asks for more time to practice.

"Just two more hours, I promise," she says, sitting on the floor surrounded by a storm of note cards.

"All right. Michael, let's go get snacks before the store closes. Tia, when we come back you better be ten times more calm, or I'm sending you to bed. Let's go, let's go," Charo says.

Michael jumps out of his seat, excited to get away from studying. Charo runs upstairs to grab her coat. When she returns, Clint calls her into the kitchen. The phone, he mouths. She furrows her brow, but he shrugs, passes her the phone, and goes back out to the living room, where Michael waits.

"Hey, glad I was able to reach you," the voice says nervously. He explains he got the number from Ella and apologizes for calling out of the blue. He says this, *out of the blue*, and Charo imagines him emerging from the blue sheen of everything she's outrunning. It takes her a few seconds to register who it is.

"Yeah, no problem, Vance," she says.

He makes small talk, asks her about Pennsylvania, about Ella's hometown. He speaks as if he's trying to soothe her, which only makes her feel more guarded. Vance, always accommodating, even when his help is not wanted. She tells him briefly of the diner, then offers condolences about Aunt Meena, if only to shift the conversation from herself.

"All right, so . . ." Charo says when the well of small talk runs dry.

"I wanted to get your opinion on something," he starts, finally arriving at the point of the call. "You're Sal's best friend, so I wanted to ask."

He got a job offer in Los Angeles through one of the officers who funds his work. They want him to fly out in February to lead a community project for a few months, some initiative in Hollywood centering gay rights. The company promises there'll be an opportunity to stay longer, but only if he wants. Vance underscores this flexibility. He wants Charo to know nothing is set in stone. But it's clear he wants to go, that he wants to take Sal with him. He wouldn't be calling otherwise.

She sees no reason why Sal should leave his life in New York to move across the country for Vance. Her instinct is to protect her friend. And maybe it's a bit of her own life that inspires this bitterness, everything she's given up to stay beside a man. New location, new lifestyle, new people. What if Sal leaves everything for him and the relationship sours? New York has given them enough disillusionment to last them a lifetime.

"Do you want to go to LA, Vance?"

"I want to go. It would be nice. With Aunt Meena gone, there's not a lot keeping me in New York. Just Sal now. If he would come, I mean, yeah."

"That's the best thing you can do, with Sal. Make sure you know what you want. He'll make up his own mind, you just have to make sure you're clear about you."

This seems to satisfy him. She knows by the way he breathes a muffled thank-you into the phone.

They flirt the entire trip to the store. Michael doesn't have the cool swagger that usually attracts Charo. But he's smart, wears nice do-rags, and his lips—she's curious. In the line as they wait to ring up their snacks, he comments on her smile, but he stutters, and she pretends she doesn't hear it.

In the car, she opens up a bag of chocolates. Charo throws a velvety square into her mouth and exclaims about the tart raspberry filling.

"You got me?" Michael says. He keeps his hands on the steering wheel and opens his mouth. The chocolate square grazes his bottom lip. Velvet to velvet. She lets her finger linger there for a second, just long enough to signal her want. He parks the car a few blocks from the house. The streetlight above them is orange and dying. They kiss as if they're running out of time. And they are. Their friends are waiting, hungry, anxious. But Charo squeezes into the backseat, slips off her jacket, folds her scarf. She showered when she got home from work, but she smells herself while he's not looking. She wants to make sure she's all right. He opens the windows a sliver. "Air, it's good for you," he says, chuckles, and suddenly she feels ridiculous about the whole thing. Maybe they should go back, meet their friends, be part of the group again. But just as quickly as doubt forms, he sits next to her in the backseat, and then he's kissing her neck, running his tongue down her chest. He palms her breasts. She palms his pants where his stiff bulge should be. It's some time before they realize that Michael can't get hard. After she's put him in her mouth. After he squeezes his head as one might squeeze life back into a dying bird. It's anxiety about tomorrow; he doesn't have to say it.

"I'm sorry," he whispers.

He searches for her eyes in the dark, but she looks away. She wants to be good and kind, but she's repulsed by his impotence. Robert was anything but in bed. The thought of Robert makes her angrier. She leans forward to grab her shirt, but he puts his hand on her stomach to make her lie back again.

"What are you doing?" she says sharply.

"I want to try something."

She wants to get up and walk the rest of the way home, pull Tia aside, tell her what a loser Michael-not-Mike is, but she's still curious. Michael kisses her thighs before putting his lips between her legs. He is patient and stays there for some time, longer than any man has ventured to stay. The car windows dampen from their body heat. He works his tongue with precision; her mind melts and she is slack and thoughtless in her body. When she comes, it's in waves. Her body shakes but he holds her steady until her trembling slows into heavy breathing.

"Thank you," she says when they're dressed again. A cold breeze enters the car and cools the thin layer of sweat on her neck, down her chest, and between her breasts.

"Nah, thank you. I know it's lame when a dude can't get it up," he says.

He sounds severe, like he's made some terrible mistake. Charo can't bring herself to ask. He rarely talks about himself, and this is the first time they've been alone together, away from the group. Is it the exam? Or what it means to him? What will he do once he gets his GED? She wants to know more, if he's as lost as she. But she's not stupid, she can't confuse sex for something deeper. I'll ask tomorrow, she thinks, on the other side of the test.

The next day, work is so busy she doesn't think about much else. A drunk customer from a nearby bar stumbles in to start trouble. Jaime has to come from out back to shoo him out. A boy with sandy hair and an unreasonable overbite sends his food back twice because he doesn't like his eggs touching the waffles. Then there's Lisa, one of the younger waitresses on shift. She runs around chatting people up like the diner is a high school courtyard.

"So, like, is your dad Black? And your mom Spanish?"

"No. What? Both my parents are Dominican."

"I'm just asking," Lisa says, like she doesn't care. "'Cause you got that nice little nose. And you speak Spanish. Must be some white in there, no?"

Lisa is lighter than Charo, as are half the Black girls at the diner, but she smiles as if she's onto something. A medium-rare burger with a side of curly fries saves Charo from responding. She walks off with her table's order and avoids Lisa the rest of the shift, though the conversation is on her mind for hours. The question of her body, read by white people in Southwest as unquestionably Black, read by Black people as kin until she opens her mouth and they find out she speaks Spanish. Not for the first time, Charo finds herself longing for the anonymity gifted to her in New York. In the city, if anyone asks, all she has to do is name her country. The rest of the questions are filled in by whatever the person thinks about Dominicans. Be they right or wrong, at least New Yorkers know her country exists. Here, there is no Dominican village to disappear into, no community or stereotypes to explain her. She stands out, and a part of her resents it. But there are benefits to being the stranger, too. Because no one knows who she is or where she comes from, she can be unlike who she's ever been. Like last week, when Eve dragged her to grab some of that famous Copperman fried okra. She's always hated okra. The slimy texture, the gummy seeds. Even the name in Spanish, molondrón, makes it sound monstrous. Charo resisted, even as they stood by the side of the restaurant, plastic container in hand, Eve with a fork to Charo's mouth, trying to feed her. Girl, can you stop being so dramatic, Eve said. You gotta change the story in your head. It's not alien fingers. They're not gonna kill you. It's just okra. Eve nagged her until Charo ate a single ring of the fried vegetable. To her surprise, it wasn't all bad. Most of the slime had been fried away, and the Coppermans' spicy seasoning made it taste all right. She ended up eating Eve's container; they had to get in line to get another. A week before that, Tia drove Charo to the bank to open up a savings account. Charo has never seen the point of giving her money to the bank. But she finished paying the debt to her uncle earlier this year. Tia and Clint ask for very little for rent. And since she's arrived in Southwest, she hasn't sent her parents a dollar. For the first time in her life, she has extra cash she doesn't know what to do with. To open up the account, she deposited two hundred bucks. Nothing that would pull her through in the case of a real emergency. But it adds up with time, Tia said. It made Charo nervous to know she was putting money in what felt like an imaginary place. And what promise did she have that the bank wouldn't steal it? She called them twice the next day to make sure her money was still there. Then there are the driving lessons with Eve, which give Charo a quiet sense of control. Robert always drove. She never asked him for lessons. Part of it was fear of hurting his ego, since he took pride in driving them around. Another part of it was fear of the New York City streets, which seemed just as dangerous as the streets of Santo Domingo. I'm a New Yorker now, leave me to my trains, she would say stubbornly. Why did I limit myself like that? she wonders now. What else have I stopped myself from doing?

By the end of the shift, Charo is tired and slow. Eve yells at her to pick up the pace. Charo tells her to go fuck herself.

It's only as they pull over at home that Charo remembers the test. Charo kisses Eve's cheek and runs to the front door.

"Good night, cranky! Don't forget to write in your journal!" Eve yells from the car.

Inside, Clint is in front of the TV playing video games. Tia sits on the couch painting her nails dollhouse pink.

"Bitch!" Tia exclaims.

"It went well? How was it?"

Tia walks Charo through what she can remember of the seven long hours. The multiple-choice math section, which she's certain she aced. The long essay questions, which tired her out the most. By the time the exam was done, her head hurt; she could barely stay awake.

"I walked out of there and I didn't know where I was," she says, and laughs.

Charo tries to hold her question till the very end, to treat it as an afterthought so that it won't signal what must be obvious to Tia by now.

"Did they put you and Michael in the same room?"

Tia looks to Clint, then back down at her drying nails. Michael never showed up to the exam site. Tia waited as long as she could outside the building, then outside of the classroom. She thought maybe he was running late, that she'd be able to spot him on his way in, gasping for breath. When the exam proctor closed the door, finally, Tia had to release Michael from her mind and focus on the ready pencil in her hand.

"I tried calling him when I got home. Maybe an emergency came up," Tia says, but something in her eyes says she suspects otherwise.

Charo tries calling Michael that night. Again the evening after, and the evening after that. Finally, on her day off, she calls around noon and gets a response from a soft-spoken woman. She says Michael left town a few days ago. He's in DC visiting some cousins. She doesn't know when he'll return but says to call again in another week or so.

"He has to come back," the woman who must be his mother says, more as a wish than a promise.

In her room, Charo inspects herself in the mirror. Her hair is untied and wild around her head. She hasn't straightened it since she left New York. This untamed pajón is new for her.

"Tranquila, todo bien," she says to her reflection. She fluffs her hair to give it shape.

By the mirror lies the journal, untouched save for the few paragraphs Eve wrote before she gifted it to Charo. She's never been much of a writer. Not in school, not after. She opens the book to the first empty page and grips a pen, like that's all she has to do for the words to come flooding out. At the top of the page she writes *Michael-not-Mike*, underlines the name, and begins a list of fractured sentences to try to make sense of him. His limp dick. His lucid memory. His dark, sad eyes. She puts all of it down. After an hour, she's filled three pages all about Michael. Theories about his disappearance. Explorations of his fear. She reads her own words back, searching. But she's nowhere in these pages. It scares her, how easily she's erased herself. *I don't wanna write about myself. What would I even say?* she thinks. But in her mind, she hears Eve nagging, telling her to use the journal like it's meant to be used. *It's just okra,* she thinks. *Just okra.*

Charo sucks her teeth, flips over to a blank page, and tries.

THE PRINCIPAL WANTS TO SPEAK TO KIKO ALONE FIRST, GET HIS side of the story before introducing a parent figure. His assistant says "parent figure" but doesn't seem convinced as she measures Sal. He looks a mess, he knows, in his big blue coat, his old jeans, the right side of his hair pressed flat against his scalp from the few hours he slept last night. He sits in the waiting area and tries to look like someone who's constructing a long-winded speech in his mind. He's mad enough at his brother that he might actually scold him. Kiko was keeping up with homework, staying out of trouble. For weeks it seemed the first fight would be a blip in his sixth-grade career. His mother blamed anime. All that fighting, esa vaina e de loco, she told him once. But Sal assured her that it was a one-time thing. Kiko's not a violent kid, no amount of anime can make him so. And anyway, it was a fight for a good cause, Sal thought, though this last part he didn't say to his mother.

When Teresa called this morning, she sounded flat, exhausted. Take care of it, Salvador, she said, and hung up the phone.

Now the women in the main office shuffle around, as busy as when Sal saw them last time he was here.

"—that sixth-grade assistant position. It just opened up last week. What subject? I don't remember. Melissa, what subject?"

"Science," the woman confirms from across the office. "And I told you, call me Ms. Rogers when we're in school. I don't want these kids getting smart, calling me by my first name."

The young woman who held the position moved on to another school. They're all happy for her. She was so nice, so gentle with the kids, and so pretty too. They go on and on until they tire of the subject.

The idea forms in his mind slowly. He has his associate's degree in education to speak for him, his experience working at the garden to show that he's good with kids and science. He can even argue that being in the classroom with his younger brother a couple of times a week might tame some of Kiko's new rebellious streak.

By the time the principal's door opens, Sal's argument is laid out like a map in his mind. But what if he can't get the words out, sleep-deprived as he is? Or worse, what if all the words come out perfectly and the principal still rejects him? Just a few days ago he heard back from two of the jobs he applied to. The rejections stung. But he's been staying out of bed, remembering Don Julio's encouragement to keep him looking for other openings.

He follows the short man into the office and fluffs his hair out to make himself presentable. Kiko turns away when Sal sits next to him. This is stupid, he thinks as he looks down at his hands open on his lap. But before the principal fixes his rodent face to admonish them, Sal puts up a finger to stop him.

"I have an idea that'll help both of us," Sal starts, in his best imitation of a bargaining tiguere.

He starts teaching a few days after Kiko's fight. His first week is smooth, though kids are kids, that's no surprise. They mess up his last name on purpose, mock his accent, talk when they should be working. And though he's annoyed with them already, they each start burrowing their own place within the softest parts of his mind and heart. The riotous class clown who is actually hilarious, each joke exaggerated by the gaps between his teeth. The quiet Mexican girl who barely speaks above a whisper except for when she's with the other Mexican girls. Then she is twitchy as a squirrel; Sal has a hard time getting them to be quiet.

Sal is assigned a coteacher, Ms. Mendez, whom he'll have to work with until he gets a handle on the job. Ms. Mendez is a tough, gray-haired Puerto Rican woman who's been teaching at the school so long she's built herself a reputation made of myths. She has supersonic hearing that can catch any student talking out of turn. She goes home and eats the lab frogs after students dissect them. She's a stone butch lesbian with a motorcycle and a thrill-seeking double life. This last myth he hears in the teacher's lounge, though a few teachers admit to having met her husband. Yadiel liked everyone better as gayer versions of themselves. The thought comes to him in the middle of class as he's handing out worksheets. If Yadiel could see him now, wearing a polo shirt, speaking proper in front of a group of sardonic preteens, working next to a rumored lesbian. He can almost hear his friend calling him a vende patria, except the nation Sal betrays now is his gayness. He can't afford to lose this job too, so he's extra careful about his mannerisms and the way he talks. For at least these hours he's in school, he'll have to monitor himself, just to get by.

The most surprising part of his first week is the makeup of the room. There are kids from all over the world in his classrooms. Dominican, African American, Mexican, he expects. He doesn't expect the Ecuadorian kid who only hangs out with the West Africans, or the bubbly Bengali girls feuding with the only Polish girl in class. Even when the kids speak English, they're speaking different languages. It's no wonder there's so much fighting, Sal thinks. But even more shocking than the fights are the friendships, kids from different continents sitting side by side learning about the rain cycle, thousands of miles away from their birth places, now at home in The Bronx.

On Friday, Sal and Kiko walk home together. It's the first time they've been alone all week, though their eyes have met enough times in science class to give Kiko a lifetime of embarrassment.

"If you tell people, I'll deny it," Kiko says. "And one more thing, mi pana. From now on, you can't meet me in front of the school. I got a reputation, you know. You gotta wait for me down the block, way, way down the block."

They throw a party a week before Christmas. Everybody dresses in pajamas except for Ella, who says she refuses to end the year in a potato sack. "I'm meeting the future in style, baby!" She invites Jimmy, who is officially her boyfriend, and her number one hype man now that Charo is gone. Jimmy volunteers to make drinks for the party, Moscow mules made with authentic Jamaican ginger beer. Luis doesn't come. He hasn't been around lately. Though Mauricio doesn't talk about it, they all guess something is wrong. In his lover's place, Mauricio invites his two primas, who bring with them a glorious pernil, enough to feed the party twice over. They just arrived from Puerto Rico, so their technique is closer to the real thing, Mauricio explains. The pernil's outer layer is crispy and golden. It looks impenetrable until they slice into the smoky layers of tender meat and fat.

"So are we ready to admit Puerto Ricans have the best food in the Caribbean?"

"Best food? Hold up, hold up," Jimmy starts.

"I'm not Caribbean, but Dominican food hits different. That soup, what's it called?" Ella looks to Sal for help.

"Sancocho! That's my favorite too," Kiko says. He sits next to them with an unfinished plate of potato salad he's been ruminating over for some time.

The primas win the argument when they reveal that they've brought coquito, a mixture so rich and creamy they all down half the bottle before they feel the rum making them dizzy. The coquito loosens them into chattier versions of themselves. Even the primas, who let the food speak for them most of the night, take their turn telling stories around the circle.

Later that night, Vance calls Sal out to the fire escape. Sal leaves Kiko in the middle of a passionate card game. He can still hear Mauricio and Kiko arguing over the rules when he's out in the cold.

"I wanted to tell you, I just didn't know how to," Vance starts. Immediately, Sal feels defensive. He wishes Vance wouldn't start things in the middle. He nods to urge him on, to assure him he's listening. Vance tells him about the job offer, the prospect of living in Los Angeles, how flexible the whole thing is. He doesn't have to decide if he's staying until February. "Who knows, I might not like it."

"But you might. This is amazing, Vance."

"I was gonna tell you earlier. But you were waiting on the job applications. And then you started the teaching gig, so I didn't even want to bring it up."

"Okay."

"I just . . ." he says, then takes a deep breath. Sal can tell he's practiced the next part in the mirror. "I want to go to California in January, to see if I like the job. And I want you to come with me."

A cop car races by. Vance's face is red, then blue, red, then blue. They sit in silence until the siren fades.

"You found your sunset over the ocean."

"I did. This will be good for us, I know it."

"Vance, no," Sal says. He doesn't think of its consequence until he says it. It's so small, *no*, just a hook next to a circle. But it's so consequential, so complete as it falls from his lips.

"I know it's crazy for you to leave, I know. But you can find a teaching gig in LA. I can take care of everything until you figure it out."

"It's not just the job. I mean, yes. After the year I've just had, running around como un loco. It feels good to have something that's mine. But Kiko. He needs me right now."

"He's a boy, boys get into fights. He's gonna be fine."

"It's not just the fights," Sal says, and here his voice elevates higher than he intends. "Vance, who's gonna take care of him? Mami pretends she has it all together on her own, but he spends half the week sleeping at my place, 'cause of her overnight shifts."

"All right then. I'm not going."

"What?"

"I'm not leaving you. Your mom, your friend. I'm not gonna be another person to leave you."

Sal picks himself up from the fire escape and crawls back inside. Vance follows, asking a series of whats and whys. Sal throws off his hat to reveal his head of curls, drooping like a wilting flower.

"You're not gonna leave because I'm fucked up."

"Sal, that's not what I said. You're being dramatic."

"Now I'm fucked up and dramatic," Sal yells. The group in the living room goes quiet. They must be listening. He doesn't care. "I don't need you to stay 'cause you feel bad for me. I don't need pity."

"You think I pity you?" Vance's way of squashing an argument, turning everything into a question. Sal deflates. It sounds ridiculous when it's turned around like that.

The aquarium next to them bubbles and engulfs them in blue light. It gives the impression that they're underwater. And that's how Sal feels, like he's sinking somewhere deep and cold. He throws his coat on, stumbles out of the room to tell Kiko they're leaving. While Kiko grabs his coat, Vance barricades the door.

"You're being ridiculous. Move."

"You always do this shit. Just talk to me."

"Vance, buddy, just let him go," Mauricio says.

"Mauricio, shut the fuck up."

Mauricio stands by the couch but doesn't move closer. He's taller than Vance, and by the standards through which men approximate power, he's stronger. But there's a warning in Vance's tone. Mauricio stays away. Ella eyes them carefully. The Puerto Rican primas walk off to the kitchen like they've been called to handle some urgent task by the stove.

"I don't want you to stay. Not like that," Sal says.

"It's not up to you to make that decision. Unlike you, I'm thinking about both of us."

This natural ability to accommodate, that's what made Sal fall in love with him. But now, as he stands in front of the door, Sal is repulsed by the thought of Vance giving up his dream for him. And maybe it's cruel to lay his lover out so coldly in his mind. But the questions make him dizzy. How can a person's most virtuous trait also be a source of failure? How can Vance be so blinded by love? So stupid? And what about my own failures? Sal wonders. Vance can't be the only idiot. Why am I so defensive? Would it really be that bad, to go to California?

What if I leave? Get on a flight to Los Angeles. Move into an apartment with big windows, lots of plants, a sizable pool for the apartment complex with a view of hot red sunsets and tall palm trees. What if I let Vance take care of the bills until I can find my footing again? When I'm ready, I get a car and a stable teaching job that's not too far but still complain about the stifling hours in traffic. I hike up the city's dusty trails, visit the planetarium often, venture out to enjoy the occasional cocktail in West Hollywood. I learn where to find horchata and chilaquiles in quaint family restaurants in Inglewood. I grow increasingly apathetic to earthquakes, and complain about Hollywood's vapid culture and how much it takes from the locals. When people ask me where I'm from, by which they mean why I look the way I do but still speak Spanish, I say New York, vaguely, never the Bronx, never that other country.

In the California of my mind, there is no past life, only what the sun touches.

"Your love is very good, but I don't want it," Sal says.

Vance recoils like he's been slapped. Ella pulls him from the door, guides him by the arm as if moving an animal found lost and wounded by the side of a road. Water collects in his eyes. He's searching for something in Sal that will remind him they're together, even on opposite sides of this argument. But Sal walks out the door and doesn't look back. He wants to make it clear that they've arrived at some version of an ending.

IT'S THEIR ONLY SHARED DAY OFF FROM THE DINER IN THE WEEK between Christmas and New Year's Eve. The smell of sizzling eggs on a skillet draws Charo down from her room. Clint stands in front of the stove, humming to himself. She waves hello and sits at the kitchen table with her journal. It helps to write as the day starts. She's only had the journal for a month but she's almost halfway through the book. At first it worried her, how obsessive she's become about writing every thought and feeling. In the morning before jumping in the shower, during her short lunch breaks at work, right before bed by the television light. The source of Clint's fears. Tia's sobriety. Michael's absence. The words flow out of her unprovoked and endless. Writing helps her fill in the gaps, the places inside other people she can't know. But writing about herself is different. When her words are pointed inward, her sentences are short, metaphors spare, diction careful and unvaried. She's not verbose, doesn't focus on details like color or scent unless they're absolutely vital. Like the smell of Robert's cologne the last night they had sex. The sound of her daughter's breathing as Charo watched over her the morning before she left for Southwest. And the scar, there on Carolina's knuckle. How could I have been so cold? she asks herself, and writes that down too. It's easier to write about other people. But what she's searching for is somewhere within herself. Maybe if I write enough, I'll find it, she thinks as she fills another page.

Clint sets an omelet in front of her. She shields her journal with one hand, eats a forkful of eggs, and goes on writing about why she feels hesitant around her roommate. It hurt to find out Clint told the other cooks about her daughter. Even if, best-case scenario, he only did it to explain why there's a stranger living in his home. *Betrayal*, she writes at the top of a new page.

"Girl, you don't get tired of writing in that book?" It's Tia. She's running around the living room, gathering her things for her shift at the salon.

"That's how the crazy starts. Next thing you know she'll be writing on the walls, all possessed and shit," Clint says.

"Baby, please," Tia says, raising a hand to stop him. "But he's not wrong. Why don't you come for a drive with us?"

She gestures toward the window. It's sunny out, though the light is only an illusion. The day is frigid. She'd rather be inside writing down her thoughts, exploring new rooms in her mind, but Tia insists and drags Charo out of the house.

They wait for Clint in the car. He comes out of the house minutes later with a microwave in tow. It's heavy and he struggles to get it across the front yard to set it next to the trash can.

"Babe, what are you doing?" Tia yells through the open window.

"I told you I'm not leaving that shit in the house! You know what they saying about microwaves. Soon as the clock strikes twelve on New Year's, boom."

"I thought that was just computers," Tia says to Charo.

Clint comes around and hops in the driver's seat. He references multiple sites he's been reading, and a recent piece in the local paper. The internet is one thing. But if it's in the paper it must be true, he explains.

"Do y'all remember when Neo wakes up in the pod, breathless and shit?" he says.

Charo and Tia groan to make him stop, but it's one theory after another the fifteen-minute ride to the salon. When they arrive, Tia asks Charo what she'll do with her hair for New Year's.

"I can hook you up with some braids, if you're open to it."

"I've never done that before," Charo says, biting her nail.

"You would look so fly!"

Here, half in and half out of the car, sunlight frames Tia's heart-shaped face. Charo never sees her in the mornings when she's going to the salon. Most of their interactions are at the diner, where Tia works a few shifts a week, or after the diner when they're both exhausted. She's never noticed Tia's gestures toward beauty. The glossy lip, the pink eye shadow that makes her look girly and young. You have to be interested in being pretty to work at a salon, Charo thinks. She makes a mental note to write about it later. This clarity about Tia is worth exploring. It might even teach Charo a thing or two about why she's become so disinterested in her own looks. It was everything, when she lived in New York. How much of it was for her, and how much of it was for Robert? It's fine if it was both, she thinks. But now what do I look beautiful for?

"Fine, let's do it," Charo says.

"I got you; let's talk when I get home," Tia says. "And you, crazy, let's stop talking about the end of the world for like five minutes. Please." She kisses Clint goodbye just as he's about to form his defense.

Charo switches over to the front seat.

"I have to run one more errand," Clint says when they're alone in the car. "Wanna come with?"

Clint drives north twenty minutes into a neighboring town. But it isn't until they've crossed into the city that Clint explains that they're visiting his grandma Nettie, who lives in a nursing home. Why Clint hasn't mentioned his grandmother in the few months she's known him, Charo doesn't know.

"I couldn't come Christmas Day 'cause of work," Clint says. Charo is surprised to hear the guilt in his voice.

A young nurse meets them at the entrance. Clint must know her, because she asks about Tia and the diner. The nurse is a heavy white woman with curly brown hair and a sweet honey voice. She's delighted when she tells Clint how well his grandmother is doing. On the bad days, her memory flickers, she doesn't talk, barely eats. But on the good days, she's quick and asks question after question, curious about every passing butterfly, every snippet of rumor circling the home.

"There have been more good days than bad this week," the nurse assures Clint. "Nettie's doing good."

Charo doesn't know how someone can be so content taking care of old people. When she was a kid, she dreaded the idea that one day she'd have to bathe her mother, spoon-feed her, attend to every pill, every developing symptom, every complaint and nuance of her waning moods. Maybe care is easier when it's not your family, when you're not weighed down by a history of personal resentment, Charo thinks, and follows quietly.

They find Grandma Nettie sitting in front of a television, in a common area littered with empty chairs. When the nurse announces her visitors, it takes a few seconds for Clint's face to trigger sparks in Grandma Nettie's mind, her neurons working top speed to connect her brain to love. She welcomes him with kisses, then buries her face in his chest for a long embrace. She looks like a child next to Clint's stature, thin and short as she is.

"Nicole, this my grandbaby," she says to the nurse, as if this is the first time Clint is visiting.

The nurse leads them to Grandma Nettie's room. Before she

leaves them, she tells Clint he'll have to stop by for a formal health update just after the New Year. Charo is taken aback by the thought of the world after December.

Clint's grandmother shows them the gifts she got for Christmas. A knitted hat the color of flamingos, a deck of old playing cards, a calendar featuring photos of the Arctic. She throws on her new hat, then looks up at Charo like she's just noticed her. The older woman asks Clint who Charo is, if he's broken up with the girl who smells like bubble gum whose name she can't remember. Clint stumbles over his words. His grandmother laughs.

"Oooh, you big trouble, Clint, big, big trouble," she says, and chuckles.

Charo looks through the wall of family photos to see if she can find Ella. A portrait, a glimpse of her in the background, any blurry snapshot that will reveal what her friend looked like in her youth. It's too late when it dawns on her that Ella might not want to be seen that young. Not everyone feels reflected in how their grandparents remember them. Duh, Charo, she thinks, and feels a rush of shame for being so thoughtless. She turns her back to the photos and nods along to Grandma Nettie's gossip. The next-door neighbor who swears someone's been stealing his vintage postage stamps and using them to send aimless letters across the country. The old nurse she hates for cutting their bingo games short at bedtime.

"Do you like bingo?" Charo asks.

"The rest of these motherfuckers can't keep up," Grandma Nettie says. Charo returns her smile but hides her teeth out of respect. The old woman is missing some; Charo wouldn't want to show off.

"And how's my pearl?"

"Cousin's fine, yeah," Clint says.

"I told him not to move to that city. New York's rotten, absolutely filthy. Things are fine right here at home."

"Yeah, you know, New York's wild. But there's jobs there."

"He always been smart. Smart as he is pretty, my baby. I keep telling him, you just gotta focus on your school and forget about the other stuff. Let the Queen of Jazz do all the singing. But it was my fault. I played all those records around the house. I sure hope he don't move to no New York."

When they're back in the car, Clint lets out a huff of air like he's been holding it for hours.

"She looks happy. It's all good," Clint says, mostly to himself. He's always rapping, talking conspiracy theories, or chatting up the other cooks at the diner. But now he looks so solemn. She feels a fool for making him small and simple in her head.

"You're doing your best, Clint."

"She loves Ella, you know. Favorite grandkid, always has been. She just doesn't get it all the way, the transsexual stuff. Shit, I barely get it."

"I understand." She tries to warm her hands, but the air blows out cold. The car rumbles. It's heating up, and soon they'll be ready to go. But for now, Charo waits and listens.

"That house we live in, it's hers, you know. Ella's. I mean, it was my grandma's first. She got it from her own pops way, way back." His grandmother's father was the most respected doctor from Southwest for decades. He took appointments in people's homes and tended to poor white people and Black folks alike. He was even the pediatrician for two well-off white families across the river, in the heart of the city. That's where most of the good money came from. He accumulated enough wealth in his lifetime to own two properties. The first was his home in the city, surrounded by a bunch of white folks. He was adamant about reaping the fruit of his labor, even if it meant living around hostile neighbors. After the doctor passed, the house was repossessed by the city through nefarious means. But he left the second property to his daughter, a house in Southwest he'd rented out for as long as he'd owned it. It was a side hustle he learned to imitate from white men, the business of rental property. His daughter raised her children in the house and they lived comfortably in it. But the cultural renaissance her father envisioned for Southwest never came. The house depreciated. Decades later, when it was time for Grandma Nettie to retire, she gave the house to Ella. There was no one in the generation between them that she trusted. All three of Grandma Nettie's kids had been a disappointment. Her eldest, Clint's father, a drunk mechanic whom she got along with but couldn't trust a dollar to. The second was Ella's mother, Lori. She was rebellious her whole life, love-crazy and restless. Eventually Lori found herself a man who promised her the world but who was stealing from her to buy himself booze.

"We were teenagers when she left. Last I heard she followed some other nigga to Ohio, then out to Vegas. That was years ago," Clint explains. He breathes out misty clouds as he talks.

"And she never called?"

Clint shakes his head.

The youngest of their grandmother's children did well in school, became a dentist, married white. He left for Philly and never came back. Grandma Nettie hasn't said her youngest son's name as long as Clint has been alive. Clint's generation refers to him as "the dentist" the rare moments they talk about him, and never around their grandmother.

Grandma Nettie's grandchildren are her gems, and Ella is her pearl. Plucked right out of the sea, that's what she's always said, Clint explains. He was jealous of Ella when they were kids, and they fought often, bruising each other up and talking each other down. But all that fighting only made them closer. They were best friends, until Ella started skipping town on weekends to go up to Philadelphia with a boy from down the block. Singing lessons, that's what she said. But Clint found a flyer for a gay bar one day, poking out from under her mattress. He didn't know what to do, what to say, so he folded the flyer back under the mattress and tried to forget all about it.

"Lori spit in her face and kicked her out, first time she caught Ella in a dress. She was only fourteen," Clint says weakly, hoarse from all the talking. "Ella lived with Grandma Nettie after that. She was trying to raise her like a daughter, but they was more like sisters, I think. They were trying to fill each other up from the hole Lori left. I missed her too. Wild time, that Lori. If she was around, you knew trouble was coming. But she always made you laugh, which almost made the trouble worth it."

Clint looks outside toward the nursing home, where a new family has arrived to visit an elder. Nicole the nurse waits for them at the door.

"I think she was trying to show Ella she was safe here. That's why Grandma left my cousin the house."

The car finally warms up. Clint doesn't turn on the radio as he drives them back home. She doesn't try to fill the silence. Her mind lingers on Lori. What was she looking for all those years? Why wasn't home enough? She imagines Lori packing up her bags in the early morning, not saying goodbye, not looking back. And Ella, left in Southwest all those years, another motherless daughter.

That night on the phone with Ella:

"You didn't tell me you were your abuela's pearl," Charo says.

Charo has missed the sound of her friend's laughter. She's been so caught up running around with Eve. Trying her best to stay present where she is. She rarely calls her friends these days.

"Okay, but I have to admit something," Charo says, twirling the phone cord taut around her fingers. "I think I saw a photo of you. When you were young. I was curious, but it was probably invasive."

"Wasn't I adorable?"

"Well, yeah, but—"

"It's fine, girl. Relax. I'm not ashamed of being a woman who was a boy. Those days are important to me. Even the hard days."

Charo now knows a lot more about Ella's past than they've had the opportunity to talk about. A part of Charo feels bad about it. But Ella wouldn't have invited Charo to stay with her family if she didn't trust her.

"Southwest treating you all right?"

"I like it here."

"Oh, girl, you don't have to lie to me!"

"No, I'm serious," Charo says, and releases the phone cord. "It's funny that for you Southwest is suffocating. I mean, I get it. But that's how I feel in New York. Here in Southwest, I can let go of all the shit I'm supposed to be, and just be, you know?"

"She's a philosopher now," Ella says.

Charo grabs a pen and writes another note to herself.

"My turn to admit something."

"'Kay, go."

"He was an asshole, don't get me wrong," Ella says. "But maybe Juan had a point. About singing from a different place. Singing from the heart of things. I want to audition somewhere else when you come back."

"Yeah." Charo would go to auditions until the end of time, if it meant she might return to Ella a sliver of what she's given her. "We'll try again when I'm back."

"Soon?" Ella says.

"Soon."

On New Year's Eve, she can't bring herself to write a single word; the anticipation won't let her. She works the morning diner shift and spends most of the afternoon in her room staring at a spiderweb hanging from the ceiling. Looking at her reflection in the dirty mirror, she moves her braids out of her face. She doesn't recognize herself, and that's okay. When Eve arrives, Charo works up the courage to get dressed. She wears dark lipstick. A sleek black dress. One by one they come, with bottles and food, until the living room is crowded. They drink and smoke and talk over the music. In the midst of all this frantic energy, she arrives at a decision. She tells Eve, who holds it and gives her a drunken kiss on the cheek. They gather in front of the television when the countdown begins, teetering on the edge of panic. All except for Clint, who stands in the back like he's waiting for the television to explode. It doesn't matter that it's all pretend, that tomorrow they'll wake up and it'll be like every yesterday: their lives not enough, but almost, one day, *if only I work hard enough*. Tonight, everything will be possible tomorrow, on the other side of a thousand years. Their voices rise. A frantic three, two, one. Then a wordless cheer, a choral scream.

*   *   *

On the other side of the millennium, Sal and Vance leave their drunken friends dancing in the living room. They're not boyfriends anymore. Sex must cross some unspoken boundary between them. But they don't care. They remove one piece of clothing after another with fastidious impatience. Peeling, peeling, searching for more skin. There's nothing sexy about this drunken love. Nothing sexy about this languid wanting. They're full of resentment. Sal puts his mouth between Vance's thighs. He is sour there from all the sweating and dancing. But Sal doesn't mind. He kisses him there until Vance's legs tremble. Then Sal rolls a condom onto himself. Usually, it's the other way around. Sal being opened, being entered. Vance is tender, warm. Sal likes that. For once, to be an active verb, to be the one entering. Vance begs for more, deeper, all the way godfuckingdammit. No arrival is enough. The music in the living room shakes the walls. The fish tank bubbles and hums. They cum, their bodies writhing and drenched in spit and sweat. Then, how melancholy. How blue. Vance is leaving in two days. So maybe indigo, a holier blue, a momentous sadness to remind them: though they'll be a country apart soon, they are here together now.

THE APARTMENT FEELS VACANT, ESPECIALLY THIS DEEP INTO THE night. Don Julio left a few weeks ago, as soon as the year started. In his place he left an empty room and instructions for how to make his angel cake. A perfect recipe, he promised. That's all he said before he left. No emotional speech, no extended advice.

Vance is gone too.

Tonight Sal's sleep is brief. I must have slept a few hours, he thinks, but doesn't brave looking at the clock across the room. He knows the time will only haunt him.

When he can't fall back asleep, he throws on a coat, some thick gray socks, a long black scarf he can wrap around his neck twice. It's almost February, and winter feels endless.

In the summer there's usually a steady traffic of customers coming in and out of the bodega. But in the pit of winter, no one lingers to chat about the paper or the hottest gossip around the block, specially not in these barren hours. Now a white light flickers and illuminates the ashen sidewalk. Sal walks down The Concourse. The occasional cab passes him, black Lincolns gliding like ghosts, aimless as he is. One of them honks, asking in that nonverbal exchange if Sal needs a ride. He keeps his gaze forward as the car passes. It occurs to Sal how risky it is to walk outside at this time. His mother would call him thoughtless. The Bronx isn't safe, she'd say, like everybody else says. But Sal is acquainted with its streets, its noise, its particular rhythm. A part of him knows his home is dangerous, with its history of violence, its rampant fires and addiction epidemics. He hated The Bronx at first. But in the five years he's lived here he's had to normalize it to survive. It's just the way things are, having to look over one's shoulder, being prepared for anything to happen, not just in the middle of the night but at all hours. The Bronx has made him tougher, sharper, more alert. It's not all bad, he thinks now in the same second that he hopes he's the only lost soul bold enough to endure the cold.

He walks down The Concourse to 161, crosses the avenue, and stands in the park that overlooks the hill down to Yankee Stadium. A man stumbles by, drunk, bickering with himself. He passes Sal without looking up and walks down the hill. Sal follows behind him at a reasonable distance. When the drunk tries to sneak into a twenty-four hour diner, a waitress interrogates him at the door, then kicks him out.

"That your friend?" the waitress says to Sal when he comes inside. Her eyebrows are thin, her face mean. You gotta be tough to work at this time, Sal thinks. He raises his hands in front of him to show he comes in peace.

There are a few scattered tables of people whispering. A television plays late-night reruns. The air smells like burgers and pancakes. It surprises Sal, how much activity there is. But something about the place is bleak, missing the vitality Sal expects from diners. He thinks of how Charo talks about her new job. Every day is a new adventure, she said the last time they spoke on the phone. She sounded sarcastic, the way people complain about their jobs. But Sal wondered, as she talked about her coworkers and the regular customers, if there wasn't also a part of Charo that actually enjoyed working at her diner.

Now Sal drinks mint tea and listens to a conversation a few tables down. She's a train conductor, he's a bouncer. This is the only suitable time for them to meet, after their late-night shifts. He seems very sure of himself, but she's persistent with her questions. There are women who dance the dance and then there are women who get to the thing they're looking for, no bullshit. She asks him about kids, how his last relationship ended, what makes him think he's ready for a new one now. If Sal saw them at dinnertime like a normal couple, they might seem doomed for failure. He in his oversized jacket with his goofy smile. She in her turtleneck with her suspicious gaze. But there's something about the way he acquiesces, how he answers all her questions while retaining his lighthearted demeanor. The hour makes them honest. And they're here, aren't they? In the middle of the night at a diner in the hood, trying. Before Sal leaves, he hears her laugh for the first time. It's 3:36 a.m. He hopes these late-night lovers will prevail.

A few weeks later, in February, the teachers take the sixth grade on a field trip to the Museum of Natural History. On the way there, Sal and Kiko sit on opposite sides of the train. None of the other students know they're brothers, on account of their having different last names and Kiko's lighter skin. But it must weigh on him, to have his brother around while he's at school. In the month since Sal has been teaching, Kiko has been careful, quiet. Now, free from the school's confines, Kiko is animated with his friends. Sal turns his attention to other students to offer Kiko some relief. Next to him, Anna is going around asking people's zodiac signs. Sal tells her his birthday, and the girl responds with an exaggerated gasp. She can't believe it, but she knew it, she knew it all along. She guesses about his habits, his personality, his *true nature*. When she asks him if she's right about her analysis, Sal shrugs and forfeits nothing.

"Well, anyway, it all depends," Anna says, and her impeccable pigtails move with her shaking head. "Your rising sign, that's what dictates the houses. My mom would know. She's a professional. You can't base everything off the sun sign." She adjusts her glasses, points her nose up, and moves on to someone who will validate her well of knowledge.

At the museum, Ms. Mendez leads them through the dinosaur exhibit, where the kids are most excited, and the Hall of Ocean Life, where they stick together like a school of plankton, shoulder to shoulder, as if the giant whale floating in the middle of the room will come alive and swallow them. Ms. Mendez has been to the museum so many times she's memorized all of the permanent exhibits. Sal watches her keenly. She's cold and she scares the kids. But there's a lot he can learn from her. Finally, they make it to the space exhibit. Sal's heart flutters. The kids are allowed to explore freely, but before they scatter, Sal runs to the front to make an announcement.

"All right, class, this one's my favorite! I'll be doing a little tour. If you're interested, you know, stick around and follow me."

Kiko looks relieved when a friend pulls him away. Sal is sad to see him go. He knows his brother is tired of hearing him talk about space, but Sal wishes he could make Kiko understand what it means for him to be here. Under different circumstances than what he imagined, but here nonetheless, talking to curious people about space.

Sal leads his group to view a replica of the moon. The replica details a smattering of hills and craters, all of its wounds.

"These parts here"—Sal traces the moon with the nub of his finger—"all the dark parts you see on the moon at night, a long time ago astronomers thought it was all water. They named them the dark maria. The dark seas. Now we know they're just the result of lava flow in impact basins. But can you imagine that, a sea on the moon?"

"How did the moon get there?" It's Drew, the class clown. Sal is surprised that he decided to join his tour instead of running off with his own group of boys. Though looking at him now, Sal realizes Drew probably has no group to run off with. The life of the class clown is lonely, it seems. Sal tells him about the giant-impact theory, tries to dramatize the collision between the early Earth and a Mars-like planet billions of years ago.

"Mister, that don't make no sense," Drew says. He's disappointed, but his disappointment doesn't spread to the other kids. The rest of them offer their own myths of the moon, passed down through stories their parents and grandparents told them. Sal offers the facts he can.

"And sure, a lot of science is about evidence, but it's also about being curious and using your imagination. All theories start because people are curious."

"Look how skinny I am!" It's Riya, one of the Bengali girls. She's standing on a scale that marks the weight of humans on the moon. They push each other to take their turn. Just a minute ago they were attuned to every word coming out of his mouth. Sal is disappointed to see their attention diverted so easily. He approaches them to say something that will entice them back to his tour, but they're having their own fun, taking turns describing themselves as light objects. A feather, a match, a twenty-five-cent bag of potato chips. On the moon, they are light as they've ever been. It causes them delight to be impossible. Then Drew brings up his penis. The conversation shifts to the weight of genitals, Sal's cue to walk off on his own.

All these kids running around remind Sal of the garden. Just last week on a lunch date, Amy told Sal that Jenna was fired. It started with a prank orchestrated by Amy and some of the other workers. The plan involved pounds of powdered cinnamon, molasses, and candy canes left over from their December program.

313

Jenna was so outraged she blew up at the staff in front of Martha. That was her last shift. Jenna might never see how she wronged Sal, but he felt vindicated when he heard the story. With his relief came a newfound appreciation for Amy's rebellious spirit. I wasn't gonna let her slide for doing you dirty, she told him, and gave him a fist bump. After lunch, Sal went home and cried. He wasn't sure why he was crying. Maybe it was Amy's loyalty. Maybe the memory of his time at the garden. It was good to him, no matter how it ended.

"Mister, can you tell us about the comet?" A branch of his tour group now circles around him. Students demand so much and so little at once. The most difficult among them just want an adult they can talk back to without real repercussions, someone to test the extent of their cruelty against. Others want validation from an adult who will demand that they pull up their pants, get to class on time, treat their work with care. If I'm gonna do this teaching thing for real, that's the kind of teacher I want to be, Sal thinks as he walks them over to the comet. I want to be someone who expects the very best from them.

The giant rock before them is made of iron, weighs over fifteen tons, and has more dramatic craters and holes than the replica of the moon they saw earlier. Sal explains that this meteorite's crash on Earth was just one of many catastrophes, big and small, that occurred regularly during the early life of our planet.

"What does *catastrophe* mean?" asks one of the students.

Sal is about to explain when another voice interrupts.

"So, is this like the comets you see in anime?" Kiko stands off to the side.

"Uh, sort of," Sal says. "This is a meteorite, a piece that's broken off from a larger meteor. Kind of like debris. This probably came from a way bigger rock."

"Do you think it had cool lights?"

"I don't know."

"So it was just a useless rock, then," Kiko says.

"You can't just say that," says Anna. She points to a plaque that must be new, because Sal's never seen it. "You can't just say that about someone's religion. This rock was like a god to some Native Americans. It says it right here, they called it Toma—Toma—however you say it. But you get the point."

"So I guess it did mean something." Kiko shrugs. One of his friends swoops by and tries to divert his attention. Kiko waves him away, looks at Sal from the crowd, and waits. Sal feels a lump in his throat.

"Yes," Sal says, holding on to his teacher's façade best as he can. "The meteorite came from this huge catastrophe, all this chaos when the Earth was younger. We don't know if it was pretty, but we know it meant something to someone, eventually, way, way later."

"All right, mister, chill out. It's just a rock," Drew says through his crooked teeth.

The students laugh. Sal laughs with them.

It's been weeks since Kiko's been allowed to watch TV; that's his punishment for fighting in school. No cartoons, no sitcoms, not even commercials. Sal's been sure to follow the rule when Kiko sleeps over to avoid an argument with his mother. But a few days ago, Kiko found out about an anime marathon from one of his friends. He's been pestering his brother for days. On their way home from the museum, Sal finally gives in.

"If you tell Mami, I'll tell everyone at school your big bro is your science teacher," Sal says as they climb the stairs to his apartment.

Kiko prays in front of the television, hoping there hasn't been a last-minute schedule change.

"God, if you do this for me, I'll stop stealing Pokémon cards from my friend's house, I swear," he says as he drops his backpack on the floor. A commercial announces the marathon is still on. "Fuck yeah!" he screams, and doesn't look to Sal to apologize for cursing.

Sal sends his brother off to shower before the marathon starts. He needs a few minutes to himself after spending the whole day running around with kids at the museum. On the news, they're just ending the weather report. Sea levels are returning to normal. The floods have tempered, though the hurricane relief projects continue all along the East Coast. Sal kicks off his shoes, changes into his pajamas, not listening to anything, just letting the light and sound roll off him. Then they mention a name that draws his attention. A man on television is holding a press conference. His sand-blond hair is perfectly combed. His navy suit is sharp. He smiles, waves above his head at the cameras flashing in his direction. A woman stands by his side, keen and blonde, adorned with a pearl necklace around her thin neck. She lands a kiss on his cheek, then steps away from the podium. Sal has only seen the diplomat's face twice, both times in photographs from a Santo Domingo paper that Yadiel showed him. Loca pero ta bueno, el tipo, Sal told his friend. But it wasn't just the looks. The money, the connections, his ambiguous power. All of it added to the man's gravity. Sal and Yadiel felt it even through a grainy newspaper photograph.

Now, on television, the diplomat announces he's running for Congress in New Jersey. He loved serving America in the Caribbean, where there's so much potential, such quaint, humble people. They're not ambitious enough, but they might make something useful of themselves, with America's vision to guide them toward modernity. Now, he explains, he's ready to serve his own people. At the end of the press conference, the camera zooms in on his wife's face. She looks at him like she loves him. But Sal can see it clear as day, the theater of it all.

Sal wonders if the diplomat used his own hands to kill Yadiel, or if he had someone do it for him. He turns the thought over and over like a stone. Some clarity about that night. It would help. *Bruises everywhere*, that's what Renata said. But how to find clarity? The diplomat is on the other side of the television, on the other side of power.

"Why's the light off? Weirdo," Kiko says. He turns back to his channel, where his show is starting.

A few days later, Sal is fine when he leaves school, steady as he walks the few blocks to his apartment, but when he's back inside, his temperature shoots up, hotter and hotter, until he's so dizzy he can barely stand up. He crawls into bed, switches on the television, looks for something that will distract him from his body. Anything but the news, he thinks, and groans. He's been obsessing over the diplomat the past few days. I gotta slow down. Stop thinking. But he never really allowed himself the question. What really happened that night? It plagues him, this need to know. He imagines a hundred iterations of how the night might have gone, what Yadi might have said those last few hours of her dwindling life. It's nice to imagine his friend brave till the very end. Unfuckwithable. But he knows that's likely a fiction. His way of making the story easy on himself.

That evening, half asleep on the phone with Charo: I finally remembered my dream. It was fuzzy, but . . . I was running toward this figure on a hill standing by a tree. In the middle of this loud, crazy storm. Slapping high grass out of the way. Wiping droplets from my face so I could see. Water everywhere. I thought it was Yadiel I was dreaming about all this time. But the figure didn't have a face. And it wasn't just one person. I don't know how to explain it. But it was all of us. I was running full speed trying to save us from the rain.

Sal and Yadiel went to the beach together once. Yadiel read poesía. Sal buried himself in sand. They put together a few pesos to buy and share a fried fish, with fried plantain on the side. When they ran out of money, Yadiel stole two coconuts from a viejo who couldn't run. Sal convinced a family on the beach to gift them rum. At night, they missed the bus to go back home, so they huddled in a blanket on the sand. There's that constellation, and there's another, Sal pointed out. That one's a plane, dummy, Yadiel said. You're right, a plane! They were drunk, giggling, terrified of the roar of the sea and the dark all around them. Yadiel traced the plane's movement with his finger. That'll be us someday, he said. Sal nodded. Yes, that'll be us.

In the morning, his body is still feverish, so he calls out of work. His mother is off and he won't have to drop Kiko off at school. That helps. He wants to be alone to think, but before long he picks up the phone.

When he arrives, Mauricio welcomes him with an awkward hug. He looks different, older somehow. They haven't seen much of each other since Vance left over a month ago. Sal suspects it's secondhand hurt, that Mauricio has taken their breakup personally. Mauricio lets Sal into Vance's old room. When he comes out with a hat in his hand, Mauricio scoffs.

"That's what you came to get? A hat?"

They make idle conversation. Mauricio says he can't afford to pay for the apartment on his own, he'll have to find a new room-mate soon. Sal says the same thing about his place, though neither of them mention the obvious solution. Sal is sad they don't even joke about it. A few months ago they might have laughed at the possibility of living together. A few months ago they were friends. And now what are they? People pick their sides after a breakup, Sal thinks. People always pick sides.

Mauricio walks Sal downstairs.

"I'm gonna ask you something, but don't get offended," Mauricio says, though he's never been too concerned about offending. They stand in front of the building. The day is gray and windy. Sal turns his face away from Mauricio to avoid the smoke from his cigarette. "You didn't come here for a hat, right?" The silence between them speaks for itself. Sal turns to look at him and finally notices what's changed. For as long as they've known each other, Mauricio has had a Caesar cut, short and sharp. He is light-skinned, ambiguous enough that Sal couldn't have predicted how his hair might grow. Sal might've expected loose circles or waves of hair, but Mauricio's hair has started to curl and kink atop his head, making new shadows on his face.

"I broke up with Luis. I don't think that's what he wanted, but anyway."

"I'm sorry."

A group of teens walk by. A girl hits a boy on the head and demands she get her scarf back. The boy runs ahead, flips her the finger, and laughs with wild excitement. He sniffs the scarf like he's doing a line. She screams in disgust. Sal and Mauricio are thinking the same thing: He must really like her.

"I didn't cheat on him, by the way. I mean, I wanted to. But that's why I ended it. I've been fighting it, but I just don't think I can do a relationship like that, with just two people."

"So you want a trio?" Sal tries, but Mauricio doesn't smile.

A woman comes out of the building struggling with a cart of laundry. Mauricio carries it down the few steps for her. She tells him what a nice young man he is, though Mauricio can't be more than a few years younger than her.

"I think it's important to figure out what you want. You can't break up with someone and tell them it's what's best for them. The way you broke up with Vance, that just don't sit right with me. I don't know what's best for Luis but I know what's best for me is not, you know, that. Typical relationship shit, I just can't do it. Doesn't mean I don't love him. But I was real with him. I didn't tell him we can't be together 'cause he can't take it. I broke it off 'cause I can't. That's my own limitation. You gotta be responsible for your own shit, that's all I'm tryna say . . ." He trails off. Sal isn't sure which relationship he's talking about now, or if he's talking about all of them, all the gay lovers out there trying to fit into each other's lives.

"Make up your mind, Sal." Mauricio speaks slowly, carefully. "If you want Vance back, then call him. Don't come around here looking for ghosts."

The 4 train at 138th Street is delayed. Sal has half a mind to walk the rest of the way home. He doesn't mind the brutal February wind. But the train crawls into the station just in time. The car is warm and full. He stands by the doors and leans back. It's from the periphery that Sal notices West, sitting sandwiched between two people, her face in a book. She wears a tight leather jacket, a red scarf around her neck, her picked-out fro on her head like a halo. But the environment dulls her. She looks mundane, so different from the day he met her. Here she's just another New Yorker on her way to her life. Would she recognize him if he said hello? Or is he just another chart on her screen? One among many, as anonymous as he must be to her on this train, just a body in the crowd. The train is delayed underground another ten minutes. People groan. Time stretches. Sal's gaze keeps wandering her way, but West is in another world inside her book. Would she be disappointed that he hasn't figured out what her question means? But he's more alone than ever. With Vance and Charo and Don Julio gone. He has the same urge as last time to go ask her about his future. To try to get some clarity. Will things turn out all right? But what good will that do him, wondering about things that haven't happened? When the train screeches to a stop at 167th, Sal looks back once more at West before he walks outside.

That evening, Charo calls to check in on him. The fever is just a low hum in his body now, but he's afraid to fall asleep.

"It feels selfish, to call him."

"What's wrong with being selfish?"

"I hurt Vance a lot."

"So pide perdón."

"You say it like it's easy."

"I say it like it's true."

"I just . . . I hate being needy." He says it out loud and feels childish doing so. This angst is better suited for an adolescent, one of those kids he saw earlier today. He wants freedom from these turbulent feelings which make him feel trapped in his skin.

"I don't want to sound corny but I'm gonna sound corny. You ready?"

Sal groans.

"Believe it or not, Salvador, you are allowed to need people," she says. "Call him."

She's right, Sal should call. He puts his palm to his forehead where it's hot, looks over at the calendar stuck to the fridge. A photo of a beach on top of the month of February. It's the tenth. A few more days till Vance has to decide if he'll stay in Los Angeles. It's most likely too late. And what could he say?

But maybe what he needed was permission. For someone to

tell him it's okay to reach out after all the time that's passed. If it's okay to need people, like Charo says, then it must be all right to be needed, as well. Sal flips through his phone book, holds the receiver to his cheek, waits for a voice to break the silence.

"Hello?"

"Renata. Hi."

THEY STOP THE FIRST TIME JUST FORTY MINUTES INTO THE TRIP, at a rundown gas station too far from the highway to be convenient. Despite her friend's warning, Charo drank three cups of coffee before she left the house, and now she's bursting. She complains for a full fifteen minutes until Eve finally veers off the highway.

"I hope you peed on yourself a little."

"You're the worst," Charo says, and runs out of the car, into the gas station, where a skinny white boy hands her a key attached to a ruler. "Bathroom is outside, out back," he says, but doesn't look up at her. He's almost too careful to make sure their hands don't touch. She gets out and waves the keys to her friend, who leans on the hood of the car.

"Hurry the fuck up," Eve yells, like a parent whose patience has run thin.

There's something sickly in one of the stalls. Its horror fills the bathroom with the sour stench of rotten produce, a feral, vegetative funk. Charo opens the wooden door to a clean stall and prays that god spares her from a bacterial infection. She balances herself above the toilet, holds her breath, releases her bladder in a steady stream. She moans in relief, breathes in too much air. The acrid smell assaults her, almost knocks her out cold. She dries herself with the last bit of toilet paper on the roll, pulls up her panties, finds on the sink, surprisingly, a fresh bottle of lavender soap. She loops the ring around her pinky, afraid now of the ghosts of other hands who have held the ruler attached to the key.

Back in the store, Charo says thank you to the cashier. Loudly, to make him look up at her this time. She figures he's young and afraid of girls. Her cheeks are glowing, her jeans are tight around her globular ass. She knows what she looks like. Before she can ask about his selection of cigarettes, Eve opens the door. *Can't you see I'm busy talking to my new boyfriend*, Charo wants to say.

"We gotta go." There is a quiet alarm in Eve's voice. Charo follows her out, turns to the young man one last time to see if he's looking at them leave, but now there's something like disgust on his face. Did she bring the stench of the bathroom with her?

In the car, Eve whispers, "Bitch, you didn't see the flag?"

"Uh, the flag?" Now Charo is really confused.

"The Confederate flag! It's right next to the bathroom. And in the store. Everywhere." Eve points out the window, to the truck driver pumping gas next to them. "On his fucking hat!" Eve seethes. Charo nods as the whole thing clarifies. She's heard about the Confederate flag, but American history is foggy in her mind. All those moving pieces, those plagues of violence. It's hard to keep up.

"They don't care that you speak Spanish, by the way. This is all they care about," Eve says, and taps her arm. She starts the car. The truck owner comes around so that his line of sight aligns with Eve's window. He nods, and the badge on his cowboy hat winks like a coin. Eve drives off and complains about white people, about Pennsylvania being above some vital line that separated half the country from the other, about Charo's bladder, as if it were to blame for the whole of the American problem.

*   *   *

They've made it another two hours, almost out of Pennsylvania, when hunger wins out. This time, it's Eve who asks to stop. She mimics Charo's "I have to pee" voice. Charo laughs despite herself. Her friend is really good at impersonations. Annoying as she is, Charo can't deny it.

On the highway they pass diner after diner, but they don't budge. They agree they deserve better than the kind of food they eat at work every day. Eve points to an exit sign that promotes an Italian restaurant. Inside, they ask the host for a menu, but the prices listed are heftier than they expected. "Chicken and potatoes for twenty-two dollars? I can make that at home for seven," Eve says loud enough for the host to hear. They bow out of the restaurant feeling defeated. But across a heavily trafficked street shines a Chinese restaurant. Green and gold all over. Charo nods in its direction. *Chinese food?* Eve asks with her eyes, but she follows Charo across the street anyway.

They arrive in the middle of lunch hour. Ten-dollar buffet, drink included. Their stomachs flip with anticipation. A short woman with a smile that's all gums guides them to their seats and talks up the buffet. Best in the area, she promises. Eve grabs a little bit of everything: steamed vegetables, beef in sauce, dumplings, spring rolls. Charo places four fried wings on top of a mound of pork fried rice. This meal reminds her of her Sunday ritual a few years ago. Before she became a mother, before she became a girlfriend. Her favorite meal served in a Styrofoam container stapled at the mouth to keep the steam in until she gathered her sauces and her iced tea around her. She'd sit at the Chinese food spot alone for longer than was appropriate, watching people roll in and out. Their accents, their features, their clothes—she loved watching people she didn't know from places she couldn't imagine. New York seemed limitless back then. She promised herself she'd never be one of those Dominicans who never left their little enclave in The Bronx or in

Washington Heights. She was too curious, too hungry for a world that was different from her own. As soon as I'm done paying off this debt, this city is mine, she said to herself often.

"I wonder what it'll be like," Charo says, to release some of the tension doubling within her. "To be back in New York after all this time."

The third stop comes in the middle of a song. Charo is driving and she's steady. Not too slow on the highway, as is her habit. No sudden lane changes. She gets comfortable and drops one hand from the wheel. She revels in this newfound confidence. Then the engine sputters and the car slows down. On the side of the highway, Eve opens the hood and pokes around, but Charo knows her friend is just as clueless about car mechanics as she is. It takes a few tries to start the car again, but Charo gets it going and drives them back onto the road.

"I don't get it. Did I do something?" Charo asks.

"I don't know, but we gotta stop somewhere before it dies again."

Eve fumes quietly the whole time they search the nearest town for a mechanic. When they lose their way, Charo slows down next to a man standing on a corner. He wears a blue robe like he's in one of those cartoons Sal likes.

"You know, people call us lunatics, but it's not the moon we're worshipping. We're afraid of the unknown just like everybody else. Difference is, little lady—and here's the kicker—we're not afraid to talk about it. We're not blinded by meaning-making. And we're not ashamed that we're afraid. The world's real icy, real cold. You've seen the floods. Every evening at dusk, just a couple of minutes up this street here. We meet in a park opposite the church. We mostly read poems to each other. Sometimes we do tarot. Christians get their feathers ruffled 'cause they can see us from their window. Like they've done a better job of facing the unknown."

He hands them two flyers through the open window.

Charo pretends to look. Eve crumples it up in front of him.

"Sir, the mechanic," Eve reminds him.

"Right, right. Ten-minute drive east, should be easy to spot," the man says, smiling. Between metal wires are the remains of the man's lunch. Bits of salad, if Charo had to guess, going sour between his teeth. He's kind of hard to look at. But in his blue eyes, there's a comforting stillness. Maybe he really has found something worthwhile in those poetry books, she thinks.

Eve scolds her for stopping to ask for directions from a man in a hooded robe, while they're out in the middle of Pennsylvania. In the rearview mirror, Charo sees a second robed person meet the man by the side of the road.

"I didn't think," is all Charo can say.

"Right, you didn't."

They drive the rest of the way in silence.

"Your engine's fine. It's the car battery, burnt like a raisin. Surprised you got this far, to be honest." The mechanic's face is one sad droop. It's a quick diagnosis, but he says it with such confidence that Eve and Charo have no choice but to believe him. Charo is glad to hear the problem has nothing to do with her driving. He finishes with the cost.

"One fifty is crazy. You gotta help us out. How about seventy?" Charo stands as tall as she can.

"I can't do anything with that, that's almost what the battery costs."

"All right, what about eighty?"

Eve sits back and lets Charo do the bartering. She's too direct to get what she wants in a setting like this. At the diner, Charo has seen Eve argue about politics, justice, even the little problems in the diner's universe. She'll make an excellent lawyer one day, but this is about street smarts, not about sophisticated rhetoric in a courtroom.

Charo learned bartering from the best in her barrio. Quick wit, persistence, the push and pull like a dance. The Greeks couldn't have known about this fourth element of persuasion, because it only exists in the Caribbean. Pure tigueraje, that's the language of her people.

"I thought Pennsylvania was supposed to be friendly. And anyway, what are two young women gonna do with no car, so far from home?" Masculine guilt feels too easy. Charo starts to prepare her next argument, but something in the man's eyes changes. His shoulders drop, his eyebrows relax. He must have a daughter at home. That's it, Charo thinks. "I mean, imagine if it was your daughter out here, stranded," she says.

"All right, fine, ninety dollars," he says, and he won't go lower than that.

He points them to a bar up the street, tells them they can wait there till he's done.

One more stop on the highway, last one, Charo promises. It escapes her lips, and maybe saying it out loud will make it true. Eve sits in the passenger seat, asleep. She drank too much at the bar, met a guy with big arms full of tattoos she swore she didn't like, but liked enough to take four shots of whiskey with. She can't drive and won't be able to drive in an hour when they get to New York, if Charo doesn't pump her full of water.

When Charo returns from the store, there's a deep orange panel illuminating the car. The sunlight stretches across the passenger seat, down Eve's neck and shoulder. Charo puts her hand there to wake her friend.

"I'm sorry for being an ass earlier. I was scared."

"It's fine. You can't help being uppity," Charo says. She didn't know Eve was capable of sounding so sorry. She also didn't know herself to be so patient, to be able to wait for her friend to come back to her without nagging or probing with questions, as she's so used to doing with Sal and Ella. She draws her journal from the backseat.

"What are you writing about?"

"How I surprise myself when I'm with you," Charo says without looking up.

"Don't be gross." Eve leans back in her seat and puts the water bottle to her lips.

When it appears on the horizon, it's just a twinkle in the distance, a hazy mirage. But quickly, it opens up before them, sprawling and titanium, spears of light piercing the night sky. Driving through the city isn't as frightening as Charo thought it would be. It demands all of her attention, but maybe that's a good thing, to focus on the road and not where it leads.

By the time they arrive in front of Ella's building, Eve is awake and lucid again.

"Call me if you need anything. You have my cousin's number. I'll be there most of the weekend," Eve says.

From the good hands of one friend to another, Charo thinks, and likes the way the words have formed in her mind. She carries her bag to the front door and rings the intercom. Eve doesn't drive off till Charo is safe inside.

On the train to The Bronx, Charo holds her journal on her lap. She searches for courage there in those pages she's written to herself. She's not afraid of Robert, but she's afraid of what she'll become when she's in front of him. I want to be strong, she thinks. The journal is worn from use. It only has a few blank pages left. She tried to write something new last night, after Ella went to bed and left her alone to finish her glass of wine. But nothing came, and now, reading through her own words won't do. She flips to the first page, to words written by different hands:

To be honest, I can't relate to what you're going through. My mom was great, she was everything. But sometimes I look at you and think about what might have happened to her if she didn't have her job to keep her busy and fulfilled. If my dad wasn't so good to her. Do you think she would have left? Is that something that lives inside all moms, tucked away somewhere—this longing to leave? I don't know. I'm not you. I don't think you're a bad person for leaving, but I do think you have to go back to your baby, eventually. I'm not saying that to make you feel bad. It's just that I know what it's like to not have your mom around. In a different way, but the absence is the same. She needs you. I hope this little book gives you some solace. I know there's a lot you think about. When I was in school, I learned about this weirdo white girl from Amherst who spent her whole life in her room writing poems. They found like forty journals of her writing after she died. I'm not saying you should become a recluse. I think living is more important than writing. But you're carrying a lot. I figured I'd give you somewhere to put it all down.

—Your friend (i guess?), Eve

The train leaves the 149th Street station and a minute later erupts aboveground. At 161 she gathers herself, walks to the window to catch as much of The Bronx as she can. The stadium, Mullaly Park, her favorite restaurant just under the train tracks at 167. At Mount Eden, she slips out of the train, down to the street, where the first white flakes begin to fall.

"What's up with the hair? You think you're a morena now?"

That's the first thing he says, Robert's first proper sentence to her after all these months. It comes out of him like an impulse. He looks sorry as soon as he says it. Charo expected that he'd meet her with bitterness. She bites the inside of her cheek, waits for him to bring her a glass of water like this wasn't her home once. The apartment is different. Toys littered under the furniture. A mountain of fresh laundry piled on the couch. The glass table dusty and stained. And in a corner by the window, a large black box with flickering lights and buttons.

"You got a new radio."

"I had a life before I met you."

"Well. You didn't want to talk on the phone. So I'm here," Charo says. Her hands are still cold from the outside. She laces her fingers together.

"You left me. What do we have to talk about?"

"We have a daughter in common. We can start there."

"Now you care about our daughter."

"I've always cared about her," she says sharply. "You got me fired from my job, Robert."

"Because our daughter was in the emergency room while you were out with your friends. Remember?"

"That could have happened while we were at work, it could have happened in front of us. I can't protect her from everything."

"Then what are you good for?"

Robert looks as haggard as the apartment. Dark moons under his eyes, a messy, unlined beard covering his cheeks. A stream of pity moves within her. She wrote about this last week. Selfish as he was, she must have hurt him when she left. He had his own dreams, his own visions of his life, all of which included Charo by his side.

"I'm gonna be what I'm gonna be to you and that's fine. But I intend to be part of my daughter's life."

He massages his temples.

"I can drive now. She's not in school yet, so I can pick her up and have her stay with me."

"You want to take her."

"I want to split the time. Take her with me to Southwest every other month. It's not stable and it's not what you wanted. I'm sorry about that. But I'll be more sorry if I stay." She wrote that last week in her journal. She didn't plan to say it out loud.

On her way to the city, she was still uncertain about what she wanted to say, exactly. She might have let Robert convince her to stay with him if he tried hard enough. She misses him enough. But a few minutes ago, when she got off the train, she saw the supermarkets and restaurants and a pair of carajitos running ahead of their mom yelling in Spanish. She thought, It feels so good to be familiar here, in this little village of people just like us. I feel like I belong. But that's why I can't stay. New York reminds me of all the things I'm supposed to be. All the words for being a good mom that don't fit me like I hoped they would. In Southwest I don't have to worry about Robert, Eunice, the neighbors. In Southwest I can find my own words for being good to my daughter.

That feels right. *I'll be more sorry if I stay.*

"Aren't you tired, Robert?"

"I'm tired," he admits. That's when she knows she still loves him. He looks down at his white socks. Leans back on the couch. Drops his shoulders in defeat.

A pair of pigeons land on the fire escape outside their window. They huddle together to stay warm. For a second it looks like they're frozen there in marble. Like they'll be there together a long time. But then they're off again.

"I called Mami and Papi this morning. She didn't want to talk to me. But I told him I'll start sending them money again once I get Carolina's life in Southwest together. They'll have to figure it out alone, for now."

"They'll be all right." Robert's way of saying she's doing the right thing.

Carolina comes into the room rubbing her eyes, her head a mess of hair. She must have been sleeping in Robert's bed instead of her crib. There's a new confidence in the way her small feet slap the floor. She's older, more assured, though she hasn't been out of sleep long enough to register the world beyond her father's arms. Charo waits. Then her father props her in his seat and goes to the kitchen to prepare her milk. A simple ceremony Charo has done a thousand times. Six months away. That's all it took for her whole life to become foreign to her.

"Hola," Charo says weakly.

The baby looks at Charo curiously. There's a flicker of recognition there. There is also doubt.

"Go hug Mami," Robert says when he returns.

"It's fine," Charo says, preferring the distance between them. But Carolina walks over and climbs onto her lap.

Later that day, Charo volunteers to take her daughter out on a little trip, to give Robert a break. She's worried that the baby won't want to go out with her, but Carolina pounces on the opportunity to go out in the snow.

Outside the cab, they're met with a sweeping gust. The baby laughs and sticks out her tongue to catch white flakes falling from the sky. Sal hasn't seen them yet from where he stands, at the top of the stairs that lead to his building. It feels like a lifetime ago, their life in Santo Domingo and New York. She has people somewhere else now. How will they be friends if she's living in Southwest? It scares her, how quickly everything changes. And yet. This view is so familiar, watching Sal watch the sky. She feels it now as she approaches her best friend. What lies between them will persist, even as the world billows around them turbulent and careless.

The baby runs ahead.

"Carolina, espérame."

Charo follows her daughter through the falling snow.

There's a crowd by the gate, though they're all early by an hour and a half. A woman sits with her three kids, arguing with them about eating before they get on the plane. An old couple hold hands and whisper in each other's ears. Eventually, the crew comes to the gate, signaling that it's almost time to board.

Sal rises from his seat. Before he boards, he wants to make one last call. He follows the crowds walking to their gates, people on their way everywhere. He got good sleep last night, though it's a toss-up these days. Some nights are brief and quiet, other nights are slow and long. It helps to drink water before bed. It helps to talk with Charo about the images when he can remember them. The days he can remember are the worst. He feels like he's stuck between dream and memory. It takes hours for the fog to clear. But his students help. Their need of him. It makes him excited to return to them when school starts up again in the fall.

Now he arrives at a booth just as a woman finishes her call. He draws a warm coin from his pocket and feeds the machine.

"I was thinking."

"Well, that's your first problem," Charo says, and laughs at her own joke.

"I was sitting here looking at the planes go by."

He pauses.

"Mm-hm," she says to urge him on.

"You think if I'd been brave a little sooner, things might've been all right between me and Vance?"

In the background, Carolina calls for Charo's attention. Clint has been teaching the baby how to catch fireflies in their backyard. The ones they're keeping in a jar are awake now, and they're putting on a light show.

"I don't know if life's that simple, Sal. But it's the right thing you're doing now."

In a few hours, he'll meet Renata. She'll scold him for making her drive to the airport during rush hour. He'll compliment her on her outfit and fill her up with air. That's what it'll have to be to start, all air. They'll have to ease into it. But it'll come with time, the ability to speak earnestly again. He'll also meet up with his grandmother. They'll sit in the veranda, with coffee and bread. It scares him, to go back. But who would Sal be without Renata? Without his grandmother? And the bustling colmados, the unforgiving sun, the fractured people of his birthplace. He might blame Santo Domingo for creating the conditions that killed his friend. The gringos who use small places like his country to live out their fantasies. He might even blame New York for disappointing him equally.

I'm going back anyway, he thinks, to make himself courageous again.

"Call me when you land. And . . ." Charo hesitates, like she's searching hard for the right words. "I'm with you, even when I'm far."

An hour later, Sal boards the plane. He holds his breath those painful moments as the bird's engine roars to life. Then he's up riding the sky.

ACKNOWLEDGMENTS

I believe gratitude is the highest form of prayer, so here's a round of thanks:

To Gold Line Press, for publishing snippets of this novel in my chapbook *You're The Only Friend I Need*, when *Loca* was a very different project.

To the many organizations that have supported my work: The Dominican Writers Institute, LAMBDA Literary, Dominican Writer's Association, and especially Trinity College's Ann Plato Fellowship (and the whole English department), which supported me as I finished writing *Loca*.

To Yahdon Israel, for believing in my vision, for helping me transform it into something lucid, with a proper form. I'm grateful for your passion, intelligence, and honesty. I feel very lucky to have you in my corner. Thank you to my entire team Simon & Schuster, including Martha Langford and Anna Skrabacz, and special shout out to Sophia Benz, for your care.

To my friends, too many to name here: thank you for sharing your lives with me. Everything I've learned about the importance of friendship, of community, I've learned from you.

To my teachers at the Hunter College MFA: Sigrid Nunez, Peter Carey, Rivka Galchen. And to my cohort: Josie Sloyan, Joshua Barnett,

Alex Richardson, Balim Barutcu (and honorary member Silas Jones!). Thank you for your candid advice, and for reminding me writers can be great people, too.

To my teachers throughout the years: Jerry Philogene, Elise Levine, Susan Perabo, Siobhan Phillips, Mariana Past, Poulomi Saha, and so many others.

To my mentors: James Hannaham, for always offering a listening ear and critical eye, and Adam Haslett, for pushing me to create the best version of this novel. I wouldn't be the writer or thinker I am without your guidance.

To Meredith Kaffel Simonoff, for your grace, your genius. None of this would be possible without your vision and love. Thank you for reminding me that all great things happen by faith, just as much as by ambition and rigor.

To my family, for telling me your best stories, for your unending support and patience. I know I disappear a lot. Thank you for letting me return to you, time and time again. Los quiero mucho.

To Michele Meredith, thank you for teaching me how to love books. Thank you for saving my life.

To John, thank you for, you know, *everything*. When I look at you, I'm home.

ABOUT THE AUTHOR

Alejandro Heredia is a writer from The Bronx. He has received fellowships from LAMBDA Literary, Dominican Studies Institute, UNLV's Black Mountain Institute, and elsewhere. He received an MFA in fiction from Hunter College. *Loca* is his debut novel.